I0583366
I'D
FIND
YOU
IN
THE
DARK

Copyright 2025 AB Publishing

All rights reserved by Arielle Bitetti

I'd Find You In The Dark

All rights reserved.

No part of this publication may be reproduced, stored in a retrieval system, or transmitted in any form or by any means, electronic, mechanical, photocopying, recording, or otherwise, without the prior permission of the publisher- except for the use of brief quotations in a book review.

The characters in this book are purely fictional. Any resemblance to actual persons, living or dead, is entirely coincidental.

No part of this work was written with artificial intelligence. I support human creativity, not generative forms of AI. No part of this work may be used to create, feed, or refine artificial intelligence models for any purpose. I do not consent to or permit any part of this book to be used in AI technology. Without limiting the authors' exclusive rights, any unauthorized use of this publication to train generative intelligence (AI) technologies is strictly and expressly prohibited.

Published by AB Publishing

Cover Design by Arielle Bitetti

Edited by Samantha McDaniel

Proofread by Mandy Tayian

December 2025

Paperback: 979-8-9926695-2-7

Epub: 979-8-9926695-3-4

For the readers ready to curl up for the next 24 hours to bed rot and enjoy the pleasures of a good-ole-fashioned smutty romance. I sincerely hope it's raining, that your coffee is hot, and that there's no one at home to interrupt your much-needed self-care time.
Now read on, reader... the spice awaits.

Hello dear reader,

For those of you who wish to go into this book blind, feel free to skip this page. For those who like an appetizer before the main course, this is for you. This book is entirely a work of fiction. It is a very spicy romance, a standalone, forced proximity, age-gap, detective/survivor love story with a happily-ever-after ending.

Mental Health Disclaimer

Please be aware that there are elements of violence, sexual assault, torture, parental loss/grief, PTSD, and murder. Proceed with caution and don't get lost in the dark, darling. If you are a survivor of sexual assault, please take care and caution when reading this book.

California Victims of Crime is a real organization that connects victims with therapists. If you are interested in supporting or connecting with this organization, check them out here:

https://victims.ca.gov/for-victims/

Many victims of sexual assault do not report out of fear, confusion, or shame. Many sexual predators continue to harm because of victim-blaming and societal shame/doubt. If you need to talk to someone or know someone who does, please contact:

https://rainn.org/help-and-healing/hotline/

You're not alone.

THE PLAYLIST

Seasons- Chris Cornell

Alligator- Reignwolf

You Shook Me- Muddy Waters

All My Life- Foo Fighters

Big Bad Wolf- The Heavy

Into the Dark- Danielle Ponder

Capital G- Nine Inch Nails

In-A-Gadda-Da-Vida- Iron Butterfly

Layla- Derek & The Dominos

Ain't No Grave (feat. Adam Christopher)
[Epic Trailer Version]- Hidden Citizens

Bad Company- Bad Company

Save Me- Hanni El Khatib

Wicked Good Come- Blue Saraceno & Nine One One

Killing the Fly- The Union Underground

Safe Word- Eyes Eternal

The Stroke- Billy Squier

In the Dark- Reignwolf

Can't You See- The Marshall Tucker Band

Back Where I Belong (feat. Avicii)- Otto Knows

ON SPOTIFY & APPLE MUSIC
"I'D FIND YOU IN THE DARK' BOOK PLAYLIST

CHAPTER 1

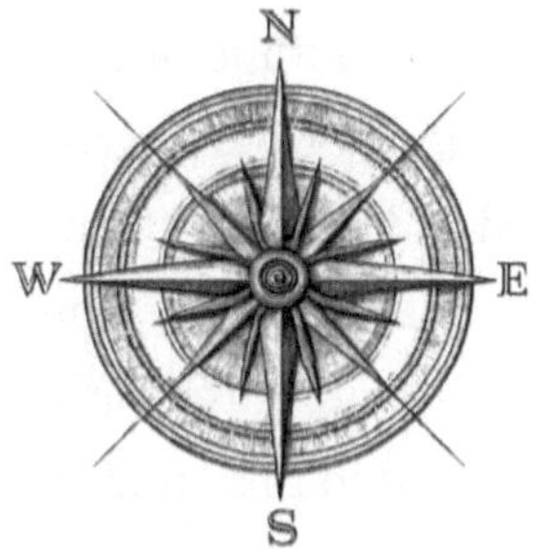

His legs were heavy as he stumbled through the dark woods. Everything hurt. His skin, his limbs, his bones—his fucking soul. But he couldn't think about any of that right now. He just had to run.

Run. Run. Run! Keep moving. Keep going. Don't fuckin' stop.

It took everything in his power not to look behind him because he knew what followed him and knew it would certainly carry his death on swift wings should he stop.

Lungs burning, he swallowed the dry spit in his mouth, trying to keep his pace despite the weight of his legs. Branches cut across his face, whipping past him as he barreled through, tripping over a fallen tree he hadn't seen in the dark. The fear rippling through him kept him on his feet and scrambling through another thicket of bramble and trees, his eyes caught hold of something—light.

A porchlight.

Thank fuck!

Heart racing, lungs gulping air, Colton rushed forward, barely making it up the front porch steps before slamming his entire body against the hardwood of the door and thumping wildly against it, hoping to God—to the Universe, to the grand entity that listened and granted mercy—that someone was inside.

He heard a dog yelping and movement from inside, and another light flickered on, illuminating the outline of a figure behind the window curtain beside the door. The dog barked again, and a male voice hushed it silent as the lock clicked and the door swung open.

Colton sighed, relief flooding him as he stood before the stranger, lips dry and cracked, still trying to catch his breath. He wasn't sure how long he'd been running until he found this cabin. But it didn't matter now.

A beautiful white and gray husky pushed excitedly past the man's jean-clad legs and sniffed Colton's bare, scraped, and bleeding legs.

"Colton Sacks?" The man's voice was rough from sleep and surprised.

Colton whipped his head up to the man who said his name and stared, bewildered. He stared into nearly black obsidian eyes, knowing he would remember those eyes. So, how did this man know him? He didn't understand or know. He was tired, so very fuckin' tired.

"Yeah," Colton murmured. "That's me."

"We've been looking for you," the man said to him.

Looking for me?

"Come inside, please," he said urgently, opening the door wider and ushering him in.

Colton stared vacantly, unmoving, as the icy cold fingers of fear slid up his spine. He was defenseless, naked, and about to walk into another room—another locked door keeping him inside.

"No," he murmured. "I ain't fuckin' doin' that."

The man at the door understood and nodded, hands carefully held out before him. It reminded him of what his father would sometimes do when approaching a spooked horse.

"My name is Eli Winter," he said gently. "I won't hurt you. I'm a Detective with the Placer County Sheriff's Department. I've been assigned to the task force looking for you." He reached for something hanging by the door, and Colton straightened, drawing back, preparing his body for another attack. He glanced at the sleeve of a leather jacket the man reached for, withdrawing a piece of white paper from the coat's pocket, along with a gold badge.

Detective Winter opened the piece of paper quickly and handed it to him. It was a flyer with Colton's face on it with big, bold red letters that read: MISSING.

"Are you hurt?" Detective Winter asked.

Unexpected emotion clogged Colton's throat as he stared at the flyer, blinking hard, fighting back the welling of tears. He hadn't cried in years, not since his father left.

"You're bleeding," the stranger said. "Please, let me help you."

Colton felt the husky's soft fur touch the side of his legs and glanced down to see sky blue eyes peering curiously back up at him.

He suddenly imagined this pretty, innocent dog running out into the forest, into the dark—and never being seen again.

"Do you have a gun?" Colton asked, voice raw and cracked.

Something shifted in the man's expression, and he glanced knowingly behind Colton, to the forest beyond.

"Get inside," Detective Winter commanded quietly, and Colton did.

The husky hesitated on the porch, eyes darting to the forest, and Colton, on pure instinct, reached for the dog, fingers wrapping in her thick fur, not wanting her to race out into the dark.

"Sierra, come," Winter urged, and the husky, with white-tipped ears, perked and trotted back inside.

Winter closed and bolted the door behind Colton, and he stood, paralyzed in the entrance. Winter seemed to understand his shock and motioned to the living room. "Here," he pulled off the throw blanket on the back of the couch and held it out for him. Colton stared, not approaching. Winter leaned forward, handing it to him. Colton, with dirty, bloodied hands, took it.

"Let me get you some clothes. I'll be right back."

"Do you have a gun?" He asked again, this time impatiently.

"I do. Now sit down, please. You look like you're about to fall over."

"They're coming for me," Colton finally said the words that chased him through the forest for what felt like an eternity before he found this cabin.

"They?" Winter asked.

"They."

Winter pointed to the couch. "Stay away from the window. Give me two minutes."

Winter ran to the back of the house, and Colton listened to the beep of a gun safe and the sounds of cabinets and rustling. The man—this stranger—came out moments later, carrying a medical kit, clothes, and a gun belt secured around his narrow waist with a pistol on his hip and a rifle over his shoulder. He frowned when he noted Colton still hadn't moved and placed the clothes on the back of the couch before taking a seat on the edge of a reading chair next to the fireplace, pulling on a pair of weathered hiking boots.

Colton had no concept of the time or day. He didn't even know if it was early or late. The room they kept him in had no windows or clocks, only a bed with iron bedpost rails that they cuffed him to, a double-locked door, and silk black sheets. His fingers could somehow still feel the stark contrast between the silk and the simple cotton shirt in his hands.

Winter stood, leaning his tall frame against the side of the window, peering out, flipping off the lamp next to it. "How many?"

Colton pulled on the black basketball shorts and T-shirt, covering his nudity. The clothes hung a little long on him, but it was still better than going into this next round of fighting or running or whatever the fuck he had to do to survive, completely naked.

"Two."

Winter flipped open the medical kit and pulled out gauze and bandages. "Give me your arm."

Colton, who had yet to comply with this stranger's requests thus far, was surprised to hear the cutting command in Winter's tone now, and like an obedient child, he lifted his arm, noticing the smear and trickle of fresh blood. Surprised, Colton stared, watching, annoyed as Winter made quick work of the gauze, wrapping the white material over the wound. He wasn't sure how or when this happened, but it was bleeding like a son of a bitch. Winter's touch was warm and firm, calming him somehow.

"Are they armed?" Winter asked.

Colton nodded.

"Can you shoot?"

Colton nodded again, which seemed to please Winter as he handed him the pistol. "The cabin is remote—no cell service. We gotta get to my truck. Can you run?"

Colton hesitated. His legs, which had been immobile for the last few minutes, felt like jelly beneath him. "I can manage."

"You've gotten this far without any help. I think you can manage a couple more feet," Winter said with a slight edge of praise that unexpectedly filled Colton with renewed energy. But not to run.

Colton gripped the hilt of the pistol, thinking of his father's armory of weapons at his disposal, and hesitated.

"I'm better with a rifle," Colton said, thinking of the skeet shoots in the countryside with his father's 'hunting parties'. The decadent, self-indulgent life at his father's estate for nearly his entire life felt out of place in this moment. "Skeet shooting. I'm good at following a target at long range."

Winter's curve of a smile shone a startling white flash of teeth, which made Colton think of a wolf for some reason. "Sorry, kid, you'll have to manage with the pistol."

Colton wasn't a child. He was 20 bloody years old. He attended university and was here on holiday with his American mum. He was a man, and at the moment, despite his condition, a very angry one.

Winter glanced out the window, eyes intent on the trees surrounding the cabin, looking for signs of movement. "This is how I see this playing out. You go for the truck first, I'll give you the keys, and Sierra will follow ya. I'll bring up the rear and give us cover. You got that?"

Colton's heart thumped in panic at the mere thought of going back out into the dark—into the woods.

With them.

Winter's voice was strong and low, settling over him. "This will all be over in a few minutes, all right?"

Colton felt his body tremble weakly, unsure if he could make it another couple of feet to safety.

"I'm right here with ya. No one's gonna hurt you, and if they try, they're gonna have to come through me first," Winter said, eyes locking with his in the darkness of the home. Colton let out a breath and nodded, believing him.

Sweat drenched Colton's back from the run, and it was beginning to trickle low, too low—touching the raw skin of his backside, which was bruised with welt marks and torn with teeth marks.

"Follow me," Winter directed quietly. "Stay low and close to me."

Colton followed, staying close to his back, smelling gun oil, pine, sweat, and blood.

"Sierra," Winter beckoned with a soft whistle, and sensing a change in him, the white fluffy dog bounded ahead of Winter toward the back door of the house that led through the kitchen. Winter plucked the truck keys from his jeans pocket and held them out to Colton.

"The doors are locked, but don't hit the unlock button. It'll beep and give you away. It's a sensor. Wave it over the driver's side handle and it'll unlock automatically. Get in and wait till I clear the house before you start the truck."

Winter handed him his cellphone. "If I don't make it, my passcode is 5595. Look up Jim Emerson in my contacts. He's the Placer County Sheriff. Tell him where I am and what happened. Just follow this road straight out for about six, maybe seven miles. It's long and windy, but you'll eventually hit the main road that connects back to the highway. You got all that?"

Colton slid the phone into his shorts, attempting to steady his breathing. "5595. Jim Emerson. Six, seven miles till the main road."

"Good. Now, run like hell."

CHAPTER 2

A few hours later...

The hospital lights were so bright against the black of the night that it took her a moment to realize where they were.

Miles, her best friend and partner, accelerated the last few yards, jerking the car to a halt in front of the emergency hospital doors. "Go!" He said urgently, "I'll park the car and find you. Go."

Grace leapt out of the car, her eyes blurry with tears, her heart racing. The hospital doors slid open and the cool, fresh mountain air mixed with the smell of disinfectant slammed her nostrils. Panic rose in her throat. She hated hospitals.

She barely made it to the front station, where a nurse sat, nearly shouting her son's name. "Colton Sacks. I'm his mother. Please, where is he?!"

The nurse's eyes widened and glanced over her shoulder at the deputy Sheriff, whom Grace hadn't even seen upon entering. The nurse and officer, dressed in blue-green and khaki uniforms, led her down the longest hallway of her life. The bright fluorescent lights seared through her retinas, making her squint.

Everything felt so bright.

Too bright.

And it hadn't helped that she was going on nearly 48 hours of no sleep.

She caught a glimpse of her reflection in a window of one of the rooms and saw the hooded bags around her eyes, the tangled waves of her dark blond hair wrapped in a messy bun, and the dress she wore, which Miles had picked out for her. She nearly left the rental cabin in one of her robes when Miles grabbed her at the doorway and quickly helped her into a clean dress. It was one of her favorites, too. Long, the fabric brushing her ankles as she walked, and a dark nutmeg color with white polka dots.

"He's here," the nurse said softly.

Grace pushed past them and immediately felt the cool night air, noticing the low lighting in the room, as though someone had opened a window and dimmed the lights. Already, it calmed her frayed nerves, as her hands anxiously twisted at the strap of her purse, and she saw the sheer white curtain around the bed, blocking the view of her son.

The door behind her softly closed, and the noise of the hospital and the searing brightness were gone. The suffocation of the hospital eased from her limbs as she slowly opened the curtain, her body braced to see her son and the results of being in the hands of the North Tahoe Ripper for almost two days.

With a trembling hand, she pushed the curtain open and froze. Her son lay quietly on the bed, sleeping, his face riddled with small and big cuts, his lips chapped, his hair tangled, resting on his side, with his arm outstretched and the IV taped to his sun-kissed skin, and his hand...

Grace glanced at the man, the stranger who sat beside her son, confused.

He didn't look like a doctor or nurse.

His black hair was short and curled in waves on the top of his head, with a few days' worth of stubble adorning his chin and cheeks. He was handsome. She could tell even at the angle his head rested on the chair in which he sat, his long legs splayed out in dark jeans. His plain white T-shirt made the darkness of his hair more stark by contrast. The dark lashes of his eyes were closed as he slept beside her son's bed, his hand lying beside Colton's.

Their fingertips were a breath apart.

Something moved through her, something protective and warm. The scene felt intimate, and she was the intruder in it.

The breeze from the open window fluttered over her skin, making her shiver even though it wasn't cold. Her mother always taught her to listen to signs and trust her instincts, and she felt the universe now, powerful and flowing through her. Once upon a time, she had dismissed her mother, believing magic wasn't real. But as she aged and matured, Grace wanted to believe in nothing but magic, especially now after Colton had been taken and returned to her.

Grace listened, feeling the calmness and the strength, the light and the dark.

She hadn't seen her son in almost two terrifying days, and seeing him alive, sleeping and safe, made the black hole inside her chest slowly come together again. Her eyes moved curiously to the man again and noted the gun on his hip, next to the golden badge clipped beside it.

The man with the badge stirred, and she held her breath, unsure all of a sudden. He didn't see her at first, his brown, nearly black eyes returning immediately to her son. His hand, unconscious and sure, reached to touch him, studying his face before glancing at the monitors at the opposite side of his bed.

Grace took that moment to walk to the foot of the bed, and the man sat back, releasing Colton and standing. He was much taller than she had initially thought. But he no longer mattered now as she rounded the bed and touched Colton's arm, tracing her fingers over his bruised and cut cheeks, tears flooded her once more—relieved and grateful. So, so grateful.

"You must be Grace Sacks?" The man said in a husky voice.

She sucked in a breath, tears leaking uncontrollably from her eyes, but she didn't care. "Yes."

"He looks like you," he said softly.

She raked her nails through her son's dirty hair, feeling the oil and grime, wanting to bathe him like she did when he was a baby, and to never let him out of her sight again.

"He's only been sleeping..." The man glanced at his wristwatch. "About thirty minutes. I apologize for the delay in calling you. Colton had a hard time remembering your phone number. Shock can sometimes make us forget simple things. Once forensics and the doctor were done with him, and he was able to rest, he remembered your number."

She glanced up at the man with the dark eyes and saw then the deep, jagged scar beneath his jaw and grazing the side of his neck. "You were the one who called me," she realized, recognizing his voice.

He nodded, "Would you like me to get the doctor for you?"

"Have you been here the whole time?"

He hesitated and nodded again.

"Then you can tell me," She stated firmly, listening to her gut. And her gut was inclined to trust this stranger. "Start with your name. I know you told me on the phone, but I don't remember. I'm sorry."

He smirked slightly, and it vanished as quickly as it came. "Detective Eli Winter. And don't apologize, I imagine you heard the best news of your life and heard nothing else."

She bent and kissed the side of Colton's face. "There are no words for it..."

"He's fearless. I don't think I've ever seen such courage."

Grace wavered, and Detective Winter gestured to the chair he had just vacated. "Please," he indicated for her to take his seat, and she did so, reluctant to stop touching Colton.

She nearly collapsed into the chair, but sat forward, slipping her hands into her son's, clutching, grasping for anything.

"Is anyone else joining you?" Detective Winter asked.

"Colton's father won't be here until the morning. He's flying here now. Miles, my partner, will be in shortly. But it's fine, you don't have to wait."

Detective Winter hesitated, seeming to struggle with what to say.

"You don't suppose courage can be genetic, too?" he asked curiously, and she frowned in confusion and then stilled, understanding dawning in an instant.

Did she have the courage—the strength to hear what happened to her son? Grace knew herself well enough to know that she didn't. But that didn't mean she lacked courage. Fear can be just as resilient, especially for parents.

"I want to know everything, Detective Winter. Don't spare me, please."

"Call me Winter," he murmured and let out a long exhale, as though it had been trapped in his chest for a long time. "He has a lot of superficial abrasions and wounds from running naked through the woods in the dark. Scrapes, bruises, nothing deep. Both his hands are severely bruised, and his left thumb is broken. He has a..." Winter's voice caught, and she glanced up sharply, waiting. Winter shifted uncomfortably. "He has a burn on his pelvic area, it looks like some sort of brand. It's small and will likely be permanent. I believe whoever held him captive branded him."

Bile rose to her throat, and she gripped her son's fingers, glancing down at the white blanket that covered his waist.

"He was sexually assaulted..."

The emotions came swiftly and devastatingly. Her throat clenched, and the sound that echoed from the chambers of her soul was low and whining, mixed with ferocious anger.

No...not my baby. Not my baby.

"I'm so sorry," Winter said in a tremulous voice. "I can give you some space..."

"No! No," she snapped, wiping the tears away with the back of her hand. "Tell me. I can take it. I have to."

Winter's penetratingly stern gaze held hers, and she wondered for the briefest of moments if he wouldn't tell her. "He alleged there were two men responsible for his rape."

She gasped, "Two?"

"One has been... killed—the other, we're not sure of his whereabouts yet. Deputies are currently searching the forest, following Colton's trail. We'll have better luck in the morning, and when we find the last known location of one of the men who was killed tonight."

"Sheriff Emerson told me he believed the North Tahoe Ripper took Colton," Grace said, hands shaking. "You're saying there are two...?" She couldn't say the word 'killers' out loud. Not yet, at least.

"Yes."

"And one of them is dead?"

Winter's expression never changed, hard and almost stonelike. "Yes."

She wanted to scream, her throat burned with it, while the other part wanted to cry out in joy. She knew it was wrong to celebrate the death of another, but this man—this killer, this rapist—took her son, with the intent to brutalize and kill. People like that didn't deserve the breath in their lungs.

"How?" she asked quietly through her tears.

"A shotgun to the face," he remarked coldly. "And had I thought about it, I would've shot him between the legs first to make him suffer.

Maybe with the next one I'll get the chance."

Her mouth fell open at the casual violence spoken and yet, Detective Winter had protected her son. That's all that mattered.

She swallowed the swirling emotions lodged in her throat. "How did you find Colton?"

Winter's dark gaze flicked toward him, a flash of something in his expression she couldn't decipher. "He found me. He managed to escape somehow. But I haven't asked yet. We haven't gotten that far, and considering what I did tonight, the Sheriff will have to do the questioning, not me. But I can sit with him in the interview room, and so can you, if he wants you to."

Colton found this man in the dark, she thought, staring up at the eyes of a predator and a protector.

"Guessing from his broken thumb and bruising around his hands, I think he slipped out of a pair of handcuffs," Winter deduced. "His right thumb isn't broken though..."

"He dislocated it last year in a fencing tournament."

Winter looked mildly impressed, "Fencing? Fancy. He also mentioned he could shoot."

"Skeet shooting with his father on the Stanton Estate."

"A hunter."

"Not really," she murmured. "He's more of a poet, and a burning, raging star that doesn't know when to quit."

Winter stilled, looking thoughtful. "I said almost the same thing to him. Not knowing when to quit."

She smiled bravely, staring over at her most precious thing in the world. "The audacity to live..."

"...to survive," Winter finished, and something passed between them as the gentle night air settled over the room, reminding her of the magic of new beginnings and endings. Her son was alive, and one of the perpetrators who did this to him was dead.

The door to the hospital room opened.

She glanced up and saw Miles, who was panting, face pinched in frustrated confusion. "Sorry, I got turned around and I forgot where the nurse told me to go."

"Winter, this is Miles, my partner," she introduced, and Winter shook hands with him. Miles barely reached Winter's shoulders in terms of height and was older and softer than the Detective, yet he was the kindest man she knew, who loved her absolutely, and that was a gift.

Winter glanced between the three of them and the door. "I'll give you some time with him. I'll be back in a few hours."

She nodded, grateful, wanting him to stay, but knowing she couldn't ask more of him. "Thank you."

Winter glanced one more time over Colton with that same mysterious expression before he nodded politely at her and left.

She sat for a long time staring at Colton, and after a while she glanced out the window, into the black night sky.

Colton was alive. Alive and breathing, and he would heal. She was confident in that. And she knew, too, that her son and she would do whatever it took to help heal the unseen wounds he would surely have from this ordeal.

Detective Eli Winter was now a part of her, like he was of Colton's life.

And she would be forever grateful to him.

Ten years later

Winter glanced moodily at the extensive picnic grounds that hosted the annual Heroes in the Park Festival. It was a massive event that somehow grew larger each year, hosting and parading Tahoe's first responders—firefighters, police officers, doctors, nurses—and adding a new category this year: mental health workers, such as therapists and school counselors.

And it had landed in Winter's lap this year because his office was next on the list to help organize.

He gritted his teeth, annoyed that his boss, Jim, had saddled this to him. The festival was already practically done in terms of logistics. Winter was merely there to give final approval and provide the official rubber stamp from the Placer County Sheriff's Office.

The team he met with today was a diverse group, comprising representatives from the mayor's office, City Hall, and the privately hired event coordinator and her team. She was a petite woman with thick red hair and freckles, dressed in a modest black business suit. Her bright green eyes flashed with excitement as she clicked the tablet in her hand, using an app to show him the layout of this year's festival.

Not that Winter cared much, but he was polite enough to pretend that he did.

"The theme this year was a blast to work with," she said, beaming up at him. "So much better than another brewfest. But there will be plenty of booze! You can't have an event without it these days, and, of course, good food. Hired some amazing food trucks—award winners from Sacramento and some local vendors of our own, of course." She gushed, "I'm so excited." She waved a hand over the tablet display. "So, with the throw-back high school carnival theme, there will be a dunk-tank, pie tossing, carnival games—the works."

He glanced at the tablet, which showed a mockup digital layout of the space, with a faceless avatar walking through each booth. He sighed, wondering when this would end and if he would actually attend this year. He skipped the last two.

Winter felt his phone buzz in his back pocket and gave her a flat, apologetic smile while glancing at it, hoping it was Jim telling him to go home, but it wasn't. Irritation washed over him as he read who the text message was from, then he shoved the phone back without opening it.

How many times did he have to tell him, Winter thought, mashing his teeth together. How many times would it take?

Another buzz.

Winter was sorely tempted to toss the damned phone into his truck or, better yet, the lake and let it sink to the bottom.

"I think the nostalgia and fun games will be something that everyone can enjoy," she continued. "Play is tough to come by as an adult, and our company really loved the idea of letting officers like you cut loose and throw a pie or swing a mallet. Have a little fun! What are your thoughts on the dunk tank? We can offer a charity throw option to incentivize participants. Toss a couple of softballs for a new fire truck or police cruiser. Red versus blue."

He nodded patiently, knowing the firefighters and cops would hate it. "Sounds great."

His phone vibrated once more, pinging multiple times now, and Winter was unable to focus on the elaborate dunk tank display the event coordinator was insisting on showing him.

He held out a finger, pausing her. "Give me two minutes."

"Of course!" She said happily and instead showed the mayor's assistant the plans for the dunk tank.

Winter opened his phone and quickly read the text messages:

Please…!

I'm sorry!

I'll behave this time. Let me show you what a

good boy I can be.

Good boy, my ass, he thought irritably. Winter could tolerate a lot of things—in fact, the list was pretty long. But cheating, he drew the line.

I don't know what I was thinking. I wanted your attention and…

The text bubble stopped and restarted.

I've never felt like this with anyone. Please! I will do whatever you want, Winter. Whatever. You. Want.

Typically, something like this would compel Winter to consider giving a second chance. After all, everyone made mistakes, but he had been very clear on his non-negotiables right from the start. Winter always was. It was essential to lay the ground rules for his bedmates and to make sure everything was consensual and, most importantly, that they too wanted everything he gave them.

Being in Winter's bed had requirements, and this man—this man-child—wasn't it.

Winter liked order. He liked consistency and appreciated predictability. His job was hard enough, and he didn't have time for personal drama outside the office. And his job at this very moment was to give the thumbs up to a fucking dunk tank.

Winter typed his response.

Goodbye, Trevor, and good luck. It was fun.

Trevor's response was fast.

This is your fault! You set me up to do this.

Winter felt the line in his jaw twitch. This was the problem with liking and actively pursuing defiant, overly confident young men who had egos the size of Mount Everest. They tended to blame him for their shitty behavior.

> You knew the rules. Goodbye. Stop texting me.

Winter shoved the phone into his pocket and refocused on the event team.

The hot summer sun was beginning to beat down on the open grounds, and the only cool place was the shade cast mercifully on them by the towering, faded green sugar pine trees. He raked his fingers through his hair, feeling the sweat bead on his brow and upper neck, as he pushed up his aviator sunglasses onto his nose and began rolling up his khaki long-sleeve button-up. He was grateful that he no longer had to wear the official sheriff's uniform on hot days like these and could wear more discreet clothes. He wore his gun and badge on his hip, faded jeans, and worn-down hiking boots that he probably should replace soon.

He was about to return to the group when he spotted the sheriff's white SUV haul down the side lane into a park next to his truck. Jim jumped out, looking upset. Winter frowned and gave the group another pausing wave as he approached Jim, feeling the weight of their curious eyes on them.

"This is a pleasant surprise," Winter said drily, knowing the group could overhear them.

Jim glanced over his shoulder and motioned him between the SUV and Winter's truck, out of eyeshot and hopefully earshot. Winter's frown deepened, unsettled by Jim's behavior. Usually, Jim would be downright jovial to see Winter being tortured like this, knowing how much he hated these sorts of things.

Once blocked by the truck, Winter leaned against it.

"A body's been found off the North Tahoe Trail," Jim informed him, launching right into it. It was then that Winter saw the wrinkles on Jim's face deepen with tension, making him suddenly look much older than his 68 years.

The pit in Winter's stomach opened into a void, dropping rapidly.

North Tahoe Trail. The last time they had found a body near there was ten years ago...

Jim pulled out his phone and showed him a picture of the missing young man in his mid-twenties, wearing a baseball shirt and khaki shorts, with sun-kissed skin, strawberry-blond hair, and a wide smile. He was handsome, full of life. Winter had been working on the missing person case for the past week. It was him. Bryan Douglas.

"Damn it," Winter hissed, and Jim scrolled to the next photo, and everything inside him stilled.

He heard Jim's voice, but it sounded distant, eyes fixated on the image. "He was found only a mile from the trail. Bound and gagged, tied to a tree, naked, strangled. The coroner's office has him now. I knew you'd want to see it."

Winter grabbed Jim's phone from his hand, zooming closer in on the burnt brand on Bryan Douglas's groin area. It looked nearly identical to the one he saw ten years ago on Colton Sacks. The second Ripper was back. Every instinct in his gut said this was him. Grace Sacks had told him, years ago, that the second Ripper wasn't done.

It was starting all over again, and already they had a body on their hands, which meant that another young man would be taken any day now.

Winter tossed Jim back his phone and pulled the keys to his truck out of his pocket, already mentally driving to the coroner's office to inspect the body himself.

"Winter!" Jim said, halting him. "You said ten years ago there were two of them..."

Winter's hand clutched the handle of his truck, mind racing. He never said there were two Rippers—Colton did.

"We never found any evidence of the second Ripper," Jim said in a low, almost pleading tone. "It's been ten fucking years. It can't be that. We closed the North Tahoe Ripper case. Barry Pollock is dead. He worked alone. This can't be him—this has to be a copycat."

Winter yanked open the door and climbed inside. He nearly shook his head. Jim was a good man, and he tried not to judge him too harshly for wanting to convince himself and Winter that this was a copycat. He could understand why Jim had felt it was necessary to close the North Tahoe Ripper case all those years ago. North Tahoe was supposed to be a safe place for families and tourists. It wasn't a place where serial killers stalked the woods. And when Jim had officially closed the case, all of Tahoe sighed in relief, trusting their Sheriff over the sensational media headlines caused by the Sacks family, who initially claimed there was a second serial killer still out there.

"Tell yourself whatever you want, Jim," Winter clipped out. "I'm not waitin' for you this time."

Jim sighed, raking a hand over his balding head, before fingering his bushy mustache over his upper lip. "It's a copycat. Ripper made national headlines cuz of that damned family—that's it. Don't go lookin' into this for somethin' it ain't."

Winter roared his truck to life, wanting to drown out Jim's bullshit excuses. "You givin' me the case then?" He asked it casually, yet his heart was racing a mile a minute, eager to get started with fresh evidence.

Jim's muddy brown eyes locked with his. They had a total of five detectives in their county. One was on maternity leave, the other two were fresh into the department and working more minor cases, and the other was handling abuse and domestic disputes.

Jim's jaw cracked, and he snorted, "Fine. But if you so much as say that family's name..."

Winter put his truck into reverse, aware of Jim's hatred for the Sacks family. Despite the evidence Colton had provided, they had never found the alleged second Ripper, and the media frenzy had publicly humiliated and questioned the Sheriff at the time.

Winter rolled down his window, "I follow the evidence, Jim. You know that. You gotta trust me."

"It ain't you I don't trust," Jim muttered as he stomped off toward the festival team, taking over for him.

Winter accelerated onto the road, pulse racing.

It had been ten years since the North Tahoe Ripper had struck. Ten years since the last known killing. Ten years since the infamous Barry Pollock was shot and killed.

Ten years since Colton Sacks spoke to him.

Ten years too long, he thought. Winter had a sinking feeling that the man would want nothing to do with him.

It had only been five years, and in that time span, Colton Sacks had only grown more stunning. He had already been striking for his age when Winter first met him. But now, he was downright blinding.

Colton's jawline filled out with a thick, short-cropped blond beard. His lips were curved into a devilish, arrogant smile as he spoke to two beautiful women at the bar, leaning in close. His dark blond hair, cut short on the sides and left long in the middle, sweeping back in the classic warrior style, suited him perfectly. Winter noted the fine lines of tattoo ink on Colton's neck, dipping low and out of sight beneath the collar of his black shirt.

Colton had information on the second Ripper. He was his only survivor, and Winter knew that the investigation at the time had overlooked Colton's victim statement because they had their man—Barry Pollock.

Winter hadn't been in charge back then. So, the decisions that were made were out of his hands, but he knew Colton never saw it that way. It's why, even at Grace's funeral, Colton refused to speak to him.

Winter studied him from the back of the crowded bar, unnoticed.

He preferred watching.

He was good at seeing what others hid in plain sight, and even though he had seen Colton Sacks before, it felt like he saw an entirely different man today.

And damn him to hell, he couldn't help but watch only him. Roping muscles clearly defined like an ancient Greek statue, with tanned, golden skin that glistened with sweat as he reached for glasses and poured drinks. He was almost overly confident, winking and smirking like he owned the place.

And maybe he did for all Winter knew.

Lord Charles Sacks Stanton came from a legacy of wealth and British prestige, which included a Viscount title. Colton was his only child, born to an American woman, Grace Sacks, with whom he had lived until her death five years ago. He had assumed Colton would return to London and was surprised to find him here instead.

The bar was indeed a vibe in its own right, with crimson red wallpaper adorning the space in a 1920s speakeasy aesthetic, featuring rustic candelabras on the shelves alongside old radios and vintage books, beautifully colored bottles and black-and-white photos of other bars from that era. A three-piece blues band sat on stage at the back, the smoky voice of the man and his guitar adding to the place's timelessness.

Colton dressed the part, keeping the modern flair of his T-shirt with the added brown leather suspenders that were tightened around his shoulders and back, sharply tailored black pants, and a black bar towel dangling from his back pocket. This wasn't just any bar. It was a bar that demanded class from everyone who walked through those doors.

And by watching Colton for less than five minutes, Winter knew precisely what kind of man Colton Sacks had become. He'd seen this thousands of times and could spot his type from a mile away. The cocky arrogance of a man who swaggered like a lion, all tooth and bite, purr and play, but when pressed, they liked to be controlled and told what to do. Essentially, they were pleasers disguised as predators.

Fuck.

If Winter had a weakness of any kind, it was this—his own special kryptonite.

He could hear Mal's voice in his ear, fifteen years ago, when Winter had first discovered he even had a type. He could remember it like it was last night, the feeling of walking into a pleasure club like the one Mal had taken him to for the first time—the jittery excitement of what was waiting for him on the other side of the double doors.

The club was very similar to this bar, with its walls lined with heavy theater velvet curtains to muffle the sounds from the other rooms. Black wallpaper, velvet, and leather sofas surrounded the stage and bar area, while the backrooms were occupied with whatever kink was on the menu that night. And nearly everything was available.

It had been Winter's first time at a place like that, different than a dirty strip club on the side of the highway. This sex club felt tasteful, respectful, and rich. Everything Mal was. Mal had been his best friend since high school and accepted Winter right away when he came out, because Mal was gay, too.

Mal was also much more fashionable than Winter, and the expert in all areas of carnal appetites, had insisted that Winter wear a suit—black Armani, with wingtip Italian leather shoes.

"Black brings out your eyes," Mal had drawled, telling him to leave the tie in the car, which he did.

Mal had reserved a table and was given a drink menu upon sitting.

The music pulsed to the tempo in his veins, as Winter let out a nervous breath, unbuttoning his suit jacket, trying his damnest to relax. This was Mal's arena, not his.

"Sometimes I wish you'd drink to relax," Mal murmured, waving the waitress-bartender down to place their order, which included a club soda for Winter.

After several minutes of sipping their drinks and acclimating to their environment, Winter felt himself ease just slightly more in his chair.

"How does this work?" Winter asked, watching the men and women on the stage, doing an aerial rope dance that was very naked and very stimulating to watch.

Mal smirked, his classically handsome features looking even more striking in the darkness of the club. "Think of this as a buffet—sometimes, all you can eat. Other times, you may just want one. Some are sex workers, some are performers, others are here to be seen and fucked, others to simply watch. Or be watched while fucking. Take your pick."

Winter sucked in a breath, suddenly doubting if this was for him, as he surveyed the room.

It wasn't exactly his style, and maybe he shouldn't have agreed to come here. But he had been in a dry spell—a very long, very dry spell—with little sexual enjoyment of late. And Mal knew this, hence the weekend getaway just to come here.

Winter swallowed, attempting to drown the anxiously fluttering butterflies in his stomach with another long sip of soda. He never liked being on display. He preferred watching in the shadows. He'd always been like this, but especially after a car accident left him with a rather noticeable scar on his neck and upper jaw.

It didn't matter that Winter had multiple jaw and skin reconstruction surgeries, because what was left with nearly a seven-inch scar, deep and thick from beneath his neck to the edge of his jaw, an inch away from the corner of his lip. The scar got a lot of attention, but so did he.

Winter was tall, over six feet, with wavy black hair and eyes as dark as obsidian. He also knew he was handsome. He got his looks from his father, a selfish man who would use his good looks to ensnare rich women, leeching off them through his next bender or two.

"The three at the bar," Mal commented, his finger twirling to indicate where to look.

Winter's gaze moved away from the exotic dancers and saw the three young men, all dressed in suits, as though they were told the dress code and went rental shopping. They looked eager and yet out of place. Obviously drinking to cut the nerves of being there. It was an exclusive club with an even more exclusive membership. Mal was allowed one guest a year. Clearly, these men had wealthy fathers who got them a ticket in. Or they were part of tonight's menu, bought by the club.

Winter clenched his jaw, "Too young."

Mal tsked disapproving, "Just watch."

Winter, deciding to trust Mal, let out a slow exhale and did.

The three boys jostled and joked, and one, with bright red hair, punched the blond one in the shoulder, egging him on. The blond-haired young man pushed back roughly, cursing and saying something cutting to the redhead, who paled. The middle one, with dark hair, shoved both away and was clearly the mediator, the level-headed one of the three.

Mal's eyes were riveted on them.

Curious, Winter continued to look and couldn't help but watch the blond, the one who looked a breath away from giving the redhead a black eye. Instead, he pursed his upper lip and leaned heavily onto the bar top, calling over to the pretty bartender in a tight black dress, and with the swiftness of a Bengal cat, changed from aggressive irritation to sweet and smoldering.

Winter felt his blood tick and his heart oddly accelerate.

The pretty bartender poured him a drink, laughed kindly at his flirtation, and sauntered off. The blond's face dropped in angry disappointment, and he tossed his drink back, pouting.

Fucking pouting.

Winter's jaw clenched, a dark swirling clenching his gut.

Mal glanced over to Winter, "See it now?"

He did. And he fucking wanted it.

"I want the dark-haired one in the middle," Mal said, sipping his cocktail as his eyes danced with delight. "I do love a good pleaser. Let's see if he wants to please me."

Mal stood, not waiting for Winter to join him as he strode determinedly, yet casually, to the three men and began smooth-talking, eyes fixated like a hunter on the dark-haired man in the middle. Winter watched, curious to see what would happen. Mal made his intention known almost instantly, and the young man blushed, glancing nervously between his friends. The blond intervened, looking downright hostile at Mal.

So damned rude, Winter thought. Unable to tolerate the childish antics anymore, he was on his feet and at the bar before they could blink.

"I was asking your friend, not you," Mal said flippantly, yet his eyes were edged with something Winter rarely saw in his best friend, anger.

The blond's nostrils flared, "We ain't gay."

"That's yet to be determined," Mal remarked. "Why be here if you're not willing to explore all sides of yourself?"

The blond sneered, and Winter stepped to the side of the bar beside him, intentionally brushing his shoulder against him. The young man straightened, sensing his imposing presence, and turned to look over his shoulder at Winter. His eyes, as everyone's usually did when they first looked at him, traveled over the length of the menacing scar before meeting his gaze.

The young man tensed, and Winter saw the breath expel from his lips. Arousal. Curiosity. Aggression.

Winter saw it in a split second, and his heart hammered excitedly.

This was what he wanted, he realized. He wanted the chase, the fight, and the surrender.

"We're customers, we're not, uh, workers," the dark-haired man said quickly.

"We know," Mal drawled. "Now c'mon, sweetheart, let me buy you a drink and tell me why you're here."

Mal held out his hand to him, and Winter watched, mildly impressed as the young man nearly tripped over his feet before clasping Mal's hand and letting himself be led back to their table, away from the friends.

"I don't know what that asshole thinks he's doing, but we're here for the girls," the blond-haired man spat acidly, and the redhead, glancing only once at Winter, took his drink and headed toward the stage to watch the show.

"You're here for sex," Winter said flatly.

The blond shifted but didn't back down, squaring his shoulders, as though flashing his feathers at him—either to draw him in or away, he wasn't sure.

"Fuck off, dude, I ain't into guys."

Winter saw the young man's throat bob nervously as he licked his lower lip.

When Winter didn't make a move to retreat, the blond turned angrily on him, "What are you, dumb? I said fuck off!"

Winter's control snapped and he pivoted on his back heel, pushing the asshole against the bar with his chest and grabbing his throat, his fingers digging into his flesh. His broad shoulders and height caged him to the bar, and he felt the man's pulse skip wildly beneath his fingers.

The desire tightened his expression, and he slackened in Winter's hold before tensing once more, resisting himself—resisting Winter.

He grabbed at Winter's wrist and reared up against him like a feral animal. Winter smirked, unfazed by the lackluster attempt to get out of his grip as he angled his hips and ground into him, forcing him hard against the bar.

The blond let out a surprised gasp, and through the thin material of this man's rental suit, Winter felt the stiff bulge press against him.

Blood roared in his ears, feeling the hot breath strain against his hand, and his cock hardened like a cinder block between them.

Excitement like nothing he'd ever felt before rushed through Winter's body, and he nearly trembled with it. But instead, maintaining his composure, he leveled his gaze at him.

"Here's what's gonna happen," Winter instructed calmly. "You're gonna come with me to a room."

The blond pushed back, "Fuck no!"

Winter smirked, closing his hand tighter around his throat, and the man moaned, actually fucking moaned. Dear Christ, this was gonna be fun, Winter thought, gaze dipping over the plump pink lips that he intended to kiss and suck and fuck.

"You behave from here until we get to the room. And if you wanna bullshit me some more, go right ahead, but *only* when we're in the room. Because we both know you want this." His free hand moved between them, stroking the length of the bulging cock. The blond weakened his struggles, his moans becoming trembling whimpers.

Winter gritted his teeth, refusing to touch other than the light graze of his fingers and the hold on his neck. He wouldn't rub himself off here in the middle of the damned club. He would wait. He could be patient when necessary.

"Say it," Winter demanded hoarsely.

"Fuck," the man hissed out, glancing around to see if his friends were watching him, and swallowing hard, his hips humping Winter's fingers in the darkness of the bar.

"*Say it*, or I leave you here," Winter hissed, withdrawing his fingers, and the blond moaned weakly, cock straining at the air. "Your choice."

The blond licked his lips, looking scared but mostly excited. "I haven't done this with a guy before."

"Do you want to do this or not?" Winter asked coldly.

He sucked in a breath, "Yeah, yeah. Fuck it."

Winter arched an eyebrow and released him.

They spent two hours in a dark room at the club together, and when Winter finally left, his black suit jacket tossed casually over his shoulder, sweat beading his brow, he glanced back at the blond. He was lying naked and beautiful on the black silk sheets, all hard muscle damp with sex and sweat, limp and soaked, and begging for Winter to stay—for more. But Winter didn't need more. He knew his limits and had been thoroughly satisfied. He had finally quenched his thirst from his dry spell.

Later that night, on the drive back to the hotel, Mal teased him about liking brats.

Winter scrubbed a hand over his jaw, over the deep line of his scar tissue, relaxed, content even. It had been a long time since he had that much fun.

Winter laughed, "Brats?"

"In my world, they call someone like you a brat tamer."

"That sounds ridiculous," and yet, it stirred his blood at the idea of 'taming' someone. Of correcting their brutish, rude, or even downright hostile behavior. And they, in return, needed to be controlled, to be told what to do, and ultimately taken care of however Winter wanted.

Winter learned so much about himself in that experience that he returned to the club a few more times to learn more.

Fifteen years later, Winter had accepted this part of his identity and all the dark facets of it. Because being a tamer, of any kind, required dominance, control, patience, and power.

And Colton Sacks wasn't just any brat; he was a spoiled one with a rich daddy who threw money at problems to make them go away. Winter saw it firsthand. And the entitlement dripping from Colton was just as bad as the shit he had to scrape off his boots. Grace Sacks, however, was the exception. Colton's mother was as kind as she was brilliant. But she had passed away five years ago, and he couldn't turn to her for the information he needed, which meant he had to go to the source.

Winter watched as Colton's fingers fidgeted with something on the bar as he spoke to the two women. It shone briefly in the dim light of the bar, reflecting a silver glint of a metal lighter as he tapped it three times, before sliding it into his pocket. His muscles bunched and coiled into a tight band as he pushed himself off the back of the bar, reached for a bottle of tequila from behind him, and lined up three shots. The women giggled and swooned, happily taking the free drinks. Winter observed Colton's smile, noticing that it didn't quite reach his eyes.

Winter narrowed his gaze, curious if this was all just a ruse. A play to make customers happy. Free shots, uncaring smiles, and shameless flirting.

He wondered what would make Colton Sacks genuinely smile.

Maybe my hand around his throat? Winter bit back a curse. Focus, he told himself firmly. Colton Sacks was off-limits. He was a key witness and the only survivor of the second Ripper. Winter couldn't jeopardize the current case by having any dirty thoughts directed at the handsome blond behind the bar.

He had to toe the line.

There was too much at stake. Because the second Ripper was cunning. Bryan Douglas' body had been spotless of evidence, and the only thing connecting him to the North Tahoe Ripper case was the brand—the brand Colton Sacks had. It was one of the reasons Winter was here.

It was then that a large man, wearing a business suit, wrinkled from a long day at the office, loudly slammed his beer bottle on the bar top, demanding attention from the bartenders.

Colton lazily glanced up at the sight of the rude customer. The other bartender, a gothic young woman with red eyeliner and pitch-black hair, whipped around to glare hotly at the man in the business suit as she busily poured a beer for a different customer, intentionally ignoring him.

Colton drifted over to the demanding asshole.

Winter watched, fascinated by the play of events.

In less than a minute, the businessman's tense shoulders dropped and he laughed, his sour expression changing into a blush. Colton was flirting with him, too, and waved a finger at the man to lean further toward him from across the bar. The man, looking dazed by the cosmic pull of Colton, complied, and Colton proceeded to fix his tie, and Winter caught a glimpse of his finger brushing underneath the man's jaw.

The man's cheeks were a fiery red now, and he was gulping air as he leaned back into his barstool, while Colton fixed him a drink. The female bartender said something as she walked behind Colton, who tossed her a cool smirk. Then, the two women at the end giggled and gushed some more, attempting to capture Colton's attention again.

Apparently, whoever fell in the line of fire of Colton Sacks became wooed. It was a magnetic power that Winter had to see for himself.

He pushed his back off the dark wall and took the only empty barstool, sitting next to the flushed-faced man in the business suit.

Colton seemed as though he hadn't noticed him as he finished the drink and handed it to the man with the crooked tie.

"Drinks on me, luv," Colton drawled in that deep British accent. "Sorry again for the wait."

The man spluttered. "It's fine. I come here all the time. You guys are normally really good."

"All the time, eh?" Colton asked. "Any reason why?"

The man's face, impossibly, reddened some more. "No reason. Just like the, um, vibe."

"Well, how 'bout next time we're taking too long for you, why don't you come right up to me, yeah? I'll take care of ya."

The man licked his sweaty upper lip and practically fell out of his barstool when one of his office colleagues, dressed in similar after-work attire, clasped him hard on the shoulder. The businessman abruptly turned away, trying to regain his composure in front of his workmates.

"You spyin' on me?" Colton's voice dropped low, directed at Winter.

Winter's eyebrows arched in surprise. "I didn't think you noticed me."

Colton's chin pursed upward with his lip as he frowned. Pale, sky blue eyes, riveted on his face. "I saw you the moment you walked in, Detective."

Winter hesitated at the purring drawl in Colton's voice and felt his stomach clench.

This was what Colton had done with the last three customers. Winter could've smiled, but didn't.

"What's it been? Five years?" Colton slid his hand into his pocket, plucking out that silver lighter and tapping it on the bar top, his full attention on Winter, scrutinizing him. "A little grayer around the edges, old man, but it looks good on you." Colton's eyes slowly dipped over his body. "Real good..."

Winter knew that Colton didn't possibly mean any of that. This was a power play—a fun one, but a game nonetheless.

Winter smiled blandly, "Thanks. And I'm not that old."

"How old are ya now? 50-something'?"

Winter aged at hearing the high number and bit back the curse on the tip of his tongue. Another jab, another poke. Colton was testing him, and he couldn't fight back the way he usually would, so instead, he continued his polite politician smile, "I'm 45."

"It's a bit old for a lesson on what a proper watch looks like. Is that plastic?"

Jab, jab.

God, Winter would've given anything to reach across the bar and teach him some manners and maybe do it with his hand collaring his throat and...

Winter blinked and felt strong, sure fingers grasping his hand, dragging him forward to inspect the watch. Colton initiated the contact, bold and unafraid. This caught Winter off guard.

"Jesus Christ, mate. You could do better. Does this have a fuckin' compass on it?" Colton asked incredulously.

Winter, stunned, laughed. "Who are you? And what happened to the Colton Sacks I once knew?"

Colton tossed him a wicked, almost insolent smile, "He's dead, mate. Died ten years ago."

Winter saw a flash of that night. Of blood spraying the air, and the sound of a shotgun blast. Barry Pollock's body was pinned like a helpless deer by a ruined, crashed truck against the base of a tree.

Colton noticed something shift in his expression. His sparkling blue eyes sharpened, "You rememberin' that night like I am?"

Winter stiffened.

Colton hummed at his reaction. "I remember everything."

Winter held his gaze. He wasn't ashamed of anything he had done that night—nothing. He did what he had to.

His fists tightened into knuckles and he sat back, attempting to move away from this conversation somehow, when Colton's fingers squeezed his wrist, drawing him closer.

"Well, that just proves what a dangerous man you are, Detective Winter. That you can kill a man, and not even blink about it afterward."

Winter snapped his wrist back, goose bumps erupting up his neck, as he shifted in his seat.

"You want something to drink?" Colton asked casually, as though he hadn't brought up the subject of him killing someone.

"Club soda," Winter gruffed out.

Colton looked mildly impressed and, with a quick twirl, grabbed a couple of pints off the shelf behind him and made two club sodas, one with lime and the other with cherries. He placed both in front of him. Winter chose the lime, and Colton smirked, taking the cherries.

Winter noticed the outline of the tattoo on Colton's forearm, a dark forest scene that looked almost menacing, with black trees lined and grouped tightly, drawn in thin lines and sharp detail, snaking up his forearm and bicep, with hints of it on his neck, the rest hidden by his black shirt.

Colton took a sip of his soda. "How'd you find me?"

The bar was beginning to fill now with the demands of people crowding around Winter.

"How do you think?" Winter asked.

Colton gave a careless shrug, "My lovely father, I presume."

Winter sipped his soda, pulled out his card, and handed it to him. "We need to talk."

The man beside Winter tapped his beer on the bar top again, this time smiling teasingly at Colton, attempting to divert his attention. Colton, for the first time all evening, frowned, his jaw tightening beneath his dark blond beard, looking impatient and angry. Winter felt something tighten over his chest at the leveling gaze Colton gave him.

"About?" Colton asked.

Winter paused, lips pursed, knowing full well he wasn't about to have this conversation in a crowded bar.

Colton suddenly, unexpectedly, let out a long, dramatic sigh, looking disappointed. "So, you're not here to ask me out?"

Winter's stomach swooped suddenly, throat tightening.

Ask him out? Christ, he was good.

It was a rare thing indeed to disarm Winter, let alone challenge him.

He never experienced this part of the game so well. In fact, most of the men he pursued folded like a deck of cards when Winter set his sights on them. But he wasn't setting anything on Colton. Hell no. This was work, not play, and he needed to get the fuck out of this bar and clear his head.

Colton Sacks was just barely a man when they first met. The man before him today was charming, dangerously so, and naturally charismatic in a way he hadn't anticipated. He hadn't expected his physical reaction to him either, which was ridiculous, given that Winter had always known there was something unique—something intriguing—about Colton Sacks.

He should've been more prepared for him.

Colton, ignoring the people at the bar, snatched the card from Winter's fingers and leaned forward, his lips so close that Winter could feel the heat of his breath on the side of his face. It took everything in his power not to turn his chin and stare him down. He didn't like being on display or noticed, and what Colton was doing was drawing attention. His jaw hardened like a steel plate against his teeth.

"I have a feeling..." Colton murmured smoothly. "You don't date—you fuck. I can tell just by lookin' at ya. But you ain't here to fuck me. You're here for business. I get off at one. Or you wait, come by this address tomorrow around three." Colton pulled a pen out from behind the bar and scribbled on the back of Winter's card, and handed it back to him. "I'll meet you out front. You can buy me lunch since I bought you a drink."

Winter hesitated before taking the card.

Colton didn't, grabbing his hand once more, and flattening the card into his palm, patting it three times, before forcing his fingers closed around it. "Now with the deepest regards, I kindly ask you to fuck off. You're distracting me. Or..." Colton's voice was a husky rasp. "You can sit here all night and let me look at ya. Cuz bloody hell, sweetheart, you're just my type. I gotta thing for older men," he winked, followed by the most arrogant smile Winter had ever seen.

His cock twitched.

Holy fucking shit.

The man in the business suit beside him gaped and shot a furious look at Winter, eyeing him up and down as though he was competition for Colton's priceless attention.

What the hell just happened?

Winter watched as Colton slipped away, sliding the lighter into his pocket and taking charge of the chaotic bar that it had become in the last few minutes. He boldly held out his arms and yelled loudly at the clamoring customers. "We will be with you shortly, my luvs, don't you fuckin' fret!"

Winter, for the first time in ten years, understood why the North Tahoe Ripper chose Colton Sacks. Not just for his obvious, handsome looks, but for this—his casual, undaunted confidence that oozed from his very pores as though he was born with it. And miraculously, he still had it—after everything he endured at the hands of the Rippers.

Heart thumping, Winter stood, slid the card into his pocket, and walked out, his mind racing and stuck on the words: *"I gotta thing for older men."*

CHAPTER 3

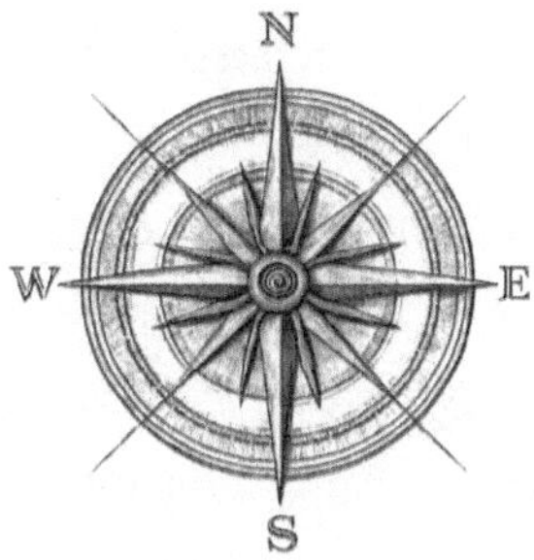

Colton cradled his mug of tea and sat perched on the padded bench in front of his loft apartment's windows, overlooking the sleeping, dark city. His thoughts swirled as he glanced at the phone on the cushioned seat, debating. His beard still felt damp from the shower as he sat in nothing but a simple white T-shirt and black boxer briefs, his bare toes digging into the cushion, his back firmly against the wall, breathing slowly in and out, grounding himself.

He could hear his best friend's voice in his head already: "Just call me, silly. I'll always answer. You know that!"

Without waiting for more doubts to creep in, Colton leaned forward and called the second person on his emergency contact list.

It rang only twice before he heard Jamie's sleepy voice answer, "Everything okay?"

After years of no longer being roommates, Jamie always anticipated a late-night call if Colton had one of his nightmares.

No nightmare tonight, he thought, *just my past coming full circle.*

"Hey," Colton drawled casually. Too casually. "Sorry to bother you so

39

late."

The sound of bed sheets rustling, and her whispered voice became slightly clearer. "You're never a bother, Colt. Give me a sec, I don't want to wake Tess."

Tess, the happy yet bittersweet reason he and Jamie were no longer roommates, was Jamie's partner, going two years strong now. They met at work. Tess was a traveling nurse who came in on a rotation for one of Jamie's hospice patients, and somehow, despite the hardship of working with the dying and the grieving, they found each other.

They found each other in the dark, his mother had once said that to him in reference to someone who had once been found in the dark.

"Wow," Jamie marveled. "I can't remember the last time you called like this."

Colton let his head drop back into the cool glass of the window, staring vacantly into the black sky. "Me either."

"That's good though, right?"

It was always good not to have those nightmares. "It's something else," he dragged out. "Someone came into the bar tonight."

His words choked on the name—Winter. Colton was afraid to say it out loud for some reason, unsure how to start this conversation, as if telling his name would conjure up memories—or worse, feelings —from the past he would rather not dredge up.

He closed his eyes and sighed. "Superman."

Jamie let out an audible gasp. "Like as in *the* Superman?"

The name Superman had come from Colton's mother. She had dubbed him that ten years ago, and the name stuck—maybe it was because of Winter's dark black hair and even darker eyes. His formidable size, with the broad chest and corded arms that looked to be made out of steel. Yet he moved like a dancer, graceful and light, never once making his 6'3" size intimidating, or even noticeable. Mum said if she hadn't already been head over heels with Miles, she would've easily swooned over the man who saved her son.

She had always been overly romantic in that way, a sucker for a good love story.

Jamie had been his mother's hospice nurse. That's where their friendship started. That's when she, too, found out about what happened to Colton and who Superman was. Mum, even in the late stages of her cancer, would still talk about Winter, how kind he was, how handsome, how caring, as though he were still active in their lives somehow.

"Jamie," Colton groaned, pinching the brim of his nose, his pulse skittering in his veins, thinking about how handsome Winter had looked tonight in the darkly lit bar, his rough hands grasping the soda, the slight graying black stubble on his cheeks and sharp jawline. And his lips, good God in heaven, those lips were as sinful as those black eyes of his.

"No, no running away. You called to tell me about him—now you have to share," Jamie pressed. "What's it been? Five years?"

Colton stilled and suddenly felt the rush of the memory from his mother's funeral—the drizzle of the rain sprinkling over the bleak skies of Sacramento. Colton, suspended in grief, was stunned to see him there. He stood far back from the rest of the crowd as they lowered his mother's coffin into the ground. Colton hadn't invited him, and in a way, he didn't want the memory of his past there. So, he had coldly brushed past Winter, without a word, refusing to acknowledge him.

"He wants to talk," Colton finally said.

"About?" Jamie asked.

"I think it has something to do with the case."

"Shit."

"Yeah."

Jamie paused a long beat before asking quietly, "Are you going to?"

His fingers bent the paper of the tea wrapper, a low-grade anger pulsating through him. "Why should I?"

"Colt..."

He heard something in her tone he didn't like but couldn't name. "It doesn't matter what he did back then. It matters what he did the last eight years."

Jamie sighed, "I know you're angry, Colton. I know. And you have every right to be. But he's here now. That has to mean something?"

"It means bloody nothing."

"Then why did you call me?"

He hesitated, a murmured curse breathing from his pursed lips.

"It's cuz of her, isn't it?" Jamie asked knowingly.

His mother. His mother—the one who never gave up on him, on anyone. Including Detective—disappointing-fuckin'—Winter. His eyes flicked to the silver lighter glinting at the edge of the bench, staring up at him.

Jamie let out another long breath, her voice edged with anxiety. "There's something I need to tell you, Colton."

His shoulders tensed, "What?"

"It's about your mom. I didn't understand at the time when I overheard her talking, but I think I know why he was there that day at her funeral."

Colton pressed the phone harder into his palm.

"Sometimes when I was at the house, she'd be on the phone with someone. It was always hushed. I tried my best not to listen in, but it was hard with her, you know what I mean? She was so infectious and bright, even when she was serious. I heard her talk about you and the case. And I remember hearing her say: 'Someone has to keep looking when I'm gone'."

He remembered his mother's boxes of files on the North Tahoe Ripper case and how, after she died, he had the violent urge to destroy them all. Instead, he boxed them away in a nameless storage unit and left them to rot indefinitely. The only thing he kept was her laptop.

"You think she was talking to him?" Colton asked, irritated by the notion that his mom possibly kept a secret from him. They told each other everything. Why would she keep this from him?

Because she knew how I'd react.

He took another forced breath, trying to calm his anger.

"Maybe," Jamie offered softly. "She never talked about the case with anyone—not even you."

"Because the case is fuckin' closed."

Because of Winter, he thought.

Barry Pollock, the North Tahoe Ripper, was barely dead in the ground for two years when Winter had sent him an official notice in the mail that the Placer County Sheriff's Department and Northern California FBI office had closed the case. The letter was cold and sterile. And in that moment, the man he had trusted with his life had betrayed him through a fucking letter. Winter hadn't even bothered to pick up the phone and call him.

Colton lost all respect for the man after that and refused to speak his name out loud for years. It was his mum, his bloody loving mum, who insisted that Winter was just doing his job because the trail for the second Ripper had run cold. That there were no new suspects, no new abductions or killings. And the biggest factor in all of this is that no evidence was discovered to suggest that the second Ripper ever existed, outside of Colton's statement and the brand.

The North Tahoe Ripper was dead.

Case closed.

"It was never closed for her. She believed you—I believe you. You were so stuck on him that you didn't see the people around you who still knew that what you said was true."

Colton set down his mug, needing something stronger than tea to get him to bed tonight. "I need to get some sleep. Forget I called, all right?"

Jamie's voice was quiet as she asked, "Are you going to see him?"

Colton had given Winter the location to his second job for tomorrow, but he had regretted it after giving it to him, not sure if he wanted to talk. It was one thing to flirt and tease, attempting to get Winter to storm out of his bar and leave him the hell alone. But the man, resolute as ever, barreled through his charm offense without batting an eye. That's what men with steel for spines often did. They didn't wilt easily under the intensity of the sun. And Colton had pulled out all the stops to make that man wilt.

The fucker didn't.

"I dunno," he admitted.

Jamie sighed, "Text me in the morning?"

"Yeah, all right. Good night," he murmured. "Thanks for picking up."

"Always."

He slept like shit and woke up feeling hungover despite not having a drop of alcohol in him. Colton went through his routine just the same and made sure to arrive at the gym before heading to his second job. Boxing always made him feel grounded, channeling his anger into something besides himself—or worse, others. His anger often got him into trouble in his younger years. Boxing had been the only thing that seemed to stick with him after everything else faded. His dad encouraged Colton's love of boxing through his usual methods of finding the best coaches and trainers. Luckily, some of the best boxing gyms were in London and LA. Two places he frequented. Though he hadn't been back in London for a while, he knew a trip to see his dad was long overdue.

After beating the hell out of a heavy bag for an hour with intense weight training, Colton felt better, showered and changed for work, and walked the mile to the local YMCA.

"Yo, yo, yo! Big man brawler comin' in!" Shouted Ty, one of Colton's favorite youths who frequented the center. Ty's mom, a single parent, worked three jobs and barely had time for Ty and his two younger brothers, so Colton made sure to always carve out time for them.

Colton smirked, "Well, looky here," he taunted. "Are those new kicks I see?"

Ty, with his freshly cleaned Nikes, beamed, racing up to him with a basketball in hand. "I got these yesterday at the mall. Mama says they will give me an extra jump on my game."

Colton scoffed, "Please. I'd like to see you try, little man."

"You callin' my mama a liar?" Ty accused with a dazzle of bright white teeth.

"What's one of our rules, Ty?"

Ty's smile wavered, and he grew serious, "Never disrespect your mother. She is the bread we eat, the air we breathe, the laundry we clean, the chores we do, and the love we receive."

"Good man," Colton said proudly. "And no, I wasn't disrespecting your mama—I was challenging you and those posh Nikes you got talkin' up a big game. Now, get your brothers and the rest of the gang. I'm in the mood to wipe the floor with you lot."

Three o'clock had arrived quickly, and Colton had felt eyes on his back for the last twenty minutes. He knew who was watching him. Ever since he was 20 years old, he had known when Detective Eli Winter was in the room. To this day, he still hates how his body reacts to the feeling. That stirring pulse of excitement thrummed through him like a live electrical current.

After years of therapy, Colton realized that his basic attraction to Winter was because of two things: Winter had saved his life, and Colton, at the time, was a hormonal young man with daddy issues.

Trauma can cause people to form attachments, sometimes too quickly. And that's all that ever was between them. A fucked up trauma in the woods with a psychopath chasing him, intent on killing him, and Winter intervening.

Colton left the basketball court, a couple of kids calling after him. He gave them a dismissive wave, grabbed his gym bag, and wiped his face with a towel before stuffing it back in and tossing the bag over his shoulder, heading toward the parking lot.

Detective Winter leaned casually against his gunmetal gray truck, his hands crossed over his chest, his aviator sunglasses pushed up the brim of his nose, keeping the smoldering glare of the sun off his face. His pressed khaki shirt was buttoned, and the long sleeves neatly folded up over his elbows, showing the tanned skin of his forearms, smattered with dark hair. The shirt was tucked into his dark blue jeans, the gun belt secured on his hip with a holster gun and a shiny gold sheriff's badge. His eyes traveled to the sharp, flat stomach and lean legs that supported the tall man. He wore worn-down hiking boots and that silly plastic watch, and yet somehow looked like a goddamned model that belonged on a calendar or poster somewhere. Not here, picking him up in a dirty parking lot, in a low-income part of the city.

Though Detective Eli Winter would never be a model with a scar like that. Too garish for slick magazine covers. People didn't want to see something that dark—that violent—reflected on such beauty. He remembered not seeing it that night at all—too frightened by what was coming for him.

"You work here?" Winter asked curiously, his husky voice caressing a fine line of sweat between Colton's back as he straightened.

"No, I just like playing basketball with underprivileged children in my spare time." Colton snapped open a couple of buttons at the collar of his throat, attempting to cool his sweaty skin.

Colton motioned to his truck. "Don't wanna stand outside on the pavement with these fuckin' kids. They're the biggest gossipers on the block. Let's go."

Winter nodded, and they climbed inside.

"Didn't expect you to be workin' here," Winter remarked, turning on the truck, letting the AC cool the cab. "Goin' from the bar to this, I mean."

Colton rolled the sleeves of his shirt up to his elbows. His uniform at the YMCA required him to cover his tattoos, which he didn't mind, but it was a bit bothersome when he spent days like this beating the blacktop with a basketball and twenty eager, energetic boys to keep up with. He reached for the towel in his bag again, wiping his forearms, tempted to change into his gym shirt from earlier, but that too was probably still sweaty from the boxing club.

"They had an opening, so I took it. Jobs a job," Colton said with a shrug. "The other option was the orphanage a couple of blocks over. But this one was closer to my apartment, and they have a basketball court."

Winter arched an eyebrow. "Sorry, I don't mean to offend. I suppose I wasn't expecting..."

"What?" Colton rolled his head against the seat, eyeing him coolly. "What were you expecting?"

The last time Winter had seen him, he was grieving and lost. It had been five years since his mother's death, and ten since Pollock's.

Colton wasn't the same person he was all those years ago. And the man beside him was still a stranger, despite what they had gone through together.

He glanced over the older man, seeing the telling lines of his age and the veins in his hands—hands that he had once held close, soothing and calming him—that slow, dark drawl of his voice flickering across his memory.

"You're safe. You're safe with me..."

Winter's silence now seemed to echo in the space between them.

Colton pushed up his sleeves past the elbows, the material tightening around his thick biceps. "I'm hungry. Skipped lunch to do this with you, so if you don't mind, I'd like to eat before we get into it."

Winter put the truck in reverse and maneuvered out of the parking lot. "I hear the homeless shelter has good soup on Tuesdays."

Colton, unexpectedly, laughed.

CHAPTER 4

C olton chose a sandwich deli shop in a busy part of town, and inside the restaurant it was even busier. *Not exactly a discreet location to have this conversation*, Winter thought.

Colton entered first, the shop bells ringing to announce their arrival, and he shouted over the crowded line of customers to one of the men behind the counter. "Jose!"

Jose, a burly man who had the speed and accuracy of a front-line chef in a five-star restaurant, glanced up from the sandwich he was carving. He cracked a smile at the sight of Colton. "Colt—the usual?"

"Ya, make it two. We'll be in the back."

"Sounds good, bro."

Colton led Winter around the side and down a hallway into a usually quiet dining hall that was empty of customers except for a couple of old school arcade games.

"We won't be bothered back here," Colton said. "No one actually eats here."

Winter sat across from him in a very clean booth and removed his sunglasses, raking his hands through his hair, which drew Colton's eyes before he quickly looked away and leaned heavily against the puffy leather booth.

"You aren't what I was expecting either, you know," Colton said.

"And what were you expecting?"

Colton's sky blue eyes flickered over him, and he furrowed his brow, intentionally letting the question hang in the air.

Their gazes held a long minute, and Winter wondered if this was how all his interactions with this man would be—tense, or flirty, or both. Goddamn, Colton was gonna give him whiplash by the time they were done talking.

"So, what did you order me?" Winter asked, drawing the conversation back to a more neutral topic.

"The best damn sandwich in the city. You'll like it. Trust me."

Winter smiled faintly, unable to decide if he trusted him. He trusted his mother, as sentimental and good-hearted as she was. He supposed he would have to wait and find out about Colton.

"Tell me," Colton tapped his fingers on the wooden table between them. "What were you expecting when you saw me, Detective Winter?"

The boy had certainly grown into a man, and after some of the things he said to him last night, Winter realized he was woefully unprepared for him. Not to mention his aching cock this morning that was literally leaking, demanding his attention the second Winter's eyes opened in his hotel room.

It had been a long time since he woke up that hard and nearly stumbled into the shower, mind still blurry with sleep, the need to release coursing through him like a blazing bonfire. The second Winter had touched his smooth shaft, barely even pumping, he was so ready to go off, and all it took was his touch—and seeing a flash of a wicked, knowing smirk and pale blue eyes.

Winter grunted and cursed himself as hot, streaming ribbons of cum coated his fist and the wall of the hotel shower, as he dropped his forehead and arm against the cool tile, wondering how the hell he was gonna get through this investigation with his head on straight.

Winter glanced at the neck tattoo and pointed to his own neck, pushing away thoughts of this morning's shower.

Colton shrugged, leaning against the booth, letting his arm drape across the top, the well-defined curve of muscles also catching Winter's gaze, and glanced back.

"Yeah, got that on a dime spent in Folsom," Colton drawled casually.

Winter hesitated.

"Christ, Winter. It's a joke. I know you probably checked my record before you came here."

He did. After the events in Tahoe and the ensuing media circus, Colton disappeared. He assumed it had a lot to do with his dad, Lord Stanton, keeping him away from the spotlight of being the Ripper's only survivor.

"You're the same," Colton said with a slight shake of his head. "Serious and annoyingly fuckin' quiet."

Before Winter could reply, Jose burst into the dining hall, arms loaded with sandwiches in red plastic baskets and two beers. Colton rose, taking the sandwiches, before giving the man a brotherly hug and pushing a couple of twenty-dollar bills into his hand. Jose attempted to protest, and Colton waved him off.

"Keep it," Colton insisted. "You mind bringing us a couple of sodas instead?"

Jose nodded, clasping his hand on his shoulder in gratitude. He took the beers away and strolled out of the dining room.

Once Jose left, Colton returned to his seat across from him, opened the white paper wrapping around the sandwich, and took a hungry bite. His throat worked as he swallowed, looking too damn tempting. Winter was momentarily mesmerized, irritated by his reaction.

"He didn't want you to pay for the sandwiches," Winter stated, needing to distract himself.

Colton hesitated on the next bite, the sandwich an inch from his full lips. "He owes me."

"For?"

Colton paused, looking annoyed. "You gonna let me eat first before the 20 questions start, Detective?"

This shut Winter up and he relented, eating their thick, meaty sandwiches in silence, as both of them were hungry. Jose came in with the sodas a few moments later, leaving with another thump on Colton's shoulder.

Once finished and full, Winter wiped his lips on the paper napkin and sipped his icy soda. Colton had devoured his sandwich and was sitting patiently, a slight smile dancing across his lips, unabashedly staring, as though wanting to get a rise out of Winter.

Usually, Winter would be unfazed by something as insignificant as this. But Colton was different because he was off-limits.

Very, very off-limits.

"I spotted Jose's niece trying to get into my bar one night and got her out of line before the bouncer did for the fake ID she had," Colton said, answering Winter's earlier question. "She's barely 18."

Winter tossed his napkin into the sandwich basket. "That was kind of you."

"No," Colton replied. "It wasn't. She nearly tore my head off for it, and her mother laid into me the next day. Jose is the only one with any damned sense in that family."

"How do you know them?" Winter asked.

"Jose sometimes spars with me at the club. Used to be a heavyweight back in his day."

"The club?"

"Do you just repeat everything I say?"

"Habit."

"It's a boxing club. Been goin' there a few years now. You got any hobbies?"

Winter frowned, eyebrows arching as he sat back, folding his hands into his lap. He had always been awkward in conversations with people. He blamed it on the job. So accustomed to interrogating that he had forgotten what regular discussions were.

"Aw, c'mon, Detective Winter. Sharing something about yourself won't hurt—or maybe," Colton's boot toe brushed against his under the booth, stretching out lazily, "it will."

Winter's awareness sharpened, wondering if he should shift away from the boot or stay perfectly still. "I golf sometimes. Tahoe has some nice greens."

Colton smirked, seeming pleased by this. "Thrilling. What else?"

"I joined a bowling league last year."

"Jesus, how old are you?"

"I already told you last night."

Colton scoffed, "Hell, I'm sure my grandma would've loved to play bingo with you."

"I don't mind bingo."

"Of course you don't."

"I like to cook," Winter heard himself admit. He hadn't told anyone, not even his best friend Mal, about it.

Colton waved his fingers encouragingly, "Go on."

"Every Friday night, if work permits, I go to the Italian Cultural Center and learn how to make dishes. I made pasta from scratch in the first lesson, and I'm working my way up to traditional Italian breads."

Impressed, Colton's expression softened. "Does the missus join you?"

Winter sipped his soda and shook his head.

Colton's eyes narrowed. "No Mrs. Winter or...Mr. Winter?"

Winter tried to ignore the silky, low tone and straightened. "I'm single."

"But dating?"

"I don't care to talk about my personal life."

"So that's a no," Colton stated simply.

"I didn't say that."

"You did."

"I didn't."

"Agree to disagree."

Winter felt his knuckles tighten around the pint glass and sighed heavily through his nose. "You don't know when to quit, do you?"

Colton's smile edged with a flash of something Winter couldn't decipher. "A quality you once praised."

Winter felt his chin hitch back, reeling. He suddenly remembered that moment, remembered the praise, and nearly choked on his soda. The young man, with scraped knees, bloodied lips and nose, eyes sunken and hollow, stared helplessly at him. And Winter had praised him, held him, reassured him, and Colton clung to him like a vine in a storm.

Winter didn't see a trace of that boy in the man before him now.

This man was confident, brazen, and angry.

"What's your favorite Italian dish you've made so far?" Colton asked the question, throwing Winter slightly off balance.

"A lemon—pasta something. It was good."

Colton hummed, swirling the ice in his soda. "So, Detective Winter, why are you here?"

Winter leaned forward, feeling the tension in his spine, wondering if this was a good idea—or a horrible one.

It was hard enough being a survivor of a serial rapist murderer, let alone one that made international news due to Colton's privileged status. But to be asked to return to an investigation that had been officially closed, after dismissing his claims of the second Ripper, felt like opening a can of worms after years of letting it rot on the shelf, untouched. But Winter rarely did anything easy.

Winter slowly withdrew his phone from his back pocket and showed him the picture of the two young men on the screen. "You recognize them?"

Colton leaned forward, scrutinized the photos, and after a moment, shook his head. "No. Should I?"

"Details of the investigation haven't been made public yet," Winter explained, his tone lowering. "I asked Sheriff Jim Emerson to let me meet with you first before this news went public."

Something in Colton's easy-going expression changed.

"The first victim went missing three weeks ago. His body was found last week off North Tahoe Trail. The second victim was taken shortly after. He's been missing for four days now."

Colton's jaw twitched. "What does this have to do with me?"

Winter flicked his screen and showed him the next photo. Colton sucked in a breath, face paling.

"I'm sorry," Winter said thickly. "You were right ten years ago. There were two of 'em."

CHAPTER 5

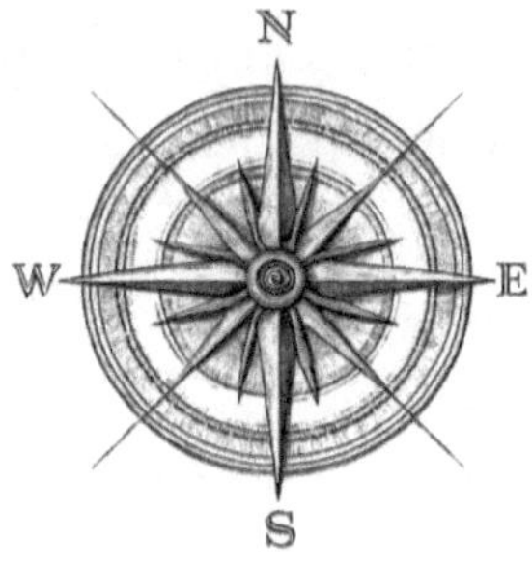

The hard vibrations of his fists slamming into the heavy bag ricocheted up his arms and chest. He couldn't hear the music. Couldn't hear his coach or anyone else in the club. All he heard was Winter's voice, *"You were right ten years ago. There were two of 'em."*

Two.

And the last victim that was taken could've been Colton's fucking brother. He looked almost identical to him. It was downright eerie as he stared blindly at the picture Winter showed him. It took everything not to snatch the phone right out of his hand and stomp on it. So, what did he do instead? He stormed out of the fucking building like it was on fire, unable to cope with the reality of hearing that the Ripper—the man that had brutally raped and tortured him—was still alive and killing again.

Twenty minutes later, drenched in fresh sweat, emotions swirling, Colton jogged home. It was only a couple of miles, but he hoped it would clear the fog in his mind.

He turned the corner of his block and his breath hitched in surprise at the man standing on his front porch, arms crossed over his chest, aviator sunglasses perched high, and looking far too relaxed, like a horse that had fallen asleep standing up.

Colton ignored the galloping race of his heartbeat and chalked it up to the hard run.

"What are you doing here?" He asked, noticing it came out much louder than he intended.

Winter's head angled upward, "Hello to you, too, Mr. Sacks."

His drawling voice soothed his frayed nerves, and he sighed. Colton had left their conversation fairly quickly once Winter dropped the bomb on his head about the Ripper killing and kidnapping again.

"Can I come in?" Winter asked politely.

Colt nodded, sucking in a deep breath, knowing that this conversation wasn't finished.

He unlocked the front door of the apartment complex and led them inside. A few minutes later, they were in his loft apartment. The cool air from the AC felt refreshing after the workout and run. He gulped down a water bottle from the fridge.

"Can I get you something to drink? Water? Iced tea?" he asked as Winter strolled into the open space of the loft.

The living room and kitchen were an open-floor concept, and the upstairs area consisted of his bedroom and bathroom. Two towering, expansive windows took up one side of the apartment, while the stairs and a TV occupied the other side. Winter walked to Colton's favorite spot in the whole place, the windowsill bench, which was well-worn and had a coffee table beside it, his tea from the night before still sitting there, along with a book and his notebook. He stilled, oddly anxious at Winter spying on his personal things.

"Iced tea would be lovely, thank you," Winters said, the ever-polite gentleman.

Colton knew a thing or two about being a gentleman. The problem was, he bloody well didn't care about polite manners when it came to this man.

He grabbed a cold bottle of iced tea from the fridge and walked it over to him. Winter straightened, slipping his sunglasses into his shirt pocket, smiling thinly. "Thank you." He motioned to the open book resting on the coffee table, "*Meditations*, that's a good book. I read it in college."

"You have power over your mind, not outside events. Realize this, and you will find strength," Colton recited easily.

Winter nodded appreciatively, "I like that line, too. One of my favorites is, 'The best revenge is to be unlike him who performed the injury.'"

Colton's fingers rolled into his palms and he stepped forward, his voice cutting. "Is that you askin' for forgiveness, Detective Winter?"

Winter stilled and returned the hard stare. "You'll know when I ask it."

Colton studied him, feeling the whoosh of sensation in his lower belly, and he forced himself to take a step back, flopping down on his couch, attempting to look bored. "You're back—so soon? I must be a popular guy."

"At the moment," Winter unscrewed the top of the tea and took a sip.

Winter reminded him of a dark, thoroughbred stallion—all muscle and black hair— who seemed relaxed in his loft, and he hated how easy he made it look. It took years of practice and patience for Colton to find that strength, that sense of comfort within himself. Winter made it look as natural as breathing. He hated him for it.

"What else do you want, Detective Winter? You've already notified me, I think we're done, yeah?" Colton asked, unable to hide the irritation in his tone.

Winter cleared his throat, still standing, "I have a few more things I'd like to discuss."

"Well, go on then, I have work later tonight."

"We need evidence to confirm that this is the same Ripper from ten years ago," Winter said, holding his gaze steady. "Evidence that connects the recent murder with the old case."

Colton shook his head, not following.

"I went through your old record and saw that the photo of the..." Winter cleared his throat again, "brand. It was blurry at best, and I would need another updated picture."

Blood drained from Colton's body, and yet the anger, impossibly, raged. "You wanna picture of my dick?"

Winter pursed his lips into a firm line. "Bryan Douglas has a similar brand in his groin area, and the other bodies that were found ten years ago were set on fire by the Ripper, so I can't confirm this is the second Ripper—not yet. But Douglas's body was left in good condition, and we were able to see his brand clearly this time. Almost like this second Ripper is demanding our attention now. And you are the only one who has this mark, the only one that can connect the cases. Because right now, this just looks like any other murder."

Colton, feeling reckless, stood up and reached for the waistband of his basketball shorts. "So, you wanna do it, or you okay with a selfie?"

Winter's black eyes somehow darkened for the briefest of seconds before answering, "Whatever you're comfortable with."

"I ain't comfortable with any of this, so what choice do I really have?" he shot back.

Winter carefully set down his tea, his movements slow and calm, as though not wishing to startle the bear in the room. "We don't have to do this now."

Colton snorted, "Please. You want evidence. You can't protect me from being evidence—just like I can't escape this. So might as well get on with it." Colton dragged his sweaty hoodie off and tossed it on the couch, followed by his sneakers. He reached for the edge of his waistband, but Winter's hand captured his wrist, stilling him.

Colton could feel the heat of his strong fingers and felt goosebumps race up his arms.

"Do you want to try to take a picture of it yourself?" Winter asked softly.

"I can't," he admitted roughly. "The angle is fuckin' impossible to do with one hand. If you get my meaning."

Something passed over the older man's features, tight and controlled, and he nodded, turning his back to give him some privacy.

Colton refused to acknowledge the hard beat of his heart against his ribcage or the shortness of breath suddenly gasping from his lungs as he lowered the shorts and undershorts. Naked from the waist down he took a seat on the couch, grabbed his black hoodie, and with gritted teeth he brushed his cock to the side of his leg, splayed out to reveal the small brand that the Rippers had burned into his flesh.

"All right," Colton said with a shaky voice, averting his gaze as Winter slowly turned. His ears felt hot, and the back of his neck prickled, but he didn't move, knowing Winter would be professional about this.

Winter pulled out his phone, and Colton noticed the man wouldn't come any closer. He frowned, "You're gonna have to get closer than that."

Winter let out a puff of breath from his lips, and Colton glanced up, seeing a hint of discomfort on the man, and this, for some reason, calmed him.

"I won't bite," Colton snapped.

Winter's eyes flickered up to him and he took two steps, standing between Colton's open legs. Winter angled the phone and took a picture, but due to his height and the low couch, Colton wasn't sure the picture would be good enough.

"I'm going to have to get closer," Winter said.

Colton nodded and closed his eyes, refusing to watch this next part. He felt Winter shift and heard him drop to a knee, his massive frame filling the open space between Colton's legs. He caught the scent of pine, coffee, and firewood. His cock twitched.

Fuck. Fuck. Fuck.

His stomach clenched as he listened to Winter's gruff drawl, "The hoodie is blocking a part of it."

Colton's eyes opened, and Winter's handsomely tense face greeted him. His expression was stormy and almost violent. Surprised, Colton glanced away, pushing the sweater over, jostling his stiffening cock and grinding his molars down to ash, resisting the building pressure cupping his balls.

Winter let out a hard breath, chest heaving as he held his phone out over the brand and snapped a few photos. Colton's eyes were transfixed on his mouth, watching him suck in his lower lip before releasing it, coating it with his saliva.

Bloody fuckin' hell, this man was beautiful and the sexiest thing he'd seen in ages. Colton never denied his sexuality, especially after the trauma he endured. That was the one thing he appreciated about his father, insisting on all the intensive therapy treatment after the 'event' as his father deemed it. Flying in every trauma specialist known to the universe to work with him. Colton had done the work and was grateful for it. And he learned a tremendous amount about himself in the process.

He spent less than 48 hours with the Rippers.

Sexually assaulted twice, lasting a total of five hours.

Five hours versus the rest of his life.

He had a choice. To choose to live with it, or let it kill him. Stay the victim, or become the survivor. It took work and time, and eventually he became a survivor, no longer dictated by what happened to him. He still had the occasional nightmare or flashback; those things he could handle. The things that helped him the most were the support of his mother, his father, and his friends. And even Winter.

The memories of Winter were ingrained in his soul from that one night. That night changed his life in more ways than one.

How many times had he imagined Winter just like this?

How many times had he played out the fantasy of Detective Eli Winter on his knees—for him?

They were strangers to each other, and yet they were connected by the Rippers—by that night. And that felt intimate, strong and unshakeable, as if he was tethered to him by a delicate string, one he wasn't sure he wanted to cut or pull closer.

He saw a flash of a memory—of Winter's hand on the rifle, his boot heel digging into Pollock's leg, and without hesitating, without so much as blinking, fired point-blank range, right between the eyes. The blood shot upward from the impact, splattering Winter's jaw and cheek. He had seen firsthand what Winter was capable of. His polite manners and stoic mask were to protect everyone else from seeing the violent man beneath.

Winter's dark eyes dropped to the tented hoodie and quickly glanced away as he got to his feet, slipping his phone into his back pocket. Heat flooded Colton, not sure if it was embarrassment or pure, unfiltered lust.

"I'm—sorry," Winter said hesitantly, almost awkwardly, as though he were the one embarrassed, despite having seen Colton's semi-hard-on, and politely turning his back to him.

Lips pursed, Colton dragged his sweaty shorts back on and strode into the kitchen, grabbing another bottle of water from the fridge and drinking it down, trying to rein in his idiotic cockstand.

"What else do you need from me?" Colton clipped out, leaning against the black marble island of the kitchen, regaining his composure.

Winter turned, "I'd like you to help me on this investigation."

"What?"

"You're the only living survivor. You interacted with both Rippers."

"Are you fuckin' serious?" Colton asked incredulously.

"Deadly. One man is dead, another was taken four days ago. It's only a matter of time before his body is found, and another is taken. This is almost the same pattern as before, except that the victims are missing longer. This has to stop."

"It could've stopped ten bloody years ago," Colton hissed through his teeth.

"I know."

"You know, but didn't care."

"I care, Colton. I cared a lot. I still do," Winter retorted, his calm composure cracking slightly.

"Then why ask this of me, huh?" Colton scrubbed a hand over his jaw, "I don't have anything else to give you."

"You have memories, details that can shine a new light on the evidence this time. You may see something that I don't, something that I'm missing."

Colton raced a hand to the back of his neck, unsure. "You're the detective, not me."

Winter hitched his head back, a glint of something lethal and cold in his gaze. "This is the second Ripper—I know it in my gut. He's calculating and patient, until he's not. He's organized, methodical, and obsessive. He's a clean freak. Douglas's body was nearly pristine when we found him. He was bathed multiple times. Forensics found traces of Neosporin on every single cut on that man's body." Winter slowly walked out of the living room, the kitchen island standing between them. "I remember touching your skin that night—it was oily and felt like some sort of balm was all over you."

Colton glared, fingers digging into the counter, his heart thumping.

"I have a working profile of the second Ripper—but I need you. This case needs you. We have to do this together," Winter said firmly.

"*We?*"

Winter's chin tilted back as though Colton had just sucker punched him.

Good, he thought irritably, *feel the sting that I've lived with the past eight years, you twat.*

Winter may have been here now, asking for his help, but it didn't change that he failed him—that Colton had trusted him to keep going after the second Ripper. But he didn't.

It took another death for Winter to do something.

Colton wasn't sure he could ever forgive him for that.

"There is no *we*, Detective Winter," Colton ground out. "If you'd so kindly see yourself out. I have nothing else to say to you."

Winter hesitated, pulled his card from his back pocket, and set it down on the marble island. "If you change your mind, I'll be stickin' around town a couple more days. My number, just in case." Winter paused at the door, his hand on the doorknob. "What happened out there. What happened to you? It matters. It still matters. I wouldn't be here if it didn't. Have a good night, Colton."

CHAPTER 6

Winter bit numbly into the French fry served with his burger from the hotel restaurant, and he clicked through his old notes and photos of the case, his mind buzzing. He stared at the picture of Bryan Douglas's body, unburnt, and left for the animals tied to a tree.

The brand on the victim's body matched without a doubt the one on Colton's.

It wasn't a copycat. It was the second Ripper—the one still alive.

He rechecked his phone, waiting and hoping Colton would call him and agree to work on the case with him.

If not, he'd ask him to at least go on record about everything he could remember.

Colton's cooperation was key to this whole investigation. Colton had spent time in the same room as the other killer—and possibly had remembered details about him that would help the investigation. Sure, he has his victim statement from ten years ago, but memories change, and details come back—he'd seen that firsthand in multiple investigations over the years. Plus, Jim had done the interview, and he hadn't been convinced there even was a second Ripper, so his questions on the record were lackluster at best.

So far, even with the new evidence of the brand matching, they had limited information to go on.

Sheriff Emersen had taken his deputies around some of the popular hiking trails and tried to find any cellphone or camera footage of Douglas' whereabouts before he went missing.

Winter tapped once more on his laptop screen, rotating from picture to picture, seeing but not seeing. He wanted to return to Tahoe as soon as possible, but he couldn't without Colton.

He was aware of the gravity of the request and hoped that, given time and some space, Colton would come to realize that he didn't have a choice.

Neither of them did.

He stared at the photo of Colton's aged brand and the intimate location of it along his pelvis on the upper side of his cock, where the hair had been burnt away with the brand, leaving bare skin and scar tissue. His jaw twitched in fury. Who could do this to someone?

Winter leaned back in the desk chair in his hotel room, eyes surveying the mark and the black hoodie that covered his penis, except the material had been drawn further away in this photo. He could see the stiff, curving side, the flesh ripe and soft, veined. His pulse leaped, and he reached out, slamming the screen down, refusing to acknowledge the stirring in his chest as he got to his feet, raking a hand through the black curls on the top of his head.

Fuck, he thought with a long breath.

Winter couldn't forget the sound of Colton's slight intake of breath and the way his pupils dilated when Winter knelt between his legs. And he had known, seen it in his periphery, Colton's cock stiffened under the black hoodie, and it had taken all of Winter's control to look away.

All of his fucking control, which seemed to get worse the longer he was around him. This had never happened to Winter before. He could always rein it in and knew how to manage himself, because he was the epitome of control. But that didn't stop the swooping sensation in his belly and the tingle at the base of his balls whenever he thought about that black tented hoodie.

Under no circumstance was he permitted to touch Colton Sacks.

It's not that fucking hard, Winter.

This had to stay professional; otherwise, the investigation could go sideways fast, skewing his perspective, and Winter couldn't allow that.

And he couldn't sit around waiting for Colton to decide either. It was time to make one last stand and see if he could persuade him to join him.

Winter arrived outside the bar, and was pleasantly surprised by the ample parking, despite the people crowding the outside patio, and the busy line to get in. He parked his truck and was about to step out when he noticed a flurry of movement around the side alley of the bar. A man dressed in slacks and a muted purple button-up shirt, accompanied by an obnoxious golden chain necklace and a balding hairline, stumbled toward the sidewalk, yelling.

The bouncer by the front entrance, a large bruiser of a man, motioned for someone else to keep checking IDs while he headed toward the commotion. It was then Winter saw him—Colton. His hand grabbed the man in the purple shirt by the neck of his collar, and with a furious jerk, wrenched him back. The man let out a throaty gag and stumbled back, slipping on his overly flashy shoes.

Winter was out of the truck and running. He rounded the alley just in time to see Colton slam the smaller man into the brick walls of the opposite building, delivering not two, but three stiff jabs into his solar plexus. The man yelped.

"Fuck, Colton!" The bouncer materialized beside Winter and rushed Colton, heaving him off.

Colton's face was twisted with rage as he slipped out of the bouncer's grasp, eyes locked with the man slumped against the brick wall, ready to unleash another torrent of fists.

Winter was there this time and saw the rearing of his arm and, without thinking, stepped between him and the man against the wall, catching the raging fist.

Winter's hand stung by the brute force of the impact, feeling the unhinged strength for himself. Colton blinked hard, staring at him, breathing fast.

"Enough," Winter said calmly, his voice a low but firm whisper. "Enough."

Colton looked far from done as the muscle beneath his beard clenched and unclenched ferociously.

All of a sudden, a horde of women came rushing out the side door, phones in hand, yelling and screaming. "He fuckin' groped us!"

The bouncer, who had been helping the man against the wall, shoved him hard. "Is that true?"

"Someone call the cops!" another woman yelled.

"This shit is going viral—fuckin' hit that asshole again!"

"Pervert!"

Colton's fist bared down into Winter's hand, and he felt the weight of it, and he pushed back, refusing to let Colton Sacks be filmed while beating a defenseless man to a pulp. This would not help Winter's investigation, and it certainly wouldn't help the already tattered relationship between the Placer County Sheriff's office and the Sacks family.

"I am the cops," Winter said, raising his voice only enough to be heard over the chaos. "The situation is under control. Go back inside. We'll need all of you to stay put so we can get your statements on what happened."

"Bitch!" One of the women yelled at the man in purple, flipping him off and storming back inside. The rest of the young women followed.

"You really a cop?" the bouncer asked behind him.

"Sorta," Winter replied, releasing his hold on Colton and stepping back. "I'm a bit far out of my jurisdiction, so you'll still need to call the local police."

The bouncer led the man in purple to the front of the bar and pulled out his cellphone, already dialing, glancing back at Colton.

"You good, Colt?" the bouncer asked, phone already pressed to his ear.

"Yeah," Colton grumbled. "He's the groper, by the way."

The bouncer's bushy eyebrows rose to his hairline as he gripped the man in purple even harder. "No shit? We've been lookin' for you for a while, asshole." The bouncer took the man away to the front of the bar and out of sight.

Winter turned to Colton when he saw a flying fist and felt the impact of it on the side of his cheek. He reeled, stumbling back against the wall, grabbing his jaw, blinking through the tears that had automatically filled his eyes.

The rage in Colton's face had vanished, replaced by something else entirely—something cold and unforgiving.

"You had that comin'," Colton said without a trace of remorse.

The sharp sting in his jaw no longer bothered him as much as the way Colton was looking at him, as though he were nothing but a bug—meaningless and insignificant.

At first, he didn't understand, but as the tension thickened like a damned wall, he knew. Colton had never forgiven him for breaking his promise—the promise he made ten years ago.

Winter swallowed the blood coating his mouth from his teeth, scraping the thin tissue of his inner cheek. "Yeah, I know."

The tension in Colton's shoulders eased, seeming surprised but also suspicious.

Winter straightened, "Got any more sucker punches you wanna dish out this evening? Or maybe, you wanna just say what you need to say?"

"You're a fucking coward," Colton shot back. "A letter? Really?"

Shame washed over Winter, remembering the formal letter he had sent to inform Colton that the Ripper case had been officially closed, as there had been no further evidence of the alleged second killer.

"I'm sorry," Winter murmured. "I truly am. You're right. I should've called. I should've done more."

"I really wanna fuckin' hit you again." Colton's gaze pinned him to the wall.

"Then do it if it'll make you feel better."

Colton seemed to consider it.

"Why are you still here?" Colton asked, scowling.

Winter scrubbed his fingers over the spot on his jaw, knowing there would be a bruise there by tomorrow. "I need you."

Colton's chin jerked, eyes narrowing.

Winter cleared his throat, "This case needs you. But I'll understand if you don't want to do this. I'll officially reopen the North Tahoe Rippers investigation. I'm sure the press will find you pretty quickly, I know I did." He paused before adding, "You can go back to your life and pretend that the other bastard who did this to you ain't doin' it to others. Maybe you'll sleep," Winter's eyes scrutinized him. "Maybe you won't."

Colton's nostrils flared, and he looked a breath away from punching him again.

"The other option, the one I prefer, is…" The weight of his words dropped into his stomach like a fucking brick: "You come with me."

Back into the dark.

Back into the woods.

Back to where all this started.

Colton's pale blue eyes stared, seeming to search for something in Winter. Trust, maybe? He felt helpless in this whole damn situation, and he fucking hated it. He messed this up years ago, and there was no going back from that—only forward. He intended to mend the bridge that had been burned between them.

And if Colton came with him, Winter planned on making this right, whatever it took.

"You work with me on this investigation. You're good with people, damn good. You'll be my consultant. Walk me through any memories or ideas you might have. You are their only living survivor. You have somethin' the others didn't have."

"And what is that?" Colton asked coldly.

"The audacity to live," Winter retorted simply, remembering what Grace Sacks had said the night she had seen her son in the hospital. "You don't want that to go to waste."

Colt cocked his head to the side, "And what if I don't want to do this?"

"You do," Winter replied with a certainty that he didn't have until this very moment. He pushed off the brick wall, "You almost beat the shit out of that man. Because?"

Colton shifted, throat bobbing.

"Because you needed to," Winter said darkly. "You needed to because this isn't over for you—just like it ain't over for me. We both need this, Colton. Don't pretend that you don't."

Winter knew he was getting a little too close, and damnit, he couldn't help himself. Colton Sacks was the sun, a spectacular, fiery burning star that exploded as much as it warmed. "You're not done. You wanted a reason to beat that man to hell and high water. But it wasn't him you wanted. I saw the way you touched that man at the bar the other day."

Colton stiffened, for the first time since he stepped into this alleyway with him, the younger man wavered.

"You're checking them, aren't you?" Winter whispered knowingly.

Colton's silence was deafening.

"You told me you cut the second Ripper under the chin." Winter dragged his knuckle beneath his chin to indicate where. "And I think, for the last ten years, you can't stop yourself from making sure it isn't him sitting at your bar—hitting on you."

Colton swayed and looked away, reminding Winter of the lost boy coming out of the woods, scared and alone.

"Tell me I'm wrong—tell me to go to hell." Winter wanted to shake this version of Colton. The angry one he could deal with—this one—this one looked too damn vulnerable, and made every muscle in Winter's body want to comfort and soothe.

"Go to hell," Colton managed out, looking at him with just enough spark in his gaze to give Winter hope.

"Tell me when to pick you up tomorrow morning," Winter said confidently.

Colton blinked, "nine o'clock. And you'd better bring coffee. Your treat."

CHAPTER 7

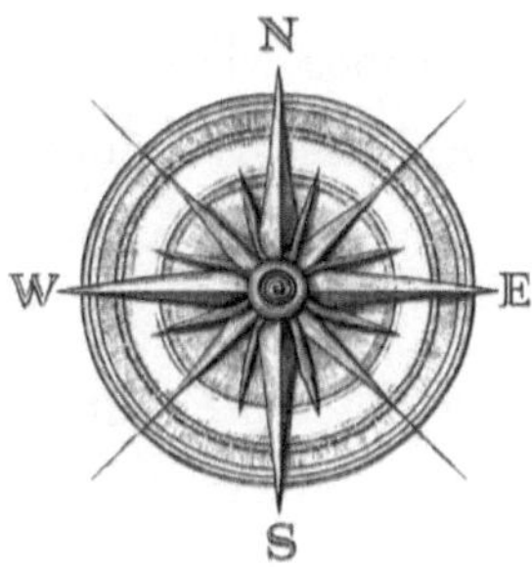

"You were so romantic once," she said at the end of the bar, the lights had been turned off for the night, leaving her illuminated only by the bar lights that he used to finish cleaning up.

Colton recognized her voice and felt the ache in his heart, glancing over his shoulder at her. She was dressed in red tonight. Her long, flowy, strawberry-blond hair curled and layered down her back, her face bare of makeup, with full pink lips and a light array of freckles dancing over her nose and cheeks. Her pale blue eyes were a replica of his. Her long, velvet-red robe was tied at her waist, with a deep blue silk slip beneath. Her feet were bare as she crossed her legs, sitting at his bar, watching him with that faint, loving smile of hers.

"I was wondering when you would show up," he murmured.

His mother smiled, leaning against the bar counter, her hand and elbow propping up her head as she side-eyed him. "Did you hear me?"

"Aye," he drawled irritably.

"You used to be so romantic—about *him*."

Colton sighed, knowing she was right, because she had lived with him during his romantic phase of Eli Winter.

"Once upon a time," Colton tugged up one of the barstools and plopped it on the countertop. "...when the nymphs did roam, and faeries flown, and men like him were made of stone. It was boys like me, made of glass and sun, waiting for their winter to come. So hopeful for the day, and that day did pass. And pass again, until the glass turned to stone and the heart lost its glow. The glass boy turned rotten because love was forgotten."

She sighed sweetly, "I always did love your poems. Especially the tragically romantic ones."

Colton snorted and leaned over the counter, grasping the neck of a bottle of whiskey and a fresh glass. "You would be. You preferred the tragic romances over the happy ending ones. You'd say..."

"Love does conquer all, even in death!" She fisted the air, looking victorious and self-assured.

He smiled, pouring whiskey into his glass. "I blame my hopelessly romantic heart on my swoon-worthy mother."

"Swoon," Grace Sacks hummed. "I always loved that word." She paused, scrutinizing him. "So, when did you stop?"

He sipped the amber liquid. "Stop what?"

"Being romantic."

He shot a look over at her, savoring the memory of her like this, emotion clogging his throat. "When you died."

Her face softened sadly.

"I miss you," he breathed, swallowing hard.

"Try being me, missing you," she countered teasingly, her eyes dancing with that glint—that spark.

He drank down the entire contents in one swig, knocking it back, needing the burn to push down the rising swirl of grief.

"I feel like it's been a long time since we last talked," she commented.

"Jamie," he rasped.

She sighed dreamily, "That's right... Jamie. She moved out to be with her partner, Tess. And you were so sad, all the grief came back that first night you were left alone. You thought about me. Her. Him."

He closed his eyes, "And I conjured you up like a madman conjures up water in a desert or lost at sea."

"Oh, Captain..."

"My Captain," he finished.

She smiled wistfully, "I'm so proud of you."

He twirled his fingers over the glass.

"You said yes," she said.

Colton knew what she was referring to, and that was why she was here tonight—his vision of his mother came only in moments of true vulnerability. He sometimes wondered if it was her magic—or his love that made her feel so real in these moments.

"I did it for you," he replied.

She beamed and shook her head, "No, you did it for him. For you. For another chance."

"There are no chances, mum. There never was."

"*Never was?*" she scoffed, and a drink appeared in her hands, her expression hardening. "*Never was?*"

He stiffened. "Don't start that."

"Never is a word I hate. I hate it. I heard it so much, all the time. People telling me there *never was* a second Ripper—*never was* another man out there, still alive, still breathing from hurting my son. There *never was*...it was all a dream—a delusion from trauma and fear..." she sneered. "It really gets my goat when I hear that word."

He smiled lazily at her, liking the way she sounded almost British there for a minute. Whenever she'd get fired up, she sometimes sounded like him or his father.

"And now," she sat up, furious. "He's alive and at it again because no one believed you at the time when you could've stopped him, had they listened."

"Had Winter listened."

She stiffened, "He listened. He heard you. He believed you. I know he did."

He poured another shot. "It doesn't matter. He gave up before. He will again. Forgotten and turned rotten..."

She reached across the bar top, as though trying to reach through time and space to touch him again. If only, he thought miserably.

"I wish I were here to see you through this part," she whispered.

"I know. Me too."

"Will you forgive him?" she asked quietly.

He sucked in a breath. "Should I?"

"Only if you can."

"And what if I can't?"

Her vision began to fade into the dim light of the bar. "You can, my love. And you will. Because you are sunshine, reflected in starlight, and don't know when to quit. So don't give up yet."

"I love you," he said, tears welling in his eyes, unable to watch her disappear from his life again.

"I love you so much more," she murmured. "Now go get that bastard who tried to dim your star and take you from me. I'll be there, every step of the way."

His mother vanished from the barstool beside him. Leaving him once more, all alone and lost at sea.

※

Colton informed his boss that he'd be taking an extended leave due to a family emergency. The director of the YMCA, Teresa, whose warm voice on the phone said he'd be in her prayers, added before hanging up, "Ty's gonna miss you. Hope you come back soon."

"Me too," he said, ending the call, thoughts straying to Ty and the other young boys and girls that he had gotten attached to over the course of his work there. He was good at working with kids, having a knack for it, especially with the troubled ones, likely because he had been a mischievous youth in his own day.

He still wasn't too far from that life now. Ever since his mother passed away, his life seemed to be at a standstill, just drifting through the days. Five years later, at 30, he had no direction or purpose, serving drinks, playing basketball, wrangling drunks, and listening to kids vent. It didn't seem like much on the outside, and yet, it was the only thing he had. It kept him tethered to the world and allowed him peace outside his head—outside his anger.

Colton leaned back against the passenger seat, watching the endless blur of trees pass by on the highway. "So, wanna tell me how this is gonna work?"

Winter's arm rested on the console between them, taking up far too much space in the cab. "Well, I suppose that depends on you."

"What do you mean?" Colton asked.

"How far are you willing to go?" Winter kept his gaze level with the road, his aviator sunglasses framing his face, and the dark shadow of two-day-old stubble unable to hide the purple bruise forming along his jawline.

"Why don't you just spell it out for me? Cuz clearly, I ain't followin'," Colton drawled irritably.

"I want you everywhere I go. You may see something, hear something, that can give me the direction I've been missing the last ten years."

"Eight years," Colton corrected, remembering the letter in the mail.

"Right," Winter nodded. "Having you is essential, but I don't wanna push you."

Colton retrieved the lighter from his pocket and slid it in and out of his fingers, thinking. "Well, Detective Winter, I appreciate the concern, but I think I can manage."

"You said that to me before."

Surprised, Colton glanced at the man and felt himself transported back to that night, holding the pistol Winter had given him, ready to run but mostly, ready to kill.

"It was true then as it is now," Colton retorted. "I can take care of myself."

"And if you can't...?"

"What are you, my dad?"

Winter shot him a look across the cab, "I'm allowed to be concerned, Colton. Your memories are attached to the trauma of being held captive for nearly two days and everything else you experienced at the hands of those men."

Colton bit his lower lip, flicking angrily at the lighter in his hand. "Well, considering you don't know me, Detective, I'd say you should wait before gettin' yourself all worked up about something you know nothin' about."

The sigh that escaped Winter's pursed lips was long. "My name is Winter, not Detective."

Colton rolled his head to the side to look at him, studying the way the sunglasses framed his stupid, handsome face, all the way down to the veined lines of his strong, masculine hands that gripped the leather steering wheel.

"I thought your first name was Eli," Colton said.

"It is. I prefer Winter."

Colton smirked, so did he. It suited him far better than Eli.

Winter glanced over at him, their eyes locking briefly. "Whatever happens, I'm here. I'm not leaving this time, you can trust that."

Colton slammed the butt of the silver lighter into the car windowsill, feeling hope spread through him like a thunderclap. He wanted to believe him—desperately. But how could he? Winter gave up the hunt for the second Ripper, the one Colton knew in his bones existed. But the evidence had never been there, and the world called him crazy, saying he dreamt of the Boogeyman in the forest that night—that it was Barry Pollock, the middle-aged truck driver, who was the only North Tahoe Ripper.

Winter's phone rang, and the console screen read the name Sheriff Emerson. Winter answered, putting the Sheriff on speaker.

"I'm on my way back," Winter informed him at once.

"Fuckin' great timing, then, cause we have another one."

Colton's stomach clenched.

Winter said nothing at first, but Colton could see his fingers tense on the steering wheel and the sudden acceleration of the truck. "Where?"

"I'll send you the location. A bit off the beaten path this time. Fucker is getting smarter. It didn't help that social media spread the last location of the body like wildfire, and I had tourists in the station for days claiming they saw him. Everyone just wants to go viral these days... Christ, humanity has sunk to a new low. I need to catch this fucker so I can retire already."

"Jim," Winter said in a direct tone. "Text me the location and I'll be there soon."

"There's a warning of a possible electrical storm comin'. Get here before it does." The line went dead, and his phone pinged with the text message of the location. Winter cursed, attempting to open the message and connect it to his maps, but he couldn't do that while driving.

"Need your reading glasses, old man?" Colton teased, snagging the phone from Winter's fumbling hand and punching in the location so it read on the console screen. It added thirty minutes to the trip. Winter muttered thanks and snatched his phone back.

"Tell me about the case so far," Colton commanded coolly.

"Thanks to you, I was able to match the brand with Bryan Douglas, confirming this is the North Tahoe Ripper. We haven't released that information to the public yet, and no one has caught on that this is the same serial killer. Their motives are similar, but their style is different. Pollock used fire when he disposed of the bodies."

Colton nodded, "Hence why you could never get an exact match on my brand with the other men."

"I always knew you were smart under all that—blond."

Colton, for the first time since starting the journey back to Tahoe—back to hell—smiled.

Winter glanced over at him and smirked, "I should tell blond jokes more often."

"Not unless you want your face to experience another shade of purple, you won't."

Winter's halfhearted smile eased some of the tightening in Colton's limbs as he listened to the details of the case.

"How is this Ripper's style different?" Colton asked.

"Fire cleaned the crime scenes of all evidence with Pollock. This guy—he leaves evidence out in the open." Winter reached for his jawline, fingering the deep scar tissue and grazing the pad of his thumb over his mouth in deliberation, seemingly unconscious of the movement as he continued. "First thing is the brand. Clearly, this came from him, not Pollock. It doesn't really fit Pollock's style anyway. He was more brute strength and luck—this one is methodical and wants to show off. He needs to brand them—mark his victims with his emblem. And he does it somewhere so vulnerable, so..."

He trailed off. Colton fisted his hand over the lighter.

"Obvious. As though staking his claim—the final claim on his victims, as if no one could touch them other than him, even after death."

Colton swallowed, shifting in his seat, trying not to think of the fucking brand next to his cock and how much his father insisted on buying the most skilled plastic surgeon on the planet to cover it for him. But he never did. For some reason, Colton kept the mark.

"He strips them naked, sits them on a blanket in the middle of the forest, and strangles them from behind, unable to look at them while he does it."

Colton shivered.

"The blanket is generic, cheap, and almost every department store has it. The same applies to the rope, which is generic and available at any hardware store. No prints or DNA have been found, and if the bugs and animals don't get to the body first, the weather always does. And Tahoe has been hot lately, which adds to the degradation of evidence."

"What about his victim...?"

"Attending a bachelor party with friends for the weekend, but they were more the hiking, exercise type, rather than the boozing partiers."

"That's not what I was asking," Colton said.

Winter's brow furrowed, confused.

"Was he...?" Colton's throat tightened. "Was he raped?"

Winter let out a breath, "Yeah."

"Any evidence there?" Colton asked because he knew that neither Ripper nor Pollock used protection with him. But one of them cleaned him, thoroughly, every time.

"None so far," Winter replied, knuckles cracking the leather steering wheel beneath his hands.

"What about the skin?"

Winter paused, glancing over. "What about it?"

"Lotioned—oiled up?"

Winter nodded, "Yeah. The Neosporin and oil..."

"Eucalyptus?" Colton finished.

Winter let out a surprised curse, "At first, I thought it was pine, but it was too sweet. If this body has it, we have a confirmed serial killer on our hands, connecting him to the bodies ten years ago."

Colton released a pent-up breath and glanced up at the gray clouds looming over the forest up ahead. "I'm going with you to the crime scene?"

Winter hesitated, "Can you?"

"Let's find out."

CHAPTER 8

In less than a few hours of Colton agreeing to join him in the investigation, he had already revealed a crucial bit of information that connected Douglas to the actual Ripper ten years prior. It wasn't a copycat. It was the second Ripper. There had always been a second Ripper.

Vindication and adrenaline fueled his lead foot as Winter sped the last few miles to the location of the crime scene. He was deep into the woods, off a side trail from the paved road, noticing only one or two cabins, but not much activity in the area. He spotted the yellow crime scene tape and a few police cruisers. He parked and hesitated, hand on the door handle.

"You ready?" Winter asked the younger man beside him.

For a moment, Winter didn't see Colton Sacks as he was today. He saw the twenty-year-old—messy, dirty hair, scrapes and cuts along his face and neck from running blindly through the dark woods—and wearing Winter's clothes, an old button-up plaid shirt, and a pair of basketball shorts. He wasn't swimming in the clothes, but they didn't fit him either, making him look small, and his boyish face even younger than he was.

But that was not the man sitting next to him. This man was stronger, more muscular, fuller, and a hell of a lot angrier.

"Yeah," Colton said with a tense nod and got out before Winter did.

He bit back the urge to sigh and took the lead, walking to the forensics officer who, without a word, handed him a pair of latex gloves. He motioned to Colton, and the officer gave him a pair as well. Colton, for a moment uncertain, took them, slipping the lighter into his pocket and putting them on.

"Where I go, you go," Winter instructed Colton as he pushed up the crime scene tape. Together, they joined Sheriff Jim Emerson and the other two officers who were waiting for them.

"Jim," Winter said, and the older man, dressed in his uniform today with the matching forest green button-up and pants, relief reflected in his eyes.

"You remember Colton Sacks?" Winter motioned with his chin to the man beside him, and Jim arched his eyebrows high, blinking.

"I surely do," Jim hesitated before reaching out to shake hands. "Winter mentioned he wanted to bring you in..." He glanced irritably at Winter, and clearly had a lot to say, but instead said, "I'd say it's good to see you, but under the circumstances..."

Colton, jaw tense, merely nodded.

"Local trail," Jim said, turning to Winter. "Leads to a private residence a couple of miles up, and a neighbor that way," he motioned with his fingers in the other direction. "Not exactly a popular tourist spot. Locals mostly use this trail. He's getting better at hiding them. He's been out here two days from the state of him—the coroner will know for sure."

"Who found him?"

"A local woman and her labradoodle who were out for their morning walk."

"Forensics finished?" Winter asked, confirming that he could adjust or touch the body.

"He's all yours. They've been told to wait until you're done." Jim glanced up at the cloudy sky above them. "Summer storm is comin' in fast. I suggest you don't dally."

Jim motioned to the other deputies and waved them off back to their cars. "Give them some space."

Winter watched as the others cleared the scene, leaving just him and Colton with the body. He saw the large tree with the rope strung around it, and the hands knotted at the base of the trunk. But from the angle of the trail, he couldn't see the body, just the hands. In fact, the tree was so wide that the hands themselves were barely visible on the sides. They were lucky a dog had sniffed him out.

Winter approached the tree and felt Colton behind him, stepping to where he stepped, mindful of himself and respectful of the crime scene. He rounded the tree, dried twigs and dirt crunching under his boots, eyes trailing over the knots and blood pooled at the tips of the victim's fingertips.

He saw the naked legs and bare feet, spread out beneath a cream-colored blanket that looked soft to the touch. The legs were not bruised or scratched. There were no visible marks on his feet either. It wasn't until his gaze traveled upwards that he saw the teeth and nail marks around his upper thighs, torso, and crotch on the pale, grayish skin. The way the body was sitting so straight against the tree, Winter was unable to see the brand. He squatted down and carefully widened the legs, shifting the body. And that's when he saw it, the burned and puckered flesh on the groin area near the penis.

Anger rippled through his muscles, and he sat back, breathing hard, and then he caught the scent—something faint but there. He dropped a knee onto the blanket, leaned forward, and saw the oil still lingering on the naked upper chest. Leaning as close as he could, Winter took in the odor and knew it immediately.

"Eucalyptus."

"It's him."

Winter nodded, "Yeah." Eyes traveling over the rope at the victim's throat and seeing the red and torn skin of being roughly strangled to death. He noted the amount of stubble on this victim's cheeks and frowned.

"He's older than the last one," Winter said and got to his feet, turning to glance at Colton, and he stilled. The young man was almost as gray as the corpse behind him. "You all right?"

Colton's eyes were fixed on the man's face. "He looks almost just like me. So did Douglas."

Winter turned back and studied him, contemplating this. There were similarities, but no one looked like Colton. But maybe there was something to what Colton said—what if the Ripper was trying to recapture the 'one that got away'? Winter had considered it briefly as a working theory after the first victim. Now with this latest victim, it felt true, and Colton saw it, too.

Something heavy fell hard through his stomach, and he cracked his knuckles.

"Do you see anything else?" Winter asked him curiously.

"The marks on his torso and..." Colton gestured to the groin. "Pollock never did that to me. But the other Ripper did. He'd get so worked up, almost in a frenzy, and would scratch and bite and..."

"And?" Winter pressed gently.

"Get me to like it," Colton seethed out. "Almost like he wanted me to like the pain. He'd work really fucking hard on getting me off when he was like that."

"How often was he like that?"

Colton paused, "Every time."

Winter sucked in a breath and glanced back at the victim. "He was reported missing five days ago."

"I was taken for two—escaped the night of the second, before he could have at me again. The Ripper and Pollock were once a day fuckers. So, this poor bastard was probably fucked and manhandled right up until the cunt put him here."

"The marks look fresh," Winter commented. "So does the brand."

Colton cursed and stepped back, "I need a fuckin' drink." And with that, Colton slipped away, peeling the gloves furiously off as he went. Winter followed, deciding he had enough visual evidence for now. He wanted a closer look at the rope and the body, but only that could be done at the coroner's office.

Colton brushed past the other officers, and Winter gave the forensics team the go-ahead to cut the rope and collect the evidence.

The storm clouds were getting thicker, and the wind was starting to pick up, howling through the burnt summer trees, causing leaves and debris to be swept up in the air and drop around them. He could smell the rain on the way as well, and heard the distant roll of thunder. He was grateful that Pollock was dead, and they didn't have to deal with a burning body, starting a wildfire in the midst of a crime scene. It had been a dry couple of summers, and Tahoe would suffer should a fire break out.

Colton was already pulling open the truck door, about to climb in, when Winter said, "I can take you back to the station? Or the cabin."

Colton hesitated, eyes vacant. "Cabin?"

"My place."

"What?" Colton shook his head as though clearing away a thought.

"Like I said before, you go where I go. You're not sitting in a hotel room. You're crucial to this investigation, and I would like to keep you—"

"Under lock and fuckin' key?" Colton snapped.

Winter tensed, finishing his statement, "Close. I wanna keep you close."

Colton looked ready to break the handle off his truck.

Winter held his palms out in defense as he slowly approached. "I moved a couple of years back. I have a place next to the lake, lots of space. I'll stay outta your way, and you'll have plenty of privacy. We can work on the case there. I prefer it to the station anyway."

Colton seemed to deliberate this and then shook his head, "I'll think about it, Detective Winter. Right now, you're gonna take me to a fuckin' bar."

He climbed in and slammed the truck door with a resounding bang, finishing the conversation. Winter narrowed his eyes irritably.

Colton certainly did like to boss him around, he thought, as the undeniable sensation swooped low in his belly and the all-too-familiar tingle around the base of his spine alerted him to how his body felt about such behavior.

Off-limits, Winter, *he is so fucking off-limits, he might as well be on the moon.*

Winter swallowed, tamping down his need to 'correct' Colton's attitude.

He decided to take Colton to a local bar, rather than a tourist one, and somewhere closer to his cabin. He pulled up to the nondescript brick building with a neon beer sign illuminated in the window, and the rain began to patter on his windshield, lightning flashing overhead in a bursting white display.

Colton flung open the door before he barely rolled up to the curb and, without a word, began heading inside.

"Wait—" Winter yelled out, rolling down the passenger window.

Colton tossed him a hard look over his shoulder, the rain sprinkling his white V-neck T-shirt and over the black ink on his tanned neck. "You're not invited, Detective Winter. I've got your number. I'll call you when I need an Uber."

Blood roared in his ears as he watched Colton wave him away with a dismissive hand and stroll into the bar alone. He gripped the steering wheel hard enough to hear the leather crack under his fists. No one in his life had the balls to treat him like that.

Winter only ever allowed his lovers, his sexual flavor of the week or month, to challenge him like this. Because when they did, and they really got under his skin, they knew what they would be rewarded with—him. And everything he would give to them. After, of course, they begged and pleaded.

But Colton wanted nothing to do with him. The big flirtatious act at the bar when he had initially approached Colton had all been an act—something to scare Winter off. Whatever physical reaction Colton had back at his apartment hadn't been intentional. And it didn't matter anyway if Colton wanted or didn't want him—Colton couldn't be pursued.

And it certainly didn't matter that Winter had already imagined his fist around that perfect fucking throat, watching those pale blue eyes spark with rage and lust, wanting to fight him and fuck him as he sank to his knees like a good fuckin' boy and put that impetuous mouth to work.

Stop it right fucking now, Winter.

Colton may have been the perfect blend of sass and ass, but he had trauma—heavy, deep-rooted trauma around violence and sex. The last thing Colton probably wanted was another man controlling and punishing him in the bedroom.

Winter scrubbed a hand over his jaw and to the back of his neck, massaging the tense muscles, guilt flooding him. He felt like dirt. No, he felt lower than dirt. He shouldn't be having these thoughts. It was wrong, and he needed to clear his head.

He parked, pulled out his phone, and irritably snatched the reading glasses off the dashboard, then opened the text to Trevor. Without giving himself a chance to think, he texted his former lover.

Where are you?

Sent.

Winter sighed, staring at the forming bubbles of the immediate response, and felt his insides coil in disgust.

"Fuck," he hissed out and tossed the phone onto the console.

"Going back to an ex is like trying to push shit back up your ass," Mal had once said in a passing joke.

Mal, he thought, could he swing by his art gallery while Colton got hammered? And then he was going to have to deal with drunk Colton, which felt somehow more dangerous than the sober version.

"Fuck, fuck, fuck," Winter grumbled and sat there, watching the lightning flash and the rain sheet his truck, listening to his phone ping more than the rolling thunder.

CHAPTER 9

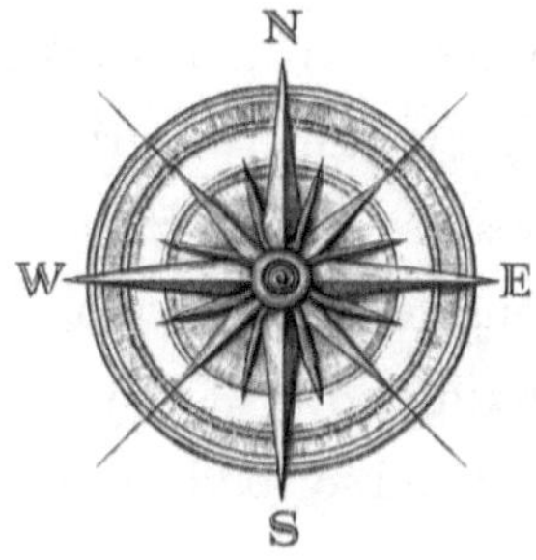

Colton touched the soft hair of the pretty young woman, practically sitting in his lap, as he sipped his beer. She blathered on about the hike she had gone on earlier in the day and her plans to go clubbing that night with her girlfriends, who were also at the bar with her.

If she sat back, the dark lighting of the booth would make her hair a shade darker, almost like Winter's. Except she was too young to have grays.

Fuck, why am I even thinking that?

Well, probably cuz I don't wanna think about what I just saw in the fuckin' forest.

He drank down another long swig of the amber liquid, nearly cursing himself and his ridiculous thought. Because damn him to hell, Winter was a far more distracting relief than replaying the image of the Ripper's latest victim, bound and strangled, his eyes closed and lips parted in a silent scream of pain.

Colton shivered, wishing he hadn't seen it—wishing he wasn't fucking here again. He never thought in a million years he'd come back to

Tahoe, but he was, and there was no going back to his comfortable life in Sacramento, knowing what was happening here.

He ripped his fingers angrily through his hair, pulling at the roots. The pent-up energy of this entire day had him feeling on the edge of a cliff. And all he wanted to do was jump. Recklessly, blindly jump into the bottom of a bottle of something, or perhaps he could sink into this carefree woman, who was also looking for a release. Or maybe—what he really needed was strong, firm arms holding him, while he listened to that calm, steady voice washing over his frayed nerves. Winter was all of it, intoxicating and steady, and so goddamned perfect that he, in some ways, hated him for it.

Colton had thought of nothing else since their brief encounter in his apartment the other night. It had taken every ounce of self-control he possessed to fight off the urge to grind himself against Winter like a horny dog when he was that close. Because he was too fucking gorgeous, and seeing those black eyes up close, the way his sculpted mouth parted in a sharp breath, and the chiseled jawline dusted with sexy stubble.

He went to the gym before Winter had arrived this morning, trying to beat the thoughts out of his head, and when that didn't work, he practically sprinted home, hoping the vigorous workout would kill the desire roaring through his bloodstream, but that, too, failed. It wasn't until he was in the shower that the pulse in his cock ticked like a time bomb, demanding release. And damn it, he did. He pulled himself root to tip, already wet with precum, thinking about that moment with Winter between his legs.

Because Colton had seen something. Brief but fucking real.

Winter's eyes had darkened with awareness, glancing at the bulging press of Colton's cock beneath the hoodie. And it was arousal. Hard and violent like a punch to the face.

Colton rationalized it away as embarrassment at first, but when he went to bed that night, thinking about their conversation, about that moment—that look—he recognized it for what it was, and something opened inside of him.

Something wide and deep, yearning to be filled.

Something he'd felt before.

Something he couldn't allow himself to feel again.

Winter had brought him here purely to help with the investigation. He wasn't here to live a lifelong fantasy of fucking Detective Eli Winter.

Colton nearly groaned in his beer at the mere thought, hating himself for being so stupid, so easy. And then, when Winter brought up taking him back to his cabin, after feeling so bloody vulnerable seeing that poor fuck in the woods, measuring every little detail and similarities he saw in the man with himself, down to the tattoo on his arm and neck.

Christ, it was creepy.

And then Winter opened his bloody mouth, while Colton was leaking like a damned wound, and said: *"You go where I go...I wanna keep you close."*

So simple. So safe.

Winter's natural protection was like the warmest blanket he had ever felt, and he wanted nothing more than to wrap himself in it and let it smother him.

The woman slid her finger over his short beard, grazing her nails through it, simpering weakly. He smirked down at her coyly, but he didn't see her. He saw him.

Fuckin 'ell, I'm not drunk enough.

The beer tasted bitter on his tongue, and he needed to get something much stronger if he were to sleep under the same roof as Detective-Come-Fuck-Me-Eyes.

He clenched his jaw and grabbed a thick potato fry off his plate, jamming it into his mouth. The woman he was sitting with ordered a round of shots and another couple of beers without asking him, and he merely smiled blandly at her. Jess something—Jessica maybe.

The door to the bar opened, and his stomach tightened.

Winter walked in, taking off his sunglasses and hooking them to the top button of his khaki shirt. His golden badge caught the dying gleam of the sunlight as the door closed behind him, and his gun was securely attached to his hip in his black holster. His dark blue jeans were worn from years of wear, looking almost soft to the touch, curving to his tall, lean legs and perfect damned ass. His hiking boots fit the ranger detective look, and the watch—that watch. It was the cheesy kind that hikers wore with a built-in compass and shit. He wondered briefly what this man would look like in a nice black suit, with gold or silver glinting from his wrist rather than leather and plastic. He knew already that Eli Winter would clean up like a pretty penny.

Everything about Winter was methodical and precise.

He was the epitome of control—over his emotions and his behavior, rarely breaking that stoic reserve.

And Colton wondered what it would take to break that illusion and see the man beneath.

Winter went to the bar, nodding to the bartender, and exchanging some words, smiling cordially at him. Obviously, they knew one another. Winter's smile, brief and warm, was startling. Startling because it was genuine, and damn it if Colton didn't want to see it again, but just for him.

He nearly facepalmed at his own betraying thoughts. He wasn't allowed to like this man, let alone be attracted to him. This man was nothing but a false idol whom he had spent years fantasizing about, hoping he'd find the second Ripper and vindicate him after all this time.

But Winter never did. He closed the case after a two-year search.

Because that was what Winter was: empty—nothing but cold stone.

Loud music suddenly erupted from the jukebox in the corner, and the woman beside him jumped in excitement, "Oh, I love this song. Dance with me?" She puffed out her big red lips, and her friends, the other tourists visiting for the weekend, were on the dance floor, swaying to the song.

She dragged Colton out of the booth, and he made it a point to stroll up to the bartender and take the shot lined up for him, while she giggled on his arm. Winter side-eyed him with that uncrackable face of his, not a hint of expression as he watched. Colton shot him a reckless wink and daring smile, tasting the burn of the whiskey in his mouth as he slid onto the dancefloor with the young woman and her three friends.

He wanted to forget Winter.

Forget the Ripper.

Forget seeing the dead man in the forest—strangled, exposed, and cruelly left to the elements of nature.

Winter believed that Colton's memories from ten years ago were blurred, fogged by pain and trauma. Colton had even told his mother the same thing, that he had gaps—that he couldn't remember everything.

But the truth was...he remembered everything.

Everything.

And he knew that drinking, fucking, dancing, and fighting wouldn't make any of that shit go away. It finally took his father convincing him to go to therapy for things to start to change for him. That he could touch another person's body, be touched in return, without clamming up—without turning away or dissociating. It took time, and a hell of a lot of patience and love—to himself, from his mother, and a bit from his father.

Yet he never settled down with someone, despite all the work he had done. He never wanted to feel committed to someone.

Perhaps it was because he never felt settled within himself.

Maybe because he had unfinished business with the final Ripper.

And with Winter. Today proved it to him. Seeing that man, knowing it could've been him ten years ago, stirred up a rage that felt like the crackling storm outside—waiting to set fire to something—or someone.

Confidently, Colton twirled the woman in his arms. The pull of the music led her to ride and grind against him, while her friends clapped and cheered along. Colt knew he fit the bill for the bad boy, with his throat tattoo, classic good looks, bright blue eyes, and dark blond hair, slicked back and cleanly cut. His thin white T-shirt was pushed up around his forearms, revealing the ink there, along with the silver rings glinting on his fingers. His dark jeans and black boots made him look more like a biker than a hiker.

Her group of girlfriends began to crowd them, and he felt hands drift over his upper back, and he stiffened. Another flutter of hands over his ass, and his jaw twitched. He'd been in situations like this before, dozens of times. He worked at a bar, for fuck's sake.

Sweat beaded his brow and trickled down his neck, his heart rate quickened, and he could no longer hear the music.

Another touch.

Another brush around his cock.

A wave of nausea swept over him, and he saw claw marks on the pale, gray skin, bare legs, splayed and cold. The burnt, charred skin of the brand. The same brand he had on his body...

Colton swayed, unable to breathe, and before he realized it, strong hands were around him and pulling him out. The women protested, but he didn't hear it—he could only hear Pollock panting in his ear—of the second Ripper, humming and moaning in pleasure.

Winter led him through the back bar room door and out onto the employee balcony outside, away from the crowd. He pushed himself out of Winter's grasp and flung himself against the iron railings, gripping the cool bars, eyes fixed on the glorious forest and dark blue lake stretched out before him. Electric bolts of lightning flared, bursting to life with such power and vibrancy that he shivered, sucking in a lungful of pine and fresh rain, scrubbing a hand over his beard to steady his breath.

"You all right?" Winter asked.

Colton tilted his head up, feeling the soft misty rain on his face, and took another long breath. "I don't need you rescuing me."

"Then don't put yourself in situations where you need rescuing."

Colton rolled his eyes, hearing the reproach in his tone and continuing to keep his back to him. He didn't want to see him. Didn't want to see the pity, the concern. He couldn't fuckin' stand it.

"How'd you know?" Colton asked quietly.

Winter hesitated. "You had that same look in the woods."

Yeah, I bet I did, he thought, raking his fingers through his hair.

"Do you wanna talk about it?" Winter asked softly.

Colton scoffed out a dark laugh. He arched his eyebrows high before finally turning to look at him over his shoulder, still clutching the iron rail. "Seriously?"

Winter shifted, his thumbs hooking into his jeans pockets, releasing a sigh. "If you want."

"You don't wanna know that shit—only if it's valuable to your investigation."

Winter's eyes narrowed, "That's not true."

"It is," he said flippantly, turning all the way around to lean heavily against the balcony railing, his feet outstretched before him, his hands tight around the iron bars. "So, ask."

The lines around Winter's lips deepened into a frown.

"Here, I'll do it for you," Colton began casually. "Colton, after viewing the body of the dead man, the Ripper's *second* victim—the Ripper, who I thought never existed in the first place, and oh, whose latest victim looks almost exactly like you, did you discover any new helpful tidbits?"

Winter crossed his arms over his chest, glaring.

Colton continued, jaw twitching as he tried to appear indifferent. "As a matter of fact, I did. I remembered one of the Rippers smelled like body odor, which, from my novice assessment, would be Barry. He was a bit pig-like, snorting and huffing, especially when he fucked."

Winter's expression chilled.

"But he didn't last long. He was a one-two-three, pump and dump kinda guy. Didn't have the stamina like the other one." Colton's throat bunched. "The other one…"

"You don't have to," Winter stepped forward, looking fierce.

Colton ignored this, waving him off. "The other one smelled clean, too clean. Almost like disinfectant. He liked to take his time with me."

Winter stilled, dark eyes watching him closely.

"Hours," Colton choked out. "But unlike Barry, he tried to make it hurt. And then when it was done, he'd treat me like a fuckin' king. Applying ointment to my wounds, massaging my body, washing me, smearing that fuckin' oil on me." Colton shook his head, disgusted. "He spent a total of six hours with me. Six hours versus the rest of my life. Fuck that—fuck him—and fuck you for giving up on me."

Shit, he hadn't meant to say the words. Colton, flushed with frustration and embarrassment, tried to turn away, but Winter's hand was on his shoulder, stopping him. He refused to meet his gaze—refused for him to see his swirling, fucked up emotions.

"Look at me," Winter said in a quiet and compelling command.

Colton swallowed, resisting. Winter's fingers began to trail upward, as though wanting to capture his neck, but stilled at the base of his throat. This made Colton look, seeing the storm, almost just as violent as the one overhead, reflected in Winter's dark eyes.

"Just so you know, I was forced to close the investigation. I had no choice."

Colton sneered at the excuse.

"Christ, Colton, I ain't the bad guy here," Winter seethed, his fingers inching to his throat, breath coming hard out of his nostrils, looking ready to toss him over the railing or...

His heart skipped in his chest, and his body began to respond, heating from the inside out. Winter's expression tightened in a tight grimace, gaze dropping to Colton's lips and holding.

Bloody fucking hell.

Harsh, horrible desire flooded him. Every limb went tense, and he waited breathlessly for Winter to lean in and take—taste.

Sudden laughter from the other side of the patio shattered the tension between them, and Winter took a quick step backward, releasing him. Colton saw the screen that the bar had put up to give the employees some privacy, and heard the women on the other side.

"Get back inside!" one of the women laughed, "It's raining!"

"Looks like a tornado is coming!"

There was more chatter, and the women retreated inside the bar.

Colton glanced up at the gray skies, flashing with light, as the rain and wind howled between them. Rain pattered on his face, and he slicked it off and stilled. Winter's dark gaze was locked on his body, eyes moving from his chest, down his flat stomach, and to his crotch before slowly working his way back up, making Colton's stomach tighten, and his cock began to ache against the stiff denim of his jeans.

Before, he had been embarrassed by the physical reaction he had in his apartment to Winter—now, he would use it.

A reckless thrill coursed through him, desperately needing to see Winter's resistance crumble. He reached between his legs, making a show of adjusting his cockstand, dragging his shirt slightly up, revealing the sharp muscle V that pointed down to his sex. He knew he was all hard muscle from years of boxing and conditioning.

Winter's chest expanded, and his eyes—those rich, warm brown eyes—darkened with heat. Colton nearly groaned in relief because, for a moment there, he believed Winter didn't want this—him.

And a small, unknown part of him was intimidated by this man. So strong, so masculine, so smart and wildly sexy.

"I've always loved a good thunderstorm." Colton leaned back farther on the railing, giving Winter permission to look.

Winter's dark eyes drifted over his body hungrily, yet his hands remained fisted at his sides.

"You done?" Winter asked hoarsely.

Colton smirked, enjoying the conflict on his face. "Ready to take me home, Detective Winter?"

"Winter, dammit."

"Such a pretty name for such a pretty man," Colton drawled, deciding then and there that he really enjoyed irritating Winter. "Normally, the people who hit on me are eager, practically begging me for a night." He let his hand rest on the waistline of his jeans, his shirt riding up just enough.

"Was she?" Winter asked.

Colton eyed him curiously, knowing he was referring to the woman he was drinking and dancing with. "Jealous?"

"Not really."

"Nor should you be," Colton replied coolly. "You don't seem the type anyway. Too bloody sexy to be worried by such nonsense."

"Stop it."

"What?" he asked innocently.

Winter, to Colton's delight, was on him in three wide strides, eyes flashing. "You know exactly what."

Colton nearly fucking purred. "How 'bout you spell it out for me."

It took everything not to undulate his hips forward the moment Winter was in striking distance of his cock. So instead, he raised his head, challenging him.

"This remains professional, Colton. So whatever little game you wanna play, I ain't playin'."

"Sure you are," Colton whispered huskily.

"I'm not that easy, you know," Winter shot back arrogantly.

"Then why does this feel so easy?"

Something broke in Winter's face, and he touched him, and his fingers reached behind Colton's neck, drawing him close. Their breaths mingled, lips inches apart.

Yes!

Colton couldn't look away, feeling Winter's hand sure and controlled, forcing Colton's face back, tipping his chin upward. The rain was slowing, and the wind became a faint whisper as the raging storm above began to break apart. But he didn't want that. He wanted thunder, lightning, chaos, rage.

Colton, letting the last dregs of the storm seize him, impulsively angled his hips and brushed his aching cock against Winter, and let out a humming sigh, feeling the weighted bulge of Winter's hard dick.

Thank fuckin' Christ.

He gripped the iron bars of the railing behind him, refusing to touch more than this. Winter's eyes were black, fully blown out, and his fingers reached up to Colton's hairline and dragged his head backward, revealing his vulnerable neck and forcing his back to arch and spine to push outward, now fully pushing his cock into his.

Colton gritted his teeth, resisting the urge to rotate his hips, despite the furious demand stretching between his legs.

"Does this feel easy?" Winter asked, his tone laced with bitterness.

Colton twisted his knuckles on the railing. "Actually, it feels pretty fuckin' hard."

Winter cursed, yanking Colton back harder by the hair and again forcing his hips into his, and he whimpered. Colton cringed, not at the way Winter was holding him, but at his ridiculous whimper. It was so needy—so goddamned needy! He was never like this, not with anyone.

But Winter was the exception.

Always the exception.

Winter's fingers raked through his scalp, cradling the back of his head, and with a slight push of pressure, Colton, for the first time, felt him move. It was subtle but there, and Colton sucked in a short breath, arched and rotated, jerking against him and feeling their sexes press, briefly. He whimpered again, and blushed.

Winter hummed in approval at the sound, "Do you want me to let go?"

"Fuck, no." Colton flinched again at his eager response.

Winter, though, seemed to like it—a lot, as his cock twitched and his stance bore down on him, caging him against the railing and riding him. The sensation was as glorious as it was tormenting. Colton's fingers itched to touch—to take—greedy for this man in ways he hadn't expected.

Something he shouldn't be doing because he was supposed to hate this man. But his body didn't understand that.

Suddenly, Winter's phone vibrated and rang in his back pocket. They both stilled, and Colton felt Winter retreat from him once more, and he had to bite his tongue from moaning in protest.

Winter, chest rising and falling with clipped breaths, eyes hooded, reached for his phone in his back pocket and let out a stream of curses before answering it and walking away.

Colton exhaled, releasing his white-knuckle grip on the railing, and turned to look out over the forest and lake. The storm had broken, and the sun was already peeking out from behind the gray clouds.

God, he wanted to keep touching him. To rake his fingers through that salt-and-pepper hair, wanting to feel those thick waves break under his hand. Instead, he twisted his fists over the railing, willing his body to relax and his breathing to even. But it was hard to calm his raging cock because that was possibly the most deliciously erotic thing he'd ever done. There was sex, and then there was this—angry foreplay that felt violent and exhilarating and glorious.

And he wanted it again.

"Let's go," Winter's voice was rough as he yanked open the employee back door, not even bothering to wait for him.

CHAPTER 10

*D*amn it, damn him, damn everything! That wasn't supposed to happen! Fuck.

All it took was three seconds and he'd lost control—something he never, ever did.

The pads of his fingers burned where Winter had gripped the back of Colton's neck.

Christ, Colton's hair had been achingly soft and smooth under his firm grip. His hair had been the only soft thing about him. All solid, unmistakable muscles, bound and rippling under the thin layer of clothing.

And he should have known better. But he had been baited, and Winter fell for it, hook, line, and sinker. That never happened to him. He wasn't like the men he pursued, who folded within minutes of meeting Winter. He was far too adapted for that lack of discipline. He controlled his impulses and urges—not the other way around.

But it had been Colton's desire, etched on his face, open and hungry, and his vulnerability. So raw, so pure. So emotional and real that Winter nearly shivered from the display and felt the first crack echo like a bullet through the wall he had erected between them. Maybe it was the storm above them, and the vision of Thomas McNamara's body seared into his skull, that added to his crumbling resolve.

For the first time in years, the well-laid brick wall, reinforced with steel, that Winter had built up inside him, trembled. It trembled the day he met Colton Sacks. And it trembled now, violently. Panic welled in his throat at the mere thought of that wall crumbling to ruin—because the last time it did, Winter lost control and nearly destroyed his life and the life of someone else. He couldn't risk that again, not ever.

Yet his body tingled with heat, unable to shake the feeling of Colton's rampant desire pressed into him, with just the simple brushing of bodies. And the whimper, fuck, the sounds that came from the back of his throat when Winter had finally touched him were so goddamned hot. It was possibly the sexiest thing he'd ever heard, and he knew he couldn't hear it again. And knowing he couldn't cross that line and hear that sexy little whimper made him want to punch a hole in the wall on his way out of the bar.

Fuck—what was I thinking? I know better than being trapped like that!

Colton had laid out all the trappings of a seduction, and Winter fell in like a bumbling bear, so desperate for the sweet honey that he didn't see the spikes underneath him.

I am a damned idiot.

Winter slammed his hand into the exit of the back room, returned to the bar, and walked blindly into a woman with red hair, surrounded by a group of people. He paused and nearly cursed under his breath, and caught it in time, as she beamed up at him, all wide teeth and freckles.

"Detective Winter! It's so good to see you!" She said chattily, reintroducing him to the group of colleagues.

Shit. Another trap.

He didn't have time for this. He needed to get home and...and what?

Colton would be coming home with him, and he couldn't very well do any of the things they had started on the patio. He couldn't escape the man for the next few days, maybe even longer, depending on how much progress they made in the investigation. Colton would be underfoot, in the way, and fucking with his head the whole goddamned time, especially after what just happened.

Damn it, shit, fuck, piss!

Maybe this was karma, he thought irritably. Karma for playing the field for as long as he had and never considering the damage of ruined hearts that he had stepped over, on his way out the door. Yeah, he thought, this felt like a punishment from the universe to have the epitome of his desire and sexual longing sleeping under his roof, drinking his fucking coffee, teasing and toying with him the entire time.

"Well, well, who is this?" Colton drawled directly behind him, his hand brushing the lower part of Winter's back, unseen by the rest of the group.

Winter straightened, teeth mashing together.

The redhead beamed, "Yes, hello!" She reached out a hand to Colton, who took it instantly, looking pleased. So goddamned pleased with himself as he glanced at Winter, "You gonna introduce us?"

"Raquel, this is my..." he couldn't say associate or consultant on the investigation, because once people started finding out Colton Sacks was back in Tahoe, they would assume the worst—that the allegations he made public all those years ago were true. Besides, they hadn't made the community aware just yet of the serial killer, which would certainly not help during Tahoe's peak tourist times outside of ski season.

"He's being shy," Colton said silkily, sliding his hip against Winter's against the bar, casually draping his arm behind him, without touching him. "We're friends." He made sure to emphasize the word 'friends' to give everyone the idea that they were more than that.

Winter wanted to break something.

"Raquel, this is Colton," Winter bit out.

"Oh!" Raquel said happily, "Wonderful to meet you!"

"So, how do you two know each other?" Colton asked curiously.

"Detective Winter has been our liaison with the Placer County Sheriff's Office for the past month, coordinating the Heroes in the Park festival," Raquel replied.

Colton's eyebrows arched, head tilting up at him. "Heroes in the Park?"

"It's Tahoe's big annual fundraiser for first-responders and mental health workers. It's gonna be a big one this year, we're nearly sold out on tickets." Raquel's pretty face turned to Winter then, looking excited. "And I'm so glad I ran into you—I spoke to CalVCB and they are so excited to partner with us. Thank you again for suggesting them. I think their organization is the perfect fit for this event."

"Cal—what?" Colton asked.

"California Victims of Crime," Raquel explained. "They're a state-organized service that supports victims of crime in working with a therapist. It pays for their therapy. It's fabulous."

Colton straightened, something shifting in his demeanor. Winter released a reluctant sigh. He had reached out to Raquel a few days after his abrupt departure from their last meeting at the festival location and made the recommendation for a charity they could add to sponsor this year.

"I was thinking we could have them be a part of the carnival games," Raquel added. "So, every ticket purchased for participating in the dunk tank, or ring toss, etc., that'll go directly to Victims of Crime."

"Sounds brilliant," Colton said, and Winter felt the brush of his fingers along his back once more, and he let out a hard breath through his nostrils, remaining perfectly still.

"We thought so, too!"

Colton leaned in toward Raquel, giving her a slow, mischievous smile, which had Winter sharpening his eyes like daggers. "I heard you say dunk tank, luv."

She beamed, nodding.

"How much do you think we could raise if we got this man…" Colton hitched his chin to Winter, without looking at him, "Sitting on that platform in the dunk tank?"

Raquel laughed, and the others behind her nodded in approval.

"I bet people would pay handsomely to see this man soaking wet. I know I would," Colton finally looked at him, grinning. "In fact, I'll promise to donate five thousand dollars if Winter agrees, right now, to do it."

Winter felt his jaw unhinge. He hated being on display and doubted that anyone would want to see him…

The thought trailed off as he glanced around and saw them all nearly dancing with excitement about the prospect. For the money—or him? Or both, probably both, he thought irritably.

Fuck.

He couldn't say no. It was his cause he championed for, and now Colton was putting him on the spot to show up for it.

"So…? Is that a yes?" Raquel pressed, beaming.

Winter sighed, "Yeah, of course. Anything for a good cause, right?"

Colton snorted behind him, which was covered by Raquel's squeak of delight, and the rest of her team celebrated.

"I think this calls for a round of shots," Colton announced and turned to the bartender, waving him down. Winter balled his fingers into a tight fist and a moment later felt the club soda pressed into his hand.

Colton then returned to the bartender, helping him line up the shots, but he didn't take one—instead he had a club soda, too.

Winter dropped his forehead against the cool tile walls of his shower, letting the streaming water pound his shoulders and back, demanding his body relax. But he knew what would ultimately help the coiled tension knotted in every limb since he walked through the front doors of his house.

He had somehow managed to walk out of the bar, becoming the hero of the evening with Raquel and her event team, and drove home with Colton sitting beside him, looking like the cat that had caught the damned canary.

When they reached his cabin, Winter led Colton through the house, showing him the guest bedroom and private bathroom, along with anything else he might need in the twenty minutes Winter needed alone to deal with himself.

"I'll cook dinner in a bit," Winter informed the younger man and strode off to the master bedroom, nearly slamming the door behind him.

He wasn't about to go an entire evening inconvenienced by his dick. Or vividly recalling the press of Colton's body against his, their need for each other, in lust alone, imprinted on his brain like a fucking forest fire. All he could feel was him, all he could see were pale blue eyes that were nearly gray in the light. He could still hear Colton's quick intake of breath when Winter finally touched him. In that moment, Colton had looked like something out of his best erotic dream. Wet, panting, edging himself against him, looking like a glowing star, with his dark blond hair slicked back from that boyishly handsome face.

And those lips, pink and plump, begging to be licked and sucked.

Winter released a shuddering sigh as his hand finally grasped the heavy weight between his legs, and he stroked himself from root to tip. He knew it wouldn't take long. The building anticipation had peaked the moment he stepped into the shower.

If this was what Winter had to do to keep his composure the rest of the evening, so be it. He could permit himself to lose control here in the sanctity of his shower, behind a locked door, away from temptation. He couldn't feel the stream of the hot water, mind fully elsewhere—on a patio, overlooking a storm, of dark green forest and of Colton, taunting him—challenging him.

Winter fisted his cock and shivered. The velvety smooth skin of his shaft flexing hard in his grasp, pulsating with such need, he fisted his free hand into the tiles, digging into the marble. He felt so achingly swollen and hard that just by clenching himself over the straining muscle and giving himself a few tugs, the orgasm was there, rippling through his limbs, crashing over him in wave after wave. He shivered as ribbons of cum coated his fist and the wall, waiting for the relief and relaxation to settle over him like it normally did.

Except it didn't come. He blinked, still half-hard and breath coming out fast.

The noise of the shower roared back to life in his ears, and the moment was over. And the release may have been had, but the tension curled in his gut like a spring coil that had yet to ease; if anything, it retracted further inward, keeping him edgy and keyed up.

Christ, this was going to be a long couple of days, he thought.

He rinsed himself and the shower down before turning it off. He toweled off and dressed in the stiffest pair of jeans he owned and a gray and black flannel, which he buttoned up and was rolling up the sleeves to his elbows when he headed out of his room to the kitchen, his hungry stomach making itself known now that he had the attention for it.

Colton was nowhere to be seen, but the guest bedroom door was closed. Winter pulled out his overly expensive cooking wear and went to work. It was then he heard Colton's voice drifting through the open slider of his porch patio and he saw him there, on the phone, pacing idly back and forth.

The patio furniture was still wet from the storm, and so was Colton as he smiled to himself and to whomever he was talking to. It was a beautiful smile, deep and sincere, and Winter hesitated. Colton had asked him earlier if he was jealous of the women fawning over him in the bar, and he had meant it when he said he wasn't.

But right now, he was. The feeling was sharp and unfamiliar as he twisted his hand on the fridge handle before yanking it open and grabbing the ingredients he needed for dinner. Winter had only been jealous once before in his life, and it didn't end well.

He swallowed, refusing to think about that or the ridiculous sensation gripping his guts like a vice.

His phone pinged a text on the charger he had in the kitchen, and Winter, allowing himself the distraction, glanced over to it and was relieved to see the name of his best friend.

> I have your dog. And I know you're home.

Winter quickly grabbed his spare readers from the kitchen drawer and replied.

> I'll pick him up tomorrow morning if that's all right? Long day.

> How about you come to my dinner party tomorrow night instead? You can pick him up then.

He frowned, knowing Mal had been trying to lure him back to his popular bi-monthly dinner parties for a while now. They were lavish spectacles because Mal was a bit extravagant. He enjoyed hosting parties and spending time discussing art, wine, and other topics he didn't particularly care for.

Colton's laughter floated over his thoughts, and he released a breath and texted.

> Can I bring a friend?

As long as it's not a brat, sure.

Winter smirked.

> He is. But he's not my brat.

Not yours…yet?

He pinched the brim of his nose. Mal knew him too well.

> Off-limits.

???!!

> Colton Sacks

He watched as the bubbles typed and stopped, and then typed again.

Why does that name sound so familiar?

> Probably because you haven't heard it in ten years. NTR case. He's staying with me for a bit.

Holy shit. *Why* is he with you?

> Long story. So, can he come?

Absolutely. Hopefully, he can stand a little ogling by my guests. It's not every day we get a local celebrity at one of my parties.

> Thanks.

Btw Trevor popped by the gallery today…just so you know…

Winter cursed.

Why do you date such needy little things again?

They only become needy after they've been with me.

Mal sent him several eye-rolling emojis, making Winter chuckle as he set down the phone and started cooking.

Winter heard the slider door open ten minutes later, and Colton walked in.

"Smells good," Colton remarked, shutting the door behind him, eyes dancing over Winter.

He ignored the way Colton's eyes made a show of moving over his body, and turned back to his sauce, scraping and stirring it in the pan. The large stainless-steel pot of water was beginning to boil.

"Food should be ready soon," Winter informed him.

"Fantastic, I'm starved. Mind if I hit the shower real quick?"

"Go ahead. The shower in the guest bath leaks. Use mine."

Colton hesitated before heading to the guest room down the hallway, and then to Winter's bedroom. Colton appeared almost exactly ten minutes later, freshly showered, wearing gray sweatpants and a black T-shirt with the logo of his boxing gym on it, padding out barefoot and smiling. "Smells divine."

Winter had prepared their plates and was working on the iced tea when Colton strode into the kitchen, Winter's shampoo wafting over him, making his knuckles go white over the glass handle of the tea pitcher. He didn't want to like the smell of himself on Colton's body, and it took everything in his severely tested self-control not to react.

"Thank my Italian teacher for this recipe." Winter gestured to the table jerkily, attempting to remove Colton from his proximity as quickly as possible. Colton, with a nod and a thanks, took the seat opposite him.

"Molto bene," Colton said upon the first bite. "Fuck, I haven't had a home-cooked meal in a while."

Winter, deciding that there was nothing wrong with a bit of conversation outside of the investigation, asked, "What do you normally do for dinner?"

Colton sighed in pleasure after the second bite. "A lot of frozen and take-out, mostly. My mum cooked all the time when I lived with her. It was bloody fabulous, and I, the self-indolent idiot I am, never saw how good I had it until I moved out."

"When did you move?"

"I moved in with her right after Tahoe," Colton admitted. "Mum didn't want me traveling, and I didn't want to go back to university yet. So, I stayed. Thought it would only be for a month or so—turned into ten years. I visit my dad usually a couple of times a year. Haven't gotten around to it yet this year, though, which, knowing him, he'll be informing me of his displeasure any day now."

Winter smirked, "That sounded very British."

Colton chuckled. "Jamie says my accent gets a bit more—posh—whenever Daddy gets mentioned."

"Jamie?" Winter plunged his fork into his pasta, ignoring the tightening around his chest.

"My bestie. She was my mum's hospice nurse. That's how our romance started. I call her my platonic soulmate." Colton leaned back, sipping his iced tea. "What about you?"

"What about me?"

Colton's eyebrows arched, "Do you have a platonic soulmate?"

Winter finished his bite of pasta. "Mal—Malcolm Connell. Met in high school, haven't been able to shake him since."

Colton's smile was bright and radiant, and Winter tried his damnest to ignore that, too. Still, it felt downright impossible not to notice the sparkle emanating so naturally from the younger man across the table from him.

"He currently has my dog," Winter added roughly. "Mal dog sits whenever I have to go out of town."

"I saw the picture of Sierra." Colton's voice was a tight murmur. "When did she pass?"

"A couple of years ago—cancer. She was one of a kind."

"She certainly was," Colton said, throat bunching. "I don't think I've ever met a dog like her."

"She was special," Winter managed with a tight smile, trying not to let the grief of her passing swallow him whole. Because the fact was, he still missed her. It had been one of the hardest days of his life when he had to say goodbye.

"I'm so sorry for your loss," Colton whispered. "I only knew her for a short time, but I'm pretty sure I fell madly in love anyway."

He cleared his throat. "What about you? Any pets?"

"I'm never home long enough to keep a bloody plant alive."

"Two jobs and the gym," Winter motioned to the shirt. "You seem busy."

"I prefer it that way. After mum passed away, I've sorta just..." his words trailed off. "Floated. I suppose she was a bit of my rock after everything happened here. I love my life, though. I really love working with kids, to be honest. And bartending. Seeing people, all kinds of people, ready to have fun and cut loose, it's thrilling to watch people be honest with themselves."

Winter blinked, "At a bar?"

Colton shrugged, "Liquid courage and a flirty bartender can open people up a lot faster than a couple hours of therapy, trust me on that."

Winter chuckled, thinking about the sex club he frequented in his self-discovery years and how true that statement was, even though he never drank. He supposed Mal was his form of liquid courage, always inspiring him to challenge and test himself.

"So," Colton said, standing to get another helping of food. "Did you always wanna be a copper, or did you have other ambitions?" He paused, "Another round?"

Winter sat back and handed him his plate. "Sure, thanks."

He watched as Colton scooped pasta onto their plates and returned to the table with their second helpings. Winter nearly smiled. He couldn't remember the last time someone served him something from his own kitchen. The men he dated were accustomed to him taking care of them, and some even expected it, which left a sour taste in his mouth after a while. Ultimately, he supposed, that's why none of them lasted.

It was in these simple, polite gestures of consideration that love grew.

Stop it, Winter chided himself irritably, as he tapped his finger on the icy wet condensation of his pint glass. Just because his control broke today, it didn't mean this man still wasn't very much off-limits.

"So?" Colton asked.

Winter exhaled, returning his attention to the conversation. "No, I didn't always want to be a cop. I gave serious thought to being a pilot."

"Really?"

"I liked the idea of having my life in a suitcase and being able to pick up and go anywhere—anytime."

"Sounds romantic," Colton said wistfully.

"Yeah, well, being that I didn't have the patience for flight school and figured out I was color blind, my hopes were dashed, and I thought the next best thing was to be a cop. I saw some things happen as a kid with the justice system, and it took a few more years for me to figure out that if I wanted something to change, I had to become it—become the change…"

"…you see in the world," Colton finished the quote, and Winter smiled, surprised. "It pays to have a rich education."

"Wealth doesn't equate to knowledge, or age to wisdom. You're smart, Colton, and fearless. I saw that day one."

"Careful, now. That sounded almost like a compliment," Colton drawled, his eyes lingering over Winter's mouth as he splayed his legs wide beneath the table, leaning far back in his chair, giving him the best come-hither look Winter had ever seen.

Colton was as subtle as a brick wall smacking him in the face as he clearly offered himself up to Winter to be the mouth-watering dessert after tonight's meal.

"It is," Winter retorted smoothly, refusing to get drawn in. "Can I ask you another, more personal question?"

Colton angled his head to the side, "Isn't that what we're doing?"

"Feels like small talk to me. Though I am pretty outta practice when it comes to normal conversations these days."

"And why is that?" Colton asked.

"Being a detective as long as I have, and maybe living alone, I forget how to lead up to the big questions. I usually go straight for the jugular."

Colton smirked, looking pleased.

"Fuck small talk," Winter heard himself say out loud before he could stop himself. "Show me a glimpse of your soul."

Colton's gaze wavered, the hands around his lap stiffened, and his eyes sharpened.

Winter stilled.

Colton shook his head, his expression softening. "My mum used to say somethin' like that. Show me your soul, is what she'd say as a way to disarm people."

Winter, careful with his gaze, took a slow sip of his tea.

"So, what do you want to know, Detective?" Colton said with a light tone.

"You told me about why you work at the bar—what about the YMCA? What do you like there?"

"Oh, just about everything," Colton replied, softening. "The kids remind me of myself. I was once a wayward youth, defiant to authority, preferring the tempo in my own head and heart rather than listening to some random teacher's suggestion on how I was supposed to live my life. My father tried a bit, I'll give him that. It took a lot to get me through high school. Once university hit, well, the gloves were off, and dad stepped outta the ring for that round. I only attended for about a year before everything that happened here. And then after that, well, my life kinda veered off on its own course for a while. I found YMCA by happenstance. I fell in love with the kids, the staff, and the freedom of it. If I were to go back to university, I think I'd get a degree in psychology—work with kids."

Winter studied him, imagining Colton being a champion or advocate for kids, and how suited he seemed for the work.

"Why don't you?" Winter asked.

Colton rolled his shoulders in a careless shrug. "Never got around to it, I suppose."

"I don't believe in excuse-ology."

Colton laughed, surprised. "You callin' me out?"

Winter sipped his tea, smirking. "Maybe I am."

"Fine, all right—I was thinking about applying to a university this fall—maybe spring next year, happy?"

Winter cocked his head to the side and nodded, "That's incredible. Good for you, Colton."

"Aw, shove it. I don't need a fuckin' pat on the back, Winter."

"That's not what I'm doing. I'm serious. It takes a lot for someone to find their calling—and a helluva lot of courage to pursue it."

"All these compliments, luv. You're making me blush."

Winter saw the hint of amusement and seduction in his gaze and merely shook his head, unwilling to get trapped by this man again. And besides, they had work to do.

"I'd like to ask you some more serious questions now, if I can. There's a lot of information you have that I need for the case."

The younger man let out a disappointed sigh and nodded. "Of course. Let me do the dishes. Cook never cleans, at least not at the Stanton Manor."

"Manor?"

Colton tossed a broad smile at him over his shoulder, "My father made sure I grew up in an equitable home, even with servants."

Winter had always lived in a rough or rural area. Luxury to him was clean sheets, a long shower, and a roaring fireplace. Maybe a new pair of hiking boots on rare occasions.

He slipped his reading glasses into his pocket, feeling suddenly ancient as he headed into his living room, flipping on the Tiffany lamps and setting the box of files on the floor next to the coffee table. He caught a glimpse of his dog's bed, blanketed and empty, and frowned. Frank was his elderly Pitbull, tanned and white, and grayer than Winter, whom he adopted a few years back when Frank's prior owners placed him up for adoption. Winter didn't like the idea of elderly dogs spending their last few years in a cage.

He was surprised how much he missed the old bastard, even though Frank didn't do much but sleep and cuddle these days.

"Should I put the kettle on, or are you all right with iced tea?" Colton asked from the kitchen.

Winter wouldn't admit to his hot chocolate indulgence as his evening nightcap and instead replied, "Iced is fine."

Winter tapped the audio recorder app on his phone. This was the first time in ten years Colton Sacks would be re-interviewed, and he wanted to make sure he got it right this time.

"Setting the mood, are we?" Colton teased, bringing in fresh glasses of tea.

Winter eyed the man and hesitated. "I'd offer you somethin' stronger, but I don't have anything."

Colton, unperturbed, plopped down on the couch, draping an arm across the top. His lean body took up far too much space as he seemed to like spreading out wherever he went. "I'm not worried, Winter. I trust you'll go slow with me."

Winter caught the heat in his tone and refused to acknowledge it. "May I record this?"

Colton nodded, his humor draining a bit, noting the level of severity that had come over the room. "All right, where do we start?"

"The first day you arrived," Winter pulled out his notepad and pen, reluctantly withdrawing the reading glasses from his pocket. Colton arched an eyebrow in amusement but didn't tease him for it.

"Okay, let's start from the beginning of the day," Winter said.

"Don't you have this already?"

"I do, but it's always good to hear it again. And now that we know for a fact there's a second killer, this will be more important."

Colton nodded. "I flew in around 4 am. The only person who saw me in the house was mum."

Winter tapped the edge of his pen on the notepad, referring to his notes. "You reported at the time that the only people who saw you arrive in Tahoe were the pilot, stewardess, and driver."

"Father insisted I take the jet, so I did."

"Driver was already vetted back then. His alibi was his wife, and he didn't fit the description of the second Ripper you gave me."

"The pilot and stewardess?" Colton asked.

"Their alibis were each other at a hotel by the airport in Truckee."

Colton smirked, "So cliché."

"So, no one else could have possibly seen you? Maybe someone at the airport?"

"I don't remember seeing anyone up and about that morning. It was too early. And besides, Dad had a private car waiting on the field strip for me. So, I didn't really dally before gettin' in."

Winter ticked irritably against the inner cheek with his tongue. "This is the only glaring hole in the entire investigation."

"What?"

"You."

Colton frowned, leaning forward with his elbows on his knees. "How so?"

"The young men prior were all taken from different locations, but most were consistent in that they were taken while on a hike. You were taken from your bedroom, and without having even set foot on a trail or even in town."

"Maybe it's confusing because the profile you made back then was based on one killer, not two," Colton suggested.

"I thought about that, but a Ripper took you. At this point, they saw their victims on hiking trails, which again was the working theory at the time. You— from your bedroom. And—no one saw you. So how could they? How could they possibly have known you were even there?"

Colton scrubbed his hand over his jaw. "No fuckin' clue."

"So, this leads me to the next point of questioning."

"Fire away."

"Tell me what you remember about both of them—but mostly the second one."

Winter watched as Colton tensed and his jaw muscle flared, but his eyes held steadfast to his. "How they differed in fucking me or how they behaved?"

Winter's fists clenched over the notepad. This was the part he didn't want to know, but he had to. He was a coward in that way, he supposed. He had heard Colton's story a long time ago, when he was a vulnerable young man, helpless and broken. Now, he was a man—strong and confident, arrogant even, and...

Winter swallowed.

Colton didn't belong to him.

He knew that, but his body and his swirling emotions didn't understand. Something was building between them. Something unnamed and unknown, and he feared what it would do to him to hear it now. It had been different ten years ago when he could detach himself from Colton Sacks. And he wasn't sure he could let go of him so easily again. The thought was paralyzing and Winter stilled, unable to say a damned word.

Colton understood his silence as something else and sighed. "Sorry, I know, you're just tryin' to help. Alright, so here we go. I remember waking up, wrists handcuffed to a bed railing above me, on a rather posh bed."

"Posh bed?"

"Silk sheets, laundered, well cared for—the bedsheets anyway."

"What color were they?"

Colton hitched his head, surprised, "Why?"

"Just curious."

"Black. Midnight black."

"Tell me about the room."

"Clean, smelled like sanitizer and disinfectant," Colton said, rubbing his hands together as his eyes glazed over, as if he was transported back in time, recalling what he could. "Nauseatingly strong. It was a bit spartan—not many decorations, just a plain room with plain gray walls, wood floors, and a steel iron railing for the bedpost I was handcuffed to. There was a bedside table in a way, but the second Ripper rolled it in. He never once left it in the room."

Winter arched an eyebrow curiously.

"Like a nurse's cart, you know the ones. Jamie had one for my mum in hospice, it had everything. Wipes, nail file, clippers, lotion, ointments, you name it. His was just like that, but with an additional drawer for...toys. The spicy kind."

Winter's teeth clamped down, but he said nothing.

"He only used one of 'em on me. Though I doubt anyone would say it was for that purpose," Colton scoffed. "He liked to tase me. I fought him hard, especially after Pollock. But it didn't matter. The fucker tased me right on the spine."

Winter recalled the multiple taser burns on Colton's back, and his throat tightened.

"I figured out later why he used it so much on me." Colton squeezed his fist, opening and closing it in front of Winter. "The muscles contract when you're tased. It's brief but strong. When his dick was inside me, he'd hold me down and tase me. Did it a few times. I'd clench, and he'd groan like a fucking stuck pig."

Winter had assumed the taser burns had been for subduing purposes, which was half correct, he supposed. But to hear the whole truth made his insides coil and his stomach seize in disgust. Unable to sit, Winter stood, restless, burning energy coursing through him.

"You want me to go on?" Colton asked, eyes trailing over his features.

Winter nodded.

"I knew the second man was different from Pollock on behavior alone. Pollock was like a raging bull. He stomped into the room like he owned the place. I called him the Panter."

This was new information to Winter, and he glanced up from his pacing.

Colton shrugged, "A name I coined for him in therapy."

"You went to therapy?"

"For a long time," Colton said easily. "Mum and dad. I suppose money buys its privilege. I had the best trauma therapists workin' with me for years. The only things they couldn't work out of me were three things."

Winter waited, curious and wondering if Colton would share with him.

Colton hesitated, eyeing the recorder and leaning forward to say, "And that's not for you silly police bastards to hear."

Winter nodded and waved his fingers to continue, "Tell me more about Pollock the Panter."

"He panted while he fucked me," Colton bit out. "I don't say rape, and it's intentional on my end. That word feels like a dagger to the scar tissue. And I don't like it. I had one therapist tell me that whatever language I used to describe what happened to me, took the power back—the ownership of the story. Cause we're all stories in the end, aren't we? So, I was fucked. Without my consent, mind you. Pollock, thank God, was a 1-2-3 kind of man. He came quickly and left quickly. Panting the whole damned time, thought the bastard was gonna keel over on me."

"Did you see him?"

"Blindfold, remember?" Colton said, catching his gaze. "Every time. Except once. Couldn't have been blindfolded to make my daring escape—that would've been fucking extraordinary."

Winter absorbed his words before saying, "It was extraordinary you escaped in the first place, Colton."

Something passed between the two men, and Winter watched the tension ease from Colton's body before continuing, "Pollock was clumsy and rough. He manhandled me in ways that made me think this man had no experience with sex. At the time, I wasn't that experienced, so I didn't know much. But now that I do, I know for a fact that what that idiot did to me wasn't anything close to it. It almost seemed like he didn't want to be there."

Winter frowned, contemplating Colton's story.

"Once Pollock was through, I knew he'd be next," Colton sucked in a breath. "The Snake."

Winter remembered Colton calling him that last time, but he never pressed for an explanation as to why. "Snake?"

"The song he'd play: *In-A-Gadda-Da-Vida*."

"You never told me he played a song," Winter said.

"I blocked it out, honestly. It took a couple of years of therapy for me to remember. I did some brainspotting treatment where she made me look at a pointer—anyway, it doesn't matter. The important part is, I remembered." Colton took a sip of tea and sighed. "I wish he hadn't chosen that song. My mum loved it. She loved all that hippie psychedelic shit growin' up. Anyway, the song is about the Garden of Eden, of wanting to be accepted and loved. Except that what he did wasn't very accepting or loving."

Winter watched Colton's throat bob as he swallowed. "He'd come in, check the handcuffs on my wrists, make sure the blindfold was still secure, and then I'd hear the rolling cart being brought in—I saw it on my escape and put the pieces together later. He'd bathe me with a sponge, listening to that song the whole time. Once the song was over, he was done cleaning me. He would turn me over and stimulate me until I got hard. He knew exactly what buttons to push to get me going. He knew a man's body, unlike Pollock. He'd make sure to get me close to comin' before he'd suck me off. He was quiet up until that point, and then he'd mewl like a fucking cat the second I'd come, using sex toys and shit on me to make sure I did. I'd spew in his mouth, and he'd swallow it. I'd hear him groaning like he fuckin' came, not me. I'm surprised I never threw up on him. He was disgusting and pathetic and wanted me to want him. Or like what he did to me. I never did. If anything, it made me hate him more."

Colton scrubbed a hand through his beard. "I realized a few years back when I stupidly fucked an old flame, and felt how needy and desperate he was for me—that was the way he was. Like the song—wanted to be loved by those he had trapped in his fucked up garden of sex toys and handcuffs, soap and oil."

Colton exhaled sharply. "Anyway, after he was done with the foreplay, he'd flip me onto my stomach, and that's when he got cruel. He'd fuck to punish. To make me bleed. He'd scrape his teeth and nails all over my body. He never used lube, but maybe spit. He wanted to make it hurt. And it did. Every time. I'd fight and buck, and he'd laugh and hold me down. Whenever I stopped fighting, he'd tase me. He liked that I fought him."

Colton retrieved the lighter from his pocket and tapped in tempo on his knee, seemingly unconscious of it.

"He liked to slow down and then speed up. Take his time, unlike Pollock. And when he finally did orgasm, the same sounds of pathetic mewling. Then he'd restart the song, clean me, and massage me with the oil. It was so strong it'd sting my fuckin' nostrils. He massaged me, making sure he 'took care of me'," Colton said in air quotations. "Sick fuck, is what he is."

Winter hadn't realized he was leaning heavily against the brick fireplace mantle until Colton's story paused.

"Did you ever see anyone else?" Winter asked softly.

"No, I never saw any of the other men, if that's what you're asking."

"What about when you escaped?"

"I saw the room I was held in, but nothing helpful there."

Winter nodded, a tightness around his chest constricting his breath as he asked, "Do you need to take a break?"

The silver lighter stilled, and his gaze flicked up to Winter. "Do you want me to?"

Winter was surprised by the question. "Only you can answer that."

"Yeah, but you're way over there, lookin' like the big bad wolf."

Winter's chin jerked up, and he released the breath caught in his lungs, raking a hand through his hair. "Sorry."

"Don't be," Colton murmured, his expression stayed on Winter, softening, warming, holding him like the fucking sun. Yet, it was his story of trauma—of pain and suffering, and it almost felt like the tables were turned and Winter couldn't handle it.

What the hell was wrong with him? He'd heard countless victim stories—witnessed the worst of the worst in humanity, and yet...his fingers gripped the mantle as though he could break the brick apart, piece by piece, with the intensity of the emotion flaring inside him.

"Come here," Colton whispered thickly.

Winter hesitated.

"Please," Colton added.

He pushed off the fireplace and sat down across from him on the couch. Once he was comfortable, Colton sat back, legs splayed as he did, letting his knee brush Winter's leg and holding. Winter, for the first time, didn't resist and allowed the touch, not sure if it was for him or for Colton.

"What's your next question?" Colton asked.

"Tell me about the escape."

Colton hummed, looking pleased for the first time as he dragged a hard knuckle beneath his chin. "That's my favorite part."

Winter stared in awe at the burning delight in Colton's blue eyes.

"I'd been there two days too long and decided it was time to go," he began. "I hadn't started boxing back then, thank God. My dad preferred the gentlemen's sport of fencing. I had gotten pretty lean and had strong hands and wrists and knew I'd heal for what was next. I managed to twist my arms up, got the blindfold off, and slicked my hands first with all that lovely fuckin' oil. Then the hard part," Colton let out a breath. "I used the iron railing of the bedpost, broke my thumb and got out of the first handcuff. I had an old sports injury, dislocated my other thumb, and slipped out of the second cuff. Thank fuck I was able to pop my thumb back in place, cuz I needed at least one good hand. I searched the room next for something to use as a weapon. I found a tiny, rusted nail from the corner of the floorboards and used it to pick the handcuffs off the bedpost."

Colton smirked, and it was downright diabolical. "Then...I started singin', *In-A-Gadda-Da-Vida*, at the top of my lungs. I didn't want Pollock. I could tell by his size alone that he'd be hard to fight one-on-one without a weapon. But the mewler—the pathetic one, I could handle him. And sure enough, like a whale call, he came runnin'. I was butt naked, sore ass, marks all over my body, and alive. I had a chance. The door swung open, and I saw the mask first. It was a plain, black mask, no markings, and he was wearing a black hoodie, pants, and gloves. Smart fucker. And I knew it was him."

"Where were you?" Winter asked.

"On the bed, waiting." Colton flipped the lighter in his hand. "He just stood there as I yelled the song at him—it took a little encouragement on my part to get him to where I wanted him."

Winter eyed him curiously.

"I may have called him a few colorful things, something about a small dick, can't remember. He flew at me, enraged, and that's when I punched him. He lifted his chin up, grabbing the mask, and I sliced him with the open steel of the handcuff, right under the chin." Colton laughed, "he gasped and sounded almost feminine. I hit him a few more times, and that's when I heard Pollock—the bull above me—and I realized then that the place I was at was underground. I had to get out, so I ran."

Colton sat back, releasing a long breath. "I found a hatch, it looked like one of those hunter's traps, and climbed out. I remembered coming outta the ground and seeing nothing but a black sky and stars, surrounded by a forest. I didn't know where I was, so I ran, lookin' for light—anything. I ran for miles through the forest, my feet were bleeding and sore, but it didn't matter. And that's when I saw your porchlight. The rest is, well…"

"How did you know Pollock was following you?" Winter asked.

"He shot at me, but he couldn't see shit, and it was wide. I heard a vehicle of some sort, but didn't know what it was. The engine sounded too small to be a truck or car. So, I knew he was following me, trying to find me in the dark."

Winter knew the next question would be difficult and leaned forward, lightly touching the knee that was resting against his. "You skipped something."

Colton's eyes lingered on where his hand lay. "What?"

"The brand."

Colton released a hard breath, all humor draining away, leaving nothing but an emptiness in his eyes. "Right."

He dropped the lighter and leaned forward on the couch, his fingers grazing over the back of Winter's hand. The tightness around Winter's chest eased with a simple, almost delicate touch, which felt opposite to the violence of Colton's story. "He did that the first night."

"How?"

"He used Pollock, actually," Colton explained. "They came in after they were done with me, and I was a bit useless at that point. He used the taser a lot the first night. Pollock practically sat on me, and that's when

I felt the burn—the brand. I hadn't screamed the whole time until that moment."

Winter turned his hand over, fingers interlocking with Colton's, squeezing.

"I'm sorry," Winter murmured.

Colton pulled their joined hands to their lips and kissed them. "You saved my life," another kiss, hard and pressing. Winter shivered. "You," Colton whispered, "Glorious, big bad wolf in the woods…"

Winter's heart leapt against the bones of his chest. His mind swirled with the intimacy of this moment, of the brand, the other victims. The men—men—not young men like ten years ago, but men around Colton's age now.

The last Ripper had evolved because of Colton.

The sudden epiphany of that thought had Winter launching himself forward, grabbing Colton's face, forcing him to look at him.

"It all makes sense," Winter said. "This story—why he's choosing who he's choosing now. Why they all look so similar to you, why they're all out in the open this time…" his mind whirled. "An invitation. They're you. You're like an unfinished meal to him. He isn't done with you, and that's why he's back. He needs you."

Colton paled and trembled against him.

Winter released him and drew back, creating distance, despite the protest from his body and that tightening—that fucking restricting press against his chest returned. He stood, scrubbing a hand over his stubbled jaw, thinking.

Colton hitched his head up, bewildered. "He needs me?"

"The last ripper has been dormant for ten years, and from what you just told me, it means only one thing. He has an appetite, and he can't stop."

"But he did," Colton countered.

Winter nodded, beginning to pace. "He got scared..." he said out loud, letting his thoughts come into being while Colton listened. "From your story and how he kills, he'd be considered a passive killer, showing violence only when the victim is completely subdued. Pollock was the brutish one to handle the deaths, and the young men if they got out of line. This one, the last Ripper, was the lover."

Colton scoffed, "Fuck off."

Winter arched an eyebrow, "Think about it. He bathed you. He did thorough aftercare after he raped you. He couldn't stand the idea of you not liking him—not appreciating him—needing him. Maybe in some ways, he wanted you to love him."

Colton got to his feet, "I don't buy it. True love doesn't fuck like that."

"You're right," Winter said curtly. "It doesn't. But for him, it made sense. His love for you and hate for himself bled together. He wanted you so badly that he couldn't control himself with you. It's why he had Pollock go first."

Winter saw it all laid out, like a puzzle, combining all the old evidence with the new, letting the pieces click together. "It's why he did that ritual beforehand, with the song. He wanted to make it last because he knew he'd climax the second he was inside you, and he couldn't have that. That doesn't make a good lover, let alone an excellent one. So, he pleased you first. And when it was finally time for himself, he was angry because he couldn't."

Colton frowned, disgusted. "But he did."

"No, he didn't," Winter retorted, seeing the puzzle pieces fall into place, excitement swirling inside him. "I think he'd get too close to the orgasm too soon, and he'd retract in panic, ruining the orgasm initially. So, he'd tase you, make you clench to revive him. It was to add to the sensation, but not in the way you thought."

Colton let out a slow exhale, looking incredulous. "So, he was so in love with me—or whatever, and punished me?"

"He was angry at himself that he couldn't last and ultimately not be the lover he wanted to be with you," Winter replied knowingly. "It's why he branded you. He didn't want anyone else to touch what was his. He had to possess you, down to your skin. Almost insecure about it."

"Okay, so why now?" Colton asked quickly. "Why come back after all this time? The case was closed—he'd gotten away with it."

Winter tapped his fingers on the brick mantle, wondering the same thing.

Colton stretched, as if to release the restless energy building in his body, revealing the hard, tanned muscle of his side and the subtle curve of his hip, leading to the waistband of his shorts. Clearly, Colton ran shirtless, letting the warm rays of the sun darken his skin.

Winter's pulse skipped, unable to look away. He was beautiful, confident, so unabashedly content with himself and those around him. He was like the sun, and the world felt dark without him.

"For you," Winter whispered, the connection locked into his brain. "He came back for you."

CHAPTER 11

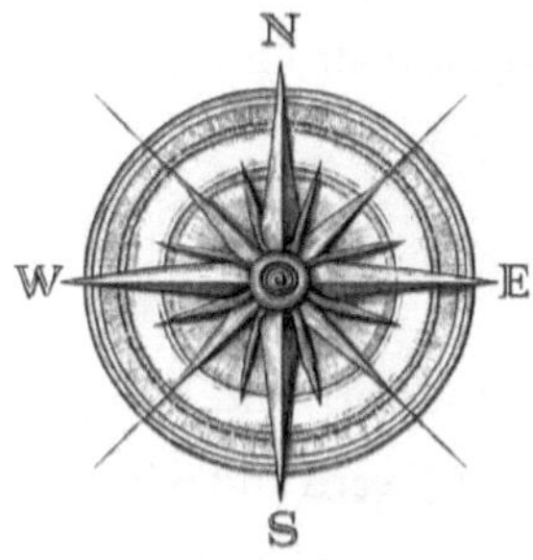

He dreamt of hands on his body, slick with oil, and then a pulse of electricity shooting through him, and then the sound of unrelenting panting, heavy and hard pressed against the shell of his ear. The memories came disjointed and quick, flashing and violent. Colton felt trapped all over again, paralyzed by fear. And then he was running. Running and running. Branches whipping past him in the dark. Nothing but black sky and stars, the moon tucked away behind a mountain. No light. No light. Until—a beacon in the dark. A burning, bright light flashed like lightning, and Colton scrambled, chasing it.

He found himself in Winter's grasp, his hand at his throat, his eyes as black as the night, and yet—he was safe, and alive, and hard. Impossibly hard, the pressure between his legs felt damn near crippling.

"Colton!"

He heard Winter's voice, but it was distant and hollow. The weighted feel of his cock, rigid and heavy, was real.

"Colton! Wake up!"

His eyes opened. The bedroom was dark except for the soft white streams of moonlight coming from the curtains of the open window. He blinked, not knowing where he was for a moment, and smelled pine and musk and knew immediately who was on top of him, hands on his shoulders, shaking him awake.

He was in Winter's guest bedroom. In Winter's sheets. In Winter's house.

Winter.

Thank fuck.

He reached blindly in the dark and, using all his strength and years of training, tilting his hips upward and without waiting, flipped Winter onto his back beneath him, straddling him. Winter let out a rush of air, hands fisting against his chest. "Colton—wake up!"

He almost purred a low growl at the feel of his naked body over Winter's, and the weight of his cock pressed between them. Colton was so bloody grateful that he preferred sleeping in the nude, so that the only barrier between them was Winter's boxers and T-shirt, which all could be easily removed.

Colton reached between them, blood rushing to his ears. Palming Winter's dick over his shorts, the man stiffened, jerking at the intrusive touch.

"Colton..." Winter whispered, voice shaking.

He could feel the outline of his thoroughly large, fat cock, and Colton nearly cursed in relief and surprise. Of course, Winter had this swinging between his legs, he thought darkly. Winter's body betrayed his resistance, as his manhood stiffened against Colton's touch, which was all the permission he needed as he ruthlessly rubbed against him. Winter cursed, hips bucking up uncontrollably, fingers digging into his chest. Colton kept himself locked against him, not moving, and letting Winter rub not once, but twice more. It was wild and almost unhinged, which caused a spark of fire to rush through Colton's veins.

Winter's hand was suddenly around Colton's throat, fingers holding him firm but not restricting airflow.

"Stop," Winter growled dangerously.

Colton grabbed the hand at his throat and squeezed, "No." He rotated his hips and ground himself onto Winter's hardening erection.

Fuck, he felt glorious.

"Colton," Winter managed out through gritted teeth, sounding like a warning.

Colton didn't want to hear the rejection—the resistance—when the hard proof was against his body that he wanted this—wanted him.

"I'm still dreaming if it makes you feel better," Colton whispered. "Touch me, Winter, please for fucks sake."

He knew he sounded desperate, but he didn't care.

After their conversation, reliving all that pain and feeling so damned exposed, so vulnerable, he watched in awe as Winter seemed more upset than him, cursing and predatory, like some dark wolf pacing in his living room, unable to do anything in the cage but listen. It reminded him of the night Winter had protected him, and it freed all those feelings he had buried years ago. And it came back like a tidal wave, flooding him, limb for limb, and he knew then how easy it would be for him to fall in love all over again.

And damn it, he didn't want to think about any of that now. He just wanted to feel. To feel him. To touch him. To know his body, and see him tremble and shake with need, and watch his eyes darken when he climaxed.

Winter abruptly moved. He was fast and powerful, flipping Colton onto his back and slamming him down onto the mattress. Colton let out a whoosh of breath as Winter peeled himself off him, untangling their limbs and stumbling off the bed, falling backward into the dark wall of the bedroom.

Colton sat up, staring at the moonlight that illuminated the shadow of Winter, watching as his chest rose and fell in furious breaths. His hands were braced on his knees as he bent over, trying to ease the pressure building between his thighs.

"I know you want this," Colton rasped, resisting the urge to touch himself.

Winter's groan tore from his throat, guttural and angry, refusing to look at him.

"Please, Winter..." Colton wouldn't beg, but he would ask softly, gently.

Winter's jaw flexed, resisting. Colton waited, hoping Winter would break this calm demeanor of his and take what he fucking wanted.

Winter straightened and started to leave, still unable to look at him.

The weight on his chest felt like a boulder, pressing into him, refusing to be rejected. Colton sucked in a breath and, in a tone that was still calm somehow, managed to say, "I'm not fragile, you know."

He halted at the threshold of the door.

"What happened to me is for me to deal with, not you. You may have been there and seen the aftermath—but you don't know who I am now. You don't know what I can or can't do. You haven't even bothered to ask. Maybe because you're afraid to," Colton drawled, understanding dawning. "Maybe it's easier to see me as the scared victim that came running to you all those years ago." He shook his head, "But I ain't him, and I am not what happened to me either. This isn't wrong."

"It is," Winter hissed, hostility lacing his tone, surprising him. "What are the three things?"

"What?" Colton asked, unable to follow the unexpected turn in the conversation.

"The three things you couldn't work out in therapy?"

He sat up, "Why?"

Winter finally turned to face him, and that's when he saw the black haze in his eyes, violent and beautiful like a storm. "Because what just happened was not okay. I don't take anyone to bed without knowing their limitations. After everything you told me, I know you have at least three."

Colton had never seen such anger—such breathtaking fucking rage. Winter's words had temporarily nullified the stinging rejection, and Colton decided that he would correct the rest by forcing Winter onto his ground—into his arena.

Colton sat forward, needing to see the black eyes up close, to smell the pine and musk from this man's skin. He reached out, grabbing Winter by the back of the neck, dragging him close. Winter attempted to fight him off, but he wouldn't allow it, using his skills as a boxer to outmaneuver him and then roughly grab him by his throat, the way Winter had done earlier to him, forcing him within inches of his lips.

The hot fan of Winter's breath on his face and the feel of his pulse skipping beneath his fingers was like pouring oil on a burning fire, and it took everything in his control not to lick that perfect, pillowy bottom lip into his mouth.

"Number one—no massages—no oil, no pretty aftercare bullshit. I don't need it." Colton dug his free hand into the side of Winter's jaw, forcing him to look at him, forcing him to hear every fucking word.

"Number two—no blindfolds, no restraints. Unless it's your fuckin' hands, and then—and only then—you better put them here," His fingers clenched and unclenched around Winter's throat. "Cuz no man has ever touched me like that before, and fuckin' 'ell, I get hard every time you do it."

Winter's black eyes dilated, and he sucked in a hard breath.

"Fuck, let me taste you, Winter," Colton dragged out, eyes fixed on his parted lips.

Winter didn't move. "What's the last one?"

"The last one isn't sexual," Colton murmured. "So, you don't gotta worry about it."

Winter's heated gaze dropped over the contours of Colton's naked flesh, and he wanted him to look, unashamed of the erection saluting between them, the tip already leaking with precum. Ready and willing for him to be taken.

Please, just end my misery already, Colton thought, trying hard not to let his desperation show. He had waited years to touch this man—to feel his skin beneath his—to know his kiss and hands on his body.

"Let go," Winter breathed steadily.

Colton stared hard into the resolute man and dropped his hands away. Winter withdrew, shoulders tense, and hesitated at the side of the bed. Colton, knowing he shouldn't be forcing Winter into anything he didn't want to do—recklessly, impulsively plunged off the side of the cliff, sat back on his heels on the bed, cock out and exposed to Winter's scrutinizing gaze, and grabbed himself at the base. He nearly shuddered but managed to control himself and not stroke.

"If you don't wanna touch me," Colton rasped. "You can watch. It won't take me long, but I can drag it out if you'd like." He pulled upward, stroking his shaft in front of him, thumbing the wet tip and letting out a tight breath, resisting the urge to moan, sucking his lower lip.

The darkness shrouded his features, and yet he remained perfectly still, watching.

He had his attention, if only for a moment. Colton slid his hand slowly down, his stomach muscles bunching and legs tensing beneath him from the building pressure already pushing at the base of his spine. He could see the outline of Winter's neck, the throat bobbing as he swallowed, his chest rising and falling in short, choppy breaths.

"Goodnight, Colton."

To his stunned amazement, Colton watched as Winter turned his back on him once more and left the bedroom, quietly closing the door behind him.

The rejection came swiftly and painfully, piercing his heart like a needle. He dropped his hand away from his body and fell backward onto the bed, staring blankly at the ceiling and the moonlight reflecting off the wooden beams of the bedroom, knowing himself well enough to know he wouldn't be getting any more sleep tonight.

His chest heaved, sucking in the fresh pine air as he collapsed onto the beach in front of Winter's home, letting the morning sunlight beat onto his chest, sweat dripping from his forehead and slicking his back. He had already been up before the sun, and as soon as it was light enough, he grabbed his running shoes and disappeared into the forest, needing a grueling run.

He had lain in bed a long time, thinking about what had happened, and wondered if Winter would ever come to him, would ever cross that bridge and meet him halfway. Or maybe, he couldn't. Maybe all Winter would ever see whenever he looked at him was a victim—this sensitive, delicate thing who was too fragile to touch.

Colton sneered at the thought, grabbing the shirt he had taken off during his run from the waistband of his shorts and using it to towel off the sweat on his face.

God, he thought, *this is unbearable.* He needed to stop pining. Stop wanting someone who clearly wasn't as interested as he was. Maybe he really was a bit of a masochist and enjoyed the pain of being rejected again and again.

Colton ducked his eyes away from the sun, wanting to find somewhere dark to crawl into and let these complicated fucking feelings for the Detective perish.

"Can't you see?" she said in a humming whisper.

His heart warmed at the sound of her voice, lifting his head from his shirt to see his mother sitting beside him on the sandy, pebbled beach before the vast, glittering blue lake.

She wore a forest green velvet robe, with a cream silk nightdress beneath, her bright yellow toenails pushing into the sand, and her hair slung in a thick braid along her shoulder. *She looked like a flower child today,* he thought admiringly.

He stared at the illusion—the image of his mother that he had created to cope after he lost her, knowing perfectly well this was a conversation he was having all to himself—and yet—he liked the idea that she was really here.

"See what?" he asked.

Her eyes traced over the smooth waters of the lake, taking in the scenery and the quiet.

"It's so beautiful here," she marveled with a dreamy sigh. "I forgot how quiet it was."

He nodded, tossing his sweaty shirt onto his knee as he plopped back onto his hands, lifting his chin to the rising sun, taking in the calm—the peace, knowing perfectly well it wouldn't last once the day began.

"He doesn't want me," Colton heard himself say out loud, hating how pathetic it sounded.

Her gaze returned to his, "Is that true? Or are you just wallowing because he didn't give you what you wanted last night?"

He grunted irritably. "He thinks I'm a fragile fuckin' teacup that will shatter if he touches me."

"And are you?"

"No," he snapped back haughtily.

The sun brightened the golden locks of her hair, her cheeks warm and radiant, sprinkled with freckles over her delicate nose. "I think you're going to shatter, but not in the way he thinks."

Heat spread hot and fast up the back of his neck and behind his ears.

He recognized the daring glint in her bright blue eyes and smiled back at her.

"You were a petulant child, you know," she said. "'No' to you meant a challenge, or a test—'no' was not a word you heard very often, and I blame myself for that. You were so fiery, so damned tough sometimes. So, naturally, I would give in, and you'd get what you wanted. But it was on the days that I didn't give in, when I resisted you until the last second of our day together, that you would snuggle me the tightest in bed—almost desperate for me. So affectionate, so loving."

Dead air hung between them, and all he could do was grieve. Missing her hugs, her scent, her laugh, her brightness. He missed her with every fiber of his being, and all he could do was pretend to have this conversation, wishing it were real.

"It's good he's resisting you," she taunted gently. "It only means that when he finally gives in, it will shatter you both."

Colton closed his eyes, hating himself for wanting to believe that and not knowing if he should. He spent a lifetime giving his hope away to that man. He wasn't sure he had anything left to give.

"Do you remember the story of how I first saw you after you escaped?" she asked softly.

He hummed and nodded, "Fingers a breath apart."

She wrapped her arms around her knees, looking wistful and childlike. "It was quite possibly the most romantic thing I'd ever seen."

"You are so dramatic, mum," he teased.

She bit her lower lip, unable to contain her smile. "Can't you see..." she started to sing. "What that woman, lord, she's been doing to me?"

He arched an eyebrow, "And what's that supposed to mean?"

"It means you're driving him crazy, my love. And soon, very soon, he will realize that resisting you is a futile endeavor."

"I don't want him if he's gonna regret it."

"He won't. But he might…" he shot her a questioning look. "…if you push him," she quickly added. "Winter is a still waters run deep sort of man. I can respect that. But he's also a wolf. You saw it last night—and ten years ago. Wolves are protective and ruthless over what they want."

Colton swallowed, still unsure.

"And you are a phoenix, my sweet, darling son. You brighten up everything around you, and you burn hot sometimes," she said. "Patience isn't your strong suit when you want something this much. Be careful with your big bad wolf, honey. Cuz wolves bite, growl, and devour."

Something in his pulse leapt as he said, "They also mate for life."

Her lips broke into a wide, knowing smile, "Yes, they do." She hummed the Marshall Tucker Band song, 'Can't You See?' before disappearing into the sunlight, giving him plenty to think about.

CHAPTER 12

W inter stared sightlessly out into the trees, sitting on the deck of his patio, thinking about last night. He should've known better, he thought irritably. He shouldn't have come running when he heard Colton yell in his sleep. But no, he just had to play the hero.

Watching Colton, his shadowed form held over him on the bed, thrusting his hard erection into him, had been fucking incredible. And sweet, holy hell, Winter never felt anything like it. Colton had been wild, demanding, and so out of control, as though possessed with passion. His primal power had left Winter breathless, and yet he had to regain control, and by some miracle, had managed to tear himself from the bed right when he was about to lose himself entirely into the wildness of Colton.

"I'm not fragile..." Colton's words rang in Winter's ears the rest of the night. *"This ain't wrong."*

It was wrong, he thought, raking his fingers through his hair, pulling the roots, inhaling deeply, feeling the pressure at the base of his spine, and cursing his body's betrayal.

What happened to Colton was sick, traumatic, and horrific. There were no words for it. So how could he let Colton get mixed up with someone like himself—someone that ruthlessly, and at times carelessly, consumed and dumped his lovers just as callously and coldly as the fucking Ripper?

He didn't want to hurt Colton. The young man had been through enough, and getting involved, even if it was just sex, was impossible. Winter knew deep down that Colton was different. And Winter knew, walking away from him again, especially if they started something, would be impossible. Because the truth was, the wall around his heart cracked...again. It had cracked the night he first met Colton, and now, another crack had splintered like a fucking bullet through his chest. He had felt it last night when Colton touched him.

Winter sucked in a breath, pinching the brim of his nose, wishing he could somehow forget last night, knowing perfectly well he never would. Winter had shuddered under his touch. It had been so easy, so natural, as though their bodies were made to possess one another. He nearly surrendered to the feeling of the weight of Colton's body against his—his lips. God, he wanted that. He wanted to know what his mouth tasted like. That sassy, smartass mouth that liked to tease and challenge him.

Fuck, fuck, fuck.

Winter ground his teeth, frustration mounting. He was the exact opposite of what would be best for Colton, especially in the bedroom, where he liked to be in complete control and rough, demanding every-thing from his sexual partners. Everything.

After he pressed him, Colton revealed his sexual non-negotiables, which, to some relief, were things Winter didn't require in the bedroom. But it didn't change the fact that he was a dom and he needed a sub-missive. Something he wasn't sure Colton would ever agree to because of what happened to him. And it didn't matter anyway, he thought irritably.

Colton was off-limits, and he shouldn't even be considering any of this.

He took a sip of his coffee, letting out another grumbling sigh, realizing he had let his coffee grow cold while he stewed. He got to his feet, about to get a fresh cup, when he heard a car rumble up his private driveway, and he stepped back, catching a glimpse of the silver truck, recognizing it.

"Shit," he muttered and headed inside to the front door.

"What's wrong?" Colton's voice caught him off guard, and he turned to see that the man had just stepped out of the shower, towel clutched against the side of his head, drying his hair. His naked chest was still wet as thick water droplets slid down his flawless, golden skin, traveling all the way to the thin material of the boxer briefs, which Colton must have just tugged on before stepping out of the guest bedroom.

Winter bit his lower lip, stomach tightening.

Look away. Look anywhere else.

Colton must have seen something in his gaze, and he lowered the towel, letting it drop to the floor. His eyes darkened as though a predator catching wind of prey.

"I can get back in the shower, if you'd like. And since, for some damned reason, you think you can't touch me, or whatever bullocks you got rattling on in that pretty head of yours, I'll let you watch."

Colton's fingers chased after one of those water drops with a slow stroke of his knuckle, all the way down the flat, hard muscles of his stomach. "Watch until you can't stand it anymore."

Winter balled his fingers into tight fists at his side, rooted to the spot like a damned tree, unable to tear his gaze away. Colton smiled, seeming to sense this, and casually strolled down the hallway, sliding his fingers through his wet hair, licking his lips.

"Until you get so overwhelmed, you do this..." Colton reached for Winter's hand and placed it around his throat. He felt Colton's pulse leap under his fingertips, and he knew it would be so easy to take him—right here, right now, using nothing but his tongue to lick the water from his body, listening to those smothered groans that Colton tried to hide from him last night.

"Tryin' to control me, or yourself, I wonder?" Colton murmured huskily.

He stilled, realizing that he was far too perceptive. Colton had figured out one of his telling weaknesses—the hand collar, a way to control his lovers and, in a way, himself.

And damn this man to hell, he was feeling himself cracking under the sexual tension straining between them. Everything about Colton screamed defiance, and he was a moth to a flame, wanting to burn and be burned until there was nothing left of either of them.

"Does this get you as hard as it gets me?" Colton rasped, "It has to—or else you wouldn't do it."

Fuuuuck.

Winter's fingers twitched around his neck, feeling the damp skin and the heat radiating from him. Colton's lips parted, gaze locked with his, waiting. Waiting for Winter to meet him halfway or not at all. Colton may be tempting him, but he wouldn't go any further than that. He needed Winter to want this. He had realized that last night, when Colton hadn't leapt off the bed and demanded more of him. He wasn't like the other men he had pursued before. Colton was a patient hunter, but also rash and deadly, knowing when to strike and when to back off. Winter had seen his hunter side before—on the night they killed Barry Pollock.

The knock came fast and pounding, causing Winter to tighten his hold around Colton's throat, wanting to stay locked in this moment and ignore the idiot at his door.

"Get dressed," Winter commanded gruffly.

Colton arched a defiant eyebrow, "And what do I get in return?"

Winter squeezed, and Colton hummed, eyes lighting with pleasure. The evident arousal on his face undid something in him as he tightened his hold. "What do you want?"

Colton lowered his eyes to his lips. "I want you to cook that lemon pasta dish for me. The one you were talkin' about."

Surprised, Winter nearly laughed. "That's what you want?"

"Oh, I want lots of things. Dirty, dirty fucking things, Winter. But we'll start with that, yeah? You need to go slow."

Stunned, Winter released him, retreating the same way he did the night before, except this time, he saw everything. Colton's quick breathing, the hard press of his cock, and the dangerous, confident knowing in those blue-gray eyes that said: It's only a matter of time before you break.

Fuck, I'm in hell.

Winter spun on his heel, striding down the hall, and swung open the front door, revealing Trevor—his former lover.

Yup, this is definitely hell.

Trevor was almost as tall as Winter, with broad shoulders and a lean frame. His hair was a muddy brown color and ruffled, as though he had run his large hand through it countlessly before arriving at his door. Trevor's eyes were bright green, and his clothes were a haphazard mess.

Winter had seen this look before.

The strung-out look of an addict not ready to let go.

"I'm here," Trevor said in excited relief.

"I can see that," Winter growled. "Why?"

Trevor hitched his chin up in surprise, "What do you mean? You texted me."

Winter bit his inner cheek, regret flooding him. He had. He had been frustrated with Colton and was trying his hardest not to be tempted by him, so he thought he'd nip it in the bud with sex with his former fling. Except the rest of the night had gotten away from him, and Winter neglected to check his phone, which he had a feeling was blown up right now with Trevor's frantic text messages.

"I know your booty call texts, Winter. So—here I am."

Winter released a strangled sigh, "and when I didn't text back, did you think that maybe I changed my mind?"

Trevor frowned, deep and pitying. It took serious willpower not to slam the door in his face.

"I'm sorry, Trevor," Winter said as patiently as he could. "I made a mistake texting you. It won't happen again."

"You never make mistakes," Trevor retorted in disbelief. "You're like a serial killer, methodical in that way."

Winter frowned, not liking the reference. "I'm busy. This isn't a good time."

Trevor leaned in, filling up the doorway, "So, when is a good time?"

"We talked about this."

"We did, and then you texted me."

"Like I said—a mistake."

Trevor brushed his fingers hungrily against the front of Winter's shirt, angling to touch his neck. Winter leaned back, avoiding the intrusive, unwanted touch.

"I drove all the way here," Trevor said, biting his lower lip, which made Winter pause, unable to help but compare this man to the one in his guest bedroom, who also attempted the same sort of seduction, but a thousand times better and with more class. Trevor felt like a bullheaded mule, refusing to take the hint and get off his doorstep.

"Might as well make the most of this." Trevor hooked his finger on a button of Winter's plaid shirt. "You can fuck me quick—whatever you want. I'll be your good boy..."

Winter clutched the wood of the door, digging into the grain. "Goodbye, Trevor."

He was about to shut the door when Trevor shoved him roughly backward. He stumbled, falling into his entryway vanity, slamming the back of his foot into the edge, and cursing at the jolt of pain shooting up his leg. Trevor's face was flushed with fury.

"Do you think I wanna be like this, Winter? Do you?!" Trevor's voice rose with each word. "I was normal before you! I fucked women before you! You pursued me! I was on top of the world, and then you came along and fucked my life up."

Winter stood his ground, body tensing for the fight that would surely come.

"You're a wrecking ball," Trevor seethed. "You destroy people—you break them down with your rules and your praise. I was so fucking blind! All I could think about was pleasing you, and then you left me high and dry."

"I was working a case. You knew that."

"Bullshit!" Trevor shot back. "You knew I liked you, and that's when you ran."

He felt his jaw tighten, unable to counter him because it was true. He had known for a while now that Trevor was developing feelings for him, and Winter, mercifully, had to end it. Apparently, he didn't end it soon enough.

"You can't stand feelings because they're messy and big and uncontrollable. So, like a coward, you ran," Trevor spat out furiously.

"You're right. I should've said something earlier," he admitted. "But you didn't give me any time before you imploded all by yourself."

"You set me up to fail," Trevor retorted.

"Grow up, Trevor," Winter ground out. "We're done. Get off my property."

"Or what?"

"Or I'll knock your fuckin' lights out," Colton drawled casually.

Trevor shot a glance down the hall at Colton who, to Winter's relief, was dressed, wearing faded jeans and a navy-blue T-shirt that clung to the coiled muscles of his biceps and chest. He looked downright lethal despite the appearance of a relaxed position, leaning his shoulder against the wall at the end of the hallway. His hair was slicked back from the shower as he stroked a hand through his short, trimmed blond beard. Winter recognized the latent power stirring just beneath the surface in the younger man and shot him a stern warning look.

It was bad enough that Trevor was here—let alone having Colton get involved in his personal, and now very messy, business.

Colton raised his hands in defense. "I know, I know. You can handle yourself. But this guy is really starting to annoy me."

"Wow," Trevor mocked angrily. "That was quick."

Colton hummed with a long, dragged-out sigh, "If only."

"Enough," Winter barked irritably at Colton.

"Winter!" Colton's eyes widened, and he turned—right into Trevor's punch.

CHAPTER 13

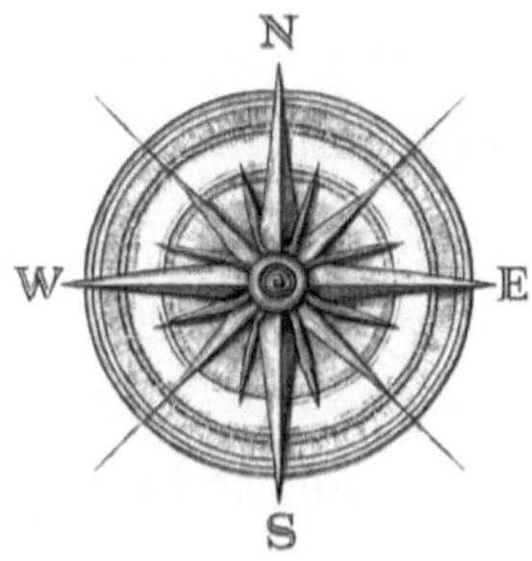

Winter dropped like a stack of bricks.

Colton was off the wall and running at Trevor a second later. He tackled the man, sending them both tumbling backwards out the door and off the porch. He didn't feel any of it, too enraged by the sight of Winter crumpling.

This man may have been taller and broader in size, but he was all soft, pillowy muscles, giving Colton the advantage.

A blasting horn and a dog barking caught Colton's attention as he kneed Trevor hard in the stomach before slamming an underhook into his balls, fighting dirty the way this man had. A punch when a man wasn't looking was fucking despicable, and he needed to be taught some manners. Colton jumped to his feet and slammed his boot into the side of the big man-child, causing him to let out a pathetic whimper.

"Stop!" Trevor groaned, waving a frantic hand out, the other clutching between his legs.

Colton glanced at the expensive car bouncing down the road toward them, and despite the rage crackling through his veins, he raced back up the steps to Winter, unconcerned about the chaos outside.

Hands trembling, heart pounding, Colton glimpsed blood on Winter's eyebrow as he slowly stirred.

"Winter," Colton said softly. "You all right?"

His eyelids fluttered open to reveal hazed dark orbs. He sat up with Colton's help and touched gingerly the corner of his bleeding eyebrow. "I should've seen that coming," Winter hissed bitterly.

"I shouldn't have encouraged it," he replied. "I'm sorry." He licked the pad of his thumb and cleaned up a bit of the blood on Winter's face.

Winter stiffened under his care, and Colton ignored it, raking his fingers through his ruffled hair, unable to stop touching him.

"I'm okay," Winter said. "I've had worse."

Colton trailed his knuckles over his stubbled jawline, his own teeth mashing together. "I should go back out there and stomp on his nuts again."

Winter unexpectedly turned, letting his lips graze across Colton's knuckles, eyes lowering as he sighed. His heart galloped at the subtle permission to touch, as he moved his hand over Winter's lips and felt the achingly soft flesh. He loved the feeling of rugged stubble and smooth lips, hearing the delicate intake of breath as he dragged his thumb across his lower lip, pulse thundering like a drum.

"Colton..." Winter grated out, but not stopping him.

His heart skipped. *Just give me one more second to touch you, you stubborn, brilliant fuckin' man.*

"Before this day is over," Colton whispered. "I'm kissing you."

Winter's eyes flared, making Colton nearly kiss him right then and there. But he knew now was not the time.

"Someone else is here," Colton said, clearing his throat, releasing him.

He stood and held out his hand to Winter, who hesitated but accepted it, getting to his feet.

Together, they walked outside, and Colton was greeted with a rather comical sight. Trevor was still on the ground, looking thoroughly put-out, while another man, around Winter's age, holding the leash of a Pitbull, was pointing a chastising finger at him as though a principal scolding a student.

"Jesus Christ, Trevor, stop torturing yourself," the man with the dog chided. "You're a handsome man. Keyword—man. Now get up and find your dignity. You probably lost it on the way here."

Trevor managed to roll to his feet and looked up to the porch where Winter stood, glowering and bleeding.

Trevor's face flooded with regret. "I'm sorry, Winter. I don't know what came over me..."

"Go," Winter said, his tone as frozen as his name, and Colton shivered, surprised by the ice there.

Trevor stumbled to his truck and got in, hauling down the road and out of sight.

"Holy hell, Winter," the man with the dog said. "You look like glorious shit."

"Thanks," Winter said without a shift in tone. "Let go of Frank."

The man did, and the Pitbull, tanned and white, with a gray snout, barreled up the steps and into Winter's legs, thick tail slapping against the railing of the porch. He bent down and lovingly patted him.

"Frank, meet Colton," Winter said to the dog. And Frank, the elderly Pitbull, turned his sights on Colton and gave him several happy licks and tail thumps. Colton leaned down and stroked the thick, muscled dog that seemed very excited to be back home with Winter. He sighed, knowing the feeling well.

"Colton, meet Malcom Conner," Winter introduced. "Mal for short."

"Life-long besties," Mal drawled, sauntering up the porch.

Colton knew a flaming gay when he saw one, and this man held no shame about who he was, or the wealth that dripped from his polished hairstyle of a faded cut of his light brown hair, to the Gucci sunglasses framing his face. He wore a Ralph Lauren white polo shirt and crisp, pressed black shorts, accompanied by bright white designer shoes. He was of average height, average build, and, honestly, average looking. If he hadn't worn designer clothes, Colton would never have noticed him. Not like he noticed Winter.

"Charmed, darling," Mal said faintly, letting his hand linger, and Colton managed to capture it for a brief handshake, unable to stop the smirk. When Winter had told him about Mal yesterday, he had not imagined a toned-down version of *Birdcage*.

"Is that blood, Winter?" Mal eyed him beneath his overly large sunglasses.

"Yeah."

"I warned you," Mal sang airily, waving a well-manicured hand as though his wrist had a hinge instead of bone.

"And when has that ever stopped me?" Winter teased, surprising Colton with a sly smile.

Mal rolled his eyes dramatically. "Never. Sometimes I think you like being tortured by all these simpering brats."

Winter grinned. He actually fucking grinned. It was dazzling, and all he could do was stare, mesmerized by the sudden transformation.

"Wanna come in for some coffee?" Winter asked Mal.

Mal tutted a dramatic sigh, "Can't—remember?"

Winter frowned and then nodded, "Of course. Busy."

Mal's eyes fluttered over Colton. "You're invited too, handsome. We love fresh meat at our little gatherings."

Colton arched his eyebrows curiously. "I feel like I'm missing something..."

"Mal and his partner, Patrick, are hosting a dinner tonight. It's…"

Mal cut in, "Not just any dinner, Winter. It's *the* dinner. My bi-monthly dinners are the most coveted invite in town. And Winter's missed the last two."

"Work has been—"

"Work, work, work," Mal dismissed with a wave. "You have to eat, too. And so does Muscles here. So come tonight, I insist! I cannot take another no, darling."

Winter's resistance melted, and Colton very much liked this best friend of his.

"Don't make me beg," Mal said through pursed lips.

"All right, fine. You win. We'll be there."

Mal nearly danced with excitement, "Finally! Okay, wonderful. Normally, I have you bring a dessert, but well, he'll be the perfect indulgence for the evening," he said, gesturing to Colton, eyebrows lifting.

Colton snorted, "I don't know if I should be offended or complimented."

"Take it however you like, handsome. I'll see you both at six o'clock sharp. Don't be late. Bye, Frank. I will not be missing your snores."

Mal twirled on his sneaker like it was a dancing shoe, slid into his all black Audi, and took off back down the lane.

Colton eyed Winter curiously, "He's somethin'."

"Yeah," Winter said, still smiling. "A lot of something. I know. But I love the damn bastard and apparently, we're going to dinner tonight."

"A posh one at that," he said knowingly. "He practically screamed money."

"He has good taste. Owns a couple of art galleries that have done very well." Winter patted Frank again. "We have time before we have to go. I'd like to go to the station and check in with forensics and the coroner. See if they have any new details."

"We should patch up your eye first," Colton suggested as they headed inside with Frank leading the way.

"Sorry for all of that," Winter clipped out.

"Don't apologize. What did Mal call him? Oh, right, brat." He emphasized the word, tonguing hard on the t.

Winter slammed the door firmly closed behind him, his movements too controlled.

"So...you got a thing for brats?" Colton hummed, following Frank into the living room and back into the kitchen, where he helped himself to the coffee, deciding that tormenting Winter was delightfully fun.

Winter followed, grabbing his mug off the counter and tossing the contents of his coffee into the sink. "His words, not mine."

"Nonetheless true."

"It's complicated enough having you here, let alone getting involved in my personal life."

Winter's lips had flattened hard as he held a towel beneath the sink and dabbed the corner of his eye. "We have work to do. I don't have time for—this."

Colton nodded, sipping his coffee, leaning against the kitchen counter. He didn't want to talk about Trevor—and he clearly didn't want to talk about what nearly happened between them last night. And never the patient man, he would have to be patient with Winter.

"I've been thinking more about our conversation last night," Winter said.

Colton smirked into his mug, "I've been thinking a lot about last night as well."

Winter tossed him a hard look, which Colton merely shrugged before adding, "Wayward thoughts and idol hands..."

Winter dropped his gaze slowly over his form, towards the waistline of his jeans, before quickly averting his gaze. "I was thinking about other reasons as to why the last Ripper went into hiding..."

Disappointed, Colton sighed. "Barry Pollock getting a shotgun to the face, maybe?"

"That's certainly a reason, considering the man who did the killing for them was gone. But there was a lot of noise around the parks at the time. The publicity surrounding the case was intense, with every news station, radio, and social media feed covering it, and it only got bigger when a rich heir to a Lordship was captured. And..." Winter cleared his throat, careful not to look at him as he said, "I think he really stopped because of you. The one that got away that would be impossible to catch again."

Colton hesitated, fisting his hands around his coffee, swallowing hard. Winter could praise or compliment him when it centered on the case. Anything outside that, he was a stone fucking statue that seemed impenetrable.

"Look, I didn't bring you up here to torture you, Colton. One word from you—and this is all over. You go home, and we both move on."

Colton carefully set down his coffee behind him on the counter, "I'm all in. I ain't going anywhere until this bastard is caught."

"You sure?"

"What's the next step?" he asked determinedly. "You have everything from me. How else can I help?"

He saw Winter's shoulders ease, seemingly relieved. "I have some ideas. First, we stop by the coroner's." He balled the bloodied rag into his hand. "I have only one condition moving forward—especially after what just happened."

"I'm listening."

"I call the shots. You listen to me, no questions asked. You just do. Got that?"

Colton cocked his head to the side, arms crossing over his chest, "You know I have authority issues, right?"

"That's my condition, Colton, or this ends right now."

Colton couldn't ignore the sinking feeling in his stomach at the thought of leaving already—not Tahoe—but him. He sucked in a breath at the sudden realization.

"No promises," Colton replied coolly. "But I'll do my best."

Something passed over the older man's face, maybe a softening, a flash of vulnerability. But it was enough to give him something far more dangerous than lust or some silly promised kiss—hope.

The first thing he noticed was the smell. It was intensely familiar, like the disinfectant one from the Ripper's lair. The coroner's office was a normal building, which was old and rustic, and with not much going on inside, besides a very polite elderly woman who greeted them at the front desk and allowed them into the back, where there were a couple of offices and a hallway that led to the room where the bodies were processed.

He supposed he had expected something cold and sterile, based on what he saw in the movies. But it was far from it. The door swung open to reveal a large window on the far wall, adorned with tall, bushy plants. The other side of the room was equipped with a whiteboard, several different scales, and tools lined the shelves, alongside more plants and six cold cabinets where bodies were stored.

On the whiteboard was the information about two people, and the one name he recognized was Thomas McNamara.

"Winter," a booming voice said from behind them, and Colton nearly jumped.

They turned, and an older woman strode towards them. She had a round, smiling face and all silver hair, cut short, wearing a white doctor's coat.

"I heard a rumor you're doin' the dunk tank at the festival this Saturday," she wiggled her eyebrows mischievously. "Please, Christ, tell me it's true."

"Who told you that?" Winter asked, frowning.

"Oh, you know—everyone." She stood before them in the threshold of the office, tall and thickly built, and Colton knew this woman worked out by her hand alone when Winter made the introductions and felt the telling calluses of a power lifter.

"Colton, this is Dr. Byne."

She waved a dismissive hand at Winter. "No one calls me that, call me Meg. Now—c'mon," she drawled out. "A couple of ladies from forensics and the courthouse need to know if this information is true because if so, we may decide to leave our husbands at home to do a ladies' night in front of your dunk tank for the evening's entertainment."

Colton snorted a chuckle and cleared his throat.

Meg placed a hand on her hip, "We all know you swing for the other team, Winter, but that doesn't mean you aren't possibly the handsomest man in three counties. So, you gettin' wet or what?"

Colton, to his delight, saw the telling signs of a blush on Winter's cheeks.

"I merely suggested another charity for the night to Raquel and her team." Winter bit out.

"So, is that a yes, you cagey bastard?" Meg asked, tapping her foot impatiently.

Colton placed a firm hand on Winter's shoulder. "Winter, you wouldn't want to disappoint your fans, now would you?"

His gaze sharpened on him.

Colton patted him roughly and turned to Meg. "He already agreed earlier this week. So, the answer is yes. He'll be getting wet for a good cause."

Meg beamed and pulled her phone from her back pocket, practically giggling. "I knew it! I'm texting everyone. Dude, you're not leaving that dunk tank for as long as I can help it. Not unless some of the guys from SWAT or the fire department want to compete with you. I can think of a couple..."

Winter looked like he wanted to break her phone, and instead shot a steely look at Colton, who shrugged innocently. A minute later, Meg tucked her phone away, smiling. "All right, you didn't come here for that. I suspect it's about McNamara?"

Winter nodded tersely, and she hitched her head curiously at Colton.

"Colton's assisting me on the case," he replied easily.

She nodded and gestured inside, "Of course."

Meg slipped on her glasses and gloves, then walked over to the cold cabinet locker, unlatched the middle door, and withdrew the steel slate that McNamara had rested.

Something shivered up the back of Colton's spine.

McNamara's pale gray flesh was the same as it was in the forest that day, but even more colorless now in the light of the room.

"This young man went through hell before he died," Meg said simply. "Reminds me of another case a few years ago... but the bodies had been pretty badly burned. Anyway," she carefully turned McNamara's wrist over, revealing the crease of his arm. "He had high doses of ketamine and Rohypnol in his system, but I don't think that's what killed him." Meg gestured to the violent rope marks at the base of his throat. "The severity of the ligature abrasions and burns suggests asphyxiation."

Colton listened. His gaze fixed on the man on the table, and he realized then that Winter had stayed perfectly still beside him. Colton's throat ached as he felt for the briefest of seconds Winter's fingers touch his before he took a step forward, seeming to want to shield him. With a violent flash, a memory pierced through his mind, taking him back ten years. They were sitting together on the bench seat inside an ambulance, and Colton had buried his face into Winter's neck, unable to stand the smell of the ambulance, clutching helplessly to him. And Winter, a stranger to him, allowed it, comforting him.

He shivered, allowing the memory to pass through him, without judgment or shame. Just letting it exist inside him and knowing that if he needed to do that again, Winter, without question, would allow it because that's who he was.

Eli Winter was more than just a good detective—he was the best man he knew.

"Theories?" Winter asked her.

She shrugged, "McNamara was a big guy, good muscle tone, strong. I think the only way his killer could get him to the tree was to knock him out with the Rohypnol and drag him." She motioned to the feet, showing the cuts and scrapes on the back of his ankles and feet. "Possibly dragged him with a blanket or tarp. These are the only indicators of vertical cuts that are consistent with drag marks. The rest of the cuts on his body are from fingernails and teeth."

Colton already knew this, but to hear it again, to be clinically diagnosed in front of the body that could've been him ten years ago, made his stomach drop.

"The ketamine could've been used for any number of reasons. Sedation of the body to move him without resistance." She pushed his leg open slightly, revealing the burn mark. "Brand mark, placed in the groin area, and at least twenty marks of teeth and nail rips around the area, and the anal area. From the bruising and tears of the soft tissue, he was sexually assaulted. There were taser burns along the spine and back of the neck. I also made a note that some of the cuts had Neosporin. There is a bite directly on the head of the penis, which was given a few hours before death."

Colton sucked in a hard breath, darkness narrowing at the corners of his eyes.

"I know I'm not the investigator here, Winter, but if I had to hazard a guess as to what this man's last few hours were... he was dragged unconscious out into the woods, and whether he was awake or not, the perp sexually assaulted him again, biting the penis, and then tied him to the tree, strangling him."

The air he was straining to capture through his nose didn't seem enough, and Colton's lungs burned for more oxygen. He mumbled an excuse to use the restroom and left, nearly running out of the building. The blinding, piercing light of the sun hit his face, and the sweet pine-scented air sucked into his mouth. His stomach swirled, and his chest heaved. Knees trembling, he stumbled to Winter's truck and, out of sight of the office building, nearly collapsed onto the truck's bumper, body shaking uncontrollably.

The fucker had escalated in violence. Colton's stomach rolled again, and this time he couldn't stop the dry heave, but nothing came out.

He raced a shaking hand over his face, sweat coating his forehead.

I was lucky, he thought. *I escaped before he could do that to me.* But Thomas McNamara was not. And it was only a matter of time before the Ripper had another one, locked in a room, doing unspeakable things to him.

He wanted to rage—to roar—to rip a tree from the roots and burn everything to the ground to find this son-of-a-bitch.

"Colton," Winter's voice, soft and urgent, came around the corner of the truck, concern etched on his features.

All he saw was Winter.

Strong, solid, powerful.

Colton felt himself being pulled into his arms, and he buried his face into his neck, his hand fisting the front of Winter's shirt, holding on while he sank into nothingness.

It felt unfair that this was happening all over again, even if it wasn't happening to him this time.

"I got you."

CHAPTER 14

The silence between them on the drive back to the house was deafening, but he said nothing, fingers cracking the leather of the steering wheel.

He couldn't stop thinking about the new evidence on McNamara's body—the bite mark and the sexual assault right up until his last moments of life. Disgust and hatred raced through his veins and he barely saw the road home, knowing he had to stop this sick, twisted fuck before he struck again. He'd already taken two lives—two lives too many, he thought angrily.

"I need to make a call," Winter said, pulling up to the front of his house.

Colton nodded.

Once the truck was parked, Colton opened the door and left without a word. Winter didn't stop him. He watched him take the path down to the lake, knowing he needed space after everything he had just heard and seen. Maybe it had been a mistake to let Colton see the body... maybe he made another mistake with him. He sighed, pushing his fingers beneath his sunglasses, rubbing his eyes, before tossing them onto the console.

He dialed Jim's number. It rang twice before his gruff voice answered.

"What do you have?"

Winter glanced toward Colton's direction, seeing his back as he walked out of sight. "He's getting more violent," he said. "Douglas was a test run for him, to see if he could stomach the kill. I think he discovered that he could and liked it. McNamara was assaulted right before death, unlike Douglas. He's getting more confident, taking his time in broad daylight, and now he knows he can kill without Pollock."

"Jesus..."

"I think this son of a bitch is gonna do it again and again until we stop him."

Jim let out a stream of curses, and he heard a door slam in the background. "We need to set up warning flyers—"

"We got Heroes in the Park tomorrow night, Jim. We've got half the states' firefighters and cops coming here with their entire families. It's the perfect hunting ground."

"We can't cancel the damn thing less than 24 hours out," Jim snapped.

"We need to think of something."

"I know!" Jim sighed and then added more gently. "I know. Sorry, it's been a hell of a week. Has Colton been of any use?"

Winter relaxed against the driver's seat, exhaling. "Yeah. He's confirmed it's the second Ripper. His story matches the evidence from McNamara and Douglas, and so does his brand."

Jim let out a long breath. "Christ, I owe that kid an apology."

They both did.

"I can come over tonight, we can talk strategy on tomorrow night's event," Jim suggested.

Winter nodded, "It's gonna be hard to stake out an event that large, Jim, especially with our small team."

"Do you think he'd try to take a cop?"

Winter's eyes moved to the beach where he knew Colton was, but just out of sight. A sudden anxious dread filled him. "I don't know. Let's talk tonight, all right? I'm gonna swing by Mal's for an hour or so, and I'll text you when we're back."

"Sounds good," Jim clicked and hung up.

Winter climbed out of the truck and headed after Colton, unable to stop himself from nearly running to the beach, and slowed when he spotted him, heart thumping.

Colton sat on the small beachfront in front of his house. The vast, glistening lake spread out before him as the sun drifted slowly behind the mountains. Winter would often come to the exact spot, usually with Frank, to escape his thoughts—to find solace in the world that felt violent and at times cruel beyond reason.

He took a deep breath and sat down beside him, feeling the coarse sand beneath his hand before draping his wrists over his jean-clad knees.

"I don't wanna talk," Colton said quietly.

"You don't have to," Winter replied, picking up a rock between his legs on the beach and thumbing it. They sat like that for a long time, neither of them speaking.

"I envy you, you know," Winter heard himself admit.

Colton's eyes shot to his, surprised.

"You're fearless, Colton. I saw it ten years ago, and I just saw it today when you walked into that room and looked when you didn't have to. You didn't have to come here. You didn't have to do any of this. But you're a fighter and possibly the most courageous person I know."

Colton averted his gaze, jaw twitching. "This doesn't feel like courage."

Winter nodded in understanding. "I once heard that it takes five seconds of courage or fear to change or ruin your life."

He twirled the stone in his hand. "I had that moment. But mine was fear. I was seventeen when I fell in love, or so I thought. I'm sure we all think lust is love at some point. We played on the same football team. He was the star quarterback, Michael Drake. Everyone loved him. He was confident, handsome, and brilliant on and off the field. And somehow he noticed me."

A warm summer breeze drifted over them from the surrounding trees, and Winter felt the gentle kiss of it.

"One day after practice," he went on. "He took me under the bleachers and kissed me. My first real kiss. And it was good," he said with a faint smile. "I had kissed a few girls before, but he opened a floodgate, and I knew I had finally met a part of myself that had been so lost to me. Before that kiss, I thought I was broken somehow because I wasn't chasing after the girls or feeling much attraction to anyone at all.

"After that, the story in my head vanished, and I knew who I was. It went on for a while like that—stolen kisses in passing, quickies in the locker room before anyone got there. I lost my virginity in the back of my grandparents' old pickup. I became obsessed, consumed by him. And he knew it..."

He released the stone, letting it drop back into the sand. "Then one day, I found him kissing another boy under the bleachers. He laughed at me when I confronted him, and that hurt more than his betrayal. I tried to walk away, but then I saw a baseball bat left out on the field, and... Five seconds was all it took, and I crushed his most prized possession. I thought my life was over when the ambulance took him away. I had become my father, out of control and so full of rage.

"I was sure he'd press charges, but he didn't. He was humiliated because he had to explain how he lost one of his testicles. It exploded like a tomato from one hit between the legs. His football career was over because the scouts didn't see him play his senior year. I graduated from high school, went off to college, earned my degree, and then went straight into the academy. If he had made a different decision, my life—this life—wouldn't be here."

Winter finally turned toward Colton, and he saw the focused intensity in his gaze, causing him to shiver.

"It took you five seconds of courage to change your life," Winter whispered. "Mine was five seconds of losing absolute control and realizing I could never do that again—I couldn't be like my father, my worst impulses. I couldn't..."

He shut his eyes hard and felt Colton's hand capture his, squeezing. The tension in his body slowly eased from his shoulders, and he opened his eyes, the blue lake unusually still.

"You're a better man than me, Colton," Winter said, finally meeting his gaze.

Colton reached for him, grabbing him by the front of his shirt, and kissed him. It was slow and thorough. His body trembled, and he nearly whimpered, emotion flooding his limbs as he reached for him in return, raking his fingers through his thick blond hair, opening his mouth to the force of his tongue, desperately needing to taste him. He had to know what Colton tasted like. He tasted surprisingly sweet, and somehow spicy—a sweet heat that set his blood ablaze.

Colton matched his intensity, letting him drive into him, over and over.

Winter never felt anything like this. Never been so lost in the wildness of a kiss—never allowed it. But this was different because he was different. Because it was Colton. A part of him that had been locked away breathed back to life and he shuddered, reaching for him, dragging him closer.

Colton, however, was not satisfied with that and pulled Winter down on top of him. Winter braced his hand in the sand beneath him, the other holding Colton's face as he dominated the kiss. Colton moaned, and it was the sexiest sound Winter had ever heard in his god damned life. He wanted more. He wanted to hear nothing but him moaning and gasping—whimpering and begging.

He sucked his tongue greedily into his mouth, devouring him and sampling him simultaneously. Because he was both soft and hard, kind and mean, greedy and generous, and that was what this kiss was. Colton dragged his fingers through the back of Winter's hair, over his stubbled jawline, his other hand frantically pushing their bodies closer, desperate for more.

More, more, more.

Winter exhaled, lifting his head, seeing the red puffiness of Colton's perfect fucking mouth and thumbing it hard, opening his mouth, liking how willingly Colton surrendered to him. His cock pushed dangerously against his jeans, demanding his attention.

Colton swirled his tongue around the thumb and then sucked, breathing hard through his nose. It was Winter's turn to moan at the sensation.

"We do this," Winter ground out, shifting his weight so his cock would be granted momentarily relief from the mounting pressure. "We do it with rules."

Colton arched an eyebrow, undulating beneath him, feeling the need of his body dance against his.

"First fucking rule," Winter bit out, barely hanging on to his sanity, as thoughts of driving his cock into Colton's mouth preoccupied his brain. "We have to establish a safe word so I know when to stop. I don't want to hurt you."

Colton stilled, eyes reflecting the palest of sky. "You could never hurt me."

Winter studied him, emotion building inside him that he didn't want to acknowledge—not yet. "Tell me your safe word."

"Fine, how about...Frank?" Colton said with a laughing smirk.

Winter sighed, slipping out his thumb, and unable to stop touching him, bit his sexy lower lip, sucking it. "Frank, it is."

"Second rule," Colton husked, hand reaching between them, and Winter finally broke, a deep growling groan erupting from his chest as Colton's hand stroked his cock over his jeans. "You have to trust me."

Winter gritted his teeth and, with a terse nod, agreed, letting Colton unbutton him, reaching beneath the fabric and taking him in hand, grabbing him root to stem, precum already slickening his tip. Colton let out a moaning sigh, biting his lower lip as he stroked him, right there on the beach, before a vast blue lake, the sun holding them in its last dying embrace.

Colton pushed himself upward, flipping Winter onto his back, hand on his chest, pushing him down into the soft sand, the other hand languishingly between his legs. The younger man, with the most insolent, wicked glint in his gaze, lowered himself over Winter.

Winter reached for him, ready to stop him when Colton's chin tilted defiantly. "I'm a big boy, Winter. If I wanna suck your cock, I'm gonna."

He fisted his hands into the sand beneath him and nodded again, watching as Colton freed his erect flesh from the confines of his clothes, and Colton licked his lips.

"I didn't get to see you the other night," Colton murmured, eyes heavy with anticipation—with hunger. "I fuckin' wanted to. I knew you'd feel good in my hand, and Christ, you're beautiful and bloody 'ell, you might just break me in two with this fuckin' thing." He hummed a purring growl. "I can't wait for you to fuckin' try."

Winter gasped at his words and then gasped again at the feel of his mouth nearly swallowing him whole on the first go. It took every ounce of his self-control not to buck upward as Colton took him wildly, angrily, victoriously. There was no preamble, no foreplay, no waiting—not anymore. Winter groaned so loud now that he was sure the cabin nearby could hear, but he didn't care because he had the most glorious mouth around his cock. Colton bobbed over him, sucking down his thick shaft, using his teeth and tongue in ways Winter had only fantasized but never experienced. The lovers he took were selfish and demanding—Colton was that, but also generous.

Winter's rigid control wouldn't allow lowering his guardrails for even a second, and yet he could feel the dismantling of it beneath Colton's touch.

This man's wildness was infectious and intoxicating.

It was exactly what he needed, and he never knew it until this moment.

Winter arched slowly, trying not to push too fast or roughly down Colton's mouth and into his throat, because he knew he was large and didn't want to hurt him.

Colton seemed to sense this and sucked up the tip, tonguing him hard before shooting him a fiery look. "What the fuck did I just say about takin' it easy on me?"

Winter would've laughed but couldn't, because Colton, as though to make a point, swallowed him down again, but this time gagging himself over him, his throat contracting and saliva pooling. Winter couldn't breathe. The sensation of his cock being aggressively sucked to prove a point was invigorating and infuriating because Colton was in charge—he was demanding, telling him what he wanted.

Winter needed to get out of his own damned way and just give in already.

Dragging his hand out of the sand, Winter clasped the back of Colton's head, nails biting into his scalp.

"Take a breath," Winter hissed.

Colton hummed eagerly and sucked in a breath, and Winter pushed him back down, hard, bucking his hips upward and spearing his cock down his throat and holding him against him. Colton gagged, settled, and sucked. Winter released him, and Colton came up gasping, eyes wide with lust, and grabbed Winter's hand at the back of his head.

"Do that again—and again—until you fuckin' come down my throat you bastard," he commanded.

Gasoline had already poured into Winter's veins, edging him toward combustion, but hearing Colton's permission to use him—to do what he pleased...

Fuuuck.

Winter dragged Colton back down and fucked his face again, without mercy this time. Colton moaned and reached between his own legs, shoving a hand into his jeans. The heat of Colton's mouth consumed him. The sensation of sucking and tonguing sent him teetering to the edge of the universe. He was so fucking close, he could feel the tingling at the base of his spine and the tensing of his stomach muscles, and with one final thrust, he sat up, grabbing Colton's throat and back of his head, simultaneously squeezing and pushing.

Colton jerked, and the moan that came out of his mouth was absolute wanton submission mixed with primal need.

Winter held him there and spewed down his throat, hard and violent.

Colton took it all. His throat contracted as he swallowed the hot seed.

Winter released him, and Colton slowly eased up, sucking as he went, causing him to gasp his name until finally his dick went soft in the younger man's mouth, and Colton sat back on his heels in the sand. Sparkling blue eyes watering and breathing hard, Colton thumbed the moisture from his lips.

It was—he was—the most gorgeous fucking thing Winter had ever seen in his life. The gasoline sparked, and fire raged in his soul.

He grabbed Colton and kissed him hungrily, thoroughly.

"Such a good fuckin' boy, aren't you?" Winter murmured against his mouth.

Colton shivered, trembling against him.

"How can I take care of you?" He rasped, biting his earlobe, palming the hard press of Colton's cock. "You have the mouth of a fucking viper. I don't think I could top that, but damn, I'll try."

Colton groaned, "Just touch me—keep talking...I'm close. So fuckin' close..."

Winter shifted Colton between his open legs, peeling his jeans back, touching the rigid flesh, and feeling Colton buck upward at just the feel of his fingertips grazing across his head.

"Had I known you had such a good fuckin' mouth, I would've done this sooner," Winter praised, pulling him out and stroking him lazily. "You're so damned pretty with my cock down your throat and fuck..." he dragged out the word. "Feeling my hand around your throat with my cock down it was the best feeling in the world."

Colton arched, gasping a desperate moan for him as he clutched Winter's shoulder while he fisted his hand over his undeniably hard flesh, moving the skin and muscle of the towering, leaking cock.

"I wanna see you come for me," Winter demanded harshly, unable to look away. "I wanna see how you come because that's what I'm gonna think about the next time I do."

Colton grabbed the side of Winter's face, fingers digging into his jaw, melting and tensing all at once. Colton's rapture was his rapture, and he needed to see.

"So perfect...that's it..."

Colton grated his teeth along Winter's scar tissue, angrily standing at the precipice and resisting the urge to fall forward. Winter locked his gaze with his, holding Colton back, hand beneath his jaw, pumping him ruthlessly. "You belong to me now."

Forever.

Winter sucked in a breath at the thought, and that's when Colton jerked uncontrollably, wildly, and climaxed against him. Winter watched the violence of it, the primal force of the orgasm, mixed with relief and pleasure, his body shivering as hot ribbons of cum coated his fist. Colton heaved a breath, relaxing into him as he finished. Winter was paralyzed at the rush of emotion flooding him, his heart kicking frantically.

Fuck. Colton was perfect. Everything about this moment was perfect, and he couldn't go back now. The guardrails around their relationship evaporated with that kiss. And he wasn't sure how he felt, only that he needed more of this, more of Colton, in his bed, in his truck, smiling at him, climaxing for him, but most importantly, needing him in return.

Winter blinked, rattled by the sweeping thoughts and feelings.

"Christ, Winter," Colton panted, shocked and awed, mixed with the afterglow of his orgasm.

Winter kissed him, loving the way Colton was looking at him.

"Let's get cleaned up, we have a dinner party to attend." He helped him to his feet, wiping Colton's bliss on his jeans and shirt.

Unable to stop touching him, Winter tucked him back in, and Colton, docile as a kitten, let him, watching him with hooded eyes as he buttoned his jeans.

"Do you always talk like that during sex?" Colton asked, his voice soft, body sedated.

"Yes," Winter admitted. He would be honest about how he was in the bedroom, because in a way, he was a different man—one that Colton was only just starting to see glimpses of.

"And what we did wasn't sex. It was sexual and..."

"Hot," Colton finished, with a slow grin.

Winter smirked, buckling Colton's belt for him. "Yes, it was. Minus the sand, but yeah."

Colton laughed and batted his hands away, taking care of himself. "Is it just words—or do you mean it?"

Winter stilled, seeing the challenge—the intensity return in Colton's gaze, and he realized then what he had said. *You belong to me now.*

It was one thing to say something in the heat of the moment, but to admit the feeling that was laced behind it felt dangerously close to something he wasn't sure he was ready to think about yet.

"I belong to you?" Colton traced his fingertips over Winter's stubble, nails biting into his cheek.

Winter grabbed the hand at his face, deciding that he could rationalize those words into a boundary, rather than the whispering of his heart. "Yes. You do. I take fidelity very seriously."

"And what if I don't want to belong to you?" Colton challenged.

He gritted his teeth, "Then this ends right now. I don't share. Ever. If you want to fuck and have fun—find someone else because that isn't me."

"Loyalty," Colton murmured. "And honor. That's you. A knight in shining armor?"

He nearly scoffed, a dark burning energy building in his chest. "I'm no knight."

"Then what are ya?"

Winter straightened, fingers itching to return to the defiant throat of this man, to squeeze and make him understand that pushing him—testing him—challenging him like this constantly boiled his blood and unhinged the rigid control that was the core of his life. And by God, he loved it—loved feeling like he was standing on the edge of something, and rising every time to meet it.

"I'm your big bad wolf," Winter grabbed him, hauling him to the wall of his chest and kissing him hard, brutally so. "You've been knocking on the walls of my cave all week, Colton. Taunting me, teasing me.

You wanted me, now you have me. I don't share. I possess. I'll give you whatever you want if you respect what I ask. The second you don't…"

"You leave me out in the cold, I know. I saw what you did to that poor bastard."

Winter saw that continued flash of defiance echo in those pale blue eyes.

"Was he your good boy, too?" Colton murmured, grabbing his wrist.

Winter arched an eyebrow. "He was."

Colton unexpectedly trembled, letting out a harsh breath, "Fuck."

Pleasure blossomed in his chest at this reaction. Winter edged closer, "Only really good boys get that title with me. Is that what you want?"

"Fuck, yes," he said without hesitating, without resisting.

"Good boys listen," he said, hand sliding down Colton's body. "Give me your tongue."

His chin tilted upwards, seeming to consider.

Winter squeezed, and Colton let out a soft curse, opening his mouth. He dragged his mouth once more over his, sucking down his tongue, feeling the younger man whimper into his lips. He palmed his perfect, plump ass with his free hand, pinching.

Colton squirmed and clung to him.

"You're gonna go inside, shower, and wear something nice tonight," Winter husked.

"I didn't bring any collars, I suppose I can ask Frank to borrow his," Colton drawled.

"There goes that fuckin' mouth of yours," Winter bit on his lower lip and pinched the other ass cheek.

"Fuck, I'm getting hard again," Colton arched into him, and he felt the telling erection beginning to build. "Shower with me."

"No."

"Why the fuck not?"

"Because if I shower with you, I will most certainly fuck you, and that's for later."

CHAPTER 15

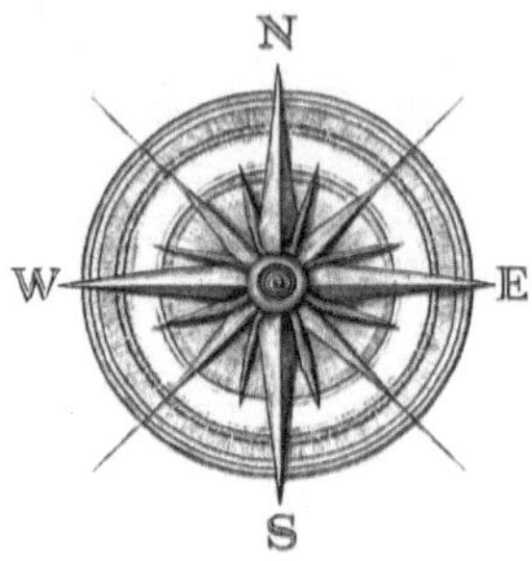

His palms itched and his leg bounced restlessly the whole drive to Mal's house.

Colton wanted to reach across the cab so badly his body ached from tamping down the urge. Because Winter hadn't reached for him. Winter was cool as a goddamned cucumber, and Colton was a hot fuckin' mess of wild, horrible need.

And that pissed him off.

He was far from a slave to sex, and he was never this damned needy for someone. But here he was, unable to stop thinking about the dark, hungry look in Winter's eyes when he was sucking his cock. And he had certainly done that. He'd given plenty of good cock sucks in his life, but that, by far, was one of Colton's proudest moments. Pleasing Winter in that way was exactly what he wanted. It was perfect, like a dance where both partners knew the movements. He could only imagine how the sex would be and fuckin' 'ell he was going to bolt out of this car and tackle Winter the second they got out.

Fuck. I'm so fucking fucked.

He shouldn't be like this already. He shouldn't be like Winter's other fuckboys, and yet—he was. Colton was just like the rest of them, and he cursed himself for it.

Anger rose quickly up his spine as he fisted the lighter in his hand.

If he were honest, his anger wasn't directed at Winter—but himself. Because he knew the second he opened the door to anything physical with Winter, of finally tasting the man of his dreams, he'd be lost. He just hadn't anticipated it happening that quickly after the first fucking kiss.

He wasn't supposed to have feelings. He was supposed to have outgrown his stupid crush ages ago. It was bloody distracting and inconvenient because, at the moment, this arrangement worked well. Him, living underfoot until the last Ripper was caught.

But what happened when this was over? What happened when Winter tried to shut the door on him, just as he had done to Trevor?

Colton was just another brat to play with. He understood that logically, and yet hated it. Hated that he could be so easily tossed out and left behind.

Winter had already done it to him once.

Who's to say it wouldn't happen again when Winter got what he wanted from him?

It was then, the lighter slipping across his knuckles and into his palm, that he decided that he would make it impossible for Winter to abandon him again. That Colton, in the end, would be the one who leaves this time.

Winter maneuvered the truck onto a smooth, paved road with a large gate to the private driveway. He rolled down the window, letting in the cool night air as he punched in the numbers on the keypad, and the iron black bars opened. He parked the truck in front of a towering mansion that almost seemed offensive in the scenic nature that surrounded it.

Expensive cars lined the driveway leading up to the front double doors.

Colton shot Winter an incredulous look as he stepped out of the truck and looked up at the mansion, sitting on a cliffside, overlooking the lake below. It dazzled in the night, with its opulence and sleek design.

"This is your friend's house?" Colton asked him.

Winter shrugged, a half-smile on his face. "What, I can't have nice friends?"

"Oh no, Winter. You're absolutely allowed all the nice things in the world, darling. But this—this is posh, even for me."

"Are you intimidated?" Winter asked. "Someone out-riched you?"

Colton was surprised by the taunt and pivoted on his boot heel, blocking Winter. The darkness and the brilliant black sky above, mixed with the fresh air and pine, was like petrol pouring in his veins. And seeing how relaxed, how easy Winter's smile was at this moment, was all the spark he needed.

Winter.

His protector—his big bad wolf.

He wanted the wolf that was promised. The heat and the command. He wanted to obey and please him.

Fuck, Colton thought, surprised he had never known that he would be the type to want to please this much—this badly. He'd had plenty of sexual experiences and thought that he had discovered everything there was to discover in that arena. Apparently, he was wrong.

He gripped Winter's wrist, maneuvering him far too easily against the hood of the truck. He heard Winter's quick intake of breath, eyes nearly as black as the sky above.

"You tryin' to impress me?" Colton asked softly. "Cuz I don't need that from you. In fact, I think we can skip this party entirely and go back to your place right now."

Winter's eyes sharpened, his face tilting forward, their breath intermingling, as Colton's pulse roared in his ears.

"We can finish what we started at the beach," Colton murmured, feeling himself so close to the edge, ready to jump headfirst off this cliff and into this man.

His lips grazed his, and Winter let out the slightest groan, so soft, too soft, but Colton heard it, and he did it again, not quite tasting, just sampling. "Take me home, Winter."

He felt Winter's hand snake around the back of his neck unexpectedly, and with a strength that thrilled him, forced Colton upward, and his lips crashed into his. It was rough, urgent, and so fucking hot.

He melted instantly into him, but did not let Winter dominate the kiss entirely. He fought back, gripping the side of his face, undulating his hips against him, pressing him back into the truck. Winter's moan wasn't low this time; it was a grasping groan, heavy with desire as he let Colton grind into him, their mouths fighting for power.

He bit on Winter's lower lip, and something snapped in the older man. He yanked back, eyes bright and something else—something Colton couldn't decipher, before he grabbed Colton by the throat, his hand fisting over him, not to hurt, and not tightly, just enough to control. Colton let out a shaky breath, so addicted to this hand collar thing he did, that his cock, already semi-hard, went full salute, pressing hard against the fly of his jeans. He seemed to be deciding something, and then glancing once at the still dark steps of the front of the house, Winter moved, pivoting on his heel and slamming Colton back into the truck, free hand on his jaw, forcing his mouth open as his tongue speared into his mouth.

Winter was entirely in control now. Taking everything from him. Colton, too stunned to think, fell against the hard wall of Winter's chest and let this man greedily tongue fuck his mouth and collar his throat, fingers pressing into him. The sound that came out of Colton's throat surprised even him as he never felt so submissive in his life, and yet, the raging fire in his bloodstream told him how much he liked Winter dominating him.

Winter must have sensed this and kicked his feet apart, widening his stance and positioning himself so that both could feel their desires, rampant and demanding. Colton's body instinctively jerked, needing to feel more, so much fucking more.

"Is this what you want?" Winter asked, his voice a husky rasp across his lips. "You want me to get on my knees and suck you?"

Colton's chest heaved, sucking in air, panting. "I—I—" For the first time in his life, he realized he didn't have the answer. Usually, in these situations, he took or gave, and there was no stopping to ask what the other actually wanted. It wasn't like he drifted through his sexual encounters, because he had a few non-negotiables that he would always manage to get around without having to explain why.

But at this moment, he could imagine Winter on his knees, taking his cock into his mouth, those black eyes staring up at him, watching him—watching him in that way that no one else did, as though he were staring into his soul and only he could see it.

Winter hummed, tilting Colton's neck to the side, giving him access to the soft spot beneath his ear as he kissed and sucked. He whimpered, goosebumps shivering up his arms and back. Winter continued to hold him, hips unmoving, yet cock achingly hard pressed against him, lavishing love bites on his neck.

"I'll tell you what I want," Winter drawled into the shell of his ear. "I want you to be speechless more often."

Colton laughed weakly, hands coming around out of their paralysis, touching the hard muscles of Winter's back.

"And what else?" Colton asked. "Cuz I can think of a couple of ways you can render me speechless."

Winter let out a growling sigh of approval, and for the first time, he hitched his hip upward, dragging his jeans cock against his. Colton clung to him, unable to stop the returning tilt of his hips, demanding himself not to hump him like a dog.

"I wouldn't mind you listening to me," Winter rasped, tonguing his lips now, opening the seam of his mouth. "Maybe even..." his tongue darted inside, sweeping through him, intrusive and demanding. "Obe ying..."

Colton suddenly understood this part about Winter, and he thought, should he ever come across someone like him, he'd be terrified. Maybe—run for the hills? Whenever someone tried to dominate their bed play with him, Colton usually responded by overpowering them and taking control instead. He never liked being under anyone's control, ever. It reminded him too much of the Rippers.

But what Winter was asking was a request—a specific request. Submit—for me—with me—for yourself.

But the power wasn't taken from him. It was given freely. It made so much sense now. Winter's demand for specificity was almost a rigid control over himself, which seemed not like armor, but a tool—a part of him fully integrated and accepted. Winter was a dom. Had that been why he resisted him? Did he think Colton wouldn't like the power play in bed because of his trauma?

Colton pulled free from their kiss and fisted his hair into Winter's. "Frank."

Winter stepped back immediately, releasing the hold around his neck, alarm tensing the lines at the corner of his eyes.

Relief washed through him, but not the way Winter assumed. It was the fact that Winter did as he asked and did it without protest. Trust, Colton thought. This would take trust to work. And he trusted Winter with his life, and now, he knew he could trust him with his body.

But what about my heart?

The front porch light flicked on, and Winter initially ignored the sound of the door opening, laughter, music, and people's voices echoing in the quiet of the forest.

"Winter?" Mal called from above. "Is that you?"

Winter's eyes were intense, focused solely on Colton as the cool summer night air flitted between them, leaving him achy, almost needing to return to Winter's arms to make the feeling go away.

"Yeah," Winter said. "Be right up."

"Hurry up, love. The Hodels have been asking about you all night."

In the light of the house, Colton could see that the concern on Winter's face had not passed. "Are you all right?" he asked roughly.

Colton straightened his clothes and slid a hand through his hair, nodding. "Always."

"That's not what I—"

"I know," he cut off. "I'm fine."

Winter's jaw tensed, looking unsatisfied with the answer. "We can leave if I—"

Colton glanced over his shoulder and saw that Mal had retreated into the house, leaving the front door open. Making sure no one was watching, he stepped forward, cupping Winter's jaw and kissing him hard and boldly, giving everything he couldn't say into the kiss.

Winter didn't touch him, seeming to fight himself, and Colton leaned back, breaking the kiss, seeing the balled fists at Winter's side.

"You didn't hurt me," he murmured. "I'm all right, really. Trust me, you'll know when I'm triggered, or I'll tell ya. You didn't do anything I didn't want."

"Then why the fuck did you use the safe word on me?"

Colton threaded his fingers into the fine silk of Winter's crisp black suit shirt. When he had seen Winter stroll out of the bedroom earlier in this outfit, it took everything not to beg to peel it off him with his bare teeth.

"I'm sorry," Colton breathed. "I needed to make sure."

The tension in Winter's shoulders relaxed, and understanding flickered across his expression. "Trust."

He swallowed, suddenly feeling exposed under those obsidian eyes. "I trust you, Winter. I do. But this is new to me. I've never been dominated by a man since..."

Winter's eyes darkened. "I'm not them."

Colton's heart ached that Winter would think that, and yet, hadn't that been the reason he just used the safe word? He stepped toward him, tentative and unsure, and so fucking vulnerable that he thought the feeling would kill him. Winter sensed it and drew him in with a strong, comforting embrace, dropping his forehead onto his. "Do whatever you have to, Colton. But I can't change who I am or what I do in the bedroom."

"I don't want you to," Colton admitted, exposing himself to that scrutinizing gaze. "I love the way you make me feel—how you touch me. It bloody scares me how much I like it. I never thought I would want something like this... but it feels, fuck, it feels natural and addictin'. Like I've been missing this my whole life cuz my own stupid fear."

"Your fear is not stupid," Winter replied gently. "It's protective, that's all."

"And so are you," Colton retorted. "You've always made me feel safe. Always."

Winter's needy low growl set fire to his soul, and he began to reach for him, when Colton took a wide step back, lips cracking into a dancing smirk. "Now, none of that. We have a party to attend, and we're already running late. I can't shame the family name by not proving I'm a proper gent at least initially to your friends."

Winter narrowed his eyes dangerously, looking very much like a wolf in the darkness of the night. Goddamn this man, Colton thought, he was far too beautiful to be real. Feeling brazen, he dragged his finger over Winter's scar tissue and to his mouth, loving the rigid flesh and how soft it made his lips feel. "The wolf suits you, you know. Not cuz of the scar. But because of your eyes. If you could set me ablaze right now, your eyes alone would."

Winter softened, "Was that a compliment?"

It took everything in his power to start walking up the driveway and not crawl into his truck and demand to be taken home to his bedroom. "Yes, it fuckin' was. Now chop, chop, wolfie. You can make me howl at the moon later…"

Winter growled and let out a long sigh, shifting his stance to adjust the bulge in his jeans.

They headed to the front steps leading up to the top of the small hill where the house sat perched, and Colton touched the side of his neck where Winter's teeth and lips had been.

"How the hell am I gonna hide a fresh hickey?" Colton snipped, titling the collar to his plaid gray and white shirt and lifting the V-necked white T-shirt upward in an attempt to cover it.

Winter, not looking at him as they entered, said so only he could hear, "I want everyone here to know what belongs to me."

Colton nearly tripped on the last step, his heart lodged firmly in his throat at the possessive words that gut-punched him.

Sweet mother of all that is holy. This man would destroy him.

Colton swallowed, mesmerized by Winter, uncaring about the party in full swing. Winter transformed the second he walked in, becoming lighter somehow, less brooding, and smiled playfully. Fucking playfully! Colton tried not to swoon visibly.

"You like your coffee and tea sickly sweet, so I'm assuming you like your cocktails that way, too," Winter said, with a devilish twinkle in his gaze.

"By all means, dear wolf, do your worst," he challenged back.

"Sex on the beach?"

Colton shrugged, giving him nothing.

"Or a cosmo?" Winter's gaze dropped to his lips. "Something pink. Like your lips." He casually raked his hand through his black and silver hair before straightening his sleeves with the fine gold clips on the end. "...lips that I imagine around my cock every time I look at them."

Colton's jaw unhinged, and before he could say anything, Winter's name was cried out in joy and he turned, without skipping a beat, to greet an older couple with open arms and a warm smile.

Yup, I am royally fucked.

And Winter had warned him he was a different man in the bedroom, but this? That dirty, wonderful mouth of his would certainly be the death of him by the end of the night.

CHAPTER 16

Winter's favorite new addiction—Colton.

He had felt his restlessness in the truck on the way up to Mal's and knew it was because of him. Watching him squirm with desire was damned invigorating. Seeing him nearly trip on the way into the party made Winter realize he no longer had to hide who he was from Colton. That he wouldn't stay quiet when Colton challenged him—taunted him. Oh, no.

It was time to let the wolf out.

The party was in full swing, and Colton made it easy to mix and mingle, seeming to know precisely how to work a room. Winter liked that, liked that he didn't have to say or do much, and whenever he drifted too far, Colton sauntered back over to him, staying close the whole night. It felt different from the others he had dated in the past, who wanted just his attention and even enjoyed, at times, teasing him to the point of distraction that felt almost too needy.

Colton didn't do any of that. He was charming and flirtatious. The sparkler in the room, laughing and dazzling Mal's guests. And when he cracked one of those brilliant, full crinkle smiles that lit his face, Winter wanted to touch him—needed to. And that laugh of his, damn, it was almost as good as his moans. Colton, somehow, had reversed the tables on him, and Winter was the needy one wanting his attention.

He internally rolled his eyes at the thought and tried to soothe the urge to drag Colton out by his neck, toss him into the truck like a conquering Viking, and take him back to his cave where he could see him shine and break, just for him.

Winter had to stay focused, though, and listened with one ear as Patrick and Mr. Hodell talked about work. Hodell worked for a large health insurance company as a director, and Patrick was an ICU doctor at the local hospital. Winter liked Patrick. He was grounded and smart as hell, and good for Mal, who tended to have his head in the clouds sometimes. The only problem was Patrick's schedule, which had been hard on Mal, who said the nursing shortage was affecting Patrick's hospital and thus extending his hours.

In his other ear and peripheral vision, he could see Colton, who was talking with Mal. Mal had designed his home himself and taken several years to complete it. It was an aesthetically modern, mid-century house the size of a mansion, that was as colorful as a black and white film. He loved Mal, but his house was a stiff, cold place that made his skin itch for cozy blankets, messily chopped wood on the porch, and books left out in odd places.

"What do you think?" Winter heard Mal ask Colton, referencing the art displayed over Mal's fireplace.

Colton shrugged, "It's a bit..."

"Garish?" Mal suggested. "I know. Patrick insisted on the thing. I would've preferred something softer, a little more color. The things we do for love..." He said with a simpering sigh.

"Love makes us crazy, and we are crazy for it," Colton said. "My mum used to say that all the time."

"Smart woman," Mal replied.

"How'd you meet Winter?" Colton asked.

Winter arched an eyebrow, surprised. He wondered if Mal would tell him the truth. He knew how Mal felt about the men he dated. Mal had a razor-sharp tongue when it came to who he believed deserved to be his best friend, and he would lash out at anyone he deemed unfit for such a position. He appreciated his protectiveness, but it sometimes bothered him. Mal tended to overstep into Winter's love life, and it usually took Winter pushing back for him to take the hint.

"In high school," Mal said. "He was a year above me, and so handsome. I had a crush on him first before we became best friends. I realize now it was more hero worship than anything. Especially when we went to college. I followed him to Sac State like a lost little puppy. But college was so good for me, I grew out of that shell and blossomed, with Winter's help, mind you. I eventually moved back here and started working on creating my gallery. A few years later, Winter moved back to Tahoe, and we picked up where we left off."

"I suppose good friendships are like that," Colton said.

"Like what?"

"Easy."

Mal laughed, "I'm sure Winter would say a lot about how uneasy I actually am. High-strung, perfectionist, tends to put his nose where it shouldn't be."

"That's probably all the reasons he likes ya then," Colton replied easily.

"That's sweet, honey, but I know I'm a busybody. So, speaking of which, you and Winter seem to be... close?"

Winter's stomach swooped.

Colton cleared his throat, "We're friends."

"Friends that haven't seen each other in—how long?"

Winter thought about intervening and almost did when Colton said,

"It's been a while, yeah."

"And you're staying with him?" Mal pressed.

Fuck, he loved Mal, but he knew Mal was one of the biggest gossips in town and didn't want Colton sharing the real reason he was up here.

"All right, you caught me," Colton drawled smoothly. "I came back to live out a lifelong fantasy of mine, and Winter was more than obliging."

Winter heard the subtle hint of heat in his words, and alarm prickled at the back of his neck.

"And that is…?" Mal asked impatiently.

"To see that man get dunked," Colton said sincerely.

"What?"

Winter smothered a laugh.

"Haven't you heard?" Colton asked. "Winter's gonna be sitting in a dunk tank tomorrow night for charity. He invited me up to the Heroes in the Park festival and, like a proper gent, let me stay in his guest room. It's been nice catching up with an old friend and even better when I can knock his ass into a big bucket of water tomorrow night."

"Did I just hear someone mention Heroes in the Park?" Mrs. Hodel asked, inching into their conversation. "Such a wonderful event! I go every year. I love this year's theme. It sounds like fun."

"Oh, it will be," Colton said, gesturing to her drink. "Can I freshen you up, luv?"

"Oh goodness, yes!"

"Let me," Mal insisted.

"No worries," Colton said. "I make drinks for a living, darling. Let me. Give the host a break, the least I can do."

And with that, Winter watched as he plucked Mrs. Hodell's drink from her hand and sauntered away toward the trolley bar. Winter followed him, and he lowered his voice as he approached. "You're good."

Colton shot him a smirk, "I know." He moved his hands easily over the ingredients for the drink. "Does your bestie interrogate all your lovers?"

Winter sucked in a breath and sighed, "Yeah. I should've warned you."

Colton shrugged, "Well, we're technically not lovers yet, are we?"

Winter swallowed, the need to touch him growing with every passing breath between them. "Wanna get out of here?"

Colton poured the contents of the stainless-steel shaker into the glass and flicked his gaze up to meet his, and all Winter saw was hunger. The same hunger he'd been feeling all evening since their kiss in the driveway.

"I thought you'd never fuckin' ask," Colton murmured. "I've been ready since the moment we arrived."

Winter smiled darkly, pleased as Colton slid past him, and handed Mrs. Hodell her drink. He excused himself again, and deciding an Irish goodbye was the best way to go, considering Mal and the others would make a big show about their departure, the two managed to make their escape.

Once they climbed into his truck and he started down the road back home, Colton relaxed into the passenger seat, pulling out the silver lighter. "I have to say it," he commented, eyebrow arched and face pinched.

"What?" Winter asked.

"His house made my skin crawl," Colton pretended to shiver as he tapped his lighter on the windowsill. "I've seen plenty of posh houses, but damn, that felt—I dunno, fake somehow."

Winter studied him across the cab and smirked, "Mal and Patrick are just—different. Not our style, that's all."

"Sorry," Colton said. "I didn't mean to offend them or you."

"It's all right. I don't like their house, either."

"Mal seems... nice."

Winter chuckled, "He's protective."

"Very," Colton drawled. "So, how many of your brats have sauntered in front of that poor love-struck man who claims to be your bestie?"

Winter straightened, "We are—just friends."

"Right, and cows jump over moons, and cats play fiddles. C'mon, Winter. Ya can't be that thick."

Winter felt his hands clench over the steering wheel.

"I'm pretty sure he loves you still," Colton said.

Winter shook his head, refusing to believe it and yet...

"Sorry," Colton said once more, this time tapping the lighter hard on his knee. "It's not my place—not my business."

"It's all right," Winter muttered. "It sometimes takes an outside perspective to see things we refuse or can't see for ourselves." He stared into the dark road lined with trees, lost in thought. "I heard what he told you about our friendship. He left a lot out."

He felt Colton's curious gaze from across the cab. "We had sex—once. I wasn't thinking clearly. I was homesick, missing the only place I ever felt safe—these woods, with my grandparents. And Mal was there. He followed me to college because I knew, deep down, he loved me more than just our friendship. Seeing him made me think of home, and I felt confused and lost. So, one night, I made the decision to cross the line, and we had sex, and I knew right away, it was a mistake."

Winter raced his fingers through his hair, guilt washing over him. "I hurt him. Bad. He left college practically the next day, and we didn't speak for a long time. It wasn't until I moved back that I started asking his forgiveness. It took him some time. But eventually, he did, and we fell back into the friendship we had in high school. But maybe I should've kept my distance..." He trailed off, wondering if he had made a mistake again with Mal.

Colton reached across the cab, taking his hand. "You didn't do anything wrong, Winter. None of us know ourselves when we're young, not really. It's not until we see the consequences, or failures of our actions, that we realize what we need or want. And you're a good fucking man to have done that. It was Mal's responsibility to say no to the friendship if he couldn't handle it."

Winter tangled his fingers into Colton's, letting in the warmth. "He can't still have feelings... It's been years now."

Colton drew their hands up, pressing a kiss to the back of Winter's hand, his beard brushing against his skin. "Patrick is nice and all, but he pales in comparison to you. And Mal knows it."

Winter glanced at him, seeing the heady darkness in his gaze, and he felt his heart kick against the bones of his chest when Colton slipped his tongue over the pad of his thumb.

"I get it." Colton opened Winter's palm, tracing the heartlines of his hand with the tip of his tongue, sending bolts of electricity up his back. "Every man you fuck falls madly in love with you. And apparently, all it takes is once."

He swallowed, licking his lower lip, jaw clenching.

Colton dragged Winter's hand over his lips, letting his fingers bury into the beard of his jawline and trail down his throat. "It sounds dangerous to get into your bed, Winter. For hearts fall and break there, don't they?"

Winter, breathing hard, thumbed Colton's lips roughly. "No one's forcing you into my bed, Colton."

"Don't you worry, I can handle myself..." Colton sucked down his thumb, taking it into the heat of his mouth. "And you."

Something tightened across his chest at the words, and Winter, deciding to let slip his inner wolf, speared his thumb into Colton's mouth, fingers digging into his jaw, heat spilling into his blood at the sound of his sharp intake of breath.

"You sure you can handle me?" he challenged, and Colton moaned, making the pressing demand between his thighs stiffen.

"How much longer until we get back to your place?" Colton asked, nipping Winter's finger.

"Twenty minutes."

Colton bit down hard, and Winter retracted, surprised.

"No touching for twenty fuckin' minutes or—" Colton shifted in his seat. "You pull over and let me suck you off in the back."

Winter groaned, accelerating down the road. "You like telling me what to do, don't you?"

He grinned, "Maybe. Or maybe I like to see what you'd do instead."

Winter flipped up the console between them and dragged Colton across the seat, hauling him against his side, his seatbelt digging into his neck, keeping him locked in place. He reached between the younger man's thighs, feeling the telling bulge, hard and pushing against his jeans, making his teeth mash together.

"I'm gonna touch you until we get home, and you can't touch me—or yourself—and most importantly, you're not allowed to cum."

Colton sucked in a breath, stomach heaving.

"Pull yourself out for me," he commanded roughly.

Colton did, hands shaking, and leaned back, eyes hooded, draping his arm across the bench seat, legs falling open. His smooth, heavy shaft was out and for the taking. Winter flicked his thumb over the sensitive, leaking tip and felt Colton's hips arch into him, his head falling back, fully surrendering his body to him.

And god damned this man was beautiful.

And his.

"Spit," he rasped, and Colton slowly raised his head, eyes shadowed as he did so into Winter's palm.

He took the moisture and used it, slicking Colton with it and his precum, sliding slowly down to the base of his erection and holding. Colton's head dropped back again, this time letting out a deep gasp.

"Watching you tonight," Winter murmured, edging up centimeter by centimeter, pulling the skin along the muscle as he went. "It was like watching a sparkler move around the room. Lighting up everything you touched. Everyone saw you—wanted you. So beautiful. Do you even know how blinding you are?"

Colton trembled.

"All I wanted to do was drag you back into this truck and do this," Winter tugged harshly, all the way to the tip.

He bucked and moaned.

"I wanted to hear you do that for me," he whispered, and dragged back down, pulling root to stem, slow and hard.

He heard Colton's fingers rake into the leather of the bench behind him and smiled darkly, knowing he was fighting to control himself.

"I would've preferred hearing you break with you fucking my mouth, but this will have to do for now...and since I can't have what I want—neither can you." Winter pumped him ruthlessly and then slowed, watching Colton's body tense and jaw flex.

He did it again, pumping him and slowing.

"Fuck," Colton ground out. "I'm so close."

Winter released him, cupping his sensitive male parts beneath his shaft. "You're not allowed."

Colton strained, letting out a frustrated growl, legs opening further apart. "Please..."

Hearing that word, so desperate, so laced with need, sent a shockwave straight through him and to his cock. He felt himself leak in his own damned jeans and rewarded Colton by returning to his heavy, erect manhood and tugging upward once more.

"I need more spit," Winter murmured.

Colton let out a whoosh of breath and leaned forward, hands still braced on the bench, and spit on the tip of his cock, giving Winter more to work with and working him in return. Colton humped upward, shaking now.

"Good boy," Winter praised, watching him fuck his fist and ride the coming tidal wave of his bliss and knowing the chase would only be a chase. And he would make him chase but never catch the wave he actually wanted.

"Fuck fuck fuck!" Colton's back arched, and Winter snapped his hand away completely, and Colton slumped into the seat, cursing him violently.

"Please don't stop," Colton finally said thickly, sweat beading his brow.

"I have to," he responded darkly. "I don't want you coming yet."

"I won't. I won't," he rasped.

"Can you hold out for eight more minutes with me touching you?" Winter shook his head, unconvinced. "I don't think you can."

Colton sucked in a hard breath, cursing him again and Winter, out of pure need to watch him like this—unhinged, wild, almost violently aroused, he stroked him again.

Colton nearly bucked off this seat, and for the next eight minutes, Winter lovingly punished him.

Once the driveway of his house was in sight, Winter knew Colton was a breath away from eruption and parked into the thicket of trees, his cock so hard he could barely maneuver himself as he got out, and walked to the passenger side, opened the door, and pushed Colton onto his back, spreading him out. Colton dropped down willingly, so crazed with lust, so desperate he would've let Winter do anything to him.

"You did so well obeying, Colton," he husked out. "I think I need to know what your cum tastes like now."

Colton shuddered, gasping a curse, need written all over his face as he allowed Winter to drag him roughly to the edge of the seat, yanking down his jeans over his hips. Blood rushed to his head as he moistened his fingers in his mouth before he lowered himself over Colton's dripping cock.

Colton sat bolt upright, capturing the back of his head. Winter shoved him back down onto the seat with one hand, sucking his magnificent cock into his mouth, slipping his free hand between Colton's legs and pushing his fingers upwards, feeling his entrance.

He only had to rub the tight hole and suck at the same time, and Colton shook violently beneath him, letting out the most guttural, moaning cry as he peeked and speared into Winter's mouth, unleashing a torrent of hot cum down his throat. Winter pushed the tip of his thumb into his entrance and hummed, knowing the vibrations of his throat would add even more sensation. Colton let out another cry, grabbing Winter's face and pushing uncontrollably, madly into him, his second wave dragging out of his body like a fight as he cursed and fumed, tensing the whole time.

It was fucking perfect.

Winter sucked it all down greedily, his hard cock pressing painfully against his jeans, desperate for his own release.

Colton's dick softened in his mouth, and he collapsed back onto the bench of his truck, gasping for breath. Winter slowly released him, wanting to spread his cheeks and lick that tight hole, knowing he'd have to save that for later.

"Fuck, I think you just killed me," Colton said weakly.

Winter, unable to stop touching him, helped him back into his jeans and slid his hands possessively over his body, helping him sit up and back into his seat.

Colton stared incredulously at him, loose-limbed and docile. "I never expected you'd be like this."

Winter tilted his head, "Like what?"

Colton reached for him and kissed him. It was slow and burning. "Take me to bed, Winter."

He nearly pressed Colton for more, but decided against it and instead nodded, got back into the truck, and continued down the winding, unpaved driveway to his home. The taste of Colton's bliss danced on his tongue.

CHAPTER 17

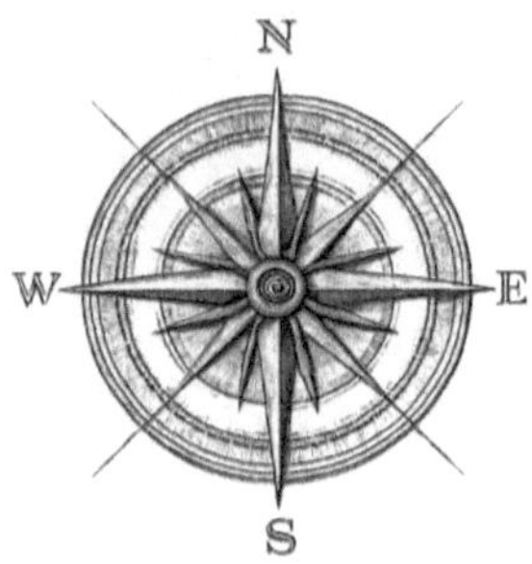

The porchlight illuminated the front of the house, and Frank's excited barks punctuated the cool night air as Winter parked the truck. Colton, feeling thoroughly satisfied and dumbly giddy, noticed something sitting on the porch and smirked, seeing the fancy bouquet of roses, finely cut in a black vase, with a card slipped between them.

Winter frowned, spotting them too.

They got out of the truck, and Colton wondered if he should make a pot of coffee to wake himself up for what he knew was going to be a fantastical night in Winter's bed. Because that man just destroyed him in the truck. If he kept up that pace, Colton would be dead by dawn.

And he didn't dare to tell Winter what he had been really thinking just now either. Maybe because anything said after sex was just the euphoria and blissed-out orgasmic high talking. And perhaps too, he didn't want to be like any of his other lovers—strung out and crazy about him after a handful of sexy blowjobs.

The evidence of Winter's ruined, broken-hearted lovers literally sat waiting for them on his porch, making Colton's fingers twist into a fist in his pocket, attempting to look casual and unaffected by yet another obsessed former lover.

"Trevor's way of an apology?" Colton asked, hitching his chin to the flowers.

Winter said nothing and held out his hand, indicating Colton to stay at the foot of the steps.

"I doubt those flowers will sucker punch you, Winter," Colton teased.

Winter walked up the steps, eyes glancing around the forest that surrounded them, his shoulders tense and his body coiled, as though on a spring, ready to jump. Colton stilled, confused.

Winter bent down and examined the flowers, then stood up quickly, his eyes darkening as he walked back to his truck. He pulled out a secured black box beneath the driver's seat and revealed a gun, along with a pair of gloves.

"What's going on?" Colton asked, alarmed.

Without a word, he pulled out the gun, tucking it into the back of his jeans, and returned to the flowers, taking a picture of them with his phone before retrieving the note placed between the red petals.

"Winter," Colton demanded. "Tell me what's going on."

Winter's chest heaved, something predatory and lethal passing over his scowling expression as he walked down the steps to Colton and showed him the note in his latex-gloved hands.

The front of the card read: Colton.

He frowned, confused. He hadn't told anyone he was coming here, only Jamie.

Winter turned the card over, his heart dropping like a stone: *"Welcome Home, My Love. Did you miss me?"* Signed with a familiar and haunting symbol.

Jim sat across from them at his kitchen table, looking tired, the bags under his eyes puffy and red from being interrupted from his sleep. Winter handed him a cup of hot coffee and sat back down.

"We can't be sure it's him, Winter," Jim said reasonably.

Colton listened to the sounds of clicking crime scene photographers outside Winter's home and the footsteps of forensic investigators collecting evidence. His house had become a crime scene, and there wasn't much they could do about it. The Ripper had been here. He knew precisely where Winter lived and that Colton was with him. Anger rippled through his veins as he sipped his coffee, eyes focused on the dark, black forest, wondering if he was out there—watching.

A thought suddenly occurred to him: what if the Ripper saw them in Winter's truck just now? What if he heard them? He closed his hand over the hot mug of coffee, wanting to stalk into the forest and find him and drive his fists into his face until there was nothing left.

What he and Winter did was private—sacred—*theirs*.

The very idea that the Ripper might have spied on it set his teeth on edge.

Winter slipped his hand into his back pocket and pulled out his phone, showing Jim the pictures of the brands from all three people, including Colton. "It's him. He signed it."

Jim cursed. "Okay, it's him. I really wish you had something stronger than coffee, right about now."

"Me too," Colton muttered, eyes cast out to the vast, dark forest beyond the kitchen window.

"Outside us knowing Colton's here, who else could know?" Jim asked.

"Everyone in the field that first day... The coroner's office, and the people at the dinner party we went to tonight," Winter said.

"Dinner party? Mal?" Jim asked knowingly.

Winter nodded, "Yeah."

"We'll need a list of everyone there," Jim said.

"Of course."

"You don't really think it was anyone from the party, do you?" Colton asked, finally turning away from the window to look at the two investigators at the dining table.

He caught the tense line around Winter's lips and the searching look in his gaze as he scrutinized Colton, looking for something. Fear, maybe? Or fury?

"No," Winter replied. "But we make the list anyway."

Colton sighed, leaning heavily against the kitchen counter.

Jim glanced between them, "You think he left any evidence on the note?"

"Probably not," Winter said.

"You wouldn't happen to have any security cameras on your property?" Jim asked.

"Outside of Frank," Winter said acidly, "no."

"Sir?" A young deputy in a dark green forest uniform stepped into the kitchen, her eyes wide. She was tall, with dark eyes to match her chestnut brown hair, and young. "Uhm, sorry to interrupt, but I found something else."

Colton's stomach knotted, and all three of them pensively waited as the deputy pulled out her phone and laid it on the table between Winter and Jim. He took a step forward, curious.

"I did an EMF sweep of the house."

"Why?" Winter asked.

"A what?" Colton asked.

"An EMF, electromagnetic field sweep for any devices in the home that the suspect might have placed." She shifted, somewhat nervously. "I dunno why, actually. I think I've been listening to the Serial Chillers podcast a lot lately. Their last episode was on stalkers, and how technology has actually helped them become better stalkers..." she pointed to the screen of her phone. "They use spy cameras, really tiny ones, about the size of a dime, and place them all over the houses of their victims. I didn't think I'd find anything when I did this. It was just a hunch. The flowers were—well, creepy."

She pointed to the master bedroom and bathroom. "Whoever left the flowers left three cameras in here, and two here."

Colton stared hollowly at the screen, his gut tightening, alarm spreading through his limbs. Winter let out a stream of curses, raking his fingers through his hair.

"Can it hear us?" Colton asked her.

She shook her head, "Considering the mic power on these cameras, I don't think so. But yes, for sure in the rooms they're planted."

Winter immediately stood and pointed to the patio, snagging the deputy's phone and ushering them all outside, slamming the thick slider glass door behind him. "Respectfully, deputy, I appreciate the theory, but I'm not taking the risk of anyone overhearing the rest of this conversation."

She merely nodded, straightening under the severity of Winter's gaze. Colton leaned against the railing of the patio, mind racing at the possibility of the Ripper bugging the house, and felt an eerie chill at the idea of him listening.

"Jesus Christ," Jim muttered. "Good work, deputy. With instincts like this, you'd better take the detective exam. Now, how do we turn these fucking things off?"

"I can disable them through the app. But he could turn it back on at any point using a different frequency. So, the best option is obviously removing them."

"Can we track him through the app?" Winter asked.

"No—it's spygear. High-tech equipment that doesn't rely on Wi-Fi," she explained with a pensive frown.

"He's a watcher," Colton said, a memory, forgotten but there, came flooding back. "He had cameras in the room just like this…"

Winter's gaze widened and then narrowed sharply.

"When I was escaping, I saw the video feed in my room attached to a laptop. He recorded us." Colton stared down at the blinking spots where the app had detected the cameras in Winter's bedroom.

So, not only did the Ripper know Colton was here, but he suspected something between them. Or was hoping for it. Either way, Colton wanted to rip apart the house brick by brick, wood by wood, until there was nothing of the Ripper touching Winter's home.

"You never told me that," Winter said, bringing his attention back to the present.

Colton blinked, "I forgot until seeing those cameras. I'm sorry."

"Don't apologize." Winter's hand reached for his and stilled, retracting. The sting of disappointment and frustration rippled once more into him. He had been a breath away from having his night with Winter, only for it to be ruined entirely by the Ripper.

If that sick son-of-a-bitch were standing in front of him right now, he'd kill him with his bare fucking hands.

"Ripper?" the deputy asked.

"Out," Jim commanded instantly. "And keep your mouth shut until I debrief you at the station, got it?"

She paled and nodded, "What about the cameras?"

"Leave your phone," Jim ordered, pointing to the slider door.

She pivoted on her boot and left, giving them the privacy they needed to discuss the case.

Winter fisted his hand over his mouth, deep in contemplation. "That could mean there is footage of what happened to Colton out there, and the other men—another reason the Ripper was able to sustain himself for so long without another victim. It all makes sense."

"Another reason to stop this twisted fuck now," Jim retorted. "Any new leads?"

Colton turned to see Winter close his eyes angrily and shake his head.

Jim let out an irritable huff from his nostrils.

"We can use this," Colton said, an idea formulating in his mind.

"How?"

"Bait him," Colton began to pace, the plan taking shape, blood pumping into his fists, ready to fight. "Get him to make a mistake and come after me again."

The cool night breeze swept through them and he stilled, seeing the fixed, almost lethal look in Winter's dark eyes. "You can't be serious?"

"Deadly."

"No," Winter growled.

"Why not?"

"It's too dangerous."

Colton's teeth mashed together. "I, of all people in this fuckin' room, know that."

Silence suspended the three men, tension thickening in the air.

"What are you suggesting?" Jim asked Colton curiously.

He sucked air into his lungs, knowing he was about to royally piss off Winter, because he wasn't going to like this plan one fucking bit.

"What if I—we—pretend that I'm with someone. Put on a show of romance and wooing, and really piss him off. Get him to do somethin' stupid, reckless even. But it's gotta be convincing enough for him to come after me."

Winter scoffed, while Jim looked intrigued. "I like this plan. But it can't just be anyone. It would have to be an officer, just in case the Ripper made an attempt on your life. I can talk to Officer Sydney, see if she would be comfortable going undercover on this."

"I think we both know what type the Ripper goes after, Sheriff. And it ain't straight men," Colton murmured darkly.

Jim stiffened, glancing over to Winter. Colton caught the look and knew that Jim knew about Winter, which was bloody convenient because that's who Colton would be suggesting for this little cat-and-mouse game.

"He's killed two men so far," Colton said, leaning heavily against the railing, boots crossing at the ankles, arms folded across his chest. "And your lot has fuck all when it comes to suspects. I've been here two days and have gathered as much. We don't want him snatching any more victims, so why not use me? The one that got away," Colton repeated Winter's very words back at him. "He clearly still wants me. That's good. So, he'll be watching me—wanting me. We tempt this bastard enough, and he'll come. I fucking know it."

Jim seemed to contemplate this, drumming his fingers on the railing, glancing into the dark ocean of trees beyond. "This is a plausible story. The media would love it, too—the Ripper's only survivor, romancing the hero detective. It would certainly catch a lot of attention, and it's an easy cover to use to keep you close, Winter. If, of course, you're comfortable with this."

Colton saw a flash of his big bad wolf before Winter quickly masked it, attempting to look neutral to the idea of them risking their lives to stop the Ripper.

Winter, without a word, opened the slider, and two minutes later came back in with the deputy, who rejoined them on the porch patio. "Officer Sydney, if you would?"

She glanced pensively at Winter, and he handed her back the phone.

"Can you tell when these cameras were installed?" Winter asked.

She clicked on the app, reading information from it before replying,

"About three hours ago. It's when it first started streaming to an undisclosed location."

"And there are no other cameras on the property?"

She shook her head.

"So, he can't see anywhere but those two locations?"

"Correct, sir."

"Unless he's sitting out in the woods, watching the circus," Jim muttered.

Winter frowned, beginning to pace, and Colton felt his heart kick in his chest, recognizing that whenever he was working out a plan—or a theory, he paced. A slight tug on the corner of his lips formed, excited that Winter seemed to be considering his insane plan.

"I doubt that," Winter said to Jim. "He doesn't want the nose-bleed seats, he wants front row to the show. Just look at where he planted the cameras."

Jim shifted his weight uncomfortably from boot to boot, shaking his head.

Winter finally stopped pacing, and without looking at Colton, his gaze cut across the trees and the lake. "So, we give him one."

Colton's pulse leapt, hands fisting against his chest, unable to look away at the detective—the wolf that stood before him.

"You can shut the cameras off from anywhere as long as you have this app," Officer Sydney said. "And I doubt he's out there," she hitched her chin to the forest. "We swept it twice."

"What are you thinking?" Colton asked Winter, riveted.

"Other than that this is nuts," he bit out. "We can use this like you said. Where are the cameras?"

Office Sydney showed him on the phone the approximate locations.

"What if we don't shut them off?" Winter said. "But instead, we cover them... but only after we trigger him."

Colton nodded, already liking the direction of the plan despite the fear coiling around his chest, not for himself, but for Winter. It was different when he was the target, but by asking Winter to join him, everything changed.

"We put on a show for him, and cover the cameras one at a time, maybe break one or two. He's a passive killer, so he won't risk doing anything tonight. He'll wait until he knows the house is empty and come back to fix the cameras."

"Heroes in the Park," Colton suggested.

"With every Tom, Dick, and Harry there," Jim replied quickly, nodding as well. "He'd be insane to try and do something in front of so many cops."

"Keeping his attention on me," Colton added.

"Us."

Heat, possessive and fiery, flooded Colton as he stood utterly still, attempting not to reveal his pleasure. The lingering scent of pine and the feel of Winter's hands on his body had been imprinted on every fiber, every muscle of his being. But it wasn't just that, he suddenly realized. This was the same rush of excitement he felt ten years ago when Winter emerged from the darkness of his home, handing Colton a weapon and the idea of them hunting the Ripper with someone else at his side—someone capable, dangerous even—felt fucking thrilling.

"Another officer and I can stake out your place while you're out," Officer Sydney suggested.

Winter nodded, his chest exhaling in a long sigh, the moonlight suspending him. "We have to really piss him off to risk him coming back here."

"And if he doesn't come here—what if he goes to the festival?" Jim asked.

"Then we put on another show," Colton drawled simply, blood

pumping, knowing he'd be ready this time.

Winter's gaze finally swung to him, an indecipherable look on his face. "It'll be in public."

Colton shrugged, "We're at war, and he is our enemy. If he wants to get caught in our crosshairs, then let's take a shot at him, Winter. He's been free to do whatever he wants for far too long, in my opinion. And I wouldn't mind makin' the bastard furiously fuckin' jealous."

There was a knock on the sliding glass door, and Winter, as though coming out of a fog, lifted his head and opened the door. Forensics informed them they were done and handed Winter a black duffel bag.

"That's the surveillance equipment," Jim said. "I had a feeling you didn't have security cameras out here. If you want, I can have a deputy come out tomorrow to help set it up."

"I can help," Officer Sydney said eagerly.

"We can manage," Winter said, placing the equipment inside the door.

"What about a patrol car out front the rest of the night?" Jim asked.

"I can set the alarm system tonight," Winter said coolly.

"So, are we doing this or what?" Colton asked him.

Winter cast Jim a weary look. "This could get messy again."

Jim snorted, "Fuck it. The only thing I care about is this town and these people. Besides, I'm retiring the second this asshole is in cuffs or in the ground."

CHAPTER 18

After the other officers and Jim left, Winter walked around the house, locking and securing all the doors and windows, relying on fans and the AC for the night. He glanced at his phone and the new app that Officer Sydney had downloaded for him, which showed the locations of the cameras in the bedroom and bathroom. He knew exactly where they were. One was placed on his vanity next to the lamp, the other by the corner chair, and the last one on his bedside. The ones in the bathroom were all pointed to the shower.

He found Colton, standing outside on the patio, staring directly into the woods, focused and intent, as though waiting for the Ripper to appear—or hoping he would.

"We need to talk about how we're gonna do this," Winter said, noting his tone was a bit rough.

Colton turned, leaning his back against the railing, a sinister grin shaping on his lips. "I love watching you work," he murmured. "It's incredibly sexy seeing a man use his brain the way you do."

"If I had any fucking sense, I wouldn't have agreed to this," Winter retorted, irritated.

"You had to, because you're just like him."

Surprised, Winter stared at him, wondering if he should be offended or not.

Colton let himself relax, his stance opening like an invitation, reminding Winter of that day at the bar, with the crackling storm overhead. "You're possessive, controlling—my big bad fuckin' wolf. You wouldn't be able to sit back and watch someone else take what's yours."

What's yours...

His breath caught, and he felt the brick wall around his heart tremble again, but this time it was Colton, armed with a sledgehammer, demolishing it one brick at a time.

Fuck.

He wanted to show him how possessive he could be, but they had work to do. He closed the slider behind him, not wanting the Ripper to hear his plan.

"We have to coordinate this like a dance," Winter said, showing Colton the app. "We cover them with clothes or knock something in front of them—but we need at least one of them streaming so that he doesn't know we know. We want him to come back and replace them."

"And we have to look and sound convincing while we tango," Colton husked heatedly.

Winter's stomach swooped. "Any suggestions?"

"Oh, I have plenty," Colton muttered. "But the real question is how far do we push him?"

Winter saw the glint of violence in Colton's gaze. "As far as we can," he heard himself say.

Colton smiled, but it wasn't like the other smile—this one was downright diabolical. "There's my wolf..." He sauntered up to him, his pale blue eyes lit by pure fire. "He liked seeing me punished. He had a raging hard-on when Pollock was done with me. So, my lovely wolf..." Colton held out his wrists. "I think it's time you get your cuffs out."

Winter hesitated, blood roaring in his ears at the thought of Colton at his complete mercy, begging and whimpering with need. He reached out and grasped his wrists, steadying himself. "Are you sure?"

Colton answered him with a kiss, strong and sure. Winter melted like steel set ablaze by the power of the sun.

He swept his tongue thoroughly through his mouth before withdrawing, "Safe word is still in play. Say it and everything stops. Agreed?"

Colton's delicious wet lips hungrily nipped at his, "Yes, my darling wolf."

He growled and kissed him one last time, knowing that this was theirs, only theirs, and the Ripper didn't get to see it.

He turned on his stereo in the front room, playing blues, letting it fill the house with the vibrations of the guitar. Winter felt his heart racing a little too quickly, wondering if this was the right thing to do. It was one thing agreeing to do something like this for his job—it was entirely something else to let Colton willingly let himself become a target again.

He raked his hand through his hair before automatically leaning down to pat Frank on the head, who was slumbering on his bed by the fireplace.

This would not only be a test for the Ripper, but for him. Everything that was about to happen in that room was to infuriate and simultaneously incite the Ripper to pursue Colton actively. It required every ounce of his will to stay in control. Because he had to stay in control, knowing full well that Colton would push him the way he intended to push the Ripper, who would be watching and listening.

Winter finally stepped into the dark hallway leading to the master bedroom and saw Colton waiting for him, casually leaning against the wall, his hand opening and closing the silver lighter. He suddenly hated how gorgeous this man was. He swallowed, his stomach twisting anxiously as Winter walked past him, trying to get his head on straight. He'd never done anything like this before, even when he went to that sex club with Mal, which had a whole room specifically for voyeurs and people who got off having someone watch them fuck.

But they weren't fucking.

They would be acting.

His jaw twitched, attempting to rein in his thudding pulse with a steel vice grip. Colton, on the other hand, looked resolutely calm, eyes fixated on the bedroom door, lighter sliding through his fingers.

"You ready?" Winter asked, noting the low grate in his voice.

Colton glanced curiously at him, scrutinizing his face. "Second thoughts?"

"Sorta," he muttered, keeping his voice low so the cameras inside couldn't hear him. "I'll state again for the record, I don't like this plan."

The younger man let his head roll lazily against the wall, looking bored and yet—excited. "I trust you. Do whatever you need to do to me in there, Winter. I give you complete permission."

Winter's stomach swooped, his fingers balling into his palms.

"I've been waiting ten years to get a go at this fucker, so I don't intend to play fair," Colton said, surprising him. "And honestly, I don't think I even know how to play fair at this point."

The darkness of the hallway enveloped them, concealing them the way a theater curtain hid the actors before stepping out onto the stage. "Whatever I say in there..." he locked his gaze with Colton's. "It's part of it, okay?"

"I know."

Colton pushed off the wall and reached for him, grabbing the back of his neck, kissing him. Winter immediately kissed him back, but it wasn't a passionate one—it felt more comforting—soothing—reassuring. And he wondered if it was more for him than it was for Colton.

Colton lifted his lips from his, blue eyes sharp and focused. "Do everything he would hate seeing someone else do to me. Make him believe it, Winter."

Something strong and protective rose in his chest, and he nodded. Winter kissed him again, and he poured in everything he had felt since seeing those damned roses and the note.

Fear, excitement, need, and something else—something he hadn't felt in a long time. But he refused to recognize it, to let it in. He couldn't imagine anything happening to Colton, of the Ripper hurting him again.

Winter had let Colton believe that this performance would lure the Ripper back to him, but he was planning the opposite. Winter fully intended to have the Ripper set his sights on him. He wanted the Ripper's rage—his wrath—his reckless violence directed at him, and only him. Because he could handle it, and he wasn't letting Colton ever be a victim of that man again. Not on his watch.

"Whatever I say in there," Winter whispered against his lips. "Just agree to it, okay?"

Colton swallowed and nodded.

Winter stepped back and walked into his bedroom.

Showtime.

The music was loud, but so was the thundering of his heartbeat in his ears as he took the handcuffs and phone from his back pocket and tossed them onto the bed, feeling the eyes of the three cameras on him.

He sat down on the edge of his bed, pulse skipping wildly in his throat, legs splayed, waiting. It was hard not to glance around the room and see where the cameras were.

Calm, cool, controlled. I can do this. We can do this.

Colton appeared then, casually leaning his shoulder against the door-frame, looking defiant, and so god damned confident. It oozed out of his pores as he smiled slyly at him.

Winter attempted to appear aloof, resting his hands behind him, try-ing hard to relax the tension rolling through his chest. Colton slipped off the wall, and Winter stopped him with a firm order. "Crawl."

Colton stilled, eyes darkening.

"Did I stutter?" He growled at the younger man.

Colton smirked dangerously, sliding his lighter into his pocket, and dropped slowly to his hands and knees. "Want me to get a leash from the closet, too?"

He gritted his back molars, "Only if I can tie you up with it."

Colton hesitated for the briefest of seconds, and Winter knew that was already too much. He knew Colton's sexual non-negotiables, and being tied up was on that list.

Fuck, he thought angrily, hating this but knowing it was too late to back out now.

"Take my boots off," he commanded roughly. This part, Colton had expected, and he made a show of crawling to him at the foot of the bed. He looked like a sleek panther, all smooth, rippling muscles and focused intention. Winter swallowed a jolt of nervous energy, already questioning his ability to maintain control. Colton reached for his boots, his hands traveling up the length of his calf, and Winter shook his head. "Just the boots."

Colton let out a frustrated growl and slowly pushed up his jeans around his ankles, unlacing the boots and dropping them behind him.

"Those are nice boots," Winter said darkly.

Colton, rising to the occasion, sat back on his heels and retrieved one of the boots. "They don't look that nice." He tossed it hard into the corner, and Winter made a show of leaning forward, affronted, but really he did a glance off his screen, which was set to the lowest dim settings, and left on.

The camera had been jarred from the corner with the toss of the boot. Colton didn't wait and tossed the other one, harder this time, even knocking the standing lamp over. The camera's sending beacon vanished from the screen, and Winter nearly smiled. Colton had somehow crushed the tiny, sensitive camera by throwing his bulky boots at it.

Perfect. Right on target.

Winter, continuing with the show of being upset, grabbed Colton by the throat and forced him upwards, the bluesy music crooning in the background. He dragged his lips over Colton's ear, biting the lobe, whispering low so only he could hear. "Good boy..."

Those words were for them. Not the Ripper.

Colton trembled, pulse leaping under his fingers. Winter felt the stirring of his cock and viciously tried to suppress it.

"One down," he nipped and pushed him back down roughly. Colton made a show of tumbling backward, letting out a curse.

Winter arched his eyebrows expectantly down at his feet. Colton sneered, but jerked off his socks next, tossing them into the same corner with the dead camera.

Colton sat back on his heels, looking up at him. Goddamn, he was a pretty sight. He desperately wanted to tell him that, and barely bit back the praise sliding off his tongue.

"Let me touch you properly," Colton demanded.

"Then by all means," he said indifferently, digging his fingers into the bedsheets.

Colton eagerly sat forward between his legs, racing his hands up his jeans, over the calves and knees, rising upward to his groin. Winter sucked in a harsh breath, knowing he couldn't stop the air from being filtered through his lungs, any more than he could stop his body from physically reacting to this sinfully handsome man with a roughish smile that could unravel him with a damned look.

He allowed Colton to touch him, but was careful not to touch back, not yet.

"Take off your shirt," Winter ordered huskily.

Colton stood, peeled off his shirt overhead, and tossed it behind him, this time, on the vanity. Winter sat back on the heels of his palms, caressing him with his gaze, and it was Colton this time who glanced at the app at Winter's side and frowned slightly.

"Take off mine," he ordered, understanding the disappointment. Colton had been aiming for the second camera.

Colton's eyes sparkled with excitement as he stepped forward between his splayed legs, his fingers slowly trailing down the buttons of Winter's black suit shirt, popping them open, a heady need in his expression as he did so. His finger dug harder into the mattress now, feeling the subtle flips of the buttons along his skin as Colton intentionally took his time, seeming to savor it. Winter nearly succumbed to the tension building between his legs, but held off, almost gulping in air through his nostrils, holding firm to his control.

Colton finally finished unbuttoning his shirt, a cocky slant to his mouth as he suddenly palmed Winter's manhood over his jeans, and startled, he sat forward, grabbing his wrist. Colton leaned forward, kissing along his neck and up to his ear. "Relax, luv. You're supposed to be havin' fun."

Winter inwardly sighed and bit back a curse. He was right; he was too focused on maintaining his control and sanity in performing this absurd act that he forgot to look the part as well.

He pushed Colton back with a firm hand, holding out his wrist. "Take these off," he instructed smoothly, indicating the golden sleeve cuffs. Colton smirked and did as he was told, easily unclasping them as though he'd done it a thousand times before.

"Put them on the dresser," Winter ordered once more.

Colton raised an eyebrow, "You gotta say please first, handsome."

His refusal was also part of the plan they had worked out. He expected this moment, and Winter grasped Colton's chin, raking his fingers through his short beard, being overly rough. "You're supposed to do what you're told..." he dipped his thumb into his mouth like Colton had done to him earlier in the truck, but this time, he was in control and pushing too hard.

Colton flinched.

Winter loathed seeing the flash of pain but knew he had to keep going. They had their established safe word. And at any point, Colton could say it, and everything would stop—he would stop.

Winter intentionally reddened Colton's soft lower lip with his thumb. "You know what I think? I think you don't want to admit how much you like being told what to do..."

Colton's nostrils flared, and he snapped his head back. Winter got to his feet and, knowing it was just an act—just a dance—pushed him backward into the dresser, knocking over a few of the things on top, listening to them fall to the floor. He trapped Colton against the dresser, rubbing himself against him like a dog, humping and grinding his hardening cock against him. Colton attempted to push him away, but his effort was weak, and Winter shoved harder, rocking the dresser back into the wall with a loud slam.

Colton gasped, jaw twitching, eyes flashing, letting himself be pinned to the dresser like a butterfly. It felt a little too good getting this rough—this raw display of power—his manhood straining against the fly of his jeans as he slammed again and again into Colton, his hips bucking into him, until nothing was standing on top of his dresser.

Satisfied, Winter grabbed him by the throat and hauled him away, pivoting and feeling Colton letting himself be pulled around, and he shoved once more. Colton's knees hit the back of the bed, and he fell onto the mattress.

Winter was on top of him in an instant, knowing that one camera was on the nightstand, and he wasn't sure if he could glance at the phone yet to see if the camera on the dresser was on the floor or not.

Colton seemed to sense what he was trying to do and attempted to maneuver Winter, his hips tossing upward and dislodging him. Winter fell and, in that brief second, glanced at the phone and saw the second camera was on the floor, lost beneath the bed.

Two down. One more to go.

Colton attempted to roll off the bed, and Winter grabbed him and threw an arm over his throat, bracing him from behind. Colton instantly struggled, growling curses at him.

Winter, knowing the camera was directly looking at him from the nightstand, and hoping to God the Ripper was watching, positioned himself behind Colton, arching his back, knees digging into the mattress, his arm bar unbreakable, as he forced open his jeans and shoved his hand inside.

Colton groaned; it was loud and full of unmistakable passion. *Fuck.* Winter nearly bit out his own needy moan.

He knew instantly what this looked like from the camera's view. Winter had forced Colton into a compromised position, with no way out, and on full display like a painting, beautiful and wildly erotic. Winter blinked, feeling his own body's reaction, his fingers touching the rigid, glorious flesh inside Colton's jeans, stroking him but not pulling him out. He would not expose him to the Ripper.

The Ripper would never get to see that much of him again.

This was all the temptation Winter would allow.

He roughly made a show of jerking him off in his pants. Colton moaned and strained against him. Winter knew he had to find a way to get to the other camera. Still, his brain was beginning to cloud—feeling the hard press of Colton's erection straining in his hand, while his own dug into his perfect ass, wanting to penetrate—to fuck him hard and rough and feel his tight hole suck him deep.

Oh god, yes.

The mere thought spiraled him off the edge and he pressed himself into him, desperate for this man—desperate in ways he had never felt. He wanted Colton—wanted him more than a possession. He wanted all of him, not just his body, but his heart as well.

Winter trembled, chest constricting at the force of the revelation.

Colton squirmed and writhed, his ass grinding against him now, and it was Winter's turn to groan. He was so aroused, so hard, he palmed Colton's hard sex and actually stroked him, rough and demanding. He needed everything from him. And he needed it right fucking now. Grasping him root to tip, he thumbed the tip of his head, feeling the needy leak, and he tugged him harder, loving the sounds Colton was making for him and the way his body responded so eagerly.

"You're so hard for me," Winter praised, unable to stop the words falling from his lips as he stroked him. "You wanna be my good fuckin' boy, don't ya baby...?"

"Fuck, Winter," Colton gasped warningly, cock jerking and spasming in his hand. "I'm gonna fuckin' cum."

He was, he could feel him leaking in his hand, and he buried his face into the back of his neck, humping him.

"Winter..." Colton gasped, arching into him, his body tensing right before the unraveling.

NO!

The Ripper didn't get to see that. He didn't get to know how Colton's face changed when he experienced the euphoric rapture of his climax.

That privilege was for him and him alone.

He's mine.

The thought was so powerful, Winter released him instantly, sudden awareness of the moment flooding back to him. He shivered, and with every ounce of control he still had, yanked his hand out of his pants, pushed him forward onto the bed, heart galloping in his chest as he peeled off his shirt, balled it into his fist, and tossed it at his nightstand and missed.

Fuck.

Breathing hard, he leaned over Colton, pushing him down into the mattress with his knee. He glanced at the phone tucked against Colton's side, his arm covering it from the camera's view, and he saw a notification on the phone, and everything in his body stilled.

The app's notification read: "Viewer linked."

The Ripper was watching and listening.

Winter released a breath from his nostrils, grabbed the handcuffs from beneath Colton, and flipped him onto his back. Colton went willingly. Eyes haunted with desire and chest heaving for air. His dark blond hair was tousled. His face riddled with fiery need.

He wanted to kiss him, but didn't.

"Cuff yourself," Winter dropped the steel cuffs onto his naked chest, and Colton licked his lips.

"Make me," Colton husked out defiantly.

Winter straddled him, jaw clenching, feeling the pressure of their aching cocks rubbing together. He knew the Ripper was watching—knew he had to keep going—but he had lost control already. He couldn't trust himself not to do so again, and hesitated. And he really didn't want to fucking cuff Colton. He refused to hurt him even though they had agreed to do this as part of the performance.

Colton's hand on the opposite side of the camera, unseen, tapped the side of Winter's leg, the same way he did the lighter, and Winter, in that moment, understood what the lighter had been for. It was a way for him to soothe himself. And he was doing it now, and also reassuring him.

Reassuring *him*!

Winter felt another stone around his heart fall, and he leaned down and kissed him, hard, roughly, angrily, putting everything he wanted to say into the heat of this kiss, spearing his tongue demandingly between his lips. Colton wrapped around him like a vine, kissing him back—this was real. And he couldn't stop. But he had to.

Winter broke the kiss, movements jerky as he grabbed Colton's wrists and dragged them above him, slipping the cuffs through the bed railing and clicking them closed. The sound of it locking together was deafening.

Colton let out a hard breath and tugged on the cuffs. Winter sat back, watching him struggle, the contours of his abs bunching as he twisted, and the sharp lines of his stomach smooth and solid, leading down to the V of his hips, his jeans covering the rest of him.

"You're trying awfully hard to break free, but we both know you wanted this," Winter said darkly.

Colton stilled, "Maybe..." he taunted.

Winter pressed his knees into the mattress, pushing his erection into him.

Colton gasped, hands instinctively coming forward, forgetting he was cuffed as he arched upwards to rub himself against him.

Winter knew now it was time to break the Ripper—direct his wrath at him, but to do it, he couldn't tell Colton this part of his plan because he knew he wouldn't do it. He stared down at him, clenching his jaw angrily.

"Tell me..." Winter said softly, hating himself, hating that he was doing this, but he knew Colton would forgive him. At least, he hoped he would. "How long have you been in love with me?"

Something cold washed over Colton, and everything in the room stilled. The music continued to croon, the camera continued to watch, but Colton was the one who changed; his pale eyes sharpened, his face tensed.

"How long?" Winter pressed.

Colton's lips flattened into a hard line. "Fuck you."

He smirked darkly down at him, stroking himself against his body for his own savage use, knowing the Ripper would react to this. "Don't worry, we'll get to that."

Colton glared, nostrils flaring.

"How long...?" Winter dragged his hand over Colton's stomach and watched him flinch and tremble, goosebumps shivering over his flesh. "The whole time?" he asked. "Ever since I killed for you?"

Colton swallowed, face paling.

Winter, hating every second of this, rocked himself against Colton's subdued body, raking his fingers down the hard lines of his muscled chest, thrusting into him. If it were too much, Colton would say the safe word. He repeated this like a mantra in his head as he dangerously crossed the line with him now.

Colton slammed his eyes shut, jaw clenching as his body betrayed him, his cock still hard between them. Winter reached for his throat and wrapped his fingers around him. "Say it."

Colton's eyes fluttered open, and he saw everything—the pain, the beautiful fury, and something else—something real—something undeniable.

"I love you," Colton whispered. "I've always fucking loved you."

The breath in Winter's chest stuttered, and he stared, thinking of the young man in his arms that night, trembling and fearless—and his.

He had always been his.

Winter let the last stone around his heart fall, and he suddenly couldn't breathe—couldn't think. He abruptly let go of him and stood, rage like nothing he had ever felt in his life pulsing through him as he somehow managed to turn on the lamp with shaking hands and searched for the camera.

"Winter…" Colton said in a tremulous breath.

Winter ignored him and spotted the tiny, black camera, sitting between two books on his nightstand. He grabbed it and placed it on the flat surface, and slammed one of the books on top of it, crushing it.

"Winter!"

He dropped to his knees and reached under the bed, his fingers searching and finding the next camera. He crushed it under the same book on his nightstand.

"Winter…"

He grabbed his phone and saw that all three cameras in the bedroom were destroyed. But the notification still read: "Viewer linked."

He ground his back molars into ash in his mouth, stormed into the bathroom, flipping on the light, and got into the shower, glancing up to the two ends, using his flashlight to spot the lens of the cameras. One was attached to the showerhead, and the other blended in with the tile of the shower. He flicked the one off the shower head and crushed it under a plastic bottle of shampoo.

He glanced at the phone. One camera left.

"Viewer Linked."

He glared at the last remaining camera, his voice a growling rasp. "He's mine. If you want him, you'll have to get through me first, you fucking limp dick bitch."

He slammed his fist into the camera this time, shattering it.

CHAPTER 19

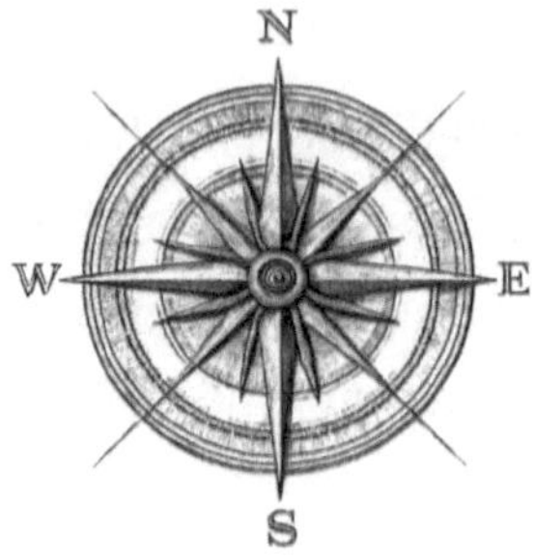

Colton stared angrily at where Winter had disappeared into the bathroom, refusing to acknowledge the embarrassment ripping apart his insides as he lay there, helpless and handcuffed to the bed.

Winter reappeared moments later, face rigid and body tense, as he pulled the key from his back pocket and quickly removed the handcuffs from around Colton's wrists, tossing the heavy steel onto his bedside.

"We shouldn't have done that," Winter murmured, face pinched with anger and regret.

Colton said nothing, not sure he could even speak as he rolled to his side, tossing his legs over the bed, unable to look at him.

"I shouldn't have done that," Winter breathed. "I'm sorry, Colton."

He swallowed the emotion welling in his throat. "That was part of your plan the whole time, wasn't it?"

Winter was quiet now, too quiet. Colton knew the man well enough to realize that he had harbored feelings for him a long time ago. And he used it as a weapon because that's what Winter thought emotions were, tools to be used and tossed aside.

"You knew all along…" His voice was steady despite his heart breaking apart all over again. It broke eight years ago with that cold official letter stating Winter had closed the case. And here he was, still hung up on this fucking man, and he hadn't learned—he hadn't learned the first time. God, he was such a fool, he thought angrily.

"No," Winter replied hollowly, anger draining away from his tone. "I didn't know."

"Aye, but you suspected." He got to his feet and turned to confront him, waiting.

Winter's dark obsidian eyes were intent and filled with remorse.

"Such a good detective when it comes to inconvenient things like love, aren't you? But when it comes to finding the man who did this to me—you're a bit lost in the woods, aren't you?"

Winter's head lifted back as though he had been struck.

"You just ruined an opportunity to capture him," Colton said through gritted teeth. "Because why, exactly?"

"Because I crossed a line," he snapped. "I shouldn't have done that to you to get to him. We can find another way."

He snorted, scrubbing his fingers over his lips, shaking his head. "It's still we, is it?"

Winter stiffened, "Nothing's changed."

"Everything's changed."

"No…"

Colton ignored him and grabbed his shirt off the dresser and headed for the door.

"Colton," Winter chased him down and into the guest bedroom.

He flipped on the small lamplight by the table beside the bed and grabbed his bag off the floor, tossing it onto the bed. Winter's hand captured his wrist and tugged him into the solid wall of his chest. Colton jerked backward, but Winter's hand collared his throat, forcing him into a searing kiss. It was hot—so fucking hot and angry.

Colton's fingers dug into his palms, refusing to kiss him back, refusing to melt so easily. Not this time.

He grabbed Winter's wrist and twisted, hard. He cursed, and his fingers released him, and Colton jabbed him quickly in the side, before shoving him away.

"Fuck off with your games, Winter. I've had enough!" Colton yelled. "I know you're doing this now out of guilt for what just happened. But I am no one's pity fuck."

Winter clutched his side, jaw clenching and unclenching. "That's not why I kissed you."

He cocked his head to the side and laughed harshly. "Sure, keep tellin' yourself that."

"Nothing has changed, Colton!" Winter shot back. "I don't fucking care what you said in that room—it doesn't matter."

"Oh, it matters, and you know it," he retorted lethally.

Winter strode to him again, invading his space, forcing him to step back. His chin lifted at the taller man, never wanting to back down to a challenge thrown intentionally at his feet.

"You're right," Winter murmured. "It does. It does."

He defiantly held his gaze, refusing to show him fear—show him how much it hurt that he knew now. But there was no going back. Only forward. And if Colton was good at anything, it was pushing through despite the chaos around him or within him.

"I realized something in there, too..." Winter's fingers reached out slowly, tentatively, stroking the side of his face, so light that Colton barely felt it, and yet he flinched all the same, unable to stand the placating intimacy, only to be tossed out with the trash. "I can't lose you."

He blinked, surprised. His heart, with an urgency and need that was crushing, hurled itself against the bones of his chest.

"I told the Ripper that if he wanted you, he'd have to come through me first. You're mine, Colton." His fingers captured his jaw firmly, bringing his lips inches from him. "You're mine."

He trembled at the words, holding back the floodgate of his whirling emotions.

"Let me show you how much I need you," Winter rasped out, and just as slowly, as though waiting for Colton to fight or resist, he pressed his lips into his and kissed. It was thorough and full of need, drawing him out and demanding more.

His pulse leapt, unsure if he should let this happen or leave to spare his heart from the inevitable rejection.

"You're so beautiful," Winter whispered against his lips, his unnerving gaze locked with his. "I thought so the first time I saw you."

Colton couldn't stop the shiver if he fucking tried.

"I knew I shouldn't have noticed." Winter traced deadly kisses along his jawline and down his sensitive neck, dragging his teeth along the flesh, causing Colton to sway against him. "I knew it was wrong. But after what you did that night, how fucking bright you were in the dark—I've never seen anything like you."

Something piercing gripped his heart, and he knew in that moment he was lost—so fucking lost to this man. And whatever resistance he thought he had was a lie.

Winter lowered him onto the bed, pushing his bag off, his lips and teeth grating against his collarbone and neck. "I understand why the Ripper left that note. He will come for you regardless of what we do. I finally see it. He wants to possess you and your light," he sighed, hand smoothing down his stomach, lips kissing as he lowered himself further, taking Colton's nipple into his warm mouth, sucking it into a hard point. He let out a hiss of pleasure, watching Winter take his body with such ease, such control, all the while Colton could feel himself breaking apart, piece by piece.

"And I'll be ready this time," Winter promised, pressing his lips into the hard contours of his stomach.

Colton reached for him, raking his nails through the thick waves of his hair, needing to touch him.

"I will do whatever it takes to protect what belongs to me," Winter breathed, eyes flashing up at him, dark and haunting. "Say that you belong to me..."

Fear tightened his throat.

"Say it... Please," Winter pleaded, hands gripping his hips, desperate and strong.

Colton knew he shouldn't. He knew he had to resist this wolf—the wolf that was intent on devouring him alive. But he was weak, so bloody weak for this man.

"I'm yours," he finally murmured raggedly.

Winter let out a harsh exhale, dark eyes sparkled with pleasure, and his lips twitched upward as he lowered himself onto the foot of the bed, his muscles bunched and moving like a predator. The heated passion in his gaze was unraveling Colton from the inside out, as his cock jerked at the magnificent fucking sight that was Winter. He grasped the edges of Colton's jeans and dragged him free of his clothes, leaving him naked, exposed, vulnerable.

Winter sat back, studying his body with an almost violent expression.

He anticipated Winter to come to his lips and claim him; instead, the stealthy bastard let his hands slide up Colton's legs, his grip firm, sending shockwaves of excitement up his body, inching closer to his sex, and unfurling his tongue as he bent. Eyes locked with his, he licked the tip of his cock.

Colton let out a gasping curse.

Winter did it again, touching him only with his tongue. It was a light press, and then a strong one, the wet muscle lavishing his aching tip with attention. Winter never looked more like a wolf than in this moment, and Colton nearly thrust himself into that teasing fucking mouth, unable to stand it.

Winter arched an eyebrow, hand clamping down on Colton's hips, preventing him from moving. "You follow every command. If you don't..." He retracted his tongue. "I stop touching."

He glared hotly down at him.

"Say yes," Winter demanded with a low growl.

"Yes, fuck..." he panted, and the tongue returned with another sensation—the heat of Winter's mouth. He gasped, his stomach muscles bunching, his legs tensing as he watched Winter lower himself over his thick cock, sucking and tonguing him.

Bloody 'ell, it was magnificent. Slow and wet and hot.

So fucking hot.

Winter released his hand on his hips, and Colton immediately bucked. He hummed approvingly, the vibrations of it ricocheting up his spine. He held himself over him, while Colton arched off the bed, deepening himself into the heated glory of Winter's mouth. He couldn't remember the last time a blow job felt this good. Fuck, he couldn't remember any blow job ever before this one. And this was the second time Winter was giving him one in less than a few hours.

Winter somehow swallowed him even deeper and Colton groaned, opening his legs, sliding his hands through the salt and pepper hair, lifting him up and down over him. And the controlling man allowed him to take the reins. Heat spilled into his lower limbs as he bucked upward, touching the back of Winter's throat. He choked, and Colton felt the squeeze of muscles contract around him and the spit slip from Winter's mouth, coating his balls. He did it again—and again. Winter allowed it, the sounds of his choking gasp and hum intoxicating.

His balls tingled suddenly, and he drew himself out of Winter's mouth, not wanting to climax yet, needing to continue the thrilling chase.

Winter understood, sucking and tonguing his balls as Colton's fingers gripped the sheets and his hips humped the air.

"Turn over," Winter commanded quietly, his throat hoarse from being fucked.

He searched the dark eyes that impaled him and complied.

Winter's hands stroked his back and ass, careful not to massage but to touch, as he slid his fingers between his cheeks, and stroked the entrance softly.

"Fuck," he suddenly cursed. "I don't have any lube in this room…"

Colton, shaking head to toe with desire, blindingly reached for his bag on the floor and dug out his own bottle.

"Such a good fucking boy," his voice was so low, so gravely, Colton barely heard it. But he did. He most certainly did, and he trembled for him—for his approval—his praise. He was putty in this man's hands, and he bloody well knew it.

Seconds later, he felt the moisture on his entrance and sighed into the pillow, breathing in Winter's scent on the sheets, his cock pressing hard into the mattress.

Winter slid a hand beneath his stomach, then his arm, pulling him upward onto his hands and knees, slicking the entrance thoroughly. Colton couldn't breathe, couldn't think—he could only feel. He was only sensation and anticipation.

"I like you like this," Winter growled darkly. "Knowing what I need and giving it to me."

Colton's cock hurt; it was so hard. He had to touch himself, and did, fisting his hand around the base of himself, back arching.

Winter eased him back again, practically sitting in his lap, as he worked his entrance, his finger slowly edging into him, as he reached around him and joined his hand with his.

"You taste so fucking good," Winter murmured behind his ear, nipping his earlobe. "I love feeling you in my mouth. And you love fucking my mouth, don't you?"

Colton whimpered, he fucking *whimpered*, his face heated with mortification. "Yes, yes..."

Winter's finger filled him, preparing him. "Goddamn, you feel tight," he rasped.

Colton's hips undulated against his finger, and he felt another one, grazing around the entrance, pushing slowly in. He moaned.

"Relax, baby," Winter commanded.

He gasped at the word and pushed himself down on the two fingers, and Winter chuckled darkly. "I think you're ready for me."

Colton was more than ready. He was thirsty. Starved. Desperate. So damned needy, he feared he would shatter the second Winter entered him.

Winter slowly withdrew from him and, surprising Colton, maneuvered him to his back, his lean body held over him. It took everything in him not to groan at the mere sight of the man—he was breathtaking. Black eyes, stubbled jaw, dark hair sprinkling his chest, trailing deliciously down his stomach to the apex of his masculinity, which was thick and long, as he stroked himself, positioning Colton's hips, lowering between them.

A part of him, the one that hero worshiped and had a very real teenage crush on this man, was stunned by the weight and feel of Winter on top of him. He had spent a better part of a decade imagining this very moment—fantasizing about Winter just like this. And holy fuck, his imagination wasn't prepared for the wolf—the ravenous man that edged the tip of his cock into his entrance.

Colton tried to relax but couldn't. Every muscle in his body was coiled like a spring loaded to snap, and Winter could feel it, easing into him slowly, barely breathing as he did, throat bobbing and face pinched in absolute control.

"Fuck," Colton gasped, feeling the thickness stretch him, the muscles widening to accommodate his fucking limb of a cock.

Winter, eyes heavy with need as his cock made the first slow thrust inside him, touched the sweet spot that had Colton instantly melting and grabbing himself, fisting hard around the base of his sex. Winter was so large that he knew he would be sore tomorrow and hoped he would be. He wanted to feel the sting—feel him.

"*Fuck fuck fuck*," Colton arched, and Winter followed, pulling out and driving back in.

Winter growled deliciously above him, his fingers reaching and squeezing around his neck, as he slowly eased back out and thrusted in. He was going slow and gentle—on purpose.

Bastard!

Colton squeezed his ass cheeks, sucking him in, punishing him. Winter gasped, his hips unable to control the immediate jerking forward.

"You fuck me properly for our first time," Colton ordered fiercely through gritted teeth.

Winter's face darkened, and the wolf reappeared, hungry and dangerous, and he squirmed, loving the sight. Winter dropped, kissing him roughly, pinning him to the bed, and pounded so hard that the headboard slammed into the wall behind them.

Colton let out a crying moan into Winter's mouth as the fucking glorious bastard did it again and again, each time harder and more frenzied, and he felt the harsh swirling of his orgasm building. Winter's cock sliding in and out, hitting the sweet spot every time, sending shockwaves through his limbs. Winter sucked down his tongue, fingers at his throat, cock deep in his ass, and he was in heaven.

This was heaven.

Surrounded by this man.

Fucked by this man. This was what he needed—this was the water he had been thirsting for his entire life.

His muscles tensed once more, and the tip of his dick tingled. Winter, sensing his orgasm, leaned back, dark eyes watching him, as he palmed Colton's manhood and pumped while he thrusted. He was lost in those obsidian eyes. He had been lost to this man for ten years. Lost and now found again, and he never wanted to let go.

This was where Colton belonged.

With him.

His heart shuddered, and his cock twitched and spewed hot ribbons of cum onto his stomach. It went on and on, all the while Winter rocked hard into him, demanding more—so much more of his body than he thought possible. And he arched again, muscles seizing, the impossible second wave of the orgasm spiraling through him.

"Good, fucking, boy..."

Winter's thrusts were losing tempo, becoming wilder, and he let out a moan between clenched teeth, unloading deep inside him.

Colton's cock pulsated once more, the sensations of it all so overwhelming that he merely lay there, sucking in air, trembling, as Winter grunted out the sexiest moan he had ever heard in his life, his face relaxing and tensing in absolute rapture, filling him to the brim with his bliss.

Winter was breathtaking. And all he wanted to do was hold him forever like this, clutched to his chest, never far from his heart. He had to clench his jaw, fighting back the swell of emotion at the power of this moment.

"Fuck you for being so bloody perfect," Colton grated bitterly through panted breaths.

Winter slowly eased out of him, also panting, eyes dancing with an elation he had never seen from him, before leaning down and kissing him tenderly. It tasted like death. Like a kiss his soul would never recover from, because he knew he would never recover from him.

Eli Winter was his death—without him, nothing fucking mattered. He couldn't go back to his life without him. Winter was his home.

Winter opened his nightstand and retrieved a hand towel, wiping Colton off before lying down beside him, and with a commanding touch, grabbed his face and kissed him passionately once more, until he was nothing but a limp, wet pool noodle. Colton pulled back, and Winter continued to brush his lips against his as though unable to stop touching him. He liked the thought and hoped it was true.

Fuck, I'm pathetic.

Something about what just happened was more than just sex. So much more. He stroked his fingers through the curled locks on top of Winter's hair, feeling the softness and the thickness.

"I knew you'd be too good," Winter admitted roughly.

"Too good?" he asked, eyebrow arching.

"You *felt* too good," he murmured, looking oddly vulnerable. Colton's heart skipped. "You're beautiful, smart as hell, and Christ, I don't think I'm ever going to forget watching you break beneath me."

Colton's chest tightened, knowing Winter had told him he was a different man in the bedroom. And maybe this man spoke pretty words that he didn't actually mean.

"You always sweet-talk your lovers after sex?" he asked, pretending to be teasing and indifferent, even though his insides were twisted into knots.

Winter dropped his forehead into his, "Never."

He tried not to notice how his stomach clenched with hope.

Fuck. Fuck. Fuck.

"I don't date them, either," Winter added.

"Really?"

"Really." He stroked his fingers through his short beard. "I wanna take you somewhere nice, show everyone that you're mine." Winter sighed, "Shit, I'm not good at this."

Colton felt himself tremble, not sure what to say. Winter had always been so strong, so sure of himself. Seeing him like this, so open and raw, exposed somehow... But it still didn't make up for what happened earlier—not yet, at least.

"You're really good at the sexy bit. Makes up for some of it." Colton reassured, sliding his fingertips over Winter's deliciously hairy chest. "And just because I let you fuck me doesn't mean I still ain't mad as hell at you for what happened in the other room."

Winter studied him and his tone dropped, "Just so we're clear, I will never stop asking for your forgiveness for that. But until you do, you have ten minutes to rest, and then I need to fuck you in the shower because I want to taste your ass with my cum inside you."

His jaw unhinged, pulse leaping. "Fuckin' 'ell, Winter. You're gonna kill me."

CHAPTER 20

The surveillance cameras were a bitch to install, but after the third one, Winter got the hang of it. And he needed to do something—anything other than to wake Colton up for the third round of rigorous fucking, because he knew the man had to be sore. Something that had been, on occasion, problematic in the initial start of his 'relationships'. And damn him to hell, he wanted to ignore all caution, all reason, and take Colton again—and again. Hard, slow, every which way possible, because he was thoroughly and completely addicted.

When he awoke this morning to Colton's soft breath on his chest, his arm draped over him, warmth spread through him like liquid fire. Not just the sexual fire, but the presence of Colton in his arms, safe, warm, his.

His.

The word shook him like a thunderclap last night. But this morning, it was now a fact.

Winter was accustomed to ownership, even possessiveness in these sorts of relationships, but this was something else. Something tethered to his heart, and he feared that should anything happen to Colton, the tether would pull at the delicate heartstrings and tear. He recognized that tug last night when Colton suggested using himself as bait to ensnare the Ripper. And after hearing Colton's forced confession of love, a confession Winter had pushed—had sensed all along and was too scared to see. It shattered the wall separating him from Colton. That feeling only got worse when he was deep inside him, watching him tense in sublime ecstasy, feeling the way his body broke against his. The way he tasted on his lips and tongue—he thought of only one thing: *his.*

Winter was a greedy son-of-a-bitch and vividly recalled how Colton looked beneath the hot spray of the shower, his muscles strained and coiled tight in his biceps and shoulders as he barely held himself upright. Winter licked his tight entrance clean, tonguing him into a harsh need that had him cursing and gasping, demanding more. He had been so close to coming from that alone that by the time he finally entered him, he was quick and damn near out of his mind.

Colton took it all—chanting his name like a prayer, unloading violently on the tiles of the shower wall, clinging to the safety pole Winter had installed for this very reason as he finished himself inside him, loving the feel of his muscles sucking him deeper as waves upon waves spilled from him.

Colton was about to turn into his arms when Winter pressed his hands onto the bar, dropped once more to his knees, and took what he wanted.

Jerking and shivering, Colton's gasp was ragged as though in pain. "Winter...It's too much..."

He liked hearing the ache in his voice and slid his tongue into his tight hole, and Colton cursed violently but didn't say his safe word. That was all the permission he needed as he lifted the young man's leg onto the step he also had custom-built into his shower, parting the space between his legs further, and placing his entire face there, kissing, sucking, touching, stroking.

"Christ!"

Winter suckled down his tightening balls, watching Colton writhe, face pinched in pleasure and pain. He felt his cock already beginning to stir, but knew he wouldn't be able to go again; but he could make Colton orgasm—one—more—time.

He lifted his head and took the semi-hard dick into his mouth, arm beneath him, sliding into his cum-slicked entrance.

"I fucking hate you," Colton cursed. "I can't!"

His cock said differently as Winter sucked, hard, revitalizing and pushing two fingers into his entrance. Colton shuddered and grabbed the back of Winter's head and shoved him all the way down his throat, holding his face into his stomach, smothering him.

"Yes, yes, yes...!" Colton gasped. "You wanted this, my devouring wolf."

Winter's cock impossibly rose from the dead, and he gasped as Colton released him, letting the air suck back into his body.

"Goddamn, look at ya," Colton murmured, "My hungry fuckin' wolf." He speared his cock back down his throat and fucked his face in the shower, spearing himself all the way down his throat and holding his face for seconds against his stomach, gagging him.

Winter looked up at him, eyes watering, "I'm gonna punish you for that... you're gonna be sore for days when I'm done with you."

"You'd better be a man of your word," Colton grated, water rolling off his shoulders, looking like pure, unfiltered defiance.

Winter flicked off the shower and grabbed Colton's hips with both hands, pushing his stiff cock into his mouth, sucking greedily. Colton let out a guttural cry, the orgasm ripping from his soul, shattering once more into oblivion. Winter opened his mouth and let the cum coat his tongue. Colton watched, panting and amazed, as Winter stood, framed his face with his hands, and kissed him, forcing him to taste himself. And he did so with a growling moan.

He had never felt so intoxicated. So crazed with desire like he was for this man. He feared the intensity of it as his heart thudded wildly in his chest.

"You've ruined me," Winter rasped quietly, stroking the side of his face affectionately.

The younger man shivered in his arms, panting. "I think that's my line."

He smirked. "I'll never want anything but your body—you mouth—your perfect ass."

Colton dropped his head onto his chest, exhausted. "I need to fuckin' lie down before I pass out, luv."

He lovingly toweled them off before practically carrying Colton to bed, and they both fell into a deep sleep in the guest room. Neither of them wanted to go back into Winter's bedroom just yet. Leaving the Ripper and the confession there and closing the door behind them.

He awoke to Colton, his hot, greedy mouth on his cock halfway through the night, sucking him to life, and off went round three.

And damn it, he wanted to go round four this morning, but he knew he had work to do and a Ripper to catch. The game had changed last night—everything had changed. Colton might be okay with putting his life on the line, but Winter wasn't, and he doubted he could change his mind.

Winter was drilling the second hole in his patio wall when he heard the slider open and saw Colton emerge, wearing nothing but a thin pair of gray sweatpants and holding two cups of hot coffee.

"My, my, what a gorgeous view," Colton drawled, staring up at him. Winter was standing on a small ladder, reaching upward, his shirt riding high on his waist.

He finished drilling the hole, shooting him a hard look over his shoulder. Colton set down the two coffee cups on the patio table, making a show of stretching his lower back. The outline of his semi-hard cock pressed into the thin material.

"Sleep well?" Winter asked, trying his damnest not to get distracted as he placed the camera over the pre-made holes.

"Like the dead," Colton murmured. "Possibly the best sleep I've had in years."

He couldn't help but smirk, knowing there hadn't been much sleeping last night.

"Need help?" Colton asked, picking up his cup and taking a sip.

"Sure, I have about three more to go. I already set up five out there," he motioned to the tree line around his house with a hitch of his chin.

"Bloody 'ell, that's a lot of cameras."

"I want to capture every angle. I won't risk your safety for anything less."

Colton's shoulders stiffened, something passing briefly over his expression before he glanced out into the forest. "You went out there alone?"

He motioned to the gun on the coffee table.

"Did you see anything?" Colton asked.

Winter shook his head, "Nothing. The deputies were thorough last night. I swept the forest this morning and didn't see anything. I doubt he would be stupid enough to linger after police showed up."

"Do you really think he's out there watching us?"

There wasn't another house for at least two miles in every direction. It's why he chose the place. The seclusion, the privacy. Now, for the first time since he moved here, it felt too isolated. Too remote. He sighed.

"I honestly don't know. He might be stupid enough to be out there, especially after destroying his precious cameras last night. These," he gestured to the cameras he was installing, "are motion-sensored, so if he decides to get close enough, they should tell us. Jim brought camouflage boxes for them, so they're well hidden. He won't even know they're out there."

Colton handed him the coffee cup. "Take a sip of your morning medicine. I have an idea for the day."

He hesitated, arching an eyebrow, accepting the cup, and sipping—the bitterness mixed with the warmth sliding over his tongue. Colton leaned casually back against the railing of the porch, crossing his ankles, looking almost roguish. Heat spilled into his veins at the powerful sight of Colton's tanned body, lean and hard, on display for him. Because it *was* for him. The challenging glint in those blue sparkling eyes told him so.

Last night may have changed their relationship, but not the reason Colton was here. They were going to catch this evil son of a bitch—together.

"I'm listening," Winter said, stepping down from the ladder, maintaining his calm despite the spike in his pulse.

"I brought my mum's old laptop, the one she used in her investigation of the second Ripper."

Surprised, he felt his throat tighten, and he swallowed another sip of coffee, concealing his reaction in reference to his mother.

"She had a lot of information on there, and I think if we look over it together, it might help," Colton offered.

"You didn't look at her research yourself?" he asked curiously. He already suspected the answer from what Colton had already told him. That he avoided delving into the investigation of the other Ripper, focusing instead on healing himself and what he went through, made logical and emotional sense. Why dig up the past and risk not finding an answer, maybe even adding to the trauma around it? It was a risk for Colton to reopen this wound. He couldn't blame him for avoiding it all this time.

"To be honest—I never wanted to until now." Colton raked his hand through his dark blond hair, exhaling. "I want to stay here today, do this with you. Put our heads together and figure this evil fucker out. And then... when we need a break..." his eyes trailed over his body with the most insolent, slow smirk. "You can fuck me into another coma."

His heart leapt at the allure and excitement of getting to have him again because all he craved, other than catching the Ripper, was the man standing across from him, looking good enough to eat for his morning breakfast. Winter was well-experienced in lustful thoughts and urges with his sexual conquests. Except Colton was something he'd never experienced before. He felt consumed and damn near blinded, because that was the truth; he was crushing hard.

And Winter had always been so careful when it came to exposing his heart, until now.

"I also think we should go to the Heroes in the Park tonight, as each other's dates. Keep the ruse going that we started last night, send the fucker into a tail spin," Colton said, pulling Winter's thoughts sharply back to the present.

He carefully set his mug down. "It's dangerous."

"His last victim practically *was* me, Winter. Same height, same build, tattoos, blond. He's got a type—me. And after our show last night, he's raging and wanting to punish me."

Winter knew all this, and yet hearing him confirm it only set his teeth on edge. He scrubbed his fingers over the tight scar tissue along his jawline and over the stubble of his cheeks.

"Or me," Winter countered.

Something passed over the younger man, and he averted his gaze back to the woods. He knew that their performance for the Ripper last night had cost Colton and him dearly—the confession had been real. When he woke up this morning, he couldn't stop thinking about it.

"I may not be able to protect you," Winter admitted, trying to regain control of his stupid, fluttering heart.

Colton scoffed, unconvinced.

He pressed on, "I'm compromised, Colton. We've slept together, and I may be distracted on our pretend date."

"There won't be anything pretend on my end, darling." The sunlight dazzled over Colton's form, the soft rays shining on his face, warming him, holding him.

"You know what I mean," Winter snipped irritably.

"How 'bout you spell it out for me?"

He bit back the urge to sigh. "You are blinding to be around. And other than my dick getting hard whenever you're fuckin' near, I'm expected to somehow function in public, kissing you, pretending to date—whatever the hell that means. While also protecting you?"

"So don't pretend," Colton whispered, flicking his tongue over the rim of his coffee mug, blue eyes dancing. "Be yourself. With me. Kiss me when you wanna kiss me, touch me when you wanna touch me."

Winter inhaled tightly, feeling that swoop in his stomach at the mere idea. He never desired to woo the men he fucked before, because he never had to. Sure, he'd cook breakfast on occasion, but most of the time, he left—or they did before anything resembling a relationship took shape.

Colton may have been infuriating and challenging at times, but why did the prospect of dating sound so—what? Winter paused, assessing his feelings and realizing in that moment, he was scared. Afraid of starting something deeper—something real with Colton, even if it was to lure out the Ripper.

"Let him see how much you like touching me. Taking me..." Colton relaxed his posture as he set down his coffee, slipping his hands free and onto the railing behind him, looking tantalizingly sexy. "Show him and the world what I am to you."

His head cocked to the side, heat racing through him. "And what's that?"

"Yours."

Winter knew it was reckless, knew he should've stayed away, but the open invitation that Colton was giving him was impossible to ignore.

The cameras around the house hadn't been turned on yet, and the ones around the forest were motion sensors within a few yards, so nothing was watching them—that he knew of.

He slowly approached him, listening to the quick intake of breath as he stroked his knuckle down Colton's stomach, feeling him shiver at his light touch.

"You came out here dressed like this because...?" Winter grated out, intentionally invading his space, forcing him to look up at him with that thrilling glint in those pale blue eyes, sparkling in the morning sunlight.

Colton's stomach muscles quivered beneath his touch. "You're the detective, you tell me."

Winter slowly trailed his knuckles further down, edging the waistline of Colton's sweatpants, his own cock stirring restlessly in his jeans as he fingered the outline of his cock through the thin material and nearly groaned, feeling Colton come to life with a simple touch.

"To punish me..." he hissed, softly stroking him.

Colton sucked in a breath, tilting his hips upward, but keeping his hands secured to the railing behind him. It reminded Winter of the bar balcony and how much he wanted to touch him just like this.

"You left me in bed, all alone," Colton rasped. "Hard as a fucking cinder block, without a thing to do about it."

Winter opened his hand and palmed the stiffening cock over the sweatpants, watching Colton's reactions of pleasure and urgent need flash across his handsome face.

"I want you to fuck me out here," Colton said, surprising the hell out of him.

Winter stilled. "Out of the question."

"Why not?"

"You know why."

"I'm not afraid of him."

"I know you're not, but that's not the point."

"We could end this all right now. No more kidnappings—no more killings. Send him in a fit of fuckin' rage, Winter. Fuck me, claim me, make me groan your name so he can hear it."

His heart raced, knowing this crossed so many lines, so many things—and yet—and yet...

Colton reached for him, and Winter blinked, letting it happen, letting Colton draw out his thick, heavy cock from his jeans and thumb the leaking, aching tip. He gritted his back molars, refusing to do something so blatantly reckless. Colton roughly thumbed him, biting his lower lip, beautifully needy. He wavered, releasing a hard breath. This man would be the death of him, he thought.

"One condition," Winter managed out, knowing this was stupid—so fucking stupid.

Colton hummed, swallowing, excited.

"Don't undress," he ordered roughly. "Come in your sweatpants and hide your face when you do. I don't want him to see you break. That's my privilege."

Colton's eyes widened, and he nodded. "What if he isn't out there?"

"He probably isn't. But do it anyway."

Winter spun him around, bracing his hands on the railing, spreading apart his legs with the swift kick of his boots. Colton complied easily, eager and ready to please.

Goddamnit, this is so fucked. So wrong.

Winter stepped back, leaning Colton's hips downwards, giving him plenty of space to hang onto the rails and also cover his face when he climaxed.

He carefully lowered his sweatpants, barely revealing his perfect, tight, muscled ass, grazing his fingers between the cheeks, and moaning at the slippery feel of lube waiting for him.

"You fucking brat," he hissed, fingering his slick entrance, hating how hard he got from Colton's game—a game he clearly just won.

Colton let out a breath, already trembling with need.

Winter reached around, slipping his hand beneath the sweatpants, grasping him from root to stem, his erection incredibly hard. Colton pressed his face into his upper arm, already tensing. "Winter..."

He fingered his entrance with his other hand and hesitated. "Are you sore?"

"Fuckin' 'ell, I swear to god...!" Colton pushed backward onto his fingers demandingly.

Jaw clenching, Winter positioned himself behind the younger man, slipping the head of himself at the entrance and groaning at the feel already. The smell of forest and coffee breathed into his lungs as he inhaled sharply upon thrusting forward, deciding that a slow, torturous, tender fuck was precisely what he intended to give his demanding brat. He thrusted into him and stilled. Colton groaned, tensing against him, and he attempted to draw back, but Winter squeezed his fingers over his hip, keeping him perfectly still.

"Don't stop," Colton whispered. "Please. Please..."

The younger man squirmed against him, letting out a hiss through his teeth. He was sore, and Winter sucked in a tight breath, not wanting to hurt him. But this was what he wanted, and the safe word was always something he could use when it got too much. And after last night, and now this, Winter wondered how far he could push him—how much he could take.

Christ.

Winter slipped almost all the way out and then thundered back inside, causing Colton to cry out, his grip on the railing making the wood crack. The tightness of Colton's body around him, the heat of him, and the sexy, breathless sounds he made, heated his blood like a volcano. He wanted to roar and howl at the fucking moon.

It felt primal what they were doing—wrong, but somehow right.

He reared back and slammed home, again and again, obliterating them both. Colton took the pounding as he clutched the railing, his head ducked, face concealed. Winter was so distracted by the feel of him that he forgot Colton's cock was in his hand and started pumping beneath the sweatpants. Colton let out a stream of angry curses through his teeth as Winter dragged the skin up and down roughly before Colton gasped, seconds away from climax.

Winter stared into the forest, into the soul of the woods, into his home, and claimed what was his. It was the most basic, animalistic fuck of his life, and he ripped away the control he had so rigidly maintained and thrusted and pumped and grasped his hip hard, thrusting so deeply, he touched serenity.

His climax was a tidal wave of devastation, flooding through his limbs as he spurted his seed inside him, filling him to the brim. It was then that he felt Colton's shuddering peak, his face turned downward, whimpering, climaxing hard in his sweatpants.

After several long moments, Winter slowly eased out of him, and Colton straightened, still clutching the railing for support of his wobbly legs.

His chest heaved at the sight of how thoroughly ruined Colton looked, and it was stunning. He grasped the side of his face, forcing his lips hard over his, dominating, claiming, devouring.

Colton collapsed into him, supplicant and perfect, melting like hot butter in a frying pan. Winter took his time with it, tasting and tonguing his mouth, leaving him weak and useless to the onslaught.

Fuck, Winter thought, as his cock somehow twitched again at how much he liked this—the thrilling wildness filtering through his blood-stream and the intoxication of his sweet mouth, open and giving, all resistance gone. His fingers raked into the back of his hair, his other hand pinning Colton against the railing as he kissed and sucked and bit the side of his neck.

Colton had created a monster—a hungry wolf out of him, and he never felt so wild in his life. Colton clung to him, letting him feast.

"Good boy…" Winter licked the bruising, sensitive flesh of his neck.

Colton arched against him, fingers digging into his back, his breath coming out in short bursts. He growled, pushing his neck back, drop-ping his kiss lower to his nipple, drawing the fine tip into his mouth and greedily taking. He finally pulled back, opened the slider, grabbed his gun off the porch table, and led them back inside, locking the slider behind him.

Aftercare for Colton would have to be different and more thoughtful, he decided, and without a word, he led him to the bathroom and turned on the faucet of his jacuzzi tub. After a few minutes, Colton slipped into the hot water, releasing a relaxed sigh. Winter turned to leave when he felt Colton reach for him, capturing his wrist.

"Stay."

He looked down at him, his body encased in the bubbling water, looking utterly spent. He had never seen Colton so still—so at peace. The man seemed to be a constant raging star, or a flickering defiant one. And he had a feeling that Colton's current state had a lot to do with him.

He swallowed the lump of emotion clogging his throat, liking the contented expression on his lover's face far to fucking much. "Are you sure? I was going to make us breakfast."

Colton's fingers squeezed, "I'm sure, luv. Now get in."

Winter did, removing his clothes and slipping into the tub, gathering Colton into his arms and trailing kisses along the side of his neck as the young man sank into him. Silence held them for a long time before Colton hummed, "I'm gonna fall asleep in this amazing fuckin' tub. Talk to me, eh?"

Winter released a long breath, deciding once more to be completely transparent, just not about his complicated feelings yet. "How should I take care of you?"

"Aren't you?" Colton drawled lazily.

He ignored this, "What do you like?"

"What do you mean?"

He shifted his legs beneath the water, accommodating more of Colton's body against his, liking how well they fit together. "Aftercare."

"Aftercare?"

"Sex—after sex. After I..." Winter trailed off.

"I've never been asked that," Colton finally replied.

He growled disapprovingly, "You should've been."

Colton chuckled, "There you go being perfect again. Stop it."

"You've dated idiots."

"I have," Colton murmured, pulling Winter's hand from beneath the water and draping it along his chest. "And you've fucked a lot of brats."

Winter tensed and sighed, "Does that bother you?"

"No," he said without hesitation. "I like that you're experienced. Your confidence is fucking astounding, and I love it. I didn't realize how much..." He stopped and cleared his throat. "So, aftercare..." he tapped his fingers into Winter's forearm, contemplating, the same way he did the lighter. "You can make me your famous hot chocolate."

Winter paused, frowning. He hadn't made any hot chocolate since Colton's arrival, so how did he know about that?

Colton tilted his face back and glanced up at him, smiling incredulously. "That night, *the* night we found each other, you made me hot chocolate, don't you remember?"

He blinked and shook his head, "I guess not."

He snorted, "Figures. You blew a man away and twenty minutes later, I had a steamy hot cup of chocolate in front of me, with fuckin' marshmallows and cinnamon sprinkled on top."

Winter couldn't help but chuckle, his hand stroking the side of Colton's stomach. "It's so automatic. I don't even think about it anymore. I usually make it every night for myself."

Colton hummed, leaning back against his shoulder. "You haven't made it since I've been here. How come?"

Heat spread over his cheeks, slightly embarrassed. "It's for kids."

"It's for everyone," Colton corrected gently. "And I happen to love it, too. So, on early nights, when we still have time, and I'm not unconscious from whatever it is you've done to me, you'll make us some, all right?"

Unexpected emotion swept through him, and he nodded. Colton lifted his hand to his lips and kissed him. The final stone around his heart crumbled to ruin, and he knew, with absolute certainty, he would never be able to let Colton go once this was over.

CHAPTER 21

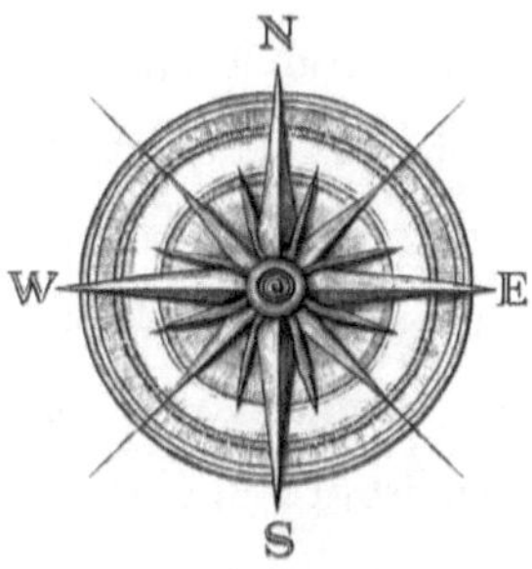

The carnival lights sparkled against the backdrop of the forest and the vast, dark lake beyond. A local cover band played classic rock on an outdoor stage as people danced or walked by with their beer, prizes, or food. Kids ran past, excited and laughing. Couples held hands, and friends gathered in line at the food trucks.

The summer night was warm, with a gentle breeze slipping through the swaying trees around them. Pine, BBQ, funnel cakes, and smoke from a bonfire on the beach filtered through Colton's nose as he took a deep breath, a silly smile dancing on his lips as he watched Winter from a distance. He was standing in front of the dunking booth with Raquel, who was talking animatedly to him as he patiently listened.

Their day had been more productive than they had expected.

His mother's old laptop had plenty of information and was well organized. Her profile of the second Ripper was nearly identical to Winter's. But there had been something in her file notes that had transfixed Colton, while Winter dug through the rest, comparing his notes with hers.

It was a drawing that she had done and scanned onto her laptop. The drawing was of the brand. His brand. The one the Rippers etched forever onto his body. She had drawn it repeatedly, breaking it apart, rearranging it, and even flipping it upside down. Winter had printed it out for him, and the suspect list she created from it. His mother's theory was that the brand was not just a symbol, but a set of letters.

He pulled out the drawing from his back pocket and read her words at the top of the page: "He used the initials of his name—I know it."

On the back of the page, she had made columns of possible initials, breaking them down into a list of names that Winter said she probably got from the county office and had requested for residents. Winter had studied the page too and crossed out a few of the names because they were either deceased, had already been vetted, or didn't exist. Colton's eyes trailed down to the end of the page, where he saw the columns and names continued all the way down, and he wondered if there was a second page she had forgotten to upload.

He folded the page and tucked it back into his pocket, wanting to enjoy the rest of the evening because, to his amazement, they had mainly worked on the Ripper case today. They took breaks to make lunch, walk Frank, and for Colton to get a run in that helped clear his head. There had been a limit to the number of Ripper things he could take.

Winter didn't like the idea of him running through the woods alone, so he went into his study and came back out with a hunting knife that he could strap to his calf.

"I'll look bloody mad," Colton snorted with a laugh at the sight of the thing.

"Take it or I run with you—with my gun."

When he came back less than an hour later, Winter had the security system around his house up and running, streaming it from his laptop to the TV, having watched the forest while Colton had been gone. Winter said nothing upon his return, but he saw the slight flash of relief as he returned to the case files with those incredibly slutty reading glasses framing his face, the hints of gray along the side of his hair and stubbled chin.

It had taken Colton less than a minute to convince Winter to take a shower break with him, and bloody 'ell, he loved getting to lather that man's body with slick, soapy suds.

His hands marveled over the contours of Winter's back and strong arms, through the dusting of hair on his chest that flowed down to his stomach and to the apex of his masculinity. Winter wasn't all hard muscle like Colton was, but he was strong and used his body naturally, keeping him fit and lean. They had kissed lazily under the spray of the hot water, taking their time, exploring each other's bodies.

It had been Winter who suggested giving Colton a break. So instead, they gripped their slick cocks together, working the rigid flesh. The sweet, intoxicating press of Winter's stiff cock against his was invigorating. Their kisses were wild and hot under the water as the tempo of their thrusting became frenzied, before finally they crashed—their sexes erupting at the same time, coating their fists with streaming ribbons of pleasure.

Winter sighed, dropping his forehead into his, saying nothing, simply holding him. So much had been said last night, and Colton appreciated Winter for not bringing up his confession when they had danced for the Ripper.

Ever since those words were spoken, Colton had known he was lost to him.

Winter had always been the one.

It took him ten years to stop running from the truth to see it. Colton expected to be more upset at himself for falling in love all over again. But surprisingly, he wasn't. He simply wanted to enjoy this moment, because it was fucking fleeting, and possibly the only time he would ever get to be with him. He wouldn't dwell on a future he couldn't control. Not now.

Colton paid for his beer at the booth and pocketed the can of soda for Winter when his phone buzzed.

He took a quick sip of the foamy beer from the plastic cup and pulled out his phone, reading that it was Jamie calling. He glanced in Winter's direction and saw that he was now talking to Jim and a few other people, who were more than likely officers too, dressed in casual attire.

"Hey," he answered, excited that she had called.

Her voice was bright with the same excitement. "Hey, right back at you, stranger. Where have you been?"

"Sorry I haven't called," he replied. "It's been busy here."

"I figured as much. How's it going?"

"Honestly, I don't even know where to begin." He knew if he started this conversation with her, everything would come spewing out.

"Tell me *how* you are at least," Jamie demanded in an almost motherly way.

He smiled, his gaze flickering back to Winter, and his heart squeezed when he saw those dark, nearly black eyes watching him. He shot him a wink, taking another sip of his beer and licking the foam off his upper lip. Winter's eyes narrowed a fraction, staring hungrily at his lips, heat spilling into his limbs instantly.

Fucking hell.

"I'm good," Colton responded, sucking in a breath, ignoring the tingle at the base of his spine.

"Really?" Jamie asked, sounding surprised.

"Really," Colton confirmed. "Superman's letting me crash at his place."

She gasped, "...and?"

He was grinning now, a blush creeping up the back of his neck toward his ears. "He's fuckin' perfect, Jamie."

She made a squeeing sound over the phone. "I knew it! Are you guys like—together?"

"We're out on our first official date right now, actually," Colton replied, trying hard not to gush.

"Then why the hell are you talking to me?" Jamie chided. "Get back to Mr. Perfect and call me when you can—I need to know everything. And I'm telling Tess."

He chuckled, "Sounds good. Talk soon."

"I love you, stay safe, please."

"Always, and I love you more."

"Impossible," she murmured and hung up.

Winter left the group and walked his way, as couples and people streamed past him, all eager for the next game. Colton slid his phone away and pulled out the soda from his pocket, handing it to him.

"Thanks," Winter said, studying him. "Who were you on the phone with?"

"Jamie, my bestie."

Winter nodded, looking thoughtful and oddly quiet.

"So, when's splash time?" Colton asked teasingly.

"About an hour," Winter cleared his throat, looking suddenly nervous. "Would you like to walk around a bit? Maybe play a couple of games?"

Stunned, Colton stared at him, knowing how difficult that was for Winter to ask. "That would be lovely."

They strolled through the event grounds, taking in the vendors and ambiance. Colton saw the massive line forming for the beer booth and glanced over at Winter. "I never asked you why you don't drink."

He shrugged, "It's complicated, and I sorta have two reasons for it." Winter sipped his soda, his face illuminated by the sparkling lights.

"I'm all ears," Colton insisted.

Winter dragged in a long breath. "The first reason is my sister. She died when I was ten in the same car accident that gave me this," he gestured to the scar along his neck and lower jaw. "Drunk driver. We were T-boned by a construction truck carrying sheet metal and tools. One of the pieces came through her window, hitting her first and then me."

Colton stared at him, a painful jolt shocking the tendrils of his heart. "Jesus, Winter. I'm so sorry."

He kept his gaze fixated on the crowd, "me too. She was only five. The only good thing in my life after our mother ran out on us."

Colton wanted to comfort him and had the urge to slip his fingers into his, but didn't, knowing this story was more important than whatever comfort he could give.

"That accident was also a big reason why I wanted to be a cop. The police officers there that night truly cared. I felt it, even with my injuries. Everyone at the hospital, too—the surgeons, doctors, and nurses. I knew then and there I had to be one of them. At ten, I didn't know much about myself yet, but the idea stuck. It wasn't until high school that I figured it out. Wasn't quite smart enough to be in the medical field, but I had one thing that stayed with me since the accident."

Winter turned and unexpectedly smiled at him. "Moral fiber. A school counselor told me that. That I had a strong trigger around social injustice and inequality, which was a fancy way of sayin' I didn't like things being unfair. So I became a cop. The rest is ancient history."

Colton arched his eyebrow, "What's the other reason?"

Winter tossed his soda into a recycling bin, the lines around his lips tightening. "The drunk driver who killed my sister was our father."

"Bloody hell."

"My father was a horrible drunk and a horrible man. I don't drink because of him—because of what happened to my sister." The festival lights illuminated over his stoic features, and Colton couldn't help but let his gaze linger over the scar along his jawline.

"The court decided that my grandparents were a better option than foster care. After my surgery, I came here. And I've lived here ever since." He glanced beyond the bustling crowd to the lake nestled quietly in the background of the carnival. "The night we first met, that cabin had belonged to my grandparents. They passed away when I was in college. I hadn't realized how much I missed the forest—the quiet. Or the dark, for that matter. I could barely see the stars in the city. I eventually moved back, spent a few more years ranking up here, and had just made detective when the North Tahoe Rippers started."

Colton stopped dead in his tracks, lips parted in surprise. "The Rippers was your first case?"

Winter nodded bleakly, "I had some experience and wasn't the lead on the case, but yeah. It was."

"Why didn't you ever tell me?" he asked, unexpectant anger swelling inside him that he couldn't explain.

He raked his fingers through his salt and pepper hair, expression strained. "I was ashamed I could never figure out who the second Ripper was. I still feel like I failed you somehow."

The anger broke into thousands of pieces in his chest, and he reached for him, grasping his fingers hard, wanting to step into the shelter of his protector's arms, but didn't. "I would've understood. It was your first bloody case, Winter. And besides, once my father got involved, well, all hell broke loose."

"You couldn't control that," he murmured, squeezing his hand. "Your father is a powerful and important man. Of course the world turned its head when something happened to his son." Winter glanced down at their intertwined fingers and hesitated. "I tried to see you..."

Surprised, Colton's chin jerked up as though he'd been punched.

"You tried to see me? When?"

"A year after it happened," Winter admitted roughly. "Your mom said you were in Santa Cruz at a weekend retreat for trauma work. I drove out there. I wanted to see if you'd talk to me, let me reinterview you."

"Why didn't you?"

Colton remembered that retreat and certainly would've remembered Winter had he seen him. It had been one of the better ones his father had insisted on, and he had been alone for the first time after the assault, minus the security team his father had bought for the weekend.

That's when his nightmares started, and when he realized being alone scared him more than it should.

"Couldn't get past the security detail," Winter said with an exhale. "Or your father."

Colton let out a fuming curse. His father loathed the Tahoe Sheriff Department and everyone there, even the man who saved his son's life. He blamed them for the media frenzy, believing they revealed Colton's identity to the press. It wasn't until years later that they discovered it had been a nurse at the hospital where Colton had been recovering who had been paid handsomely by a tabloid journalist for the information.

"But I did anyway," Winter continued, surprising him. He shot him a quick look, eyes widening. Winter's hand traced upward, trailing over his arm, seeming lost in memory. "I saw you. You had slipped past your own security detail and went for a run in the fucking woods." He shook his head. "I nearly ran in after you, but instead I waited. You came back out, unscathed, and I... I couldn't. You were glowing like the damned sun, and there was no way in hell I was gonna take that from you. I couldn't drag you back into the dark. I couldn't..."

"Winter..." Colton felt his throat ache with emotion.

It was Winter who stepped closer now, pulling Colton behind one of the food trucks and a deserted vendor supply area that was tucked out of the way.

"What happened between us ten years ago..." Winter breathed. "That night... I felt it too."

Colton sucked in a breath.

"When I saw you," he whispered. "All I wanted to do was—" Winter closed his eyes, scrubbing his hand over his face. "Fuck, I—I wanted to hold you again. I wanted to be needed by you. I knew it was wrong, and that's why I had to leave."

The tidal wave of regret and anger slammed into him, knowing that ten years had been lost because neither of them had the courage or willingness to leap to get out of their own fucking fear. Jaw clenching in fury, he reached for him, pulling him down for a scorching, furious kiss. Winter trembled against him and returned the kiss with equal fury.

His heart melded into his—his soul sparked, shook, and surrendered. This was love.

It had always been love.

Colton broke the kiss, tasting him on his tongue and staring into those eyes that haunted his dreams for the last ten years. "This was never fucking wrong." He stroked his hand across the scar, studying him, imagining Winter at the retreat, lost as much as he had been.

"We are all lost souls in the end," Colton heard himself say, the words tumbling out of his mouth the way they used to when he was young and free to be the poet he thought he was. "Neither here nor there. Neither wanted, but certainly haunted. Lost to the whims of the world and the fury of the sea. Lost souls that found each other in the dark." Their gazes fixed and held. "I'd find you in the dark. Always and forever. Lost and discovered, again and again. Our souls are bound to be found and lost again."

Winter tilted his head, surprised. "Your mother once told me you were a poet."

Colton shrugged, "I used to be a lot of things, a poet is not one of them."

"You have a gift."

"I make words sound silly when strewn together in a certain way, that's all. Nothin' fancy. Now," he said brusquely, tamping down the wildfire pulsing through his veins. "Let's attempt to be fuckin' normal and play one of these games, because I need to kick your perfectly smooth ass at something."

Winter chuckled, grazing his fingers over Colton's, before pulling out a roll of tickets from his pocket. "I believe I saw a shooting booth…"

Colton stepped back, resisting the urge to curl into the shelter of his lover's arms, and instead he tossed his nearly full beer into the bin behind him, no longer needing it. "Well, let's go then. And if I win, you gotta give me a prize."

Winter's gaze sharpened as they strolled casually back into the festival. His voice was low and commanding, "Name it."

Colton heard the slight hint of possessiveness in his tone, and his cock twitched. "I want a proper, public, showy kiss."

Winter's eyes dropped to his lips, a blush stealing on his cheeks.

"Are you blushing for me, handsome?" Colton drawled out softly.

"I've never done anything in public before," Winter admitted.

"I figured as much. That first lover of yours sure did put a lot of shame in ya about your sexuality, didn't he?"

Winter stiffened, chest expanding with a quick breath.

"I thought a lot about that story—about what he did to you," Colton murmured. "And I think I know why he hid you from the world." His fingers itched to touch, but he didn't want to push Winter out of his comfort zone too quickly. This was the hard part about being gay—the shame, the looks, the anger of never feeling comfortable being themselves in public like other couples were allowed to be.

"He didn't want you to leave him," Colton said knowingly. "Because he knew that the second you claimed who you are, and left the shame behind, the world would see how incredible you are, and you'd see all that love for yourself."

Winter hesitated, swaying slightly toward him, but still careful not to touch.

"Now, c'mon," Colton headed in the direction of the shooting gallery booth. "Let's have some fun, shall we?"

By the time they had circled back around to the dunk tank, a large crowd gathered, including Meg and a few of her friends, who were hooting and howling for the next dunk-tank victim.

"Shit," Winter muttered beside him.

Colton smothered a laugh, "I think you have fans, Winter."

Meg spotted Winter, and she descended on him with her posse, and he was suddenly being dragged away. Colton laughed as Winter fished out his cellphone and keys and tossed them to him. Colton pocketed the keys and was about to put his phone in his other pocket when he hesitated, watching Winter be pushed behind the heavy curtain, disappearing.

Curious and knowing he was snooping, Colton glanced at Winter's cellphone and clicked the screen back to life, and he froze at the picture on the screen.

It was an image of their coffee cups from this afternoon, sitting on the porch railing, sunlight filtering over them. His pulse leapt as he stared at the brief outline of Colton's side profile, leaning against the railing, looking out over the vast forest, unaware that Winter was taking the picture behind him.

Cheering and applause broke out, and Colton quickly tucked the phone away, the fluttering storm of butterflies converging into a tornado in his stomach.

Winter wasn't the sentimental type when it came to his lovers. He didn't date them, and clearly, from this evening, he didn't even know how to do it without looking ridiculously uncomfortable. But he was trying—for him. And the picture on his phone meant something—more than sex—more than their past.

Colton was tempted to look at the picture again, heart racing, but Winter emerged from behind the curtain, changed into basketball shorts and a plain white T-shirt, giving the crowd a half-hearted smile and slightly pinched expression.

Colton felt a sudden, almost painful sensation in his chest and touched the spot over his heart, digging his fingers into his shirt. Hope and love swirled inside him.

"Honey..." he heard his mother's voice from across the crowd, and he turned instantly, glancing through the busy carnival to catch a glimpse of her.

She wore one of her floppy, cream-colored hats that covered part of her face, a pretty long, brown dress with white polka dots, and wicker sandal wedges, beaming ear-to-ear at him. Miles, her late partner, materialized from the crowd, reaching for her hand. She took it, giving Colton a wink before turning into his arms, and they walked amongst the crowd.

Her words floating past him, "fingers almost touching..."

"Winter!" Meg yelled excitedly. "Detective Eli Winter, everyone!"

The crowd broke out in thunderous applause and Colton jerked his attention back to Winter—their eyes clashed and held. He saw the hint of a challenge there and strode up to Raquel, who clutched the bucket of wet softballs, dancing with delight.

"Colton!" She smiled happily at him. "We already surpassed tonight's donation goal by a thousand! And I had no idea Detective Winter would draw such a crowd!"

Meg overheard Raquel and replied, "He's our local hero! Of course he's big news around these parts, honey. And it does help that he's a looker, ain't that right, ladies?"

The women around her gushed, already pulling out wads of cash for the chance to dunk Winter.

The classic rock band roared back to life, playing "The Stroke" by Billy Squier.

Colton laughed, thinking it was the perfect song for this moment, as he pulled out his wallet to pay Raquel.

"Are you kidding me? You already paid!" She then lowered her voice and said, "We received the donation this morning from—uhm, Lord Stanton."

"Yeah, that was my father's donation. You haven't gotten mine yet." She gaped.

He had texted his father about the charity donation and received a follow-up text asking when Colton planned on visiting him. He responded that he'd come for Christmas and apologized for not reaching out sooner. His father was a good man and tried to be a better father later in his life, however it was difficult for the old-school British aristocrat to connect with him beyond the proper pleasantries of weather and equestrian pursuits.

Raquel handed him the entire metal bucket of softballs and showed him where to stand. Meg patted him roughly on the back as he took the position and set the bucket at his feet, gripping the ball, excitement pooling into his veins.

He glanced over his shoulder to Winter, who was watching him like a hawk.

"You ready to get wet, Winter?" Colton called out.

"I'd like to see you try," he shot back in a mocking tone.

He pursed his lips, locking eyes with the small, round, red-painted metal target in front of a large black net. He understood the basic premise of a dunk tank: hit the target, trigger the platform, and away Winter would splash into a large water tank.

He straightened and made his first throw —the ball slick with water —and slipped wide off the mark, missing.

"Strike one, Colton," Winter taunted, looking bored.

Colton picked up the next ball, "Oh, darling, I plan on being here all night. Don't you fret."

He threw another one.

"Strike two." Winter tsked and the crowd began to cheer him on.

He gritted his jaw, concentrating this time, and threw the ball hard, hitting the target and triggering the platform. Winter let out a surprised curse, and Colton watched with glee as he made a big splash.

The crowd roared.

Winter popped up seconds later, soaking wet, his white shirt plastered to his toned body as he raked both hands through his hair, tossing back the droplets of water and showing off his roping arms while doing so.

Meg and the others behind him swooned loudly and Colton burst out laughing, the music adding to the scene as the band sang: "Stroke me, stroke me! Say you're a winner, but babe, you're just a sinner now!"

"Christ, I need more!" Meg boomed. "Get your sexy ass back up there, Winter."

Winter laughed. It was bright and fast, lighting up his entire face as he pushed up the fallen platform and pulled himself up and back onto the seat. He wiped the water from his face, grinning at the crowd.

"Ready?" Colton asked him over the noise.

Winter looked him dead in the eyes, playful and heady with passion. Colton shivered, his fingers fisting over the softball, desire blistering his blood vessels.

"I'm more than ready," Winter ground out for only him to hear, and his heart took a solid swan dive into his stomach, knowing perfectly well that Winter wasn't referring to the dunk-tank, but something else.

In less than thirty minutes, Winter had been dunked over ten times, Meg being one of them, and a few others from the crowd—including Jim, who smirked proudly when he hit the target. Mal and Patrick even showed up halfway, and Colton held out the dripping wet softball to the couple. Mal waved away the ball to Patrick, who took it with a mirthful laugh, and took his shot at Winter, who had stripped out of his white shirt now and wore only the basketball shorts, looking pleased that his bestie had shown up.

Patrick missed, and the crowd whined.

Mal shot Patrick a stern look, "I will buy every ball here until you sink that man. Now, chop, chop."

In the distraction of Mal and Patrick, Colton retrieved his phone from his back pocket and took a few photos of Winter, capturing the smile and the playfulness of the moment, wanting to hold onto it forever.

A few throws later, Patrick finally managed to hit the target. The metal pinged, and Winter splashed loudly.

The crowd cheered, and Patrick took a bow, kissing Mal's cheek victoriously. When Winter popped up, he spotted the couple, and with a ruthless grin, splashed them. Mal gasped in dramatic outrage, dancing away in his all-white sneakers. "Winter! I swear!"

Colton and Winter laughed.

Raquel took her microphone and announced that Detective Eli Winter had raised the most out of all the dunk tank volunteers for the evening, and a smattering of applause and cheers broke out amongst the festival. Winter waved at everyone and climbed out of the tank, disappearing behind the curtain to change out of his wet clothes.

When he reappeared again in dry clothes, his hair damp and wearing a genuine smile, the crowd applauded again, and he waved politely, almost bashfully. Colton had never seen him like this. Winter was confident in all areas of his life, but when it came to anything public, the man was shy and almost mild-mannered.

Meg hugged him roughly, and a few others from the department did the same. Mal, Patrick, and Colton were waiting for him by the funnel cake food truck. The sweet smell of churros and sugary cakes wafted over them.

Winter locked eyes with them and sauntered over.

"The man of the hour," Patrick said, clasping a hand over his shoulder. "Nice work."

"Thanks," Winter replied, smiling.

"More like thirst trap of the month," Colton drawled lightly, yet his blood roared in his ears. Seeing Winter like this —relaxed, having fun, and with those very heated looks throughout had Colton nearly dancing out of his skin.

Winter moved, hauled him against him, and planted a ferocious kiss on his lips. It was stunning and perfect, and so fucking sweet. His tongue pushed through his lips and claimed Colton right there, in the middle of the festival, like a conquering hero.

Colton swooned. His mother would be so proud.

When Winter finally pulled back from the heated kiss, Colton could only stare, dumbfounded and shaking with need.

"Let's go home," Winter said.

Colton nodded weakly, too astonished to even say goodbye as Winter did it for them, leaving the carnival with his hand wrapped firmly in his.

CHAPTER 22

He maneuvered the truck out of the parking lot and onto the empty road heading home, still smiling. Watching Colton break out in a victorious smile and bark of laughter whenever Winter splashed into the tank had been the highlight of his evening.

"That was fun," he murmured, taking his hand into his.

Colton twirled his fingers through Winter's, "You were brilliant."

"I just sat there."

"And looked awfully pretty doing just that." Colton raised their joined fingers and kissed them. He tried hard not to stare at those lips and focus on the road. They had plenty of time the rest of the evening for him to take what belonged to him.

Mine. Forever.

"Did you like your prize?" he asked huskily, drawing their joined hands to his lips, dragging Colton across the dark interior of his truck.

"Yeah," Colton managed out, softening against him. "You didn't have to do that, you know."

He kissed lazily across the back of Colton's hand, unable to stop touching him. "I know. I wanted to." He liked this. He liked feeling Colton pressed against his side, his soap-and-musk scent tantalizing his nose. "Can I ask you something?"

Colton glanced curiously at him through the dark confines of the truck.

"Not to dampen the mood," he began, suddenly unsure if it was even okay to ask such a thing. "How is it you're still so—I dunno, okay? I don't think anyone tonight would've ever guessed you survived the North Tahoe Rippers."

Colton leaned heavily back against the seat, keeping their fingers locked together. "Just because someone is smiling, doesn't mean they're okay."

Winter tightened his grip.

Colton sighed, "Most days—good days like these, yeah, I'm okay. Some days, well, I'm back in that fucking room, chained to the bed with no way out. Triggers are funny that way. I sometimes struggle to control how I react or when I experience a flashback. But..." he hesitated. "I accepted what happened to me. And I accepted who I've become because of it. Do you remember the three things I couldn't compromise with?"

Winter nodded, "Yeah. You never told me the third one."

"When I went back to London, I didn't want to do much—things I used to like. Dad tried everything. Finally, one day, his driver—a big fella, built like a fucking rhino—told my dad about a gym he went to and suggested it to me. It was a boxing gym, full of hard, hard men. At first, I was intimidated, scared even. But my dad pushed me, and thank fuck he did, because the first time I learned to throw a punch and laid into one of those bags, I broke down."

He shook his head, lost in memory, "And all those hard men, they knew. They knew my story, had seen it on the news, knew who I was. And they didn't care. In fact, they were the ones who taught me to take all my pain and put it here," he raised his free hand and fisted it tight. "I went to my therapy, I worked, and I learned to fight. I learned to let go.

But I couldn't let go of the rage—the anger that sank its teeth into me because of them."

Winter felt his own anger rise, but he was careful not to show it as he listened.

"I'd get triggered in a fight, and that anger would knock someone's tooth out—or I'd go until my hands bled or I broke some poor bloke's jaw. It took years to calm down. But it never went away... My anger may never leave me. And I'll warn you now, if I ever get the opportunity with the last Ripper, I will unleash my rage and finish what we started that night in the woods. I will kill him and show no mercy when I do it."

Winter felt the darkness and weight of his words and believed him. He lifted their joined hands and kissed him. "I'll need to get you a punching bag then."

Colton's fingers tightened around him. "Don't make promises you won't keep, Winter."

He knew he was referring to more than a punching bag—but a future. Because he was, and that scared and excited him.

Colton's phone vibrated loudly, and he let out a sigh as Winter released him. He pulled his phone out of his pocket and sent a text. "It's my dad," he informed him. "Wants to know if I want to do Christmas in Italy this year."

He hummed, "Sounds nice."

"It is. Florence has an incredible Christmas market. Not a lot of tourists that time of year either, it's like you have the city to yourself." Colton put his phone away and turned to look at him. "You should come with me."

Winter's stomach swooped as though he were standing at the edge of a cliff. "You want me to?" he asked quietly.

"Only if you want to," Colton said just as quietly.

He cleared his throat, though it sounded like he gurgled nails when he spoke. "I've never been to Italy. I've always wanted to go. Never seemed to find the time."

"Or maybe the right person to go with?"

Winter reached for Colton's hand once more. "Yeah, that too."

After a long minute, the dark woods in front of them were illuminated by the truck's headlights as he navigated the winding road home. Colton finally said, "Say you'll come with me."

Winter squeezed his fingers, heart beating too quickly. Maybe it was the fun from this evening, something he hadn't felt in a long time—well, outside the bedroom—or perhaps it was the darkness suspending and holding them, or maybe it was just Colton.

He pushed his lips once more into their joined hands and nodded. "Yes. I'd love to come with you."

Colton let out the breath that seemed trapped in his chest and sat up, pressing a hot kiss on the side of his neck. Winter's pulse skidded, and desire rose quickly in his body as Colton began to touch him, in the dark, caressing his leg, his side, over the hard muscles of his chest, and lower.

He kept his hands securely locked on the steering wheel, as though with invisible shackles, letting Colton touch and freely explore his body. He leaned his head back against the seat, legs splaying, giving him permission without words. Colton stroked lower, grasping his sex through his jeans, the base of his spine arching into the rough manhandling.

Winter wasn't sure he could focus on the road and knew of a hidden, secluded alcove surrounded by trees where he could park the truck. It would be another twenty minutes home, and there was no way in hell he wasn't going to enjoy this and attempt to drive safely, too.

He was only minutes away from the alcove and felt the urgency in Colton's touch, fingers raking up and over his groin, between his legs, cupping him. He gasped and jerked, and saw the clearing, nearly cursing in relief. He parked the truck and turned off the headlights, letting the night forest blanket them.

Winter reached between the seats and pushed the driver's seat back as far as it would go to give Colton more room to maneuver.

"Take off your jeans," Colton rasped.

He made quick work of it, pulling it down around his ankles, still sitting in the driver's seat, and before he could move, Colton's hands were on him, followed by the heated wetness of his mouth. Winter let out a low moan, dropping his head back and deciding to let go of all control and surrender everything to him.

Everything.

Colton cupped his balls, sucking him down further and further, moving slow and steady, unhurried, as though he wanted to take his time with him. Winter's lungs burned as he tried to inhale enough air. Every little sensation of Colton's mouth on him in the confines of the dark truck was heightened. The sounds of Colton's moans and wet sucks unraveled him, as he bucked beneath him, deepening his sex into his mouth. Colton took it, and Winter did it again.

"Good boy," Winter whispered. "So good for me. And only me…"

Colton hummed, pumping and sucking, licking and grazing his teeth softly over his rigid flesh.

"I love watching you," Winter breathed. "I love feeling you—touching you. God, you're so fuckin' good at this," he praised into a gasp as Colton tongued his tip ruthlessly. Winter slipped his fingers through the golden, dark blond hair at the back of his head and pushed gently, easing himself deeper. Colton bobbed over him, the suckling sounds driving him mad, as the passion and desire pooled in his lower belly, tingling his balls.

"This mouth belongs to me," he husked, getting closer and closer to the edge. "This sweet fucking mouth. Damn, Colton…" he hipped upward, losing himself to the moment. "I love this—I love feeling you next to me—I love...”

"Stop," Colton murmured, withdrawing from him completely, shooting upwards to wrap his hand around Winter's throat, thumbing his open, panting mouth. "You say that word again, and I'll be forced to fuck you in this truck, Winter." He speared his thumb ruthlessly into his mouth, and Winter sucked hungrily, sparks lighting behind his eyes at the idea of Colton doing precisely that.

"Love," he grated out, challenging Colton, and he watched, in the dim light of the truck, his eyes burn with that fire—that anger and heat.

Christ, he was fucking beautiful.

Colton abruptly pushed open the passenger door and climbed out. "Come here," he commanded.

Winter did so, swallowing hard, sliding across the seat, and with Colton's help, he pulled off his boots and jeans. He reached between his naked legs and stroked his cock upward, the harsh tension of desire pulsating between them.

"Get out," Colton said, jaw twitching.

Winter stared, arching an eyebrow, stroking lazily on his cock one more time, before he got out, standing at the open truck door, wondering if Colton knew how sexy he looked—with the taunt need etched over his face.

"You're so goddamned beautiful, Colton," Winter murmured. The younger man sighed and cursed before launching himself onto him, their lips clashing together, all teeth and tongue. Colton suddenly stopped the angry, passionate kiss and turned him around, pushing him face down into the passenger seat, his hands stroking and palming his ass.

Every touch. Every trembling breath echoed through Winter's soul, imprinting on him.

Winter shook when he felt Colton's fingertips graze over his entrance, and his cock twitched eagerly. He heard the telltale sounds of spit and felt the moisture slick his skin. Winter reached between his legs and grasped his cock at the thick base, stroking upward, hissing out as Colton pushed slowly into his entrance, preparing him.

Colton widened the tight hole and slid in another finger, causing Winter to jerk at the pressure, the intrusion. It had been a long time since he allowed a lover to fuck him. In fact, it was something he rarely let his lovers do and couldn't remember the last time he had.

Colton's breathing was hard behind him as he withdrew his fingers, and he felt the push of his tip filling him.

Winter tensed and Colton spit again, slicking his shaft and easing slowly into him.

"Fuuuck, Winter!" Colton gasped, keeping himself steady, as though wanting to take his time, despite being on the side of the damned road in the shelter of towering trees. "Fuck, you feel good," Colton groaned, pushing slowly, inch by inch, filling him up before spearing all the way in, touching the sweet spot instantly.

Winter buckled and let out a loud moan into the seat of his truck.

"Bloody fuckin' 'ell," Colton eased out and slid all the way back in, thrusting hard. "I'm gonna come already—you're so fuckin' tight."

Winter felt it, too, the pressure building painfully between his legs as he barely stroked himself, the sensation of falling rapidly over the edge and into nothing but this sensation. Into Colton. He pushed his hips back, and Colton ground out a curse and let loose a wild tempo of thrusts, fucking him hard against the truck, both moaning into the dark of the forest, the sounds of their bodies slamming into one another loud in the quiet.

"Yes, baby," Winter called out, fisting himself, loving the feel of Colton's unhinged, frantic thrusts. "Fuck yes!"

Colton's punishing thrust hit once more, and Winter lost complete control, knees trembling beneath him as he came hard into his hand, soaking himself with so much bliss, he thought it would never stop.

Colton's fingers dug into his hips and he trembled, continuing the pounding. Winter cursed, another wave of an orgasm ripping from him, and he cried out Colton's name. Colton gasped, leaning over him, hands on his body as he convulsed, unloading deep inside him, moaning into his shoulder. Winter felt the tremble of his cock inside him and his stomach tightened. He closed his eyes, savoring it—him.

Colton slowly eased himself out and stumbled, panting. "Fuck, Winter..."

Winter straightened, feeling the ache behind him and the wetness of Colton's bliss, and he turned, grabbing him and kissing him hard but slow. Colton shivered and pulled back, blue eyes sparkling in the dark as he whispered, "I'm not done with you yet."

Surprised, Colton pushed Winter back down into the truck, dropped to his knees and...

Winter's whimpering moan of pleasure sounded almost too much to his own ears as Colton licked his wet entrance, pushing his cum back inside, making Winter quiver and shake.

"That's it, my sexy fuckin' wolf," Colton murmured. "I want you filled with my cum until we get home, and then I'm gonna fuck you again—maybe I'll start with my tongue first. I now understand why you do it so much."

Winter groaned and buried his face in the seat of his truck, smiling.

After several torturously pleasurable minutes, Colton palmed his cheeks, squeezing appreciatively before finally withdrawing, allowing Winter to breathe again.

Colton laughed, it was harsh and almost angry as he stood and slapped his ass cheek hard, sending shockwaves through Winter's body. He did it again and fingered his entrance before turning him around and seeing his erection at half-mast. His eyes flared with desire, but he didn't touch him again, other than to help Winter get dressed.

"I'll drive us home," Colton said.

Home.

Home was wherever Colton was. Colton was a part of him—he even invited him to Italy to meet his father for Christmas. It felt so stunningly simple and easy with him. And he couldn't wait to get home and let Colton finish what he had started.

CHAPTER 23

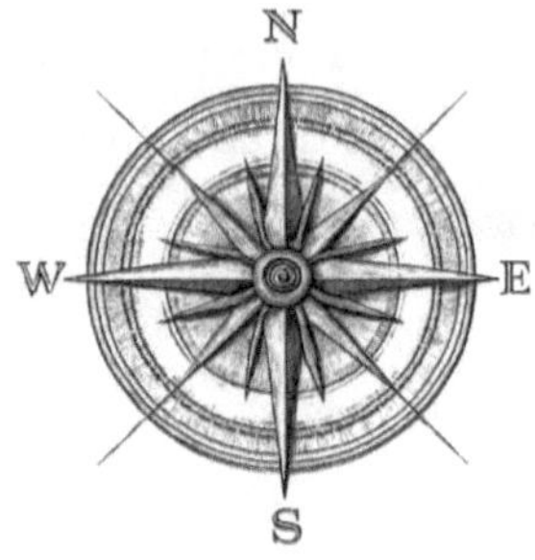

Colton never felt so fucking elated in his life and couldn't help but sit beside Winter, gloating, when he pulled up to his house.

Winter shot him a dark, knowing look across the cab. "What?"

Colton smirked, "Just happy, I suppose."

"About?"

"I just got to live out a lifelong fantasy of fucking you," Colton admitted daringly, unashamed.

Winter's eyes widened and twinkled with amusement.

"I've always imagined fucking you," Colton said as he parked the truck in front of the house, grinning devilishly at him, putting every card on the table now. "So many times and in so many ways, but that—that was better than anything I could have ever conjured up. I think I've become addicted after just one sample, Winter. So, I'm gonna need you naked and ready for me the second that door opens, because I don't intend for this night to be over until I've fucked you proper at least a dozen more times."

Winter laughed, scrubbing a hand over the back of his neck, being bashful again.

Colton leaned forward, sinking his fingers into the whiskered jaw. "I'm happy about that, *and* you agreeing to spend Christmas with me and my dad in Italy. Thank you."

Winter grabbed Colton's hand and moved his open palm to his lips, kissing it. His eyes narrowed, and he stilled. Colton then realized he wasn't looking at him, but at something else. He turned and saw Frank, standing on the front porch, the front door wide open.

His stomach dropped instantly.

Fuck. Not again.

They got out, and Winter reached for the gun he had stashed in the glove box and took the lead. Colton ground his teeth into ash, anger rising to the familiar scene of yet another shit show left behind by the Ripper. He hoped the security cameras caught him this time.

Colton followed close behind, refusing to let Winter confront the Ripper alone. Winter crossed the dark threshold and flipped on the light switch in the hallway. Light flooded the house, and Colton couldn't stop the audible gasp that followed.

Winter's case files on the Rippers were everywhere, strewn haphazardly. And his house...

"Fuck," Colton growled, staring at the ruined mess of Winter's home.

Frank barked at the wreckage of the home.

Lamps were shattered, the dining table had been overturned, and the cabinets had been left open. It looked like a bomb had gone off inside. The couch pillows had been torn open by a knife, and the white stuffing and shredded case files littered the floor.

Winter's boots crunched over glass as he slowly entered, gun out. Colton pulled his phone out of his pocket, having saved Jim's number, and was ready to call.

Winter checked the living room first, then the dining room, and finally the kitchen. He reappeared seconds later, scanning the side patio, clearing the front of the house. Colton began to follow him down the hallway to the bedrooms when Winter froze, flipping on the second set of lights. Colton peeked over his shoulder and saw what looked like handwritten letters strewn up and down the hall.

Winter, for the first time, looked upset but moved forward, stepping on the letters as he went, checking the guest room, bathroom, his office, and lastly, the master bedroom. The bedroom door was left wide open, and what looked like the heel of a boot had smashed it open.

Colton saw him enter, heart hammering. Seconds later, Winter reappeared, gun lowering. The house was empty. The Ripper had done his damage and left. He walked into Winter's room, seeing the fallen vanity, the broken cabinets, and ripped clothing. And the only thing left standing was a note, taped to Winter's bedframe.

In bold black ink, it read: ***Tell Colton the truth, Winter. Or I can the next time he's with me.***

Colton blinked, confused, gut twisting. For some reason, he glanced back at the letters scattered up and down the hallway. Curiously, he bent down and picked up a letter beneath his boot and stared at the familiar handwriting. He heard his mother's voice whisper across his skin and saw her hand grasp over his as he held her letter.

It was a letter from her—addressed to Winter?

"I'm so sorry, my love. I—we should've told you," Her pale hand squeezed his wrist, and she vanished.

An anchor plummeted in his stomach, and he stared blindly at his mother's words on the page.

He suddenly remembered what Jamie had told him about overhearing her talk to someone on the phone in hushed whispers about the case. His mother could barely hold a cup the last few months of her life, let alone a pen. And from the dates that he glanced at as he walked over the letters, there were years' worth of letters from his mother in the hallway, all addressed to Winter.

"We didn't want to hurt you," his mother whispered, and yet he heard Winter's voice, instead. He looked up and saw the anguish and guilt in Winter's expression.

"She wanted to keep working on the case and was insistent on not telling you." Winter's voice was distant and hollow. "She'd write letters of things she found, or ideas—theories…"

Colton stared numbly at the letter in his hand, dated five years ago. And it was all about him—about the job he had just gotten at the YMCA and how happy he was working with young kids. "This is about me," Colton said in a tremulous voice. He flipped the letter around, searching. "There's nothing about the Ripper here."

Winter closed his eyes, ashamed. "Not all her letters were about the case." He scrubbed a hand over his face, "Some were about her—or me—or you. We became friends. I forgot what it was like to have a mother in my life, and she…" His throat bunched. "When she got sick, she couldn't write anymore. So, she'd sometimes call. We'd talk as long as she could. Towards the end, all she could talk about was you. And I let her because I knew she wouldn't let me visit her. She didn't want you to know about this."

"Why?" Colton demanded, tears welling in his eyes.

"She thought she was protecting you from the past. A past that she—nor I could let go of."

"But you did!" Colton protested. "You sent that letter! You closed the case—"

"I was forced to close the case officially, but I never stopped working on it." Winter stepped toward him, and Colton stumbled back, needing distance from him—from this.

Winter stilled, something dangerous flickering over his face. "I've believed you from day one. So did your mom. We did the best we could with what we had, but we never had your full story. We both wanted to protect you until you were ready. But we feared the Ripper would eventually come back."

"That's why you were at her funeral," Colton said, understanding dawning, and bent down once more, collecting another letter. It was one of her last ones from the date at the top. He could see the shakiness of the words and recognized the symbol she had drawn once more, and broken down into parts, on the back, a list of suspects from the letters she had compiled. It matched the one in his pocket, and he folded it and tucked it with the other.

"Why didn't you tell me?" Colton asked. "Were you ever going to tell me?"

Winter hesitated, "I don't know."

The hurt came on swift wings, blowing a storm of rage and pain through him, knotting his guts into tight, unshakable coils.

"You don't know?" he retorted coldly.

Winter shook his head, hand at the back of his neck, remorse tightening around his lips.

"What does it take to earn your trust, I wonder?"

"This has nothing to do with trust," Winter retorted.

"Then what?" he seethed through clenched teeth. "Because right now, I feel like a bloody fool. I've been with you all goddamned week, in this house—in your *bed*..." His words trailed off, and he fisted his hand angrily over the letter. "Do you have any idea what it's been like for me without her? She was the only thing that got me through all of this, and she's *gone*. And you had a part of her here this whole time, and you didn't tell me?"

The tears welled once more, and he turned on his heel and stormed down the hallway and out of the house.

"Colton!"

He ignored him and raced down the steps of the front porch to the truck, flinging the door open and climbing inside.

Winter's hand was on the handle before he could swing it shut. "What the hell are you doing?"

Colton refused to look at him, "I ain't stayin' here. You'll call Jim, and this place will be crawling with cops again. Oh, let's not forget, it's probably loaded with fuckin' spy cameras too."

"Colton..." Winter's voice was laced with something—something heavy and desperate. It set his teeth on edge, and he closed his eyes, feeling his heart flutter like a dying bird against the bones of his chest. Winter crowded the truck's doorframe. "Stay with me, baby...please..."

Colton sucked in a breath at the stinging ache. It nearly rattled his resolve for a split second and he gripped the steering wheel. "Fuck you."

Winter reached across the space between them and captured his chin, forcing him to look at him. He saw the raw emotion etched on the contours of his handsome face and nearly melted against him. "It's safer with me."

"Is it?" he whispered.

"Don't," Winter grunted, fingers tightening around his jaw.

He knew the only way Winter would let him go was to hurt him like he was hurting. "You forced my secret out of me last night. That was *mine*—not yours," Colton hissed. "I tried to convince myself that it was never love. Just fantasy, trauma, delusion. But seeing you again, after all these years, I knew I didn't stand a chance against you."

"I'm sorry."

"I know," Colton said, resisting with every fiber of his being to touch him. He couldn't be drawn back in. "Just let me go."

Winter's hand moved to frame his face, his movements jerky. "I can't."

"You can. And you fuckin' will, cuz I'm leaving."

"I *can't*," he ground out. "I can't lose you again. I won't. I'm *yours*, Colton. Forever, do you understand?"

Colton's heart leapt at the words, and he fisted his hands into Winter's shirt, anger and love rippling through him.

Fuck.

He shoved him hard, then slammed the truck door shut and locked it. Winter stumbled and regained his footing right as Colton reared the truck to life and peeled out of the driveway. He was shaking, tears burning behind his eyes, desperate to get away—and desperate to stay.

CHAPTER 24

He felt nothing but a hollow emptiness rooting him to the spot beside the guest bedroom nightstand, staring blindly at Colton's metal lighter. He traced numb fingers over it. He had left this behind, too.

"Officer Sydney swept the house for cameras, nothing," Jim informed him at the doorway. "She's taking a look at the security footage now to see if we caught him on camera."

Winter slipped Colton's lighter into his pocket and swallowed hard, remembering the hurt on Colton's face when he discovered the letters. But the worst moment wasn't that—it was the way he shoved him away, as though violently needing to get away from him like he was the villain—the bad guy. And he was. He had kept this from him, and he knew it was wrong. He should've told him the truth—should've done it right after they kissed—after they crossed the invisible line that had been between them all these years.

Winter raked a hand over his face, hating himself. Hating that he had no idea where Colton was, and that it was his fault he was out there, at the mercy of the dark, without him. He pushed his fingers into his eyes, needing to find him—needing to keep him safe even if he wanted nothing to do with him.

"Curious, though," Jim said. "No forced entry."

Winter straightened, the fog of his emotions lifting, "What?"

"He might have had a skeleton key, or maybe you left a spare key out that was easy to find? Or lost your keys in the last couple of days?"

Winter shook his head, "I don't have spare keys stashed anywhere." Nor did he ever leave his keys unattended —except just now, when Colton took his truck; only God knows where.

"I wanna see the footage," Winter said thickly.

They headed into the destroyed living room, which the forensic teams had already swept for prints. This was the second time in less than 72 hours that his home was violated. He supposed that was partly his fault. He had, after all, threatened the Ripper over the camera stream the previous night.

Officer Sydney was searching through footage on Winter's laptop, and the second she spotted them, she replayed the hour-long footage of the Ripper arriving at his home. The cameras synced and clicked on the first video, showing a man dressed head to toe in black—a black hoodie and a black face mask—emerge from the woods. Winter stared intently at this man—the Ripper he had hunted for the last decade had finally revealed himself.

A dark thrill leaped into his veins, knowing he was that much closer to his prey.

The Ripper was of average height and build, not stocky or overly fit. He strode confidentially up the steps to Winter's place, seeming to know it was empty, and Winter heard Frank's bark over the camera.

The Ripper pulled a key out of his pocket and opened the door.

He had a key to his home.

Ice filtered through his veins as he stood there, watching the Ripper walk inside. He hadn't thought of putting cameras inside the house, so he didn't see what he had done inside. Officer Sydney sped up the footage to the moment when the Ripper left, and Winter watched as he strode back out into the woods, silent and unearthly like a ghost.

"He had a key to my house," Winter said, unable to hide his fury, and asked Officer Sydney to rewind to the Ripper at his front door, and saw a glint of a silver key in the images. It wasn't a skeleton key—it was a copy of his house key.

"There's more footage of him in the forest," she said, clicking up the images. He glanced at the times the Ripper appeared. It was around the time he and Colton had left for the Heroes in the Park.

"Do you recognize him?" Jim asked.

Winter shook his head.

"We'll have forensics take a closer look at the footage, too, see if they can get more off the feed than we can," Jim said, and spoke to the forensics lead, instructing them to take the laptop with them.

"Where's Colton?" Jim asked, glancing around, as though just realizing he wasn't there.

"He went for a drive," Winter said, sitting down on the edge of the couch that the Ripper hadn't vandalized. Frank trotted up to him, placing his big head onto his knee, looking sleepy.

"A drive?"

"Needed to clear his head," Winter muttered. "So do I, actually. I need—space."

Jim nodded, "I'm leaving a deputy out front this time."

"Fine."

"I want you at the station early tomorrow, yeah?"

"Yeah."

Jim patted his shoulder. "Sorry about your house. You sure you wanna stay here? I can talk to Susan down at the lodge, get you and Colton a couple of rooms for the night."

"Thanks, but it's fine."

"All right, call me if you change your mind." Jim turned and motioned for the rest of the officers and team to leave. Winter heard the door click behind them, not bothering to get up and lock it, knowing—hoping—Colton would return.

He stared into Frank's big brown eyes, scratching the top of his head, wondering what Frank had seen of the Ripper.

Winter's brain whirled, and he leaned forward, thinking about the video footage and how Frank only barked—once.

Once.

Frank was a protective son of a bitch, and sure, he was old, but he highly doubted he'd let anyone inside the home that wasn't someone he already knew.

Frank knew the Ripper.

The Ripper had a key to his house.

They had hoped the Ripper would do something reckless after their performance for him last night, and he had. Winter's heart kicked with sudden adrenaline, his mind racing, and he got to his feet, heading back out to the front porch, where he saw Officer Sydney sitting in her cruiser in his driveway.

"I need a ride," Winter told her. "Do you mind?"

She hesitated, uncertain.

"It's only a couple of miles up the hill," Winter said.

"Sheriff Emerson said I was supposed to watch the house."

"It won't take long."

She sighed and nodded, and he opened the passenger-side door, giving her the directions, his heart hammering in his chest as he reached for the lighter in his pocket, hoping his theory was wrong.

CHAPTER 25

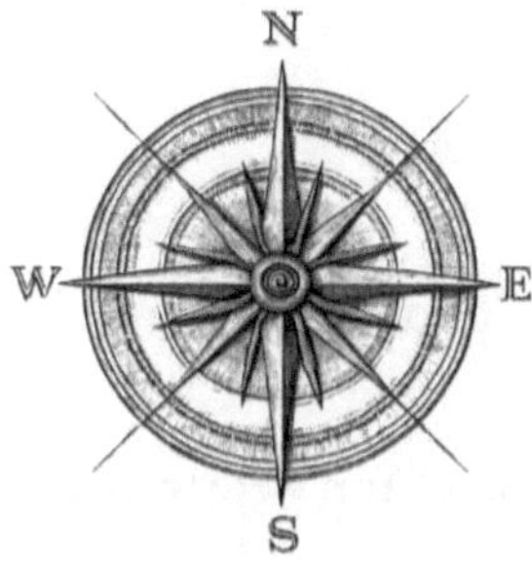

The road wasn't a familiar one, so he had to use his phone's GPS to get there. Once he saw the dirt path of the driveway, he knew where he was going and followed the uneven trail in the truck. He parked a few yards from the old house, not wanting to disturb the current residents.

He had returned to Winter's old cabin.

The place where Barry Pollock lost his life, and the night he found Winter.

Colton pulled the letter and the suspect list out of his pocket, along with his phone, and without overthinking, dialed his first emergency contact number. The darkness of the cab's interior suspended him as he gazed out into the woods, the soft glow of moonlight filtering through the trees. His eyes retraced the path he had stumbled out of all those years ago, seeing the porchlight like a beacon at sea, telling him to come home.

His father's voice was clipped when he answered, "Colton? You're actually calling?"

Colton, unable to fight the emotions clawing at his insides, asked in a strained tone, "Did you know mum kept in contact with Detective Winter?"

His father was silent for a long time before finally saying, "Yes. I knew."

Angry tears welled behind Colton's eyes, "Why didn't anyone fucking tell me?"

He sighed, "It's complicated."

"It's not."

"What do you want, Colton?" his father asked harshly. "The truth?"

"Yes!"

"Fine," he snipped coolly. "You were too delicate after what happened to you that we both decided that if you ever showed interest in talking about it yourself, without a therapist in the room, we would tell you. But you never did. Your silence was something I sometimes blame myself for," he bit out a sigh. "Her friendship with Winter was something I really had no part in. I think she knew it would upset you to know they were communicating. We all knew how much you, well..." he cleared his throat, "...were attached to Detective Winter."

Colton swallowed the ache in his throat, spreading out the letter in front of him, tracing his fingers over the curving letters, wishing he could talk to her, truly talk to her, and hear her explain this all herself.

"She wrote so many letters," Colton said thickly. "Winter kept them."

His father hummed, "She sent me many over the years as well, and I kept mine, too. She was a very special woman." He paused before finally asking, "Do you need me? I can come to Sacramento if you'd like?"

His father never asked him to visit. It surprised him and warmed him. He sighed, wiping the tears off his cheeks with the palm of his hand. Their relationship wasn't exactly estranged, but it was hard because his father was so emotionally closed off.

"I'm in Tahoe," he admitted.

His father sucked in a breath, "Why?"

"He's back, the second Ripper... Mum always knew he'd come back."

"Please, dear Christ, tell me you're with Detective Winter?" his father asked quickly.

Colton pinched the brim of his nose before rubbing an exhausted hand over his face. He called his father for information, that's all. His father lost the privilege of parenting him years ago. "I went for a drive. I needed some air."

"Well, get back to him, right now. I don't like you traveling alone, especially if the second Ripper is still out there."

"I can't."

"Why the bloody hell not?"

"I'm—mad at Winter," Colton admitted, knowing it sounded childish.

His father scoffed, "Why? He did nothing wrong. It was your mother who started it. I recall several instances where Detective Winter tried to stop writing to her. She'd work herself into a tizzy, calling me upset. She hounded that man into partaking in her obsession with the case, and he would always come back around. She was a hard woman to say no to."

Colton felt the band around his chest ease somewhat, not wanting to continue being upset at either of them. Because the truth was, his father was right.

Every time his mother tried to talk to him about the case, he'd shut her down, refuse to talk or listen. Colton had spoken to all those bloody specialists, working on his trauma. But mostly, he didn't want to hurt her by telling her the truth—the full story of what happened to him, because when it came to his mother, he was a coward. Her pain intensified his. He felt her energy and love so profoundly that he would know instantly if she was hurting. And he couldn't bear it. He loved her so much that he thought saying nothing would protect them both.

It made sense that she felt compelled to reach out to Winter. She had to talk to someone —and why not to the man who knew almost the whole story and was even part of it.

If Colton didn't fault his mother, what about Winter? Could he forgive him so easily? Winter's words came hurtling back, *"I never really had a mother..."*

Fuck. A painful tear ripped from his heart and sent him reeling back in his seat, feeling the loss in Winter's admission as well as his own grief. How could he be mad at him for seeking solace in his mum?

"She could've told me," Colton managed weakly.

His father hummed. "She wanted to, many times. But she didn't want to upset you, son."

"From what?"

"More heartache, I suspect," his father said gently.

He pondered this, letting his head thump back against the driver's seat, breathing in the scent of musk and pine. He had needed space from Winter, and yet, everything reminded him of him. It didn't help that he had borrowed his truck without asking, and he would later apologize for the theft.

Winter's touch was ingrained on his flesh, his kiss imprinted on his soul, and he needed him in ways that startled him. Colton wanted to be angry, but he couldn't. Winter had never given up on the investigation, and he had let Colton believe he had, due to his mother's insistence on not telling him the truth. And for Winter's own selfish reasons for maintaining the relationship, having a mother again.

Colton couldn't blame Winter for needing that—needing her. He had conjured up the vision of her mere months after her death, unable to cope with the loss.

He was suddenly grateful that his mother had gotten to know the man he loved, even if she never got to see them together.

Colton stared at her words on the letter—the symbol and the suspect list, and his eyes stopped on a column with the initials: ML.

"Dad—I'm gonna call you back, all right?" Colton said, sitting up slowly in his seat.

"Promise me, you'll be safe?"

"I promise."

"Text or call tomorrow, please?"

"Sure," Colton breathed. "Love you."

His father hesitated, then said, "I love you, too."

Colton tossed the phone onto the console and stared sightlessly at the dark cabin, and the memories of that night came rushing back like a monsoon.

Ten years earlier...

"...Run like hell," Winter said urgently, quietly. "I'll cover you. Go!"

Colton raced out the back door, flinging it open wide and nearly stumbling out. Sierra chased after him, and he managed to unlock the truck door using the key instead of the button, and it popped open despite his trembling hands. It was then he heard the first shot from the rifle, and he ducked low, slamming his body into the metal of the truck. Glass shattered from behind him back at the house.

Returning fire erupted from inside the cabin, and with his heart lodged in his throat, Colton yanked open the truck. Sierra bolted inside, whimpering and yelping. He climbed in and felt the whiz of a bullet stream pass his side, the tree beside the truck exploding with bark. His ears rang as he slumped into the seat, clawing his way inside. Another bullet, hitting the interior of the open truck door, shattered the window.

Sierra howled.

Shaking, breathing quickly, Colton stayed low, hidden behind the bench seats of the truck, as he pushed Sierra down onto the passenger seat floor.

She trembled and shook just as violently as he did.

"It's okay," he said, trying to reassure her and maybe even himself. "It's okay."

More return fire, bullets loud and ominous in the night, cut through the trees and into the dark forest to where Colton knew at least one of the men who held him captive had tracked him.

Another torrent of gunfire, shattering the back window of the truck now, and Sierra cried low. He gripped the seat, feeling the glass rain onto the back of his head and into his hair. He cursed, letting out a sharp breath, deciding in that instant that he would no longer be a sitting fucking duck.

Fuck this.

Colton managed to haul his body into the driver's seat, hunched low over the steering wheel. He clicked the seatbelt firmly into place and pulled hard on the belt to secure himself. He hit the ignition button, revved the engine to life, shifted the truck into reverse, and glanced at the white and gray husky.

"Sorry, girl," he whispered and slammed on the pedal.

The truck violently flew backward, speeding into the clearing in front of the house and into the path where the man had been firing. The truck barreled through the trees and into the dark.

He closed his eyes and reached for Sierra, bracing her for impact. Seconds later, the truck struck a massive oak tree. The sounds of crunching metal and a scream pierced the night, engulfing them. Colton lurched backward abruptly in the seat, his body jostled by the impact. With shaking fingers, he managed to unbuckle himself and slump forward, feeling a warm lick on his face and glancing up to see bright blue eyes staring at him, nervous but alive. They both were.

"Colton!" Winter's voice cut through the air. "Colton?"

He let out a hiss of pain and nodded, "We're good."

Winter's footsteps and direction of his voice indicated he was approaching the front of the truck. "Stay inside," he instructed sternly. "Don't get out until you hear my voice."

Colton blinked, feeling the warmth of blood on his temple, wondering if it was from the shattering glass from the bullet earlier. "Yeah."

Boots crunched beneath dried pine and forest debris, and Colton listened intently, waiting to hear more gunfire.

Instead, he heard something else, something soft and gurgling, coming from behind the crashed end of the truck. He glanced up, trying to see, but couldn't. Only darkness and the crushed metal, shadowed by a large tree, obscured the red, flickering light of the brakes.

Colton whipped the blood off his eyelid and noticed the driver's door was ajar; instinct told him to keep moving. The fight wasn't over yet.

He managed to slip out without making a sound. Sierra whined, and he ordered her to stay in a hushed whisper and went toward the sound.

Winter suddenly appeared, his gun trained directly on him, black eyes lethal and intent. Colton shivered and motioned with the hitch of his head toward the rear of the truck. Winter moved cautiously, taking the lead. Then he heard the noise—the panting and gasping.

He almost stopped dead in his tracks, but something inside him compelled him forward, and he saw Winter lower his gun toward the base of the tree, and there, pinned by crushed metal and a branch, a large man sat, chest bloodied, face bloated and puffy with flushed cheeks.

Colton stared, searching this man, this stranger.

He was balding, with a round, blotchy face, a double chin, and a large belly. His face was slick with sweat and he was breathing so heavily from the run through the forest that Colton wondered if he'd keel over from a heart attack before the branch sticking out of his chest took care of it.

Winter kicked the gun away from the man, who had been reaching for it despite the position he was in. Even though he had never seen his face, he knew the sounds of his breathing—the panting. The man's ruddy brown eyes swung to Colton, and he sneered in disgust.

"I knew you'd be fuckin' trouble," the man said fiercely. "I should've killed you..." He let out a grunting yelp, and Colton saw Winter place a heavy boot on the man's leg, pressing down on the one that wasn't crushed under the truck. It forced the man to arch his hips and yank at the leg pinned under the steel. "Motherfucker!"

Winter held the shotgun to his face. "What's your name?"

"Fuck you!"

"I'll find out soon enough," Winter said indifferently and leaned forward, continuing to put pressure on the opposite leg. The stranger hissed and writhed, cursing them both.

"Barry," he seethed, sweat sliding down his bulging face. "Barry Pollock."

"You the North Tahoe Ripper, Barry?"

Barry unexpectedly laughed and blood gurgled from his mouth. He sneered, spitting it toward Winter. The Detective didn't even blink, merely stared, waiting patiently, as though they had all the time in the world.

"I thought so," Winter murmured. "We got ourselves a bit of a situation here, Barry. See, from the state of your injuries and my lack of a truck, the soonest an ambulance could get here is probably about half an hour, maybe longer. That's if you live that long, cuz that tree branch sticking out of your chest looks pretty painful."

Barry, as though he hadn't even noticed, glanced down at the bloodied and protruding branch limb from his chest.

"Fuck," Barry muttered, letting his head fall weakly back into the tree, life quickly draining from him. They all knew that Barry Pollock had moments to live. Barry stared past Winter, flicking up to the night sky and then, as though he couldn't help himself, to Colton.

Colton almost stepped back, wanting to hide from the eyes of this man, and yet, he didn't. He stayed perfectly still.

Barry's lips twitched into a contorted smile, face paling with each passing breath. "I haven't run like that in years. Shootin' at you was almost as good as fuckin' you."

Colton's body heaved in revulsion, but he was careful not to flinch—not to show the disgust. He thought of his father at that moment. So unflappable, so cold.

"You were good," Barry purred, panting, face slackening. "I lasted the longest with you because of you buckin' and fightin' like a bronco with my dick deep inside your—"

The blast was loud and sudden.

His ears rang for what felt like an eternity, and he blinked rapidly, not understanding what he saw. There was so much blood, and chunks of Barry's face caved in and were gone.

Barry Pollock was dead.

Dead.

Winter turned toward Colton and gave him a quick study. Having seen something in his expression, he lowered the gun and bundled him against the wall of his chest. Colton fisted his fingers into the older man's shirt, the adrenaline and the fear leaking out of him as he trembled against him, burying his face into his neck, clinging to him like a sailor lost in a storm.

After a long time, Winter slipped his arm around his back, keeping Colton braced against him as he opened the passenger door for Sierra, who hopped out and raced back to the safety of the house.

Time seemed to move without Colton understanding as he blinked again and was somehow back inside Winter's cabin, sitting on his couch, a blanket over his shoulders, a mug of hot chocolate sitting in front of him, a bowl of boiling water and a rag on the coffee table.

He sat up, disoriented. The warm lighting of the living room felt cozy and almost surreal. The smell of pine and crisp summer night reminded him he was no longer in a stuffy, windowless, dark room.

The couch cushion shifted and he glanced over to see Winter taking a seat, brushing Sierra aside, who was sitting next to Colton on the couch. He hadn't noticed her, either.

Winter set down his mug of hot chocolate next to Colton's untouched one, and he swallowed, mouth dry.

"Water," was all he could say.

Winter nodded, reaching behind him on the coffee table, prepared for this, and handed him a cold bottle of water. Colton tried to uncap it, but his hands were trembling too much. Winter's warm, gentle hands were on him, doing it for him. He expected to jerk away from the brief touch, but he didn't. Something about this stranger was calming.

Safe.

He managed to put the bottle to his lips and drank greedily, not remembering the last time he had tasted something so good, or when he had last drunk anything.

"Police and paramedics are on their way," Winter informed him. "They should be here soon."

Colton finished the entire contents of the water bottle.

"You're bleeding," Winter informed him. "There's glass in your forehead."

Colton touched his temple, unaware of the pain, but he could feel the blood.

"I can take care of it, if you want me to?" Winter said.

He swallowed, keeping his gaze averted, and nodded.

Winter seemed careful of keeping a safe distance between them and reached for the tweezers he had brought out, along with hydrogen peroxide to clean the wound. Colton hadn't seen any of the items sitting in front of him. He felt the tug of his skin and let out a hiss.

"Sorry," Winter murmured. "Not exactly a surgeon… got it."

He plucked the shard out and showed it to Colton.

"You might have a scar," he said, dropping the thick glass on the table and grabbing the rag, which he dipped in the boiled water. He then gently dabbed the spot on his temple and hairline.

"Is he dead?" Colton asked quietly.

Winter glanced at him, his eyes looking black in the warm light of the lamps. "Yes."

Colton's eyes shot to the shattered front window in the living room, dread filling him. Had Barry's bullets done that, or Winter's? "And the other one?"

Winter hesitated, "What other one?"

"There are two."

Winter glanced through the broken window and back at Colton. "You sure?"

Colton nodded, "Yeah. But I don't know if the other one followed me. I—I…" he sucked in a breath. "I cut him under the jaw and locked him in the room that they—they—"

Colton's fingers fisted into his palms, balling them tight and then flinching, remembering his thumbs. He cursed, tears of welling pain springing to the corner of his eyes. "What day is it?"

"Sunday."

Colton took in the information but didn't absorb it. It didn't matter anyway. He was free.

"Where am I?"

"North Tahoe, in my cabin," Winter replied. "Once the police and ambulance get here, they'll take you to the Placer County Hospital."

"Will you stay with me?" Colton asked, not fully understanding why he did, only that Winter was safe—protective, and there was still another Ripper out there.

"Yeah," Winter nodded, "Of course."

He finally looked at the man beside him on the couch and suddenly saw everything—remembered everything.

It flooded him, and Colton felt his body tense, as the fresh memory of hands on his skin, the electricity burning into his spine, the handcuffs digging into his wrists, the way they both jerked and moaned in pleasure as they used his body against his will.

Colton sprang to his feet, bumping the table and flinging off the blanket, a wild need to run rippling through him. It was so intense that he began to pace, looking for a way out.

Get out. Get out. Run. Run. Run.

"Hey," Winter drawled in a soothing, calm voice. It was deep and warm, reminding him of how his father would sometimes talk to their horses in the stable. "You're safe, Colton. No one's out there. No one is going to hurt you again, I promise. And if they try, they'll have to go through me first, all right?"

Colton's head snapped to him and he stared, seeing that Winter had followed him, but hadn't reached for him, hadn't stopped him, and even held his hands out in a defensive gesture, as though Colton might need to know where his hands were.

"I ain't going to hurt you," Winter reassured.

He stared, heart racing, yet he stilled. "I know."

Winter studied him. "When I was a kid, I'd have nightmares, and it was too late to get lost in the woods, or do anything about it, so my grandma would sit with me. Just sit. She'd hold my hand, or me—but most of the time, her presence was enough to make the memories go away. You wanna sit? We'll just sit while we wait, yeah?"

Colton sucked in a breath and nodded, returning to the couch. Winter sat on the opposite side, moving slowly as though not wanting to startle him.

"My father has horses, thoroughbreds. Collects them more than he rides them," Colton said unexpectedly. "Sometimes he gets a difficult one and has to talk to them. Like you did just now. Can you... Can you talk to me?"

Winter's expression softened in a kind, half-hearted smile. "What do you want to talk about?"

"Whatever. It doesn't matter."

Winter nodded, reaching for his hot chocolate, taking a sip. "Well, how 'bout I tell you about—her." He hitched his chin to the husky that had finally settled on the dog bed by the fireplace, already fast asleep. "I think this is the first time in her five young years that she ever listened to me off leash and did not bolt out into the forest."

Amazed, Colton turned to her and back to him. "Really?"

"Huskies are notorious escape artists and bolters. Give them an inch, they'll take a mile—well, more like ten. We've been working on not running away, but huskies are pretty damn stubborn. They're probably smarter than German Shepherds, if they decided to listen."

"I feel like I have a lot in common with huskies then," Colton said, feeling his lips twitch in a smirk, and it surprised him.

Winter's eyebrow arched, "Stubborn? Or selective listening?"

"Both," Colton replied honestly. "You told me to run, and you told me to stay in the truck. I didn't listen to either."

"Yeah," Winter leaned forward, setting down his hot chocolate. "I noticed that." His dark gaze held him with a weight that Colton didn't understand, and yet, his palms itched and his heart sped up. "You don't know when to quit. I think that trait might have saved your life."

Colton tried hard to look away, knowing he was staring, but he couldn't. After everything he went through, he hadn't anticipated this moment. He supposed, a part of him thought he was going to die in that room. And maybe, a part of him did.

"I wasn't ready to die," Colton breathed out, unsure if he had spoken the words until Winter's eyes sharpened a mere fraction. "And I knew they would kill me."

"How did you escape?" Winter asked quietly.

Colton held up his hands in the warm light of the room, seeing the bruises and blood. But not his blood. "I..." His throat clammed up, hearing the whaling cry of the man in the mask as he dragged the grated teeth of the handcuff up and under his chin, nearly flinging off the mask.

Watching Winter shoot Pollock without hesitation—without remorse, changed something inside him in that instant. And Colton realized, if given the chance, he would kill the other man—the man in the mask.

"I want to find him," Colton said in a trembling voice. Not from pain or grief, but from rage. "I want to kill him."

Winter leaned forward, resting his elbows on his knees, "We will."

"Will you kill him like you did him?" Colton asked.

Winter stilled, his fingers flexing as his eyes darkened.

"If you don't," Colton whispered. "I will. And I won't regret it. Not for a second."

Winter slowly motioned to the mug on the coffee table, "Your hot chocolate is getting cold."

Colton snorted irritably. "I can't fuckin' lift it."

"I can—"

"It doesn't matter," Colton said, angry now, angry at himself for not being able to lift a fucking ceramic mug. He had tried initially, the strain in his hands, not just from the broken thumb and the recently dislocated one, but from fighting and resisting them, his whole body felt tired—the most tired he had ever felt in his life. All he wanted to do was sleep, but he knew the ambulance would arrive soon.

"It does," Winter said quietly, sitting forward, his knee brushing against Colton's as he picked up the mug. Colton smelled chocolate, pine, and freshly chopped wood. He decided, right then, that it was the best combination of smells in the world.

He swallowed thickly, and Winter, ever graciously, lifted the cup to his lips and Colton took a sip. He sighed the second the chocolate hit his tongue and realized that all he had tasted in the last few days had been blood, sweat, and his own saliva.

"More?" Winter asked.

Colton nodded, averting his gaze, somewhat embarrassed, yet he knew it wasn't necessary. "Yeah."

He took another sip, letting the warmth spread over his chest and into his belly. He let out a long sigh, tears pricking the back of his eyes. "I don't think I've ever tasted hot chocolate like that."

Winter, unexpectedly, smiled and set the mug down. "A couple of years back, I got lost on a hike, lost in my thoughts, not paying attention. By the time I realized I needed to turn around and retrace my steps, I'd hiked almost 22 miles before making it back to my truck. It hadn't helped that the snow had made everything so damned difficult. I crawled in, managed to get my sore, sorry ass back here, and made hot chocolate to warm up my bones. And yeah, I remember it tasting like that, too."

He wondered if Winter had come home to anyone that day. If someone wanted to make him hot chocolate and take care of him. He shifted, not liking the idea of Winter out here alone in the woods, without someone to take care of him.

Surprised, Colton glanced around the cozy cabin, with the books, the brick fireplace, the sleeping white and gray dog, and Winter. So solid, so quietly confident and strikingly handsome. His heart fluttered.

It fucking fluttered in his chest, and he knew instantly what it meant, and he stared in shock. He had literally just been through hell and yet somehow, his crazy heart was fluttering over this stranger.

Before he could process the feeling any further, he saw lights flash and sirens yell.

He sucked in a breath and shot a hard look at Winter, "You'll stay with me?"

He didn't want this man, this safe, wonderful man, to leave his side yet. The idea of going back out into the woods without Winter terrified him.

Winter didn't hesitate. "I'll stay with you until you tell me otherwise."

Once the officers and paramedics arrived, everything happened quickly.

Winter was drawn into conversation with a man in a sheriff's badge and a few other officers, explaining the body on his property. Colton watched as the paramedics brought out the gurney bed on wheels. He saw the straps and buckles and panic rose, gripping his throat like a vice. He retreated instantly, but feeling Winter's hand press into his lower back, he stilled.

"I don't wanna ride in that," Colton breathed out.

"You don't have to." Winter went to the paramedics and told them the gurney wasn't needed. He climbed into the back of the ambulance and waved Colton inside.

Winter's black hair and dark eyes looked even darker in the bright light of the ambulance. "I'd like them to check your head wound," he explained calmly. "It's about a thirty-minute drive to the closest hospital."

Once he sat down on the bench next to Winter, the smell of sterilized medical equipment made him jerk back in his seat, triggering another wave of memories of the room he was locked in and the harsh smell of disinfectant burning his nostrils.

Winter closed the space between them, careful not to touch him, his voice low. "You don't have to do anything you don't want to. We can wait until we get to the hospital."

"It's not that," Colton muttered. "It's the fuckin' smell. The room smelled like this."

He ordered the paramedic to turn on the AC and roll all the windows down. "Is that better?"

Colton sighed, breathing in Winter's scent and deciding in that moment that he would not be embarrassed anymore. "Can I lean on you?"

Winter leaned back and nodded, "Of course." He let Colton make the move toward him and swallowing the nerves in his belly, the distance between them vanished. Their legs pushed together and his arm rested against Winter's side as he turned his face into his shoulder, breathing in the pine and musk of his shirt.

A moment later, he heard Winter ask the paramedic in the back with them to turn off the lights. She did, and they were descended in darkness, and Colton relaxed even more. The rocking of the ambulance up the road soothed him, knowing he was creating more distance between him and the other Ripper.

"Does he have an emergency contact we can call?" the paramedic asked.

Colton sat up, mind searching, and couldn't find anything. "My mother—I don't—I don't remember her number right now." Panic edged his tone as he muttered, "Fuck."

"It's all right," Winter soothed, reaching his arms across the back of the bench behind Colton. "You'll remember it when we get there."

His confidence and reassurance relaxed him once more, and he slipped into the alcove of his side, face pressed against Winter's shoulder. Winter continued not to touch him, simply allowing Colton complete control. It was comforting and soothing— precisely what he needed.

The ambulance finally made it to the main road, and the smoothness of the drive lulled him. He closed his eyes, body rocking into the Detective, and miraculously fell asleep.

CHAPTER 26

The doorbell rang under the press of Winter's finger, and he glanced behind him at Officer Sydney, who was parked in the driveway. Jim had given her strict orders not to let Winter out of his sight, and he supposed he should be grateful.

Mal opened the door, dressed in the same outfit from earlier—a black V-neck shirt and dark blue jeans, paired with bright white sneakers. He smiled in surprise, his green eyes warming. "The local dunk tank star has greeted my home? Someone alert the media!"

"Ha ha," Winter said casually, a faint smile on his lips.

Mal glanced behind him, spotting the police cruiser. "Is everything okay?"

"Yeah," Winter said with a slight shrug, "Long story. Can I come in?"

"Of course," Mal stepped back, and Winter, maintaining his cool, walked inside, his heart pounding.

"Is Patrick here?" he asked.

Mal sighed, closing the door behind him and heading into the kitchen. Winter followed.

"Patrick got a call from a hospital in Truckee that needed a surgeon with his skills, so he's already flown the coop. He probably won't be back until tomorrow morning, given my luck. Can I get you something to drink?"

"Yeah, sure. You know what I like."

Mal hummed, opening the large stainless-steel door of his refrigerator, pulling out a bottle of sparkling water. Winter inhaled the sterile scent in the kitchen, the hairs on the back of his neck rising. How had he never noticed how clean Mal was…? He remembered Colton's reaction to the ambulance's smell, how he clung to him to avoid it. Winter's hand fisted over the lighter in his pocket.

Ten years and he never fucking saw it.

Ten years, and he let Colton and Grace down.

Mal busied himself with getting a pint glass and some limes.

"You don't have to do that," Winter said.

Mal waved that hingeless wrist at him and chopped the lime into slices on the granite countertop. "Do you mind if I have a drink? I had just opened a bottle when you rang."

"Go right ahead. I interrupted your evening."

"You're never an interruption, you know that." Mal tossed a glance over his shoulder, concerned. "You look—pale. Has something happened between you and Colton?"

Winter's thumb dug into the metal of the lighter, knowing Mal would ask—that the Ripper had written that note and placed the letters in the hallway, out in the open, to drive a wedge between them. He had never told Mal about the letters he had written to Grace. It took the Ripper, tearing his house apart, to find them and use them to his advantage.

"He's back at the house," he said. "We, uh—well, we fought, actually."

Mal turned, gaping. "You seemed so happy this evening. And that kiss, Winter?! In public, no less. I thought Patrick was going to have to scrape my jaw off the floor. I didn't know you had it in you." He motioned to the dining room, "Let's sit down."

He nodded and followed, hearing the soft sounds of music coming from the living room.

Winter took a seat opposite Mal, taking a long drink of the carbonated water, knowing he had to tread carefully. He didn't want to alert Mal of his suspicion, not yet.

"What happened?" Mal took a sip of wine, looking concerned.

"I don't wanna talk about it yet, if it's all right?" Winter said with a weak smile.

Mal reached across the table and patted the back of his hand, so motherly—so kind. Mal had always been good at comforting him. Now, for the first time in nearly two decades of friendship, Winter finally looked at Mal and saw the callous emptiness reflected in his eyes.

"He's different than the others, I could tell," Mal said softly. "I don't think I've seen anyone get you out of your shell like that before."

Winter leaned back in his chair, taking another sip. "You're right. He is different. Special."

Mal arched his eyebrows, curious. "What does that mean for the notoriously noncommittal Detective Eli Winter?"

"I guess I'll find out." He stroked the cold pint glass, looking across the polished and gleaming mahogany dining table at him. "You know, I could never figure out how the Ripper first spotted Colton, and that bugged the hell out of me. The other victims had been avid hikers or backpackers, spotted on busy trails and taken from there. But not Colton. He was taken from the bedroom of the rental cabin he was staying at with his mother and her boyfriend."

Mal nodded, looking uncertain. "Okay—?"

"I realized something today," Winter said, an odd stillness washing over him. "I used to walk that beach with Sierra all the time. She loved it. It was the only place she would come back to me when she escaped her leash, remember?" Winter asked. "I had been out of town that weekend, following up on a Ripper lead in Nevada, and you had been watching her for me. You met me on that beach the day Colton went missing." Winter held his gaze. "That beach had a row of rental cabins on it, Colton's included."

Mal shook his head, confused, "I don't understand."

"You saw him," Winter breathed knowingly, even though it was just a theory—a hunch. "The bedroom he was staying in had a slider door that lined up with the beach. I think you saw him that day when you dropped off Sierra. You saw him, probably just in passing, but that was enough, wasn't it?"

The record Mal was playing in the living room clicked to the next song, and the sensation of icy dread seemed to plummet him into the earth as he recognized the song—the same song Colton told him the Ripper played.

In-A-Gadda-Da-Vida by Iron Butterfly.

"It's been you this whole time," Winter said hoarsely, realizing the truth. That his best friend was a serial rapist murderer. The very one he'd been hunting for ten fucking years. The same one that had raped Colton ten years ago, and if given the chance, would do it again and then kill him.

Blinding, furious rage engulfed him.

Mal had killed two men and assisted in the death of five others. He wanted nothing more than to leap across this table and smash Mal's face into the wood and hurt him. The feeling was primal. But he couldn't. Winter had to maintain control—he had to arrest him—vindicate Colton and Grace for knowing all along that the second Ripper had always existed despite there never being any evidence other than Colton's word.

Winter slowly reached for the gun on his hip, his lips tingling and his vision blurring around the edges. He blinked hard, trying to keep his focus.

Mal smiled over the rim of his wine glass, inhaling the aroma, looking almost bored. "At first, I thought you would eventually figure it out. To me, it was glaringly obvious, but I suppose love tends to make us stupid in the end."

Winter had unlatched the buckle around his gun, but his fingers were trembling too much to hold it. He gritted his teeth and tried to move his arm up, but it wouldn't obey. It was heavy, as though stones were tied to the tips of his fingers.

Panic rose in his chest, realizing he was too weak to grip the gun. His fingers clung uselessly, forcing himself to hold it, but it was no use and he dropped the gun. It clattered loudly on the hardwood floor beneath his chair.

"That's the ketamine in your system, a high enough dose of it makes the body limp and practically useless."

Winter blinked, glancing at the bubbling water before him, throat tightening.

"I take it Colton didn't like my note?" Mal asked in a hushed, excited whisper.

He stared, watching Mal transform into the sadist, the killer, the rapist that had convinced him he was a friend.

"I had to pay you back after that spectacular show you put on for me. Or was it for you? I mean, wow, Winter, that was cold, even by my standards. Getting him to confess his love for you like that? Christ, I was so fucking hard," Mal purred, twirling his wine in his glass. "Better than porn."

Winter's jaw clenched.

"And the way you touched him," he simpered, making a sound Winter had never heard him make before, and his stomach rolled. "God, it took me back," he stroked the stem of the wine glass, face lit with desire.

"I wish I could've recorded it. I haven't climaxed like that since—well, McNamara." He hummed, "That boy was good, but not like our boy, Colton."

"He's not yours," Winter growled dangerously.

"I know, I know. I heard your sweet little threat. Seeing you all worked up like that, fuck, I'll admit it, that was the cherry on top. I came so fucking hard," he giggled into his glass, taking another sip.

Winter cringed, feeling the hatred filter through his veins.

"I never thought I'd come back, you know," Mal said. "I got away with it. No one ever knew, and it was just so... boring." He sighed heavily, "I tried everything to resist the urge. And I mean everything. I practically lived at that sex club in LA. But then I got a little too excited with someone one night, nearly strangled him, and it was so much fun." He emphasized the words as he said them, his gaze glinting with a crazed, unrecognizable look. "I got a slap on the wrist and a three-month ban. But the cat was out of the bag, and I was hungry for more. So, I went window shopping. Made a stop in Sacramento..." Mal bit his lower lip. "Found Colton at that posh little bar of his and fuck-me-sideways, that boy certainly grew into a delicious man." He hummed out a sigh, "I watched him all night—rubbed one out in the bathroom. A couple of times, actually."

Winter's body was growing heavier by the minute, and he strained to keep himself upright. Shivering in horror at the idea of Mal stalking Colton, watching him.

He could've taken him then...

And Winter would've never known...

"Why didn't you take him?" Winter asked roughly.

Mal straightened, swirling his wine. "I thought about it. Pollock was my blunt instrument for that sort of thing. I needed to practice first. So, I started with someone easier to handle. Douglas—he was sweet, begged a lot. I killed him quicker than McNamara because he was my first," he drawled airily. "I thought it would be too much for me, but it wasn't. Fuck, it was better than sex."

Winter's throat clenched with disgust.

"With McNamara, I knew I could take my time once he was dead. Winter, you haven't tasted sweet until you've fucked a corpse."

"You're fucking sick, Mal," Winter hissed, demanding his body to move, not wanting to die in this fucking house—with this horrible, evil son of a bitch.

"I thought so too at first. But he was still warm, still soft, making it easy to position him the way I wanted. I plan on doing that with Colton...take him somewhere deep in the woods...take my time...I'll keep him alive for as long as I can this time. Why starve when I can have that sweet nectar for months?" He smacked his lips as he sipped greedily on his wine.

Winter pressed his boot into the hardwood, fighting the paralytic numbness working its way up his body. "I'm gonna kill you."

Mal hummed, unfazed, eyes sharpening over him. "I know you've fucked him. I can tell. How many times, huh? Tell me."

"No."

Mal pouted and then shrugged, "Fine, whatever, be difficult. It doesn't matter anyway. I'll be his last. The last person who ever touches him. Fucking him was like touching Heaven. *Fuck*," Mal leaned his head back, palming his cock. "Just thinking about him and that tight hole gets me going. Please tell me, how is he now? Still tight? Still perfect?"

"Fuck you," Winter managed through numb lips.

He could feel his body begin to slip in the chair, and he steadied himself as long as he could with his feet firmly planted on the ground. Something shifted in his pocket, and he reached for Colton's lighter, forcing his fingers to move.

Maybe if he could reach it...

"I loved the way he struggled when he came." Mal continued to touch himself, pausing to sip the wine and enjoy the music. "He looks at you the way I once looked at you..." The music became a steady beat of hard drumming. "So much love. Christ, it's revolting but only because it's misplaced. He doesn't know who you really are. How cruel you can be. The only difference is that your victims walk away. Mine don't."

Winter gripped the edge of the chair, forcing himself to hang on just a little longer as he pushed his numb fingers into his jeans pocket, breathing heavy. He felt the edge of the lighter and forked it with two fingers, his body nearly shaking with the effort.

Mal stroked himself, "I was your first victim, wasn't I, Winter?"

Winter's breath came shallow and fast.

"You knew I loved you, and damn, when you fucked me, I thought I was going to die; it was divine. And then you left—and it was over, just like that." He snapped his fingers together, anger leaping to his face. "I hated you for a time. But the last ten years have been my payback, watching you suffer and struggle endlessly to find me."

"You were never my friend..." Winter grated out.

"Yeah, but we sure did have a lot of fun. Especially hunting," Mal said darkly. "Going to the club with you—watching you work those brats the way you once worked me. It was so fucking hot. I spied on you every time, did you know that?" Mal sipped casually, eyes dancing with malice. "The rooms have cameras. I paid a lot of money to watch you work that magical dick of yours."

Winter let out a shaky breath, trembling with rage.

"Before you pass out..." Mal said, "I want you to watch me invite Colton over for a drink tonight with me and Patrick."

Winter's heart stopped.

No, no, no!

Mal pulled out his phone, typed the text to Colton and sent it, returning his hand to his crotch, setting the phone down in front of him.

"Don't do this," Winter said, knowing it was pointless, but needing to do it anyway.

Mal ignored him and gasped in excitement, "Oh, I see bubbles!" He danced in his chair, reading his screen, "He said yes. I knew getting you out of the way would be the easiest part. He, on the other hand, well..." Mal sucked in a breath, palming his cock, eyes lowering to half-mast. "I'd better take care of myself before he shows up."

"Please, Mal..."

"I'll dose him the same way I dosed you. I'll take him downstairs so he can see you —and, more importantly, so you can see him. I won't kill you—yet. I want you to watch—you were always such a good watcher. I loved the praise when you fucked me. I doubt you will be praising him tonight. Or will you try to calm him, I wonder? Tell him he's a good boy—your boy—forever?"

"If you touch him," Winter promised, tears prickling at the back of his eyes, unable to imagine the horror Mal planned for them. "I will kill you—slowly. I will rip you apart limb by fucking limb."

Winter's body finally slumped, in full effect of the drug, and he fell sideways out of the chair, landing hard on his side. The weight and angle of his body rolled him halfway to his back, legs tangled beneath him. The lighter slipped from his fingers upwards, landing in his palm in the fall, and he felt it still there.

Thank God.

He managed, with every last ounce of strength he had left, to twist his hand over, placing the silver lighter on the ground beneath his hand. If he were lucky, Mal wouldn't see it when he dragged Winter out from under the table. But Colton might.

Mal's feet spread apart beneath the table, a mere foot away from his face, splaying his legs wide as he slid his cock out from his pants and began to masturbate.

He closed his eyes, refusing to witness this monster's revolting show of power. Winter touched the only thing he had left of Colton's, and he hoped to hell he saw it before it was too late.

And if they got out of this, he would tell Colton the truth that he loved him. That he had loved him the moment he saved his life in the forest, and he'd been falling ever since. When he saw him again, so confident, so bright and warm, the gray fog that had settled over Winter's life had vanished.

He loved him.

He'd loved him all along.

Winter kept his eyes closed, let the dark waves carry him under, and let go of the lighter.

CHAPTER 27

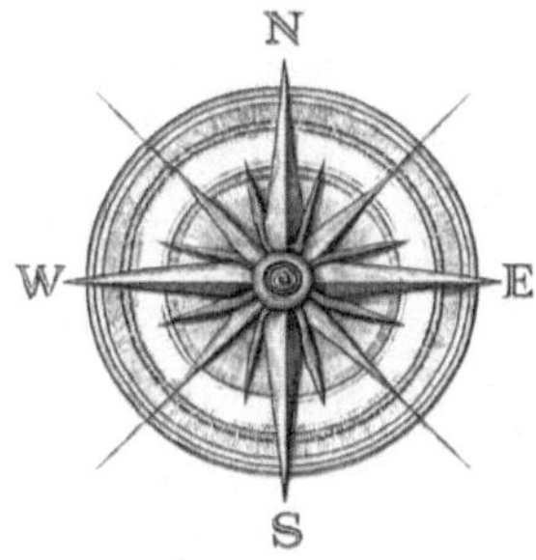

Colton heard Frank's bark as the truck keys dangled in his palm, opening the front door to Winter's house. The only light on was in the hallway, but the rest of the house was eerily still and dark.

"Winter?" He called out, patting Frank affectionately, closing the door behind him.

No response.

"I don't like this," his mother said anxiously, pacing in the living room as he entered, flipping on the light. She was dressed in the same dress from the carnival, minus the floppy hat. Her long, thick hair was braided down her shoulder, her expression anxious. "He should be here. Why isn't he here?"

"Let's not jump to any conclusions," he said, reassuring himself as he pulled out his phone and called Winter.

He may have gone back to the station after the break-in. But Winter hadn't done that last night, and Colton could tell officers had been there. Some of the mess was organized, and his mother's letters had been picked up from the hallway.

Winter's phone didn't ring. It went straight to voicemail.

The hair on the back of his neck rose.

"Something's wrong," she whispered breathlessly, her eyes widening.

"We don't know that," he retorted, trying to maintain calm. "Maybe he just stepped out for a bit and didn't want to be bothered. That's all."

He redialed Winter's number, and again it went straight to voicemail. He sucked in a long breath and called Jim next.

Frank whined, concerned, possibly picking up on Colton's energy. Jim answered right away, "Colton? You all right?"

"Yeah, I'm fine," he replied. "Is Winter with you?"

"He's at the house with Officer Sydney."

"His house?"

"Yeah, what other house would he be at?" Jim asked questioningly.

"Sorry, just makin' sure."

Jim hesitated, "Look, I know it's been a rough couple of nights. I told Winter that the Placer County Sheriff's Department would gladly set you both up at a hotel for the rest of the week if you'd like."

"I appreciate it, Jim," Colton replied smoothly, noticing his mother pace in the corner of his eye. "But if Winter is okay with stayin', so am I."

"Well, if you change your mind, the offer stands. And Officer Sydney is ordered to stay there all night just in case. Call me if you need anything."

"Sounds good. Have a good night."

Colton saw a text message notification on his screen. It was Mal. His jaw tightened as he opened it.

> Hey, you! Patrick and I don't want the evening to end and would love for you to join us. Winter is on his way. You should pop by for a drink.

Colton pulled the suspect list his mother had made and tossed it onto the kitchen counter, flipping on the light and letting his eyes fall onto one of the names.

Malcom Conner.

The letters of the brand fit.

The second Ripper was Malcom.

He expected the information to come as a revelation when it hit, but instead, it came with an anger so cold, so vengeful that only the Devil would understand it. And Winter.

Colton texted Mal back, agreeing to come over, and strode into the guest bedroom, grabbing his bag. He took out his brass knuckles and the hunting knife Winter had given him, strapping it to his ankle.

His phone dinged again.

> Winter just got here. See ya soon!

Something twisted in his gut. Winter was with Mal.

Fuck.

He raked his fingers through his hair, pulling at the roots, and he glimpsed his mother in the living room, gnawing nervously on her bottom lip. "Something's not right. Winter wouldn't have left. He knew you'd come back. Unless…"

Colton glanced at the text messages from Mal, and his stomach unraveled into a bottomless pit.

"He knows," he said in a quick whisper. "Winter figured it out. Just like me."

She glanced at the ruined house and nodded. "He went to confront Mal…"

"Without me," Colton let out a hard breath from his nostrils.

"To protect you," she whispered fervently.

"Everyone here seems to think I need protecting from the Boogeyman. Except he ain't. He's a bloody man, with my man in his fucking house, playing games." He nearly crushed his phone in his hand before sliding it into his back pocket.

She straightened, eyes flaring. "You can't just march in there. You need a plan."

"Oh, dear mum, I most certainly do," he tapped his pocket where the brass knuckles were and patted Frank on top of the head. "Hold down the fort, Frank. I'll bring your Daddy home."

He spent the last ten years fantasizing about this moment. About having his turn at the man who brutally tortured and raped him. And all the horrible things Colton would do in retribution. Except Winter was there, and he feared that Mal may have done something to him.

No. No. Winter, you better be alive and fuckin' breathing when I get there!

Speeding like a wild man, adrenaline coursing through him, Colton pulled into the driveway of Mal's home in less than twenty minutes and saw a Placer County Sheriff's cruiser parked out front and Officer Syndey sitting inside. He parked the truck next to her.

"Hey," she greeted warmly. "Winter's inside. He's staying the night. Mal came out a few minutes ago to let me know."

Colton kept his expression neutral, even though his heart leapt in his throat. He didn't like Mal talking for Winter, which meant only one thing—Winter was in trouble, and Colton hoped to God he wasn't too late.

"You're not too late, honey," his mother whispered in the passenger seat beside him. "Winter's a fighter. And if we know anything about the second Ripper, he keeps his victims alive. He wouldn't have killed him—not yet."

Colton scrubbed his fingers through his beard and allowed his lips to curve at the officer. "Yeah, Mal invited me over too, though I'm not too fond of the idea of stayin' the night."

She nodded. "Well, whatever you guys decide, Jim asked me to keep tabs on Winter and you—so, I'll be here."

Colton nodded, pondering a backup plan. "Do you mind doin' me a favor? Could you knock on the door in, say, twenty minutes? You'll be my excuse to drag Winter out."

"Sure."

"Thanks, luv."

Colton climbed out of the truck, hurried up the steps, his heart galloping in his chest, and exhaled a lung-clearing breath before ringing the doorbell.

"Winter would tell you to trust your instincts, and so would I," his mother whispered urgently, her blue gaze fixated on the door. "You have to make sure it's him first." She held out her finger and dragged it delicately beneath her chin.

"I should've checked him before," Colton muttered to himself.

"Even good men like Winter can be fooled by the devil."

For the first time in ten years, Colton felt a deep calm wash over him, reminding him of the night he escaped and took back his life. Except this time was different because he was different. And it was more than just his life on the line now, and he wanted to howl at the moon to make sure Winter was okay.

"I have made sense of the devil," he drawled in a humming voice. "And he is but a man in sheep's clothing that has ensnared *my* wolf. And for that, that man must be killed."

"Go get your mate, honey," she whispered, smiling bravely, and vanished.

"Patrick!" he heard Mal's voice through the heavy wood door. "Honey! Colton's here! Hurry up!"

He heard quick footsteps and the door swung open, revealing Mal, his handsome face beaming with pleasure. "You made it," he said, stepping back, opening the door wider. "I'm so glad you decided to come. Come in, come in!"

Colton smiled politely and did, listening to the sound of the door closing and bolting behind him.

"Patrick's such a clean freak," Mal said off-handedly. "I accidentally spilled my wine on his shirt, and he insisted on showering. I think it was the festival, too, all those people. He's a bit of a germaphobe these days." Mal sauntered into the massive living room, its floor-to-ceiling windows overlooking the dark forest, which felt otherworldly tonight. "He should be down soon. I told him that cocktail hour starts when you arrive, so follow me. What's your poison, sweetheart?"

Colton quickly scanned the house, taking note of the security cameras and alarm system. He'd seen it before but hadn't seen it. Now it felt downright insidious.

"Poison, good choice in words," Colton said. "As the great poet once said, give me libations or give me death."

Mal chuckled politely, "What poet is that?"

"Me," Colton drawled with an insolent smile. "Where's Winter?"

"Pouting on the patio. He told me you two fought."

Colton followed Mal into the posh dining room, where a massive oak table with an iron black candelabra stood in the center, candles lit and burning while soft, crooning music played in the background. It seemed almost romantic. His pulse ticked steadily.

"You seem like a whiskey man," Mal said, tossing him a dazzling smile over his shoulder while at the fully stocked bar he had pushed out on a trolley the night before. A trolley. Similar to the one the Ripper had filled to the brim with medical supplies, lotion, sex toys, and tools.

Ice trickled down his back, and he smiled blandly, "Oh, whatever you're drinking works for me, I'm not picky."

"Says the bartender. No pressure, then," Mal said, swirling the silver cocktail shaker. "Patrick says I make a mean martini, though his are better, the bastard."

"I'm sure it'll be great," he said smoothly, deciding to turn on the charm offense and see what Mal would do. "Thanks again for the invitation. I needed something stronger than tea."

"Of course. A friend of Winter's is a friend of mine. I couldn't help but notice, as almost everyone there did, the very public smooch earlier this evening. Things getting serious?"

"Possibly," Colton said coolly. "Depends on a lot of things."

Mal turned, holding two martini glasses with green olives. "Like?"

Colton shrugged, pretending not to have an answer and looking pained. "I think I need something to loosen my tongue first."

Mal smirked knowingly, waved to a seat at the table, and handed Colton the drink. He accepted it and caught a scent—slight—but there. Something familiar. His stomach heaved, and he straightened, fingers pinching the martini glass.

Mal took a seat, looking pleased with himself. "Winter was always a still waters run deep kinda guy. A guy's guy, if you know what I mean. And I loved that about him. Rugged and quiet—but the second you close the bedroom door, you couldn't get that man to shut up."

Colton felt the heat on his neck rise at the reference to Winter's pillow talk. And something else, too—something angry, bordering on violent possessiveness. The weight of his brass knuckles in his pocket seemed heavier, calling his name.

"Don't be impulsive, my love," his mother whispered right behind him. "I know you want to hurt him. However, you must ensure it's him. One more test."

Colton strolled lazily in the dining room, wanting to make a show out of himself to the man that Winter believed loved him. And if that were true, Colton had the upper hand and would use it to his advantage.

"Winter mentioned you two dated in college. How'd it end, if you don't mind me asking?" Colton asked.

"He dumped me. I think he was missing home, and I was convenient. Afterward, he said he made a mistake..." Mal gave a mocking, expressive sigh.

"That must have hurt," Colton said, pretending to give a fuck.

"It was tragic, and liberating. My silly crush was finally able to die after taking a bite out of the elusive man I had fantasized about for so long."

Colton stiffened, anger flaring in his chest.

"Sound familiar?" Mal drawled quietly, sipping his cocktail.

"I don't know what you mean?"

Mal arched both eyebrows, "You don't? You were what—19 when you first met him? So young, so naïve. It was natural to fall head over heels for the man who saved your life."

"I was twenty, and not that naïve," Colton replied flatly.

"Apologies," Mal said dismissively. "But now that you've actually had the man himself, I bet it doesn't match the fantasy one bit."

Colton felt his lips curve. "I don't think my imagination could have conjured up how extraordinary Winter actually is."

Mal rolled his eyes, "Please. That's the emotion talking."

Colton chuckled, swirling his drink but not taking a sip. "Isn't that the point?"

"No," Mal fired back. "Love is stupid and blinding. Makes us do crazy things."

He nodded, thinking about this moment and how he stepped knowingly into a trap, because Winter was somewhere in this house, locked away but not dead, because the Ripper likes to play with his meal before he eats.

Colton set down his martini. Mal's eyebrows raised in concern, "Not in the martini mood? I can make you something else."

"You said Patrick was in the shower?" Colton asked, taking a step back from the table, eyeing the decorations —the perfect alignment of the table in the center of the room, the chairs carefully positioned, and the candelabra spotless. Except for the chair he was about to sit in. It was the only thing in this room slightly off, and he stepped back further still, pretending to survey the art on the wall.

"I swear that man loves his shower more than he loves me sometimes," Mal drawled easily.

Colton pretended to admire the art in the dining room. "You know, your house is rather stunning."

"Thank you," Mal replied. "It's been a labor of love."

"Good security, too," Colton eyed the camera in the corner of the hall.

"Perks of the job," Mal smoothed his hand over the arm of his chair. "I sometimes have to house the art here before it's sent to the gallery. Gotta protect the money every step of the way."

Colton glanced back to the bar and sighed, "I think I'm craving something sweet, if you don't mind?"

"A good host never minds." Mal jumped to his feet and promptly made another cocktail.

With his back turned, Colton glanced out of the dining room and up the stairs to where Patrick was and kept his ear trained to hear movement or the shower.

Nothing.

Silence, other than the soft croon of Billie Holiday.

His eyes traveled to the back of the house, where he noticed a stairwell leading down to the lower level. Goosebumps swept up his arms, and he leaned back into the dining room, listening to the sounds of clinking ice, and moved his gaze to the dining table chair that stuck out, unlike all the rest, and caught a brief glint of something beneath it.

Colton took only a second to recognize what it was.

And his heart jumped. It was his lighter.

Winter was here—and he needed to find him—*now.*

"All right," Mal turned, "Try this one. Sweet on the tart side."

Colton thanked him, taking the cocktail glass from Mal's fingers, noticing the fine lines of his nails and the smooth lotioned hands. He placed the rim of the glass to his lips and tilted it upwards, pretending to take a sip. "Perfect."

"Excellent."

Colton set the glass on the table, once more looking apologetic, "I'm so sorry, the drive was a bit long and I forgot to use the loo."

"Oh, of course, down the hall to the left, can't miss it."

"Fantastic. Hopefully when I get back, I'll get to squeeze Patrick for info on how he managed to woo you."

Mal smiled, but it didn't reach his eyes. "I can go hurry him along."

Colton pretended to consider this. "How about instead, you wait right here and don't tell him I'm here yet. I wouldn't mind a little more... alone time with you. Winter can sulk outside for as long as he bloody likes," he said in his best sultry tone, letting his gaze drop slowly over Mal's body.

Mal let out a shaky exhale, his throat convulsing in evident excitement. "Whatever you want," Mal said, licking his lips, a twitch of a smile jerking at the corner of his mouth.

Colton, feeling bold, took a step forward, closing the distance between them and confirming the scent.

Eucalyptus.

"Good," Colton drawled huskily, resisting the urge to clamp his fingers over this man's throat and strangle, but instead, he dragged a knuckle beneath his chin and felt it. The faint but very real scar tissue from when Colton dragged the steel teeth of an open pair of handcuffs beneath the Ripper's chin.

Mal was the second Ripper.

"Be right back, luv," Colton managed to murmur, despite the fury flooding every fiber of his being.

Mal let out a tremulous breath.

He didn't wait for another display of panting excitement as he casually stepped back, strolled out of the dining room and paused, making a show of considering closing the door behind him, raking his gaze hungrily over Mal.

"I'm gonna close this. I'm not done with you yet," Colton said with a tantalizing smirk.

Mal gave him a wild hand flutter, barely containing himself. Colton closed the door silently behind him and ran straight to the stairwell leading to the lower level of the house.

He jumped over the barrister and down the steps, coming to an abrupt stop at a door with a padlock. He cursed until he realized it was left unlocked, and he quickly slipped it off, pocketed the lock, and opened the door. He was greeted by nothing but empty darkness, and he inched forward, causing the motion-sensor lights in the room to flicker to life. The light revealed a bedroom, bare except for a bed with iron bars, a toilet, and a sink in the corner. Colton stilled. It was a replica of his prison cell ten years ago. The same room Barry Pollock had built in his late mother's ruined old cabin out in the middle of the forest.

He shuddered.

The light flickered on in the back revealing Winter, and he sucked in a breath at the sight. Winter was bound and gagged, hanging by a harness from the ceiling, his arms outstretched as though hanging from a cross, his head fallen forward on his naked chest, eyes closed.

Panic spilled into his veins as Colton ran to him.

"Winter!" He grabbed his waist, feeling the warmth of his body and sighing in relief. He wasn't dead.

But he was up too high for him to reach and release him from this contraption. He quickly scanned the harness, which was attached to a track built into the ceiling, like the ones factory workers used to carry pigs across a room, dangling the helpless animal in the air before cutting their throats.

"Winter!" Colton urged again, digging his fingers into his hips, jostling him.

Winter's head rolled weakly to the side, his breathing faint, eyes still firmly shut. That's when Colton saw the leather belt wrapped around his throat. It was an expensive Italian leather belt. Something the overly conscious and fashionable Malcom would wear.

Revulsion ripped through his insides and he saw then, too, that Winter's belt had been unbuckled and the fly to his jeans unzipped. Colton's teeth mashed into ash in his mouth, wondering if Mal had done more than unbutton him—if he had touched Winter's body...

Blinding rage nearly crippled him.

"Think, honey," his mother's voice whispered calmly. "Set loose your wolf first... he needs you."

He let out a slow, controlled exhale and scanned Winter's body once more.

He couldn't reach the leather belt around his throat.

He glanced around frantically for something to stand on or to lower him back to the ground. There was a black cord from behind Winter's back, and he walked behind him and froze. Mal had upgraded from the taser. Winter was strapped to a custom-made electrified crucifix that ended at the base of his spine.

Shaking with fury, Colton followed the extension cord plugged into the electrified torture board, finding the handheld remote for the harness, which was hooked to the back wall. He carefully lowered Winter to the ground. Since he was still unconscious, he tipped over onto his side and would have fallen backward, but Colton stopped the track, keeping him dangling but upright. He unplugged the contraption and rushed over to Winter, quickly figuring out how to free him.

"Hurry up, Colton," he muttered to himself, unlatching the leather belt around Winter's neck and tossing it aside. Red marks burned and bruised Winter's flesh, and he cursed violently. He framed his face into his hands, "Winter, wake up. Wake up, please!"

He didn't respond.

Colton glanced swiftly around and saw another makeshift trolley, but it didn't have alcohol like the one upstairs. This one had medical supplies and sex toys. Disgusted, he searched through the layers of drawers and found nothing useful to wake Winter up. He cursed, glanced at the crucifix, and without options or time, he knew what he had to do. He raced back to the outlet and plugged in the torture device, grabbed the remote, and zapped Winter.

Winter jerked awake, face pinched in pain. The cry that came from his throat was rough and hoarse. Colton unplugged the damned thing and raced back to his side. Eyes watering, Winter's dark gaze blinked and found his, and Colton saw the relief and the concern all at once.

"Colton," Winter whispered gratingly. "Christ—you shouldn't be here."

"Neither should you," Colton said, framing his face with his hands, kissing him hard on his lips, but it wasn't passionate or loving—it was pure relief. Relief that he was alive.

Winter sighed, trying to move to reach him, but his arms and chest were strapped down.

"Where is he?" Winter asked, eyes darting to the door.

"Upstairs, probably nursing his cocktail and cock. I told him I was going to the loo."

"Good boy," Winter husked, and Colton hummed, heart pounding.

Colton returned his gaze quickly to the torture device on Winter's back and started unbuckling him, releasing his wrist and then his chest.

"I have so much I wanna say to you," Winter murmured over his shoulder to him. Colton's breath caught in his chest, stomach quivering.

"Whatever you gotta say, it can wait."

"No, it can't."

"You are not confessing your love in the Ripper's cellar, mate. If you do, I'll fuckin' tase ya again."

Winter let out a weak laugh and tried to unbuckle his other wrist, but his fingers trembled. Colton made quick work of it and freed him. The board fell away. Once Winter was free, he sagged against him, heavy and cursing furiously at himself. Colton supported his weight easily and walked him to the edge of the bed, where he sat him down. Unable to stand it any longer, he wrapped his fingers through his thick black and silver hair and hugged him against his stomach, kissing him repeatedly on top of his head.

"I saw my lighter," he grated out, throat thick with emotion.

"I knew you would," Winter breathed, wrapping his arms around his waist, embracing him. "I don't know if I can get very far. Whatever Mal gave me hasn't worn off."

"I can give ya another shock," Colton taunted, spotting Winter's shirt and shoes, neatly folded on the table by the trolley. He ran to it, handing Winter his shirt while he knelt and pushed on his boots. Winter tried to work his arms through the shirtsleeves, cringing and cursing some more.

"Where's your gun?" Colton asked.

"He took it," he replied bitterly.

Colton returned to the trolley, palmed the handheld taser, and shoved it into Winter's back pocket. "What about you?" He asked, voice etched with concern.

"I'm way ahead of you," Colton glanced around the room. "Do you think there's another way out other than the front fuckin' door?"

A soft click echoed through the bedroom, and Colton stilled. Winter, too, looked up, hand wrapping instantly around Colton, attempting to drag him behind him, but he was still too weak to do much.

Mal smiled in disappointment, "No, darling. There isn't."

Winter's fingers tightened around Colton's wrist.

"So, what gave me away?" Mal asked, his tone casual and cool, as if they were discussing the weather.

"A few things," he said, straightening, moving to stand beside Winter—not behind—not anymore.

"What?" Mal demanded.

"For starters, you suck at lyin', mate."

Mal's jaw twitched.

"If you're gonna say someone's in the shower, at least turn the damned thing on. You've got enough security to make me wonder what else you've got in here that ain't dreadful art. But mostly, it was *you*," he drawled, boldly stepping away from Winter entirely.

Winter tried to hang on, to keep him tethered to him, but Colton wouldn't allow it. He wasn't in fighting condition, and he wouldn't jeopardize his wolf when the devil wanted him.

He felt Winter's sharp intake of breath and pleading whisper of his name like a bullet to the chest. Colton knew his wolf would lay down his life right now to keep him safe. He knew it the moment Winter opened his door to him ten years ago, and that was the start of the end for him.

He loved him and always would. But he wouldn't allow any such sacrifice now. Not with this wretched piece of shit. Oh no, Colton intended to deal with this man—this pathetic thing, himself.

Keeping his gaze fixed on Mal, he slowly walked toward him, hands raised.

"You gave the game away, Mal," he tsked disapprovingly. "After all these years, you still use eucalyptus as a fucking lotion. Leaves a lasting imprint."

"I always hoped I did," Mal said airily.

"I was referring to the smell—not you."

Mal's smile darkened into a sneer, and then a second later, he laughed. It was cold and unfeeling.

"Oh, and one more thing," Colton said, getting closer still. "Let's not forget my mark on you," he dragged his knuckle beneath his own chin, smirking.

Mal straightened, nostrils twitching in irritation. "I had to leave Tahoe for three months until that healed. Didn't want Winter catching on. I thought long and hard about plastic surgery to cover it. However, I am very skilled at treating wounds. Speaking of, how's my mark? Or did daddy buy you a plastic surgeon?"

"He offered," Colton said with a careless shrug. "But I declined."

Mal licked his lips, intrigued. "Why?"

Colton was now feet away, hands still drawn up, gaze locked with his, uncaring of the gun. "Why do you think?"

"To remember me," Mal's excitement was building. He didn't challenge this, letting him believe whatever the fuck he wanted to believe.

"I have a lot to thank you for, Mal," Colton murmured. "You know that, right?"

Mal swallowed, eyebrows arched, curious.

"I had an awakening in that room. Not with Pollock, but with you." He drew himself all the way to the tip of the pointed gun, letting it graze his shirt. He felt Mal tremble but hold. "You."

The gun lowered, moving over his chest, grazing his nipple. Mal's dark gaze was as transparent as a child's looking at a candy shop, greedy and wanting.

"Colton," Winter's voice was harsh and scared. He ignored him. He had to. Keeping Mal's gun trained on him, his focus on him—that's all that mattered. Colton wasn't the only one willing to die to save someone he loved. He would take every bullet in that gun to protect Winter. He would even strap himself to that torture rack if it meant sparing his precious wolf.

"You're just saying all this because I have your lover," Mal retorted.

Colton felt the gun lift, as though to aim at Winter, and he stepped in front of it once more, holding Mal's attention.

"Colton," Winter rasped out warningly, pleadingly.

"I gotta thank you for that, too," Colton drawled. "If not for you, I would've never met the wolf in the woods that night…"

"Wolf?" Mal asked.

"Aye," Colton nodded, sliding a finger over the top of the gun, lowering his gaze, holding Mal's. "Mine."

He pushed the gun down hard, and with his other hand, retracting from his pocket and armed with brass knuckles, lunged forward onto Mal. The gun fired and Colton ducked, knowing the shot would be fired, and punched Mal in the solar plexus, knocking the air out of his right lung, and then, with another one-two punch and an uppercut, slammed his fists into the soft underbelly of his stomach. Mal heaved, collapsing into him like a folded book, and Colton knocked the gun out of his hand, letting it clatter to the floor.

Mal grabbed his arm, trying to pull away, but Colton held him, digging his fingers into the back of his neck.

"I knew you were the Ripper when I walked through those doors," Colton whispered. He heard Officer Sydney at the front, banging and demanding that they open the door. "I knew it was you. And all I could think about was what I heard the night Barry Pollock died."

Mal pushed against his grip, and Colton grabbed beneath him now, both hands around his throat.

"It's stayed with me for ten years," he said, squeezing his fingers. "Haunting me—driving me to this moment," Colton hissed. "I wanna hear your fuckin' death rattle."

He released him, and Mal turned, like he knew he would, and took a swing at him. Colton countered it easily and slammed his fist into Mal's throat, crushing his windpipe.

The sound was wet and gasping.

Mal's eyes widened in panic, "I can't... breathe...!" He grabbed frantically at his throat and stumbled back, eyes darting to Winter. "Winter...!" he croaked, hands reaching to his chest, clawing at it, as though he could somehow dig through the wall of skin and muscles and bone to give himself air.

"He's not gonna save you," Colton said darkly. "No one is, you sick fuck. You just trapped two wolves in your basement. How did you think this was gonna end?"

Mal collapsed, knees buckling, as he attempted to crawl to his trolley, filled with medical supplies and ointments, scrambling for anything that could relieve the pressure building in his lungs.

"You know," Colton said, watching him writhe and begin to turn purple, eyes bulging. "My mum was an excellent investigator. She had a list of suspects, and it looked like a crazy person had drawn it all together. She got a bit mad with this in the end. So fuckin' determined to find you. And she *did*," Colton withdrew the suspect list she had drawn up. "She led me here. Even the grave couldn't hold my mother down."

Mal spluttered and kicked his feet, ripping at his chest, as though a balloon was trapped there, unable to pop.

He squatted down at his side and listened to the death rattle, the gasping groans that became frantic and then stopped. His eyes fixed on Colton's, his hands dropping weightlessly, silent and still.

"I shall not mourn your death or say pretty words for this moment, only this. Thank you, dear Ripper. For showing me that I am a wolf and leading me to my mate. Rot in hell, you fuckin' cunt."

CHAPTER 28

I t had taken two days to thoroughly search Malcom's house and find proof of his crimes. He collected trophies of his victims in the form of video footage, which Jim and the forensic team made sure to collect and encrypt so that no one outside the Placer County Sheriff's department would ever see. Patrick, Mal's partner, was blindsided, having no idea about any of it, and admitted to his own workaholic tendencies and drinking abuse. He never questioned the room downstairs, as Mal had claimed it was for art pieces too valuable to display. His ignorance and addictions were to Mal's advantage, having used Patrick as a screen for normalcy.

Jim would announce Malcom Conner to the public that afternoon as the second North Tahoe Ripper, and they all knew the hailstorm that would follow. Jim was politely asked to retire early, knowing the fallout would land squarely on his shoulders, which he was more than fine with bearing. The North Tahoe Rippers case was officially closed, and the victims' families were to be notified once more.

Jim sat at Winter's dining table as Colton worked on breakfast, going over the details of the investigation, looking tired and worn out.

Winter refilled their coffee cups and sat down across from him.

"I didn't just come for a social call, Winter. There are a couple of things I'd like to discuss with you," Jim said, his tone leveling. "We found some more evidence last night on the video footage Mal had and, well," he sighed, scrubbing his fingers over his lips, looking upset.

Colton stilled, looking over his shoulder at them.

"What is it?" Winter asked gently.

"We found a video of ... you."

Ice, cold and hot, slipped into his bloodstream. Mal had told him that he watched the video from the club. He never said he had bought it from them. Bastard, he thought, teeth gritting.

"It was taken from a sex club in LA. We tracked down the source this morning. The owner said Mal paid an exorbitant amount to buy it off him. It's in evidence lockup and will die there with the rest of the footage."

Winter sat back, letting out a heavy sigh.

"Could I see it?" Colton asked over the rim of his coffee cup, giving Winter a deliciously mischievous smirk.

Winter, unexpectedly, smiled and glanced over his shoulder at the younger man. He was glaringly handsome, standing barefoot with his hair sexily tousled, wearing one of Winter's old Sac State football shirts and those wonderfully thin gray sweatpants he seemed so fond of.

"No," Jim shot back at Colton, looking mortified at the thought.

"Thanks for telling me," Winter said with an indifferent shrug. "Honestly, I don't really care. That's a part of my life I accepted a long time ago."

Jim leaned back in his chair, "Yeah, I can see why. From what little I saw, you have absolutely nothing to be ashamed about."

Colton's snort became a barely suppressed chuckle.

"Anyway," Jim said with a wave. "I'm here on other official business. Tahoe City Council asked for my top two nominations for the new

Sheriff, and I nominated you."

Winter expected this, his fingers tapping on his ceramic mug. He heard Colton's sharp intake of breath.

"Thank you, Jim," Winter replied coolly, having already prepared the answer. "I appreciate the nomination, but I can't accept."

Jim sighed, the wrinkled lines around his eyes deepening in annoyance. "Fuck. I knew you'd say that."

"What?" Colton asked, stepping out of the kitchen now, looking between them. "Why not? This is an honor."

Winter tilted his chin up to him, eyes catching and holding those sparkling pale blue eyes, feeling himself soften. "It is. But I don't deserve it. I spent ten years chasing my tail, ignoring the person right under my nose."

"That ain't your fault, luv. Mal's sheep suit was pretty thick. Even I didn't catch it at first."

Winter reached for his hand and squeezed. "There's another reason. I'd like to take a break from manhunting. See the world, get outta Tahoe a bit."

Colton stared down at him, emotion building in his gaze, and Winter's heart raced, admitting what he had been thinking the last few days.

Jim nodded and grunted, "Shit. Now I gotta tell them my lead homicide detective is going on an extended honeymoon."

Winter shot him a look and chuckled. "Really?"

Jim shrugged. "All this mooning is making my skin itch. You two are too pretty to be a real couple, and that's a quote from Officer Sydney, by the way."

"You should nominate her," Colton suggested. "She's got a good head on her shoulders."

Jim grunted, "They would say she's not experienced enough—and quite frankly, none of my deputies are. So, maybe she could be a good candidate. All right, I'm gonna head out. I expect a formal email about your time off before I leave on Monday, got it?" he said to Winter, who merely nodded, smiling.

Jim hesitated, holding out his hand to Colton. "I'm sorry for not believing you. You're a good man. Better than me."

Colton graciously accepted his hand and then hugged him. "All's forgiven, Jim. And you're a good man. You just gotta get outta your way to see it."

Jim snorted, "Sounds like therapy mumbo jumbo. All right, boys, I'll see you when I see you." He thumped Frank affectionately on the head and paused. "I'll take Frank off your hands when you head out of town. I'll need something to do with all my free time."

"He doesn't do much other than sleep and cuddle these days," Winter remarked.

Jim nodded approvingly, "Sounds perfect."

Winter thanked him, and Jim let himself out.

Once the door clicked shut, and they heard his footsteps descend and the truck rear to life, Colton pushed his foot against Winter's chair, shoving it out from underneath the table, straddling him.

Winter hummed with pleasure at the weighted feel of him sitting on his lap, sliding his fingers to Colton's hips, holding him against him.

"So, what video do you think they got on ya?" Colton asked, biting his lower lip, excitement dancing in his gaze.

"It isn't anything you haven't experienced yourself."

Colton let out a disappointed exhale, "Doesn't mean I don't wanna see it."

"Maybe when I come back from my honeymoon, I'll break in and steal it for you."

Colton laughed. It was bright and rich, warming him from the inside out.

"When were you gonna tell me you wanted to leave?" Colton asked, snaking his finger at the back of Winter's neck and through his hair. It didn't take much investigative prowess to discover that Colton had a thing for his hair.

"Today," Winter admitted. "I've been thinking about it for a long time. You just gave me the reason to do it because you're coming with me."

Colton settled into him, dropping his forehead into him. "Am I?"

"You are," Winter said fiercely, fingers digging into his waistline.

"Where should we go first on our honeymoon?"

Winter liked hearing the word honeymoon on his lips and tilted his chin back, gaze leveling with him. "London. I want to see where you grew up. I want to know everything about you because you are imprinted on my soul, Colton. You did it ten years ago. It took you coming back to let me feel it this time."

Colton kissed him hard, passionately. He groaned, allowing Colton to lead and control the rough kiss, setting his heart ablaze, knowing that this meant more than just passion—it meant love. *Their* love.

"There isn't a version of this story where you and I don't exist," Winter whispered, baring his soul to him. "I can't go back to my life pretending not to be wildly, madly, and completely in love with you."

Colton framed his face in his hands, searching. "Are you sure you want this—with me? Because I am not an easy man, Winter. I am impulsive and fiery. I do not always want to be controlled."

"I don't want to do that to you," Winter murmured. "I don't want to tame you—only when I fuck you. And I want to, all the time. I want you when, and where, and however I want because I am a selfish, hungry man that has an insatiable appetite for this," he stroked himself upward, making Colton feel the thickness growing between his thighs. "For you. I don't wanna control you. Control is an illusion. Your wildness taught me that. And I want to keep learning how to let go—surrender more often with you by my side."

"Careful, Winter, you're starting to sound like a romantic."

Winter let his hands travel up Colton's sides, grinding himself against him. Colton hummed deliciously, letting his body be used.

"You have no idea," Winter replied, throat clenching. "You wanna know why I wrote back to your mother for all those years? I wanted to catch glimpses of you in her letters. It felt wrong, and I was ashamed, and I never asked about you, ever. No matter how much I wanted to. But I think she knew, she always knew, even when I tried to stop writing, because I had to know you were okay, that you were out there burning like the sun, shining all that light onto the world, even if I wasn't there to see it."

Emotion flooded Colton's face, and he kissed him again, this time slow and deep. Winter kissed him back.

"Fingers a breath apart," Colton said, stroking his fingers through Winter's hair. Winter looked up at him, curiously. "My mum would say that to me all the time because that's how she found us that night in the hospital. Our hands were close but not touching. She said it was the most romantic thing she'd ever seen, and felt the universe move."

Winter stared up in awe, "Maybe that's what drove her."

"What do you mean?"

"Her letters, her investigation—maybe it was because of us. She didn't want us to lose each other."

"I think I just heard my mother swoon somewhere in the universe," Colton said.

Winter kissed him, holding him tight. "I wish I had the courage to find you earlier."

Colton licked his lower lip, intentionally undulating against him in the chair, and Winter nearly growled in approval. "But you did, and that's all that matters now. And besides, I like you better grayer because fuck me, you've somehow managed to get hotter with age."

Winter laughed. It tumbled easily out of his chest as he sat back, letting Colton use him.

They had made love in practically every room of his house in the last two days and yet, they hadn't done it here. The sunlight filtered through the open slider in the dining room, illuminating Colton, his blond hair seeming brighter and his curving smile more daring as he stood, lowering his thin sweatpants, giving Winter an expectant look.

Winter complied, unfastening his jeans and sliding them and his boxer briefs down over his hips and to the floor.

"Have I mentioned I like those sweatpants?" Winter drawled, his chest heaving with breath as Colton stripped out of his T-shirt next, tossing it indiscriminately behind him. The hard contours of his muscled flesh were smooth and radiant in the light, his nipples peaking and his erection thick and pulsating with desire.

Colton looked like a Sun God, chiseled from granite and possibly the most exquisite thing he had ever seen in his life. The dark ink of his tattoo blended seamlessly with the symmetry of his body. Winter now understood why men had the desire to kneel for their Gods, because he was more than ready to beg and worship his God.

"Take off your shirt, luv. I wanna see you," Colton ordered, eyes darkening with pleasure as Winter obeyed, relinquishing complete control.

Colton stroked himself unhurriedly, making Winter watch as he pumped his hand from root to stem. Winter's gaze was riveted to him, unable to look away even if he had a gun pushed into his temple.

Winter reached for his own cock, and Colton tsked, shaking his head. "You're gonna watch and that's it."

He let out a growling breath.

"You wanna practice surrendering, my darling wolf, then you must listen, obey, and trust," Colton said, tilting his head back, showing every fine line of his body, the grooves and ridges of it on full display, his throat bobbing as he pumped between his legs, his lips parting in a groan. It was the sexiest fucking sound on the planet, and Winter had to bite the inner lining of his cheek not to reach out and take what was his.

Because Colton was his.

"I need to touch you," Winter ground out.

Colton's gaze returned to his, intense and fiery. "But isn't this part of our game? You watch and I do."

"I don't wanna just watch you anymore."

"So, what do you want?" Colton asked, power glinting in his eyes.

Winter shivered, knowing he'd seen glimpses of this power before, when Colton had run down Barry Pollock, and then again, the night he captivated an entire bar with his mere presence alone. And lastly, when he killed the last Ripper, striking Mal in the throat, crushing his windpipe, and ruthlessly watching him gasp to death.

This Sun God was lethal.

Dangerous.

And so fucking hot.

"You," Winter muttered hoarsely.

Colton arched an eyebrow over his body, recklessly dragging his gaze over Winter's aching cock. He felt the stiffness between his legs, hard and long, thick and veined, his tip leaking with precum.

"You're leakin' for me, Winter..." Colton hummed. "And you haven't even touched me yet."

Winter slid out of the chair, unable to wait for the command from his Sun God, as he opened his mouth in penance and desperation. Colton's stomach sucked in a breath, and he captured the back of Winter's head with both hands, fingertips scraping through his hair, and pushing his sex into his open, waiting mouth.

Colton's moan at the feel of his wet mouth dragging over him and tongue sliding against his tip was music to his ears, and he sucked, letting Colton control his movements, rocking his head back and forth over him, taking him in deep and retreating in a slow, rhythmic pace.

"Fuckin' 'ell, you're so good at this," Colton praised, stomach visibly quivering as he undulated his hips forward, pushing himself all the way down and out.

Winter's eyes watered from the sudden intrusion down his throat, and he relaxed his muscles, allowing Colton to do it again and again, until another groan erupted from him and he pulled Winter away from him. Saliva dripping from his lips and breathing hard, he stared up at him with a painfully hard erection that he had carefully not touched throughout the duration of the cock sucking.

"Get back in your seat, luv."

Winter did so, heart racing, loving the easy way Colton commanded him.

"Keep your hands to yourself, only if I tell you to," Colton said smoothly, as he dropped slowly to his knees, cock bouncing between his legs, and took Winter's manhood into both hands, stroking him for the first time. He hissed out a curse at the sudden sensation and tensed in his chair.

Colton smiled darkly, pleased, and lowered over him, trailing his tongue over the sensitive tip and licking him up and down, making Winter let out a strangled sound from the back of his throat.

"I enjoy watching you squirm," Colton murmured before taking him into his mouth, sucking hard and almost violently.

Winter flinched, sitting forward, hand shooting out—not to stop him, but to slam him further down, but he stilled, catching himself, hand hovering over the back of Colton's head, fisting his fingers into the air.

Colton sensed his struggle and looked up, sucking his cock all the way up and letting it pop out like a lollipop. He eyed the hand above him, smiling.

"Good Wolfie," Colton drawled. "You're doing so well."

Winter retracted his hand, swallowing, breathing hard through his nose. "This is torture."

"I know," Colton grated his teeth over the tip. "Now you know how I've felt for ten fucking years. Wanting to touch you—fuck you—taste your cum on my lips and down my throat. The number of times I imagined you just like this. At my mercy, begging for me—only me."

"Yes," Winter rasped out, fisting his hands to his side as Colton sucked him down ruthlessly, like a Viking King that had won the war and wanted nothing but the spoils now. And Winter would be his plunder and riches. "Yes, suck me just like that," he whispered, arching slightly into the ferocity of Colton's mouth. "You're so goddamned good..."

He leaned back in the chair, surrendering further still, legs widening as Colton pushed his shoulders between him, and began to work beneath his shaft and cup his balls. Colton pushed Winter even further back, relaxed and at the mercy of the man between his legs, devouring him. His head tilted over the edge of the chair, his arms fell at his sides, and he glanced up through hooded eyes, Colton's bobbing head and sucking cheeks, and he felt the tingling pressure build painfully at the base of his spine.

"Fuck, baby," Winter gasped. "I'm close."

Colton hummed so hard that the vibrations rippled through every muscle of Winter's body and he bucked, his hand shooting out again and grasping nothing but air, cursing.

"Call me baby again, and I'll let you do whatever you want to me, Winter," Colton said heatedly.

"Baby," Winter growled and sat forward, grabbing Colton victoriously by the throat and lifting him to his feet. Colton gasped, biting his lower lip, the press of his leaking cock rubbing against Winter's. He reached between them, bringing their cocks together, letting them slide and pump in his fist.

Colton trembled, groaning, "Yes. Fuck. Yes!"

Winter didn't want this, though—oh no. He wanted to taste his Sun God and then drag him brutally into the heavens with him.

He released his grip on Colton's throat, but not before kissing him thoroughly, and spun him in his arms, slamming him down onto the dining table, and dropped to his knees again—this time from behind.

Colton let out a stream of curses and slapped his hand on the table as Winter, having spread his perfect cheeks, tongued his entrance ruthlessly.

"Fuck! Fuck!" Colton's body writhed against his face, and Winter didn't even have to stroke himself to keep hard. Just listening to his tortured moans was enough to keep him going.

"Winter!" Colton yelled warningly, "I'm not coming like this—you better fuck me. I swear to…!"

His words were cut short as Winter stood, and without waiting, he thrust his slick manhood into his entrance, filling him. Colton groaned into the wood of the dining table, gripping the edges, spread out before him like the best damned feast he'd ever seen. He fucked him slowly, savoring the feel of him. A deep, animalistic part of himself wanted to take him roughly. But they had plenty of time for that. This would be slow and hard, just like their passion, primal and wild, mixed with a bit of pain.

He drove them steadily forward to the edge of oblivion, thrusting at a steady, rhythmic pace until there was nothing but the sounds of bodies and their gasping breaths.

Fingers digging into his hip bone, Winter pushed down into Colton's lower back with his free hand while driving forward. Colton's groan turned into a cry of pleasure.

"Yes!" He gasped, and Winter rewarded him by slapping his ass hard, leaving a red imprint on his perfect, sweet ass.

"Again," Colton demanded, groaning desperately now, causing Winter to shudder as he spanked him once more. He bucked and whimpered against him. "Don't stop."

He spanked three more times, hard, spearing him, and that's when he felt Colton's body tighten. Anticipating this, Winter reached around him and ruthlessly pumped. He came instantly, jerking against him, tensing and drawing Winter in so deep he saw stars before the tidal wave that was his orgasm ripped him to shreds, and he unloaded inside him.

Colton collapsed fully onto the table, and Winter, breathing as though he just sprinted two miles, eased out of him and fell back into the chair, slick with their pleasure on his body.

Colton slowly stood and turned around, naked and gloriously spent.

And to Winter's disbelief and satisfaction, Colton straddled him, kissing him tenderly, gently, lovingly. Their breathing mingled, pulses coming down together.

He loved this—loved him. And he knew it would be just like this between them.

"I love you," Colton whispered, glowing with that inner light. "It's always been you."

Winter smiled wolfishly, "and it always will be."

Later that night, they booked the flights to London.

They visited Colton's father. They traveled and explored. They laughed a lot. They made love a lot more. They moved in together to Winter's place in Tahoe. They got Frank a puppy— a husky. They discussed their future in ways that left them both excited and content. They visited Grace's grave to pay their respects, give their thanks, and share their love. They had Thanksgiving with Jamie and Tess. They went to Italy for Christmas, where Colton proposed on a canal bridge in Venice—surprised to see that Winter, too, had a ring for him.

Most importantly, they lived happily ever after.

The End

Thank you so much for reading!

I am absolutely obsessed with Winter and Colton's love story. Maybe a little too much. Their story felt like a bolt of lightning that had to be told. It was a whirlwind of fun writing, and I sincerely hope you enjoyed it, too! If you enjoyed this novel and would like to stick around to read a little more of my work, I have a romantic fantasy series currently in the works. Lilith Legacy Book One is available on Amazon and my direct author website.

www.ariellebitetti.com

Follow me on TikTok & Instagram, where you can stay updated with new book announcements, sneak peeks, and bonus content. @ariellebitettiauthor

Acknowledgments

To my incredible husband, Paul. Your unwavering support, love, and encouragement got me to the next step and the step after that. I love you so damn much. Thank you for everything!

To my mom- thank you for your continued support and enthusiasm for my work, even when it surprises you ;)

To those who have supported my writing online and in person, words cannot express my deepest love and gratitude! Being an indie author is, at times, grinding work, so whenever a fan reaches out to me, it reminds me to keep going and not give up on my dreams. So, thank you.

Leave a Review

If you enjoyed this book, please consider leaving a review (even if it's in the form of stars). Anything, even a few words, can help the next reader find *I'd Find You In The Dark*.

Thank you!

Also by Arielle Bitetti

Lilith Legacy Book I

Coming Soon
The Lilith Series
Lilith Hell: Book II – Spring 2026
Lilith Paradise: Book III – TBA

About the Author

Arielle Bitetti is an indie romance author. On paper, her life is conventional, but in her mind, it's a sweeping epic with vast worlds and stories yet to be told. She lives in California with her loving husband and her young, adorably cute son whose boundless energy and love sustains her soul.

Join her Newsletter for all the fun goodies and major news direct to your email inbox at www.ariellebitetti.com. With exclusive giveaways, first look at character art/inspo, bonus chapters, and more!